BURNING BRIDGES

BURNING BRIDGES

Stephanie Harte

An Aries Book

ISBN (PB): 9781803283722
ISBN (E): 9781800245822

Cover design: Cherie Chapman

Typeset by Siliconchips Services Ltd UK

Printed and bound in Great Britain by
CPI Group (UK) Ltd, Croydon CRO 4YY

Head of Zeus
First Floor East
5–8 Hardwick Street
London EC1R 4RG

WWW.HEADOFZEUS.COM

In loving memory of my mum and dad

Two lives so entwined they couldn't be parted

I miss you more than you'll ever know

May you both rest in peace

Together forever

I

Scarlett

My eyes sprang open when the sound of roaring motorbikes woke me from my sleep. With my heart hammering in my chest, I threw back my quilt and swung my legs over the side of the bed, wincing from the exertion. Hunching over to lessen the throbbing, I wrapped my arms over my wound as I sat trembling in the dark. I was drenched in sweat; my long red hair was stuck to the side of my face like a sheet of copper.

I strained my ears, listening for the noise that had disturbed me. All was still and quiet. A very faint glow of light was coming through a crack in the curtains. Pain seared into my flesh as I got to my feet. I padded across the thick carpet, the colour of Parma Violets, my breath loud in my ears as I parted the heavy drapes where they met in the centre. I gripped the sill with shaking fingers when I peered out, but no uninvited intruders were beneath my window. The gravel driveway was deserted. The bikes I'd heard were the ones that drove into my subconsciousness every time I fell asleep.

I'd only had a hazy recollection of what had happened to me, but now that my memory had started to return, the moment I was attacked kept replaying in my mind. Every time I closed my eyes, I had flashbacks of the motorbikes, and when I did eventually go to sleep, I had vivid nightmares. Scary images walked together hand in hand through my fragile mind; their visits had become an everyday occurrence while I recovered from my injuries. The doctor said they were a side effect of the emotional burden that accompanied this type of trauma. Nothing disturbed a person's sleep more than the horror of a terrifying dream in the dead of night.

Our family home was like a fortress. The huge six-bedroomed detached house in Bow was set within half an acre and accessed by a private road. It was nestled in a secluded oasis and protected by state-of-the-art security systems, but that still didn't make me feel safe. Rio had assured me countless times that he wouldn't let anybody hurt me, but that brought me little comfort.

The experience I'd been through was as raw as the gash across my stomach that would take time to heal. My attacker's knife had penetrated deeply, piercing the layers of muscles that crisscrossed my insides, slicing open nerves, blood vessels, and lymph vessels, leaving catastrophic damage behind, which robbed my unborn baby of its first breath.

The cruel double blow of enduring the loss of my child while accepting the fact that its father had orchestrated the vicious attack was hard to come to terms with; I'd never expected to have to face mortality at the age of twenty. But I'd lost a lot of blood, and the surgeons had to battle to save my life, stitching me back together in layers from the inside out.

I was unlikely to ever be the same person as the one who'd woken up on that ill-fated morning. A month ago, I'd been high on life with a bright future ahead of me. Now I had to take morphine, antidepressants, and sleeping pills just to function to some degree. I was dosed up to the eyeballs, but the tablets weren't helping. Every time I moved, it hurt; a cough, a sneeze, even breathing could be agony. Relentless pain and loss of sensation from nerve damage had become part of the fabric of my daily existence. The doctors had told me it was too early to say whether I'd make a full recovery, so working as a dancer or actor was out of the question for the time being, which was a devastating blow to someone who had always wanted to be a performer.

I didn't like being labelled a victim and wasn't about to wallow in self-pity. I kept reminding myself that life goes on; Scarlett Saunders was made of strong stuff. I'd inherited a large measure of grit and determination. Much as my mum and sisters wanted me to forget CJ ever existed, that was never going to happen. I had too many unanswered questions floating around in my head to close the door on that chapter. He had a lot to answer for; he'd flattened my dreams and left me with harrowing memories of the night that changed my life.

As a fresh wave of pain washed over me, I gritted my teeth and vowed to track down the man who broke my heart so that I could hear his side of the story. An explanation was the very least he owed me. But there was a feeling in the pit of my stomach that maybe I should leave well alone.

2

Mia

'Good morning, ladies,' Rio said when he stepped into the garden office Mum, Kelsey and I shared.

'Good morning,' we replied in unison.

As it was such a beautiful warm August day, we'd folded back the triple glazing, which essentially removed one side of the building to let the outdoors in. The flagstone path gave way to an expanse of striped lawns and wrap-around flower beds that were a riot of colour. If I craned my neck from where I was sitting, I could just about see the tiniest tease of turquoise water. The outdoor pool was calling me, but it would have to wait until I finished work.

I tore my eyes away and concentrated my gaze on Rio. He looked as handsome as ever as he stood in front of us, dressed in a charcoal grey suit. I couldn't help thinking he must be roasting as the temperature was in the low twenties already, and it was set to be another scorcher. If he was hot and bothered, it didn't show; my dad's right-hand man was as cool, calm and collected as ever.

'Morning, all,' Jack said as he breezed into the office.

'What's on the agenda today?' Mum asked, gesturing for Rio to take a seat on the black leather sofa.

'Not a lot, really. Everything's ticking along fine, but Larry's been in touch. He's having trouble with a young guy who bought an Aston Martin off him a few months back,' Rio replied.

'What kind of trouble?' Mum asked, straightening her posture before she put her elbows on the edge of the desk and interlaced her slender fingers.

'The usual. The guy's overstretched himself. It happens all the time, especially with young lads. They want to look flash, but they haven't got the readies to back themselves up. Larry said the bloke made the first payment and then stopped bothering. He owes the best part of thirty grand.'

'What does he want us to do? Buy the debt?' I asked, already thinking the most we would offer Larry would be half, so even with his markup, he would be well out of pocket if he went down that route.

'Not in the first instance. He wants us to pay the guy a visit and put the frighteners on him. It's the cheapest option all-round.' Rio looked over at Mum to gauge her reaction. 'Darius and I will be happy to provide the muscle.'

Since Kelsey had fired Todd Evans, we were a man down on the team, but Rio's eighteen-year-old nephew Darius had stepped up to the mark and filled the vacancy. Despite his young age, he was doing a brilliant job.

'Thanks, Rio, much appreciated.' Mum smiled.

'One of you ladies should attend as well. The guy needs to be in no doubt who's giving the orders.'

Overprotective as always, Jack looked up from his keyboard. He'd been keeping his head down since he'd come in, but I could tell by the look on his face he was about to get involved in the conversation. That was the downside of having him share our office space. He knew exactly what was going on. I wasn't really sure what had prompted him to start working from home, but at times like this, I wished he'd go back to his desk at the commercial property on the industrial estate Dad used as the firm's official HQ.

'I don't like the sound of that. It's too dangerous,' Jack piped up.

'It'll be fine. I'll go,' Mum volunteered, looking sideways at Kelsey and me.

'There's no need. I'd be more than happy to accompany Rio and Darius.' Kelsey grinned.

I knew what was on my younger sister's mind. She had a voracious appetite for the male of the species, and it didn't take a genius to work out what she was up to; Kelsey was a self-confessed man-eater. Mum flashed her a warning look. She responded by grinning from ear to ear before she pulled her raven hair over one shoulder and settled back in her seat with a smirk on her face.

'Right, that's settled then. I'll swing by here at midnight to collect you,' Rio said.

'I'm glad to see my opinion is so important,' Jack muttered before he began typing away on his keyboard.

Mum waited until Rio's tall, broad-shouldered frame was out of sight before she turned her attention to Kelsey.

'Now, don't go getting any ideas, young lady,' Mum said, wagging her finger in Kelsey's face.

'What's that supposed to mean?' Kelsey quizzed, throwing her arms in the air and acting all innocent.

Mum stood up and put her hands on her hips. 'As if you don't know. I'm warning you, Kelsey, if you get involved with Darius, your days working for the firm are numbered.'

'Seriously? Spare me the lecture.' Kelsey got to her feet and started heading towards the door.

'Where are you going?' Mum asked.

'For a dip in the pool. I'm going to be working late, so I think I deserve some time off.'

Kelsey tossed her head, and her long hair cascaded over her shoulders, then she marched up the path towards the house without a backward glance.

Mum picked up her mobile. 'I need to speak to you. Can you come back to the office, please?'

I watched Mum stare into the distance with tears misting her lavender-blue eyes for a couple of moments before she turned her attention to me.

'I'm really worried about your sister. You know what she's like around the opposite sex, and the last time she got involved with a member of the team, your dad ended up losing his life.' Mum's words had a bitterness to them.

It would be hard to imagine a more devastating scenario than what happened on my wedding day. I wouldn't wish it on my worst enemy. Dad's murder had impacted our whole family. For the first time in months, I found myself crying about the tragic situation.

'I'm sorry, Mia. I didn't mean to upset you,' Mum said, reaching towards me and rubbing my arm with her soft fingertips.

'It's OK,' I replied before wiping my tears away with the back of my hand.

'I'm sure I'm worrying about nothing. Darius isn't even out of his teens, so I'm not suggesting he has a psycho wife waiting in the wings like Todd did, but I'm going to have a word with Rio all the same. You can't be too careful, can you?'

'I think that's sensible.'

It wouldn't surprise me in the slightest if Kelsey had her eye on Darius. He was a handsome young man, a younger version of his uncle, but instead of dark eyes, he had clear blue ones, which looked stunning against his caramel-coloured skin. But hopefully, she'd have the sense not to make the same mistake twice.

'I need you to do me a favour, please,' Mum said with a smile when Rio walked back into the office a few moments later.

'Fire away.' Rio stood in the doorway with his arms crossed over his stomach, one hand clasping the other at the wrist.

'Can you have a word with your nephew and make sure he understands there will be severe consequences if he gets involved with Kelsey?'

Mum almost seemed embarrassed to have to ask, but Rio didn't look a bit offended.

'Consider it done, Amanda. I've already had words with him and warned him off, not that he'd dare to go there. Todd was a rare breed; he had the morals of an alley cat. I can assure you my nephew has much better manners.'

'I don't doubt that for one minute. I'm sorry to put you in this position, but...'

Rio put his hand up to stop Mum in her tracks. 'There's no need to apologise. It's good to know we're all on the same page.'

Mum and I were sitting at the large circular glass table that overlooked the garden and outdoor pool, nursing cups of chamomile tea, when there was a knock on the back door. We both glanced up at the security panel and saw the familiar outline of Dad's best friend captured on the screen before he let himself in via the fingerprint-recognition entry system.

'Where's Darius?' Mum asked when Rio came to a stop beside her.

'He's waiting outside in the car.'

Kelsey had made herself scarce all day, which was probably a blessing in disguise. Mum seemed agitated and out of sorts, and my sister was an expert at pushing people's buttons and getting a rise out of them. Kelsey always tested Mum's role; being the peacekeeper wasn't easy, especially with my headstrong sister.

At the stroke of midnight, Kelsey strutted into the kitchen, accompanied by a waft of expensive perfume, wearing a black body-con dress, matching fitted jacket and skyscraper heels. She looked sensational. She knew she did, and her confidence was shining through as brightly as it always did. Kelsey had an aura about her. She looked as though she meant business and oozed power from every pore.

'How do I look?' Kelsey asked.

'Fantastic. That dress really suits your figure,' Mum said, beaming with pride.

Mum was good at giving compliments because she paid attention to details. She made it look so easy, but not everyone had her skill. It was a powerful gift.

'You look amazing,' I agreed.

'You're not going to take any prisoners, are you?' Rio laughed.

'You're right about that. You said the guy needs to be in no doubt who's giving the orders, so I thought I'd go for the badass boss lady look.' Kelsey grinned.

'Well then, you've achieved what you set out to do,' Mum chipped in.

'Let's get going. I'm ready to chew this sucker up and spit him out,' Kelsey said to Rio.

Mum and I glanced at each other as Kelsey's heels clicked off the tiled surface. She didn't seem the slightest bit nervous about breaking into a stranger's house in the middle of the night and delivering a threat. If anything, she seemed excited by the prospect. My sister had nerves of steel. The poor man wasn't going to know what hit him.

3

Kelsey

Oscar Myles lived in Lewisham in a purpose-built block of flats. The red-brick box-like construction didn't have much kerb appeal, but we weren't there to buy the property; we were just issuing a warning on behalf of Larry.

The weather had been kind to us, and as it had been such a boiling-hot day, Oscar had foolishly decided to sleep with his bedroom window wide open. I was a little disappointed to see that when we stood outside his ground-floor flat, as I'd been hoping to witness Rio gain entry forcibly instead of climbing through the window. In hindsight, it was probably the best outcome as we hadn't lost the element of surprise.

I leant against the brickwork, which had been like a storage heater having soaked up the warmth of the day, with my arms crossed over my chest while Rio slipped through the window with the ease of a cat.

To pass the time while Rio tiptoed unnoticed across the bedroom, I'd let my eyes roam freely over Darius's well-defined body. A smile played on my lips as I watched him trying not to squirm. He literally had steam coming out of the top of his black bomber jacket. But I was only toying with him. I had no intention of getting up close and personal with him. Not that he wasn't a great-looking guy. If he'd been ten years older, he'd have been in real trouble. I liked my men experienced; schoolboys didn't tick my boxes.

Rio opened the front door, which hadn't come a moment too soon for the young man if the look on his face was anything to go by. He signalled to Darius to pull his balaclava over his face to mirror his uncle's attire. They were both dressed head to toe in black clothing and carried extendable metal coshes in their gloved hands.

Oscar's studio flat was the size of a postage stamp. The inside was just as dismal as I'd expected. It had absolutely nothing going for it. There was a stainless steel sink with a dripping mixer tap in one corner of the room. I couldn't help noticing there were no cooking facilities, so to speak, apart from a microwave, kettle and toaster. The small section of work surface that housed them was littered with pot noodle containers and polystyrene boxes, the ones the cheap takeaways used. That must have been where the smell of stale food was coming from.

As my eyes scanned the small space, it struck me that Oscar didn't have many worldly possessions. A single free-standing wardrobe stored his clothes, and the only other piece of furniture in the room was a double bed that dominated almost the entire space. It always amazed me why people wanted to have a fancy car and then live in a shithole. Talk about having your priorities the wrong way around.

Rio and Darius took up position at the end of the bed. I stood between uncle and nephew, watching our target. He was out for the count, blissfully unaware of the fact that he was about to get a rude awakening. Oscar was lying on his back like a giant naked starfish with his mouth open and not a shred of dignity when Rio prodded him in the ribs with the metal poker. His face was a picture when he opened his eyes and saw the three of us looming over him, and I had to stifle a laugh.

Oscar started repeatedly blinking before he rubbed his eyes with his fists as though he was trying to erase us from his vision. When the penny finally dropped that he wasn't alone in the room, his face filled with terror, and he lay where he was, frozen with fear. Rio gave the signal, and then he and Darius moved towards the headboard and stood on either side of the bed. Oscar's eyes flicked between the two men. His Adam's apple started dancing in his throat when the moonlight glinted off the steel batons, and he covered his dick in response, no doubt sensing he was about to get a hiding.

'I'm sure you're probably wondering why we're here,' I began.

Oscar's eyes returned to mine, and he slowly nodded while trying to swallow down his terror.

'You owe a friend of mine a lot of money,' I continued.

At first, Oscar looked puzzled by what I'd said, and then his eyes grew wide when the realisation hit him. I could see beads of sweat break out on his upper lip.

'Did you really think Larry was going to let you keep the Aston Martin without paying for it?'

The mattress dipped when Rio sat down on the edge of the bed, and Oscar rolled towards him. He attempted to scramble away, but Rio forced him onto his back before getting up in his face.

'It's very bad manners not to answer a lady when she's speaking to you. I suggest you find your voice before I find it for you.' Rio swung his huge fist back, and when it connected with Oscar's jaw, he let out a yelp.

'Please don't hurt me,' he protested in a high-pitched, strangled voice.

It was a predictable, if not pathetic response.

'There you go; you see, you can speak after all.' Rio laughed. 'Now, I suggest you answer the lady's question.'

'Hold on a minute. There's been a huge misunderstanding,' Oscar said, holding his hands up passively in front of him.

'Larry will be expecting a deposit into his bank account for the money you owe by the end of today, plus an extra five grand for the inconvenience you've caused,' I said.

'But I haven't got that kind of dosh,' Oscar replied.

'That's not my problem. I wouldn't recommend you disappoint Larry. I can assure you that you'll be sorry if we have to come back here again. You've got off lightly so far.' I smiled.

'You aced it,' Rio said once we were back in the car.

I loved the prestige of being involved with criminals and taking the law into our own hands. It gave me a thrill. Mia and I were finally making a name for ourselves in the shadowy underworld. Rio was teaching us the ropes, and he'd drummed into us that everybody we came into contact with needed to know we were the people holding the reins. We had to gain a reputation and respect; they were essential to the firm's future.

'Thanks,' I replied, and my face stretched into a smile. 'I don't mind admitting I thoroughly enjoyed myself; it wasn't like work at all. But I have to say, I was expecting to witness a little more carnage.'

'Sometimes the situation does call for blood and guts to be spilt, but handing out a kicking wasn't necessary this time. The guy was absolutely bricking it. But rest assured, if he goes back on his word and we have to pay him another visit, he'll get everything he deserves. If you violate the terms of an agreement, you have to face the consequences.' Rio grinned.

4

Mia

Even though Jack and I worked together, we rarely discussed firm-related things. He maintained he didn't like to mix business with pleasure and didn't want to spend our free time talking shop. Work took up enough of his time without it taking over his personal life too. I got where he was coming from, but sometimes it would be nice to run things past him and have a debrief at the end of the day.

'Sorry to interrupt. Have you got a moment?' Rio asked, stepping out of the blistering heat and into our office space.

'Of course.' Mum flashed him a smile as bright as the sun. She was clearly happy to see him.

'Larry's been bending my ear again about Oscar Myles.'

Kelsey looked up from her phone and fixed her eyes on Rio. She'd been distracted by something, but he had her complete attention now.

'Don't tell me he was stupid enough not to pay the money he owed?' Kelsey questioned.

'You guessed it. The little fucker didn't part with a penny,' Rio replied, shaking his head. 'I have zero tolerance for people who try to make a fool out of me.' His nostrils flared as he stood in the doorway, waiting for our response.

'He's made a fool of me too,' Kelsey fumed, throwing her mobile down on the desk before getting to her feet.

'I can't say I'm that surprised,' Jack chipped in, and Kelsey threw him a look that could kill.

'So what does Larry want us to do?' I asked, trying to disperse the tension between my husband and sister.

'He said it's our call whether we buy the debt or just put the frighteners on him again.'

'Why stop at one when we can do both? Let's buy the debt, and then you can give him a kicking he won't forget in a hurry,' Kelsey suggested.

'It's up to you,' Rio said as his eyes rested on Mum, Kelsey and me in turn. 'But if you want my opinion, buying the debt probably isn't worth the risk. I'm not sure you'll be able to recover the money. The kid hasn't got a pot to piss in; he's barely old enough to shave, and by the looks of the shitty flat he's living in, he's got no assets worth taking. Having said that, at the very least, he deserves to be roughed up for ignoring our warning.'

'But if Mia and I manage to recover the debt, it would do wonders for our reputation, wouldn't it?' Kelsey smiled.

Rio tilted his head to one side while he considered what she'd said.

Recovering the debt was never guaranteed. That's what made the job interesting. If it was an easy line of work, everybody would be doing it.

'I'm inclined to agree with Kelsey,' I said, breaking the silence. I pretended not to notice Jack roll his eyes.

'What would Davie have done?' Mum asked.

'He would have bought the debt and gone after the fucker. Davie had a formidable reputation for being a hard nut. He wouldn't have let some jumped-up little wanker run rings around him. Darius and I behaved like gentlemen when we issued the ultimatum, but Oscar has taken advantage of our generosity. Davie would have come down hard on the bloke so that he understood the error of his ways.'

'I'm confused. Surely, in that case, we should be buying the debt from Larry. Why did you say it's too risky?' Mum asked. She tilted her head to one side and rested her index finger on her lips.

'Because the guy's broke. There's a fair chance you won't get a single penny back,' Rio reiterated. 'Davie had a better track record than most when it came to recovering outstanding money. No offence, ladies, but you're still learning the ropes and aren't quite in the same league as your dad yet.'

'Sometimes in business, it isn't about money; it's about getting even with the person who's wronged you. Davie hated the idea of losing face,' Mum said.

'You don't need to tell me that, Amanda, and if we walk away without settling the score, we'll have tongues wagging. That could undermine all the good work the girls have done so far,' Rio said, smiling at Kelsey and me like a proud surrogate father. 'It's entirely up to you, but I don't want you biting off more than you can chew.'

'Phone Larry back and tell him we'll take the debt off his hands. How much should we offer him?' Mum asked, looking in my direction.

'Oscar owes him thirty grand?' I quizzed, double-checking that I'd got the amount right.

'Yes, plus five grand for the home visit we made the other night,' Kelsey replied.

'I suggest we offer Larry fifteen and go after Oscar for fifty to make it worth our while,' I said.

'Can you phone Larry and give him the offer? Tell him he can have the cash today to sweeten the blow,' Mum said to Rio.

Rio stepped back into the office a couple of hours later, armed with the paperwork relating to the sale of the Aston Martin.

'I hope you don't mind, but I took the liberty of looking through the credit agreement. We already had Oscar's home address, but now we've got his bank details and his mobile phone number too; information like that always comes in handy. It would be a tragedy for him if that fell into the wrong hands. People can get up to all sorts of mischief with a bit of personal information.' Rio grinned.

'So when are we going back to the flat?' Kelsey asked.

She seemed keen to redress the balance and show Oscar the error of his ways.

'It's best to strike while the iron's hot. I'd suggest we go tonight,' Rio replied.

'That suits me fine.' Kelsey smiled.

5

Mia

The sound of the front door slamming woke me from my sleep, and I sat bolt upright in the bed. I picked up my phone from the bedside cabinet and switched on the screen; it was just before two. Jack stirred briefly, then rolled onto his side. I could tell from the sound of his slow, steady breathing that he was still in the land of nod, so I didn't bother to disturb him. There was no point. It was bound to be Kelsey making all the racket; something told me things hadn't gone to plan. Jack didn't like discussing business with me at the best of times, let alone in the early hours of the morning.

I threw back the sheet, slid out of bed, and then tiptoed across the duck-egg-blue-coloured carpet. I don't know why I was treading so carefully; it was so thick it could dampen the sound of hobnail boots. Mum was almost at the bottom when I reached the top of the stairs, so I stepped up my pace to catch up with her.

'Wait for me,' I called.

Mum paused and looked at me over her shoulder.

'So you heard the commotion too,' she said, sweeping her blonde pixie cut out of her eyes.

Rio and Darius were standing with their backs against the wall, watching Kelsey pace up and down as we walked into the kitchen. She spun around and gripped onto the pale grey granite work surface when she saw us approaching. Her eyes were blazing, and she was almost breathing fire like a human dragon.

'Whatever's the matter?' Mum asked. The concern in her expression grew with every step she took.

Her state of pure fury paralysed Kelsey's tongue. She was too angry to speak and stood grinding her teeth as she gripped the granite with white-knuckled hands.

Mum turned her attention towards Rio. 'What's going on?' she asked, throwing her hands up in the air.

'Oscar's done a runner. He's packed up all his stuff and cleared out,' Rio explained.

I wasn't particularly surprised. People did desperate things when they were backed into a corner.

'He obviously had no way to repay the debt, so he tried to buy himself some time by pretending it was all a big misunderstanding,' Rio added. 'But Oscar Myles has another thing coming if he thinks this is going to be the end of the matter. He isn't the only person who's given us the slip over the years. Instead of facing the problem head-on, he's decided to run. That'll only up the ante and heighten the odds.'

Mum let out a sigh of frustration. 'What do you suggest we do now?'

'We'll track the bastard down and get back every penny we're owed,' Rio replied. 'This isn't the first time something like this has happened, and I dare say it won't be the last. Davie had some very reluctant customers over the years, but he prided himself on always recovering what was owed, so I've got plenty of experience in dealing with weasels like Oscar. He thinks he's got one up on us at the moment, but he'll be sorry he didn't just do as he was told when I get hold of him.'

'So I'll leave this in your capable hands for the time being,' Mum said.

'I'll put the feelers out in the morning and see what I can find out about the wide boy we're dealing with. In the meantime, I suggest we all get some sleep. It's been a long day, and there's nothing we can do about it now,' Rio said.

'Good idea.' Mum nodded in agreement.

'I don't know about you lot, but there's no way I'm going to be able to sleep. I'm too wound up,' Kelsey snapped, finally finding her voice.

'Well, you should try. Stressing yourself out isn't going to change the situation, but you'll give yourself premature wrinkles if you keep scowling like that.' Rio laughed to try and lighten the mood.

Kelsey rewarded him with an eye-roll before she walked over to the fridge, pulled open the door and took out a bottle of chilled Chablis.

'I need a drink. Does anyone care to join me?' she asked, holding the bottle out in front of her.

'No thanks,' we all chorused.

'I can't say I'm surprised he did a runner from the flat he was living in. It was a shithole if ever I saw one.' Kelsey pulled out the cork and poured herself a large glass of white wine.

'I'll be in touch after I've done a bit of digging,' Rio said before heading for the door, closely followed by Darius.

'What a bloody nightmare that turned out to be,' Kelsey said before taking a huge gulp.

'Rio's right; you shouldn't stress yourself out,' Mum soothed, rubbing Kelsey's arm and offering her a sympathetic smile.

'That's easier said than done. Oscar Myles is a liberty taker, and I can't abide people like that.' As Kelsey downed the rest of her drink, her blue eyes flashed with anger.

6

Scarlett

Even before I'd been attacked, I'd never had the most reliable memory. I'd always been a bit of an airhead, naturally forgetful and ditzy. Mia was by far the brainiest of the three of us; intelligence seemed to be on a sliding scale in my family. By the time I'd been born, most of it had been used up by my siblings. I was definitely more in touch with my creative side. My IQ level was well below Mia and Kelsey's; my grey matter wasn't nearly as efficient as theirs. Not that that bothered me; I was the only one in the family with rhythm, and I'd rather be able to dance any day of the week than solve mathematical equations. But as I racked my brains, trying to remember the details of CJ's bachelor pad, I wished for once the split of mental capability between us had been more equal.

I readjusted my pillows and then lay back against them, staring up at the ceiling as I tried to recall even a tiny detail that might help me to locate CJ. I couldn't put my hand on my heart and say I knew that much about him. We'd only been together for a short time. The man whose child I'd been carrying was little more than a stranger. Kelsey had tried to warn me about going out with somebody I barely knew, but I was too pig-headed to listen and now I had to pay the price.

I'd only been to CJ's apartment a couple of times, and I couldn't for the life of me remember his address, but the building itself was memorable, having a gym and swimming pool that overlooked the South Dock within its walls. There was also a members' club. That should narrow things down, I thought. There couldn't be many places like that within a stone's throw of central London.

I opened my iPad and typed London apartments with leisure facilities into Google. My heart sank when I saw how many new developments came back, matching the criteria. All I could do was go through the search results one by one until I found what I was looking for; I wasn't ready to throw the towel in just yet. I spent an eternity scrolling through the various properties and was on the verge of giving up when my luck changed. The minute I saw a picture of the eighteenth-floor bar with its large terrace offering panoramic views of Canary Wharf, the Thames, and the city skyline, it ignited a spark in my brain. I recognised it instantly.

I got up from the bed and walked over to the desk in the corner of my room, pulled open the top drawer and took out a pad of paper and a pen. I'd developed a love of writing things down since losing my phone and all the information stored on it; scribbling notes had become my new obsession.

So now I knew the location of CJ's apartment, but I couldn't remember which number he lived at. All I knew was that it was on the top floor. It must have been a corner property because I remember it having fantastic views from the L-shaped balcony.

My temples started to throb; I needed a break from the screen, so I closed the lid of my iPad and looked down at the notes I'd made. I wasn't sure what I was going to do with the information. I remember turning up on CJ's doorstep unannounced once before, and I didn't receive a very warm welcome. Even though I was desperate to confront him, I wasn't sure I was brave enough to darken his doorstep. What if I plucked up the courage to go over there and he attacked me? That was a real possibility, wasn't it? My fingertips traced over the scar on my stomach. Just the thought of facing him sent adrenaline racing around my body. But being in a state of constant fear wasn't helpful. It was making me feel overwhelmed and vulnerable.

If Kelsey and Mia were to be believed, CJ had done a runner and disappeared off the face of the earth. The chances of him still living in his penthouse were slim, but I had nothing else to go on, so it had to be worth a try. The only way I'd be able to accept their account of what happened to me was to hear it from CJ's mouth. Then maybe I could start putting the pieces of my life together again. But first, I'd have to force myself to leave the house. That would require digging deep and standing up to my fears. There was nothing like having a sense of purpose to help overcome emotional trauma. Who knows, freeing myself from the past might end up being liberating. But I'd have to devise a better plan than hanging around the building, hoping to bump into my ex.

When I thought about it logically, I knew no good would come from pursuing somebody who cared so little for me. Tracking CJ down would more than likely result in even more heartache. But I couldn't seem to let go of the idea. As I began to regain my strength, my desire to track him down grew. I couldn't focus on anything else. I needed to either get myself over to his apartment or pay somebody to go there on my behalf. I briefly considered asking a friend from uni to go and knock on all of the penthouse doors and see who opened them, but they'd have a whole load of questions about why I had asked them to do such a thing, and I didn't want to have an inquisition on my hands, so I ruled that idea out almost instantly.

I picked up my mobile and dialled the number for the twenty-four-hour reception, but I ended the call before it had connected. I clearly wasn't thinking straight. What was I going to ask? *Excuse me, I know it's a long shot, but do you by any chance know what number a man called CJ lives at? He owns an apartment in the building.* I wasn't sure they'd be able to give out information like that even if they did know.

I needed help, but I wanted to protect my privacy. The idea of hiring a PI suddenly popped into my brain, but when I mulled it over, I realised I knew very little about him. I had virtually no personal information, so they'd have nothing to go on. I didn't even know CJ's surname. All I could tell them was he was a tall, dark-haired man with dark brown eyes. He had straight white teeth and was early to mid-twenties. Not a lot really to go on; they'd probably laugh me out of town. But my curiosity was getting the better of me, so I opened up the lid of my iPad again and typed 'private investigator London' into the search bar before my headache got too bad.

I clicked on the first result and read the introduction on the firm's website. It claimed its investigators would help clients collect all the evidence needed to make informed decisions. They had a track record of ninety-five per cent success in surveillance and ninety-two per cent in all other activities. Now I was intrigued, and when I read on, it looked as though I could ask a member of their team to put CJ's whole building under surveillance, not just him as an individual. That might be an option worth exploring, but I'd need to give them a call to discuss my requirements before I'd know for certain whether that was something they would be able to help me with. I didn't feel up to doing that now, but at least I'd given myself food for thought.

I attempted to let my thoughts drift away from CJ, but they kept returning to him no matter how hard I tried. Deciding what to do for the best was stressing me out. I wasn't sure why I was putting myself under so much pressure; I didn't need to make my mind up right this minute. But what was the point in stalling? The longer I had to think about things, the greater the chance I'd talk myself out of it, and my need for closure was growing stronger by the day.

7

Kelsey

'Oscar Myles seems to have disappeared off the face of the earth. I've done some digging and found out that he works at Vodafone on Lewisham High Street. Darius and I popped in there earlier, and surprise, surprise, he phoned in sick a couple of days ago, and they haven't seen him since,' Rio said when he stepped into the office.

'I'm beginning to wish we hadn't bought the debt from Larry now.' Mum looked like she had the weight of the world on her slim shoulders.

'Don't worry, Amanda. I'll sort it. You have my word,' Rio reassured her. 'I've spoken to DC Fallow and asked him to put out an alert on the Aston Martin's number plate.'

'DC Fallow?' Mum questioned. 'I haven't heard you mention his name before.'

'He's our new guy at the cop shop, and so far, he seems to be a pretty reliable source. All the information he's given me has proven to be very useful indeed. He's worked out we can potentially put a lot of money his way, so he seems extra eager to earn some brownie points with us.' Rio smiled.

'How will putting out an alert on the Aston Martin's number plate help us?' Mum tilted her head to one side.

'I'll let Darius explain.' Rio turned towards his nephew.

He was keen to get the latest recruit involved and prove that he was an asset to the firm.

Darius looked mildly horrified by Rio's suggestion but quickly composed himself.

'The police use a system called Automatic Number Plate Recognition. When a vehicle passes an ANPR camera, its registration is read and checked against database records. Anything of interest is flagged, which should help us keep tabs on Oscar's movements if he's using the road network to avoid us,' Darius said, and Rio beamed with pride.

It was touching to watch their exchange. Anyone could see the two of them shared a close bond. Rio would have made a good dad, but he'd never had the opportunity, so instead, he'd taken other people's children under his wing.

'Oh, I see. So do you think he's fled the area?' Mum asked.

'It's possible. None of his family are local. They all live in and around Northampton, so he could have done a bunk up there,' Rio replied.

Mum let out a loud sigh. 'He's not going to be easy to locate.'

'I'm confident we'll be able to track Oscar down, but it might take some time. He might think he's giving us the run-around, but he's still wet behind the ears. He'll slip up at some point, and when he does, we'll be waiting for him. He can't hide forever,' Rio said, doing his best to put Mum's mind at ease.

'I hope you're right. It won't do our reputation any good if we get duped by a man barely out of his teens,' Mum said, fixing Rio with her blue eyes.

'Oscar's not as clever as he thinks. Aston Martins are usually white, grey or black – something neutral and sophisticated – but the one the flash bastard bought was a very distinctive colour, Flugplatz Blue, so that will definitely be in our favour. It's a very unusual shade that catches the eye. Davie would have loved it,' Rio said.

Mum's eyes misted over at the mention of my dad's name, so I decided to pipe up to distract her from her thoughts.

'Tracking the little shit down is going to become my personal ambition. Nobody makes a fool out of me, so nothing would give me greater pleasure than watching Rio and Darius beat the crap out of Mr Myles,' I said, giving Mum something different to focus on.

'All in good time,' Rio replied with a slow nod of the head.

'Dealing with dickheads like Oscar makes me wish I'd never given up my old job. And to think I considered the Z-list celebrities and social media influencers I used to deal with hard work. There's no doubt they used to push my buttons, but Oscar has taken things to a whole new level.' I let out a loud sigh.

'Patience never was your strong point, darling,' Mum teased.

The corners of my mouth lifted in response. After having spent years in the company of irritating clients, I'd mastered the art of giving a bland social smile, useful on such occasions so that the other person wouldn't realise how much they were boring me. It took time to learn, but now I'd consider myself somewhat of an expert.

'Too right; life's far too short to be bogged down by things that frustrate me.' I tilted my head to one side and locked eyes with my mum.

I was quick to cull things that didn't interest me, but that wasn't a crime, so I wasn't about to apologise for being that way. I preferred to fill my days doing things that made me happy, and being given the run-around either in relationships or business wasn't something that floated my boat. Come to think of it, I was long overdue a good night out. A celibate priest had seen more action than I had recently. A bit of no-strings-attached sex always lifted my spirits and gave me a new perspective.

In the past, I'd worked for a party planning company running events for influencers and reality TV stars, and even though that wasn't my current line of work, it continued to offer perks. I was still on their email list, and one had come in earlier, inviting me to a social gathering this evening. I'd initially sacked off the idea, but after the day I was having, it was time to reconsider. A few glasses of bubbles and the chance to flirt with a roomful of hot guys who were competing for my attention was just what the doctor ordered.

The way I saw it, I had two choices. I could either spend the rest of the day trying to locate a worthless piece of scum who owed my family money or reward myself with a pampering session before this evening's event. The decision wasn't exactly a hard one to make.

'Right, ladies, I'll check back with you later,' Rio said, signalling to Darius before they stepped out into the garden.

'I better get going too,' I announced, picking up my phone and seizing the moment.

'Where are you going?' Mum asked.

'There's a function on tonight, and I need to go and buy something to wear,' I said as though that was the most normal thing to do in the middle of the working day.

'What function?' Mum's tone was abrupt.

'The firm I used to work for is hosting a cocktail evening, and I'm going along to support my old colleagues,' I said.

'Really?' Mum didn't look impressed as she fixed her eyes on me. 'What about supporting your new colleagues? I thought you said you were going to make it your mission to track Oscar down.'

'I know I did, but that can wait until tomorrow.'

Mum didn't reply, but I could see her nostrils flare ever so slightly as she bit her tongue. Another win for Kelsey, I thought as I walked past the front of her desk. I saw her look over at Mia and shake her head as I disappeared out of the door.

Running Dad's firm was more challenging than I'd expected it to be. I wasn't sure I was suited to the kind of job that meant I was working really hard all the time. When I was a party planner, I used to get to go to events and swan around in nice clothes, looking hot and being sassy, which suited my personality down to the ground.

8

Mia

'Your sister astounds me sometimes,' Mum said as Kelsey strutted off in the direction of the house.

Kelsey had never been the most reliable of people; flaky was her middle name, and she was incredibly headstrong. The two things weren't a good combination.

'I just don't know what goes on inside her head.' Mum sighed; anyone could see she was exasperated.

I knew where Mum was coming from, but Kelsey was a leader, not a follower, and she liked to march to the beat of her own drum.

'After your dad was murdered, she spent a huge amount of time and effort trying to convince me that the two of you were the firm's future. In the beginning, I was so opposed to the idea, but you know what Kelsey's like: she wouldn't take no for an answer. She was determined to wear me down, and she finally managed to convince me to give you both the opportunity to fill your dad's shoes. And look how she's repaid me? She's lost interest already.' Mum shook her head.

She usually had bucketloads of patience, but everyone had a limit, and it looked as though Mum had reached hers.

'I know how much it's frustrating you, but try not to get stressed about it. Kelsey probably just needs to let off a bit of steam.'

'The firm would fall to pieces if we followed her example and took off every time something didn't go our way.' Mum clenched her jaw. The look of disappointment she was wearing clung to her features like a second skin.

'But we're not going to follow in her footsteps; we're going to focus on the job in hand and try and find out where Oscar's hiding out. We'll bring Kelsey up to speed when she's next in the office,' I said.

'Ever since she was a little girl, Kelsey liked to think she ruled the roost. She's always broken the rules and resisted authority. That was never checked because your father saw too much of himself in her, and he liked her spirit. Now we're the ones left paying the price. The way she's behaving isn't fair on any of us, especially you. If she's not back in the office tomorrow morning, I'm going to have serious words with her.' Mum shook her head.

'I know you're annoyed, but just cut her a bit of slack. If you go in on her, pull rank and push her in one direction, you're probably only going to make the situation worse. She'll dig her heels in and end up doing the opposite anyway,' I said.

Kelsey was usually incredibly predictable in a situation like this. She didn't like being told what to do and had a rebellious streak a mile wide. I hoped for once she proved us wrong and didn't react the way we were expecting her to, but my younger sister had a habit of doing what she wanted when she wanted.

'Have you got a minute?' Rio asked before stepping inside the office.

'Of course,' Mum replied.

'I was just thinking maybe Darius and I should take a trip up to Northampton to check out where Oscar's family live,' Rio suggested. 'His parents, two sisters and various aunts and uncles are all within a stone's throw of each other.'

'That's a good idea.' Mum nodded.

'And if we're lucky, we might just spot the little fucker or better still find the Aston Martin parked outside one of his relations' gaffs.' Rio grinned.

9

Kelsey

I hot-footed it down the path with a spring in my step before Mum had a chance to say another word. Once I was inside the house, I bounded up the stairs and paced along the corridor, pausing outside Scarlett's room to momentarily catch my breath. I rapped on her door with my knuckles but didn't wait for her to reply before I opened it. Scarlett was lying on her side with her eyes closed as I approached the bed. When she realised she wasn't alone in the room, I saw her visibly jump. Guilt crept up my spine. I felt bad that I'd startled her so easily. It was clear her nerves were still in tatters.

'Sorry, I didn't mean to scare you. I just wondered if you fancied coming to Bluewater with me,' I said with a smile.

Scarlett blinked as my words registered; she looked pale and drawn. It would be some time before she was back to her old self.

'No thanks,' Scarlet replied after a significant pause.

I hated seeing my younger sister suffering like this; she used to be a vibrant young woman full of energy. Now she moved in slow motion like an astronaut walking on the moon. But most of the day, she was alone in her room, napping like an old-age pensioner as she battled to regain her health. It was almost as though she lost her spark when she lost the baby she was carrying. Her miscarriage appeared to have extinguished her zest for life.

'Are you sure I can't tempt you? You used to love going shopping.'

Not so long ago, Scarlett and I had been known to while away an entire day at Bluewater. We'd spend the morning trying on designer clothes, stop for lunch, and do the same thing all over again in the afternoon.

We could have opened our own boutique with the number of things we'd bought in the past. Most of the items were unnecessary purchases that would never leave our cupboards again. If we looked inside any of our wardrobes, we would find countless outfits that still had all the tags on; it was a needless waste, but I justified our actions because we weren't harming anybody, and we could afford the lifestyle we were living.

Scarlett shifted in the bed, and I saw her wince with pain. 'Thanks for the offer, but I'm really not feeling up to it; maybe another time.'

'Fair enough. I can take a hint.' I smiled before closing her bedroom door.

Shopping wasn't as much fun on my own, so as I walked back down the stairs, I considered whether I needed to go and buy a new outfit for the party this evening. I was sure I could find something suitable to wear. But need didn't come into it. What Kelsey wanted, she got. That was how my parents had raised me. I was happy with the arrangement and didn't feel like changing it.

I glanced at my Cartier watch. It was coming up to lunchtime. Mia and Mum would soon be taking a break, so I wanted to get out of the house before they did. My car was parked outside, so I peered out of the window to check that the coast was clear; seeing the driveway deserted, I took the opportunity to make a run for it. I opened the door of my Mercedes, sat behind the wheel and turned on the ignition.

I was about to pull away when I noticed a very faint smell in the cabin. I sniffed the air and started looking around the inside of the car, but I couldn't seem to find the source even though the aroma seemed familiar, so I filed the thought at the back of my mind and went on my way. Bluewater was calling to me, and if I didn't want to get waylaid by my mother, the slave driver, I'd better make myself scarce and get on the A2 before she ventured out of the office.

The traffic was kind to me, and for once, there weren't any hold-ups at the Blackwall Tunnel, which was a miracle in itself, and the traffic on the A2 was moving steadily, so thirty-five minutes later, I reached my destination.

I parked my car on the third level and then decided to take the stairs to the shops. I hated the idea of being in a lift when I was on my own in case it broke down. I couldn't think of anything worse than being trapped inside a windowless space waiting for help to arrive. Besides that, the exercise would do me good. It might help to clear the morning's stress from my mind.

Just as I'd descended the second flight, I heard the door from the car park above me open, and the sound of footsteps echoed behind me. I quickened my pace in response. I didn't know why I suddenly felt edgy, but it was rare for me to venture out on my own; a burly man normally accompanied me. Another four flights were between myself and the safety of other people. I was almost hyperventilating when I pushed the door open to the shops. My heart was pounding in my chest, and my pulse was jumping around at the side of my neck.

This wasn't turning out to be as much fun as I'd thought, and I was beginning to wish I hadn't come. But I was here now, so I might as well make the most of it. Once I was inside Reiss, I started leafing through the racks of beautiful clothes, and my panicked state soon subsided. It didn't take me long to find what I was looking for; I selected a bandage body-con dress in pillar-box red and took it to the changing room. It fitted like a glove and matched my personality perfectly. I didn't do wallflower. Blending into the background wasn't me. I liked to be noticed and be the centre of attention.

I'd intended to go into Hotel Chocolat and get a box of

Patisserie Luxe for Scarlett to cheer her up; they were her favourite, but I'd been a bit spooked by my earlier experience, so I'd decided to abandon the shopping trip and head for home. I wasn't going to chance walking up the stairs again even though nothing had happened, so I started hanging around by the lifts, pretending to look in the shop windows while I waited for people to gather. Sticking with a crowd seemed like the sensible thing to do; there was safety in numbers and all that, wasn't there?

Just as I began reversing out of the parking space, my mobile rang in my Coach handbag. I put the car back into park and grabbed the handle of the blush pink leather strap, hoisting it out of the passenger footwell. My hand delved inside and located the handset. The caller ID displayed private number, so I thought twice about answering it, but then curiosity got the better of me, and I decided to swipe at the screen.

'Hello. Hello,' I repeated a second or two later when the call connected, but nobody replied.

Phone reception was quite often bad at Bluewater, especially in the multi-storey, so I wasn't particularly surprised by the lack of response.

'Hello. Can you hear me?' I asked.

My question hung in the air, unanswered, so I held my breath and listened to see if I could make out any background noise, but there was nothing to indicate who was on the phone. I ended the call, reasoning that if it was anything important, the person would phone me back later. I placed my mobile in the hands-free windscreen mount before putting my Mercedes back into reverse and heading out of the shopping centre. I was keen to get on the road before the school run started and the traffic built up. It seemed to get earlier every day, and the journey, which had taken thirty-five minutes on the way down, could end up being well over an hour if I timed it wrong.

My lips stretched into a wide smile when I pulled into the drive just over half an hour later. The traffic gods had been kind to me and kept the four-wheel-drive warrior queens with weirdly named offspring away from me. These women were a force to be reckoned with on the dual carriageway driving their expensive motors like modern-day chariots of fire, changing lanes without indicating and blasting other road users out of the way while keeping the palms of their manicured hands flat on the horn. Give me a white-van man, any day of the week. If you asked me, their manners were impeccable compared to the yummy mummies I encountered on the stretch of road surrounding Sidcup, who were primed and ready to do battle.

Now that I'd made it home in one piece, I had plenty of time to get ready for the evening's event. A long soak in the tub was just what I needed to wash away the stress of the day. I'd done my best to banish Oscar Myles from my thoughts, but he kept creeping back into them every now and then.

I came out of the en suite bathroom with a towel wrapped around me, my damp skin glowing from the perfumed bubbles I'd been relaxing in, and my eyes scanned around my empty room. I couldn't put my finger on what was troubling me, but something seemed off. I sat down at my dressing table and patted myself dry before I began slathering myself in Jo Malone English Pear & Freesia body lotion. Then I started reapplying my makeup, but as I looked in the mirror, it felt like somebody was watching me. I don't know why I was being so paranoid. It was very out of character for me.

'How do I look?' I asked, waltzing into the kitchen.

'You look stunning.' Scarlett smiled.

'I'll second that,' Mia agreed.

Mum didn't comment, so I turned to look at her. She would normally have been the first to start gushing.

'You look lovely,' Mum said after a lengthy pause. But the compliment seemed begrudging.

'Thanks,' I replied.

My mum and sisters were sitting around the table. Jack was

nowhere to be seen as usual. No doubt he was working late again. He put in longer hours than a labourer in a sweatshop. It had crossed my mind that he used work as an excuse so that he didn't have to spend the evening stuck on the sofa watching Netflix with the rest of my family.

It couldn't have been much fun for him being a newlywed and having to live with his mother-in-law. Where was the excitement in that? Mia and Jack should still be in the honeymoon period, ripping each other's clothes off at every opportunity and having impromptu sex sessions all over the house. But they couldn't exactly do that with all of us rattling around. One of us might walk in on them. The thought of that brought a smile to my face; if I had been Mia, the added risk of being discovered would have made me want to do it, but my older sister was a lot more conservative than I was.

Mia was adamant that she wouldn't move into their new house and leave Mum on her own even though Scarlett and I still both lived with her. Jack knew how highly strung Mia could be, so he'd let her have her own way. He never wanted to do anything to stress her out and took the role of the concerned husband seriously, especially now that Dad was no longer around to protect her. I couldn't decide whether that was sweet or cringy.

'Right, I'd better get going,' I said.

'Have a lovely time.' Scarlett smiled again.

'You can come if you like,' I suggested.

'Thanks, but I'm not really dressed for the occasion.'

Scarlett's red hair was pulled into a messy bun on top of her head, and she had her favourite light grey lounging tracksuit on, the sleeves of which were pulled down over her hands.

'I'll help you to get ready; it doesn't matter if we're late. It's always good to make an entrance at these things.'

'It might do you good to go out, darling,' Mum encouraged.

I couldn't help noticing she was in a much better mood with Scarlett than me.

'I really don't fancy it; I'm not feeling that sociable, but thanks anyway.'

The smile had now slid from Scarlett's face. She looked stressed out that we were trying to talk her into leaving the safety of the family home.

'What about me?' Mia piped up, diverting the attention away from Scarlett. 'How come I don't get invited?'

'Because you're an old married woman,' I joked. 'I'd better make tracks; my taxi's outside.'

'What time will you be home?' Mum asked, offering me a weak smile.

I shrugged my shoulders. 'No idea, but I wouldn't bother waiting up,' I replied before turning on my crystal-encrusted Manolo Blahniks and heading out of the room.

10

Mia

'I doubt very much whether your sister will show her face at work tomorrow,' Mum said. 'I'd happily put money on the fact that she'll be nursing a hangover and spend the day buried under her duvet.'

'You might be right, but let's give her the benefit of the doubt.' I offered Mum a weak smile.

Kelsey wasn't doing herself any favours, but that wouldn't worry her. She had thick skin and didn't give a damn what people thought about her.

'It's good of you to defend her. I'm not sure Kelsey would be so generous if you tried to pull the same stunt. You girls are meant to be working together as a team. Where does it leave us if Kelsey's lost interest in the business?' Mum trained her blue eyes on me.

'I'm sure she hasn't,' I replied.

'You could always take on somebody else,' Scarlett piped up.

Mum and I had been so engrossed in conversation, and Scarlett had been so quiet I'd almost forgotten she was sitting at the table.

'I think Mia and I can handle things,' Mum replied.

Scarlett's bottom lip turned out and started to quiver. 'You said I could have a place in the firm once I finished my education, but it's always the same old story; three's a crowd, right?'

'Not at all, but you need to concentrate your efforts on getting better right now, and when you're back to full health, you can join your sisters if that's what you want.' Mum gave Scarlett a weak smile. 'I won't go back on my word, I promise, but are you sure you want to walk away from all the hard work and dedication? What about your dream of treading the boards? How does the saying go? You only regret the things you don't do.'

Scarlett pressed her hands down on her stomach. She was clearly still in pain, which reminded us that the chance of her fulfilling her chosen career was hanging by a thread.

'Do you seriously think that's still an option?' Scarlett's blue eyes brimmed with tears.

I felt myself start to well up in response. I hated seeing other people visibly distressed, so I reached across the table and squeezed her hand in a show of support. Mum leapt out of her chair and rushed over to where Scarlett was sitting. She crouched down beside her and threw her arms around her shoulders, but my sister shrugged our mum away.

'I'm going to bed. I'm not feeling well,' Scarlett said with bitterness coating her words.

Mum stood up as Scarlett pushed her chair back and got to her feet. As she walked across the tiled floor, she tried to hide the fact that she was gritting her teeth, but I could see every step she took was causing her agony.

'Maybe we shouldn't mention Scarlett becoming a performer for the time being. She's got a long road ahead of her until she'll be fit enough to audition for roles,' I said.

The future Scarlett had mapped out for herself wasn't viable right now, so everything must have seemed bleak to her.

'I suppose you're right. I didn't mean to be insensitive, but I could never imagine her doing anything else with her life. From the minute she could walk, Scarlett loved to dance and was always pirouetting around the house.' Mum's voice cracked when she spoke.

Some of my earliest memories were of Scarlett dressed in a

tutu and ballet shoes, practising her dance routines. She'd been a dedicated student and was extremely talented. It would be heartbreaking for all of us if she didn't get to fulfil her dream.

But Scarlett had a backbone of steel, and I felt confident that she would harness her inner strength and overcome the hurdles that had been thrown in her way. She just needed time and the love and support of her family. I was sure of it.

11

Scarlett

I placed one foot on the tread, but pain seared through my insides as soon as I put my weight on it. Every step I took up the staircase brought fresh agony with it. The doctors had said that my wound was healing extremely well with no sign of infection. They were delighted with my progress. Apparently, I was fortunate to have age and fitness on my side, speeding things along. But from my point of view, my recovery was dragging on and on with no end in sight.

By the time I got to the top of the stairs, I felt like I'd reached the summit of Mount Everest and had to pause to catch my breath while holding onto the bannister. The exhausting ordeal wasn't over yet. I still had to walk the short distance to my bedroom. It felt like I was embarking on a marathon. Even when I took baby steps, the wound on my stomach pulled. The surgeon had spent hours stitching me back together layer by layer, but that still didn't stop me from worrying that my skin might reopen any minute.

I pushed open my door and inched my way across to the bed. Tears of frustration rolled down my cheeks as I sat down on the edge, so I swiped at them with the back of my hand. CJ had a lot to answer for; he'd ruined my life. I couldn't even walk around without being in pain. The conversation I'd just had with Mum had highlighted how much everything had changed for me. It shouldn't have been the case, but it took her to point out what was staring me in the face. My dreams had been dashed, and the little things I used to take for granted were now huge ordeals. Anger started to rise up within me at the injustice of it all. I didn't like the label, but I was the victim in this situation, and I deserved to get some payback for what I'd been through. The more I mulled over what had happened to me, the more I wanted revenge. If CJ thought I was going to let him walk away that easily, he was very much mistaken.

I reached over to my bedside cabinet, opened the top drawer, and took out my laptop. I flipped open the screen and pulled up the website of the private investigators' firm I'd been looking at previously. I picked up my mobile and then brought it to life with the pad of my fingertip. I knew the company wasn't open now, but I dialled their number with trembling fingers anyway. My nerves were already getting the better of me, so if I waited until the morning, I would probably have talked myself out of it again. My call connected to the firm's answering machine, so I did as requested and left a message after the beep.

'My name's Scarlett Saunders. I'd like to speak to a member of your team regarding some surveillance work. Could somebody please give me a call back tomorrow? Thanks very much,' I said before I ended the call.

My heart was pounding in my chest. I hated leaving recorded messages. But at least it was done now, so there was no going back. I inhaled a deep breath, rested my back against the headboard and stared up at the ceiling. I'd only taken the first step towards tracking down CJ, but the fact that I'd done something proactive, felt like a huge achievement, and a wave of relief washed over me.

I wished I could share the good news with somebody, but that was out of the question. My family had warned me off trying to contact CJ so they wouldn't be best pleased to hear what I'd done.

I thought about reaching out to my drama school buddies, but I didn't want to suddenly phone them out of the blue. My uni friends had been really sympathetic and had all tried to rally around me after I was attacked, but I'd pushed them away and had been distancing myself from them ever since. What CJ had done to me was so humiliating; I was embarrassed by their pity. I felt like an idiot. He'd stripped me of every ounce of dignity I'd possessed. And if I was brutally honest, it wasn't just that. Since graduating, they'd all started auditioning for jobs and landing themselves fantastic roles while I'd been confined to bed like a frail old woman. I felt left out and couldn't help being envious of what my friends were achieving, and I didn't want it rubbed in my face all the time.

12

Kelsey

Almost as soon as I walked into the venue, I started to regret making the decision to attend. The place was full of loudmouth wannabes whose incessant chatter was grating on my nerves. My eyes scanned the room in search of male talent, but there was a very poor turnout indeed. If pretty boys wearing ankle-grazer trousers and loafers turned me on, I'd have been spoilt for choice. But I couldn't abide men who wore shoes with bare feet. And don't get me started on cropped trousers. I hated them. They looked ridiculous. I hadn't seen one member of the opposite sex they suited. I'd thought it was a passing trend when guys began wearing them, but now I was starting to think they might be around for a while; I was desperate for the craze to disappear. I cast my eye over the men again, but none of them were in the running; they probably took longer than I did to get ready. I wouldn't touch a guy like that with a bargepole. Just the thought of it gave me the ick.

Standing around trying to be sociable to a group of people I'd never met was harder work than I remembered. But I used to get paid to do this, so maybe that had something to do with it. As meeting the man of my dreams was out of the question tonight, I might as well enjoy the complimentary champagne and canapés that were doing the rounds, at least for an hour or two. I couldn't bear the humiliation of going home early and having to face my mum and sisters. Thankfully none of them were night owls, so

I'd only have to endure this bunch of losers for a short amount of time before I could cut and run.

To my delight, the house was in darkness when I got out of the cab. I did my best to tiptoe across the gravel, hoping my stilettos wouldn't make too much noise. I wasn't worried about disturbing my sleeping relatives, but the idea of losing face if they realised I was back before midnight was unbearable. It was unheard of for me to be home so early; they'd know without even having to ask that I'd had a terrible evening. It was a far more usual scenario for me to let myself in while they were having breakfast! When I was on a night out, I liked to party hard.

I'd been caning the free drinks, so climbing the stairs without waking the whole house took all my powers of concentration. I was more than a little worse for wear, so I didn't bother getting ready for bed. I climbed under the covers, still wearing a full face of makeup and the expensive body-con dress I'd bought earlier. Even in my drunken state, I knew I'd regret doing that in the morning, but I didn't have the energy or the inclination to carry out my usual skincare routine. My bed was calling to me, and I wasn't about to resist it.

I put my phone on the bedside table, and as I ducked under the quilt, I realised I'd forgotten to put it on airplane mode. The last thing I wanted was for my sleep to be disturbed, so I reached over to pick it up, but as I did, I accidentally knocked it onto the floor. The upper half of my body hung out of the bed like a rag doll as my fingertips searched the carpet. The handset must have gone under the bed frame, so I leant out a little further. The blood went straight to my head, making it spin further as I trained my eyes on the space under my mattress. It was difficult to see the outline in the darkness, but I made a mental note to myself to get the housekeeper to do some tidying up tomorrow as there was a sizeable pile of discarded clothes on the other side of the bed heaped into a mound.

I was just about to abandon the search when my fingers finally made contact with the case. I lifted the phone off the floor and flopped onto my back. After bringing the phone to life with my fingerprint, I scrolled down and selected the plane symbol, pressing it with my index finger before placing the mobile back on the bedside cabinet.

I must have dropped off as soon as my head hit the pillow. I was in a deep sleep when I felt a set of fingers clamp tightly over my mouth. My heart started pounding, and my eyes sprang open. A man dressed all in black was standing over me. The weight of his hand pushed my head so deep into the pillows that they had folded up on either side of my face. I had no idea how the intruder had managed to get into the house with all the high-tech security measures we had in place. But I wasn't imagining it; this wasn't a vivid dream. Somebody was in my room, and they weren't here for a social reason. Now I realised how terrifying a visit from a stranger in the early hours of the morning could be. I couldn't see his face – a black balaclava covered it – but my rude awakening made me think it had something to do with Oscar Myles.

Terror instantly filled my throat, but nothing came out of my mouth. The intruder smothered the blood-curdling scream I was trying to force out. I was desperate to raise the alarm but powerless to do so. Nothing sobered a person up quicker than finding you weren't alone in your room after all. I started thrashing around in the bed.

Whatever this person had in store for me, I wasn't going to make it easy for them. I would fight with every last breath I had in my body. I repeatedly tried to bite the fingers that were covering my mouth. My attacker pinned me down with their body weight. I thought for one horrible minute I was going to be raped in my own bed. I was so focused on that hideous idea I hadn't seen what was about to happen. I suddenly felt the unmistakable sharp scratch of a needle as it pierced my skin. I gasped when I realised the man had just injected me with something. I battled against the unknown substance that was now flowing freely around my system, but there was nothing I could do to stop the effects of whatever I'd been given from taking hold of me.

It must have taken approximately twenty seconds for him to administer the drug, and it had already started to work. A tingling sensation was spreading through my body. I felt like I was floating above the bed before I felt myself becoming limp. Any efforts I'd made to free myself ground to a halt before everything went black.

13

Mia

I couldn't get the conversation I'd had with Mum and Scarlett out of my head. She'd looked so distressed when Mum had told her to concentrate on getting better rather than taking her place in the firm. Life was one disappointment after another for her at the moment. Scarlett was turning twenty-one in less than a week, and the big shindig we'd expected to be planning hadn't materialised into anything. The idea was dead in the water. Despite Mum's best efforts to push her down that route, Scarlett was determined she didn't want to have a party or any fuss.

Birthdays were supposed to be happy occasions, but Scarlett just wanted the day to pass her by without marking it. Twenty-one was supposed to be this huge milestone where everyone did something really memorable and had a fantastic time, but her mood was low; she seemed unable to shake off the sadness and felt like she had nothing to celebrate. I wished there was something I could do to lift her spirits.

We'd considered throwing her a small surprise bash with a handful of close friends, but Scarlett was avoiding having contact with people right now, so we didn't think it would go down too well if we went behind her back. We were caught between a rock and a hard place. The last thing we wanted was for her to think nobody cared enough about her to organise anything. But Scarlett was adamant she wanted a quiet day, so we had to respect her wishes.

Mum and I were sitting behind our desks when a WhatsApp message came through on our family group chat.

> *I'm not going to make it in today. I had a blast last night and I've got the hangover from hell! K xx*

Mum glanced over at me with a thunderous look on her face. 'I told you this was going to happen, didn't I? If Kelsey thinks it's acceptable to pull a sickie because she had too much to drink, she's got another thing coming. I expected more from her. Why spend all that time convincing me that she was ready to take on an active role in the firm if she was going to behave like this? More fool me for believing her,' she fumed, drumming her long fingers on the edge of the desk. 'Right, that's it. I'm going to have it out with her.'

Mum pushed her chair back and stood up, pausing for a moment before taking long strides across the room. Pulling the walk she'd learnt as a model many moons ago out of the bag, she glided as though she was strutting her stuff on the catwalk as her calf-length chiffon dress billowed around her. But Mum wasn't in a fashion show; she was on the warpath. I wouldn't want to be in my sister's shoes right now. It took a lot to rattle our mum, but once she lost her temper, whoever was on the receiving end was going to well and truly know about it.

I was at the coffee machine making myself a cappuccino when Mum came back into the office. I looked over my shoulder and gave her a sympathetic smile.

'How did it go?' I asked.

'Kelsey's not in her room.' I was glad to see Mum's anger had subsided.

'Should we be worried?' It didn't take much to put me on high alert.

Mum shook her head and let out a long sigh. 'You know what Kelsey's like; she's probably just crashed at a friend's. She said herself, she had the hangover from hell. I bet she had a skinful last night.'

'So you don't think I should let Rio know?'

'I wouldn't raise the alarm just yet. I'm sure she'll stumble in later on. She's probably trying to sleep off the worst of it,' Mum replied.

An idea had been burrowing its way into my brain, and now that Kelsey hadn't shown up to work, I decided to share it with Mum.

'I've been thinking if Kelsey's losing interest, why don't we let Scarlett get involved in the firm? She seemed like she really wanted to pitch in last night, and it might do her good to have something else to focus on.'

It had helped pull me out of the doldrums when I was trapped in a spiral of depression after Dad was murdered.

Mum seemed genuinely startled by my suggestion. 'Oh, I don't know about that. Like I said yesterday, I think it might be too much too soon. You know yourself, this business can be extremely stressful, and I don't want anything to hinder Scarlett's recovery.'

'I understand what you're saying, but she seemed absolutely gutted when you turned her down.'

Mum blew out a loud breath. 'I didn't mean to upset her. I just want her to concentrate her efforts on getting well, that's all.'

Mum tended to wrap people in cotton wool. She'd done the same to me when I was in a fragile state of mind, but sometimes pushing a person out of their comfort zone was the best medicine. And it wasn't as though we were forcing Scarlett into anything; she was a willing party.

'Do you remember when Kelsey told me to sort myself out because I was driving all of you nuts?' I asked.

'How could I forget? Kelsey isn't known for her tact and diplomacy.' Mum shook her head.

'I know you thought she was being hard on me, but she ended up doing me a huge favour. Her words held more power than I could have imagined. I'd been trapped inside my body with only my destructive thoughts for company, but then Kelsey gave me the shake-up I needed to set myself free.'

Mum tilted her head to one side while she considered what I'd said.

'Just think about it. You were convinced it would be too much for me to take on running the firm with Kelsey, but it's been the making of me, and if we give Scarlett a chance, I think the same thing could happen.'

Mum's eyes searched mine. I knew deep down she wanted what was best for Scarlett. She was a great mum and took her role seriously. She'd thrown everything into it. Mum was patient, kind and incredibly loving. My sisters and I had a strong bond with her. She always put her girls first, but sometimes she mollycoddled us.

Nobody knew better than I did what a battle beating depression could be. Scarlett was a naturally upbeat person and had never struggled with her mental health before. Her fragile state of mind came from the trauma she'd been through.

'We need to support Scarlett in every way that we can.' My words came from the heart.

'Do you really think she's up to it? Working for the firm can be extremely stressful and challenging at times.' I could see Mum was starting to come around to my way of thinking.

'There's only one way to find out. Maybe Scarlett could start off working part-time and build up from there,' I suggested.

'That's not a bad idea,' Mum replied. 'She wouldn't need to be in the office all day; she could come and go as she pleased. Kelsey pretty much does that anyway, so what's the difference.'

'I think it would do her good to be involved in the business. It will make her feel included and supported by the people who love her most. I think she'll be a huge asset,' I said.

I hated to think of my little sister stuck in her room, isolated away from the rest of us, with only her thoughts for company.

'Do you want to tell her, or shall I?' Mum asked.

14

Kelsey

I had no idea what time it was when I woke to find my temples throbbing. I reached out of bed, and my fingers fumbled around in the darkness as they attempted to find my mobile. I always left it on the bedside cabinet, but it didn't seem to be there, so I tried to open my eyes. A simple enough task, you would have thought, but my eyelids felt like they were being weighed down by something heavy. When I managed to prise them apart, my vision appeared blurry.

With my head still glued to the pillow, I cast my eyes around, trying to locate my mobile. It took a few moments for the penny to drop. No wonder my phone wasn't where I usually put it. I wasn't in my room. I was in a huge bed, which dominated the minimal space.

I wasn't too alarmed, to begin with; this wasn't the first time I'd woken up in a stranger's bed after a night out. I allowed my mind to drift back to the previous evening, but I couldn't for the life of me remember what had happened, let alone how I'd ended up here. I stole a glance to the right and was delighted to see the other half of the bed was empty. Whoever I'd hooked up with at the party wasn't with me now. With any luck, I was in a hotel, and my unidentified roommate had already cut and run.

My eyelashes felt like I was wearing lead mascara; sleep was calling me, so I didn't try to fight it. I allowed myself to drift off, safe in the knowledge that I wasn't going to be prodded in the back by an erect penis, when my hook-up buddy suddenly decided they had to get their physical needs met before we went our separate ways.

I woke again a while later. Daylight was seeping into the room through the slits in the blinds. I tried to raise my head, but it was as though somebody had glued my hair to the pillow. I'd had my fair share of hangovers over the years, but none of them could rival this one. I was aching all over and felt like I'd been hit by a bus. I could have been for all I knew. I had absolutely no memory of last night.

I looked down at myself as I lay in the bed; I was still wearing the red dress I'd gone out in. That was a good sign, I thought. Whoever I'd come here with hadn't taken advantage of me in my drunken state. The man must have had morals, which made a change from the guys I usually went for; they were normally only after one thing and wouldn't have been put off by my paralytic state. They would have found it a bonus that I was too intoxicated to offer any resistance. The fact that a person wasn't coherent enough to say no didn't mean they were saying yes. Silence didn't equal consent, but plenty of scumbags out there pretended not to be aware of that. The idea of what could have happened made me shudder. I'd had a lucky escape.

I felt disorientated and confused, so I lay back on the pillows, trying my best to remember what I'd got up to last night and exactly how many glasses or, more likely, bottles of champagne I'd guzzled. Judging by the state of my head, it must have been a substantial number. I turned my face towards the door when I heard somebody approaching the other side of it. I wasn't alone after all, and the thought of that sent a tremor of unease rippling through my body.

I held my breath when I saw the handle depress. As the door started to open, I pulled the covers tightly around me, trying to protect myself from whoever was on the other side. I wasn't sure how effective swaddling myself in a black satin sheet would be at warding off the mystery man's advances, but in the absence of some pepper spray or any other weapon, it was the only thing I could do. My heart leapt into my mouth when Todd Evans appeared in the opening. He stood in the doorway wearing a black T-shirt and combat trousers with a cocky smile on his face.

'Hello, Kelsey, long time no see,' Todd said.

My heart started hammering in my chest. 'What do you want?' I asked, hoping that my fear wouldn't get the better of me and come out in my voice.

Todd laughed. 'That's no way to greet an old flame, is it? Correct me if I'm wrong, but you don't seem that pleased to see me.' Todd's lips parted, exposing his straight white teeth.

His tattooed arms brought a memory to the forefront of my mind. Todd had the initial M tattooed on his chest over his heart. I felt my temper spike when I remembered how he'd lied to me, telling me it stood for his love of his mum, the military and the marines. When in actual fact, it was the first letter of his wife Michelle's name.

I couldn't deny Todd was looking smoking hot as he stood in the doorway leaning against the frame, but there was more chance of him winning the lottery than getting me back into bed. A feeling of dread washed over me. It was a well-known fact that drinking too much alcohol affected a person's judgement. I hoped nothing had happened between the two of us. He might think we had some unfinished business, but I didn't believe in rekindling old flames; relationships died out for various reasons. If they hadn't worked the first time around, they were unlikely to work in the future.

'So how's the head? I have to say you're looking pretty rough.' Todd laughed.

I flashed him an evil glare but didn't bother to answer his question.

I suddenly felt self-conscious lying back on the pillows, but as I repositioned myself with my back against the headboard, my right arm felt unusually heavy and achy when I put weight on it. I remembered experiencing a similar sensation after I'd had a vaccine, and a terrifying thought suddenly jumped to the forefront of my mind. Rohypnol.

'Did you drug me last night?' I questioned.

My eyes bored into Todd's so that I could gauge whether he was being honest or not.

'What makes you think I'd do something like that?' Todd's reply was noncommittal.

'Just answer the question.'

My patience was wearing thin, but Todd's lips were sealed.

'This arm's aching like a bastard, and you don't get that from drinking too much champagne. Whether you're prepared to admit it or not, I know you've given me something.

'Well done, Kelsey. You're quite the little detective, aren't you?' He laughed.

Outrage washed over me like a tsunami. No wonder I felt like shit.

'Who the fuck do you think you are?' I was absolutely furious. 'What the hell did you give me?' I demanded.

My tongue seemed to be the only part of me that was functioning properly, so Todd should brace himself; he was in for some verbal abuse. The fact that he was standing by the side of the bed laughing at me was only making matters worse. I felt completely helpless as I tried to get out of the bed; the satin was slippy and doing nothing to aid my cause, and my coordination was all over the place.

I threw back the black satin sheet and attempted to swing my legs over the side of the bed, but as I did, I lost my balance and fell back, knocking my head against the black leather headboard. I lay there for several seconds before I attempted to sit up again.

Todd sat down on the edge of the bed; then, he ran the fingertips of his right hand down the side of my cheek. I felt myself stiffen in response to his touch.

'Here, let me help you,' Todd said, reaching toward me.

I backed away. 'Don't touch me.'

'Suit yourself,' Todd replied, getting up from the bed.

'What did you give me? Was it Rohypnol or one of those other date-rape drugs?'

Todd laughed in my face. 'Don't flatter yourself, Kelsey.'

'I have a right to know what's floating around in my system.' I could feel my nostrils flaring.

'I don't think you're in any position to start making demands, do you?' Todd grinned. He was revelling in the fact that he had the upper hand.

I'd had a knee-jerk reaction when I'd first seen him standing in the bedroom doorway, so I hadn't bothered with any pleasantries. He'd received a frosty reception, which seemed to amuse him, but his attitude was getting my back up. I'd instinctively carried on giving him a lash of my tongue, but the sensible part of my brain told me to take things down a level and tone down my spikiness. It would be stupid to do something to antagonise him while I was on my own. Physically I was no match for Todd, but mentally I could definitely give him a run for his money. Even though it pained me to do so, I'd have to try and be pleasant until I could put some distance between us. But it was going to take a huge amount of effort on my part for it to look convincing.

'I'm not trying to make demands, but I'd like to know what you injected me with all the same.'

I was quite impressed with the way my words came out. Mum would be proud of me; my manners were on point. It was amazing what a person could do when they put their mind to it. I'd had to dig deep to find the ladylike alter ego hiding inside me, but I was delighted to discover she was in there, albeit buried down in the depths and covered in cobwebs.

'I bet you would. It must be killing you not knowing what was in the needle.' The corners of Todd's mouth lifted into a smile before he walked towards the door.

Making me suffer was bringing him such pleasure. I supposed I couldn't really blame him. If I'd been in his position, I would have been behaving in exactly the same manner. I hated to admit it, but Todd and I shared a lot of similar personality traits. We were both selfish and self-centred, to name a few.

'I can tell you one thing, you're going to have plenty of time to dwell on it,' Todd said before he stepped out of the room.

I gasped when I heard a key turn on the other side of the door. 'Don't you dare lock me in here, you bastard,' I yelled.

'Unless you want me to give you a top-up dose, I suggest you shut your mouth.'

I could tell by the tone of Todd's voice he wasn't bluffing, and a shiver ran down my spine.

15

Scarlett

I was still dozing when my mobile started ringing. With my eyes still closed, my hand automatically found its way out of the covers and gravitated towards the ringing handset.

'Hello,' I said, my voice croaky and thick with sleep even though it was 10 a.m.

'Good morning; is that Scarlett Saunders?' a well-spoken man asked.

My eyes sprang open, and I cleared my throat before I replied, 'Yes.' Then I burrowed my way out of the duvet and sat with my back against the headboard as I scrabbled around in the drawer of my bedside cabinet for a pad and pen.

'My name is Hugh Oliver, and I'm phoning from Shaw's private investigators. You left a message for one of the team to call you back. Is now a good time for you to talk?'

'Yes, thanks for returning my call.'

'You're welcome. I believe you were interested in having some surveillance work done?' Hugh said.

'That's right,' I replied.

'What exactly can we help you with?' Hugh questioned.

A long pause spread out between us.

'Ms Saunders, are you still there?'

'Yes. Please call me Scarlett. Ms Saunders seems so formal,' I replied. 'I didn't mean to give you the silent treatment; it's just I find the subject quite traumatic to talk about.'

'That's understandable; take all the time you need. I'm here to help you in any way I can,' Hugh said.

I was sure he'd just recited a well-practised sales pitch, but I didn't care. Hugh had delivered the words with such sincerity that he'd put me at ease, and I was happy to sign on the dotted line before I'd even found out whether this was going to be a viable option.

I straightened my posture and took a large lungful of air through my nostrils, holding it for five seconds before slowly exhaling. It was a technique I used before a performance to help calm my nerves.

'I read on your website that it's possible to put a building under surveillance.' I paused to give Hugh an opportunity to answer.

'Yes, that's right,' he confirmed.

'Somebody I know used to live in a new development in Canary Wharf, but I'm not sure if he still does. He owned one of the penthouse apartments. I can't remember the number of his flat, but I know the name of the building. If I gave you a description of the man, would you be able to keep watch and tell me whether or not you see him coming or going?'

I wasn't ready to share the details of why I wanted to find CJ at this stage.

'Absolutely, that kind of job is right up our street.' Hugh's voice was full of enthusiasm.

I felt my heart skip a beat as the corners of my lips lifted into a smile. 'So how does it work?'

I was more than a bit intrigued, but I needed to know how much it was likely to cost before I went ahead and instructed the firm.

'Shaw's charge eighty-five pounds an hour. I'd be happy to quote a fee for an agreed amount of time if you'd like,' Hugh said.

I wasn't sure what I'd been expecting him to say, but eighty-five pounds an hour was a lot of money. Tracking CJ down could end up costing a small fortune, especially as there was no certainty on how long the surveillance might take.

'That would be useful, then at least I can see what I'll need to budget for.'

'No two investigations are the same, but we'll tailor our services to your specific requirements. If you decide to go ahead, I'll need you to give me every piece of information you have on the suspect. It's common sense really, but the more you can tell me, the easier the job will be,' Hugh said.

'The man I want you to watch, I know his first name but not his surname. Will that be a problem?'

There was no point beating around the bush. I decided to put it out there and find out if that was going to be a sticking issue before we went any further. I'd been pregnant with CJ's child, but when I'd told Hugh that I didn't have his full name, it had made me realise how little I'd known about him. I was so grateful I hadn't needed to disclose the sensitive background details of how we'd been acquainted. It was cringe-worthy to think how naïve I'd been.

'That doesn't matter in a situation like this. As long as you can give me a physical description of the man I'm looking for, I'll be able to confirm whether I see him leaving or entering the building or not. It's not essential, but if you have a recent photo, that would be extremely useful.'

I felt my heart sink. All the pictures I had of CJ vanished when my phone was stolen. The digital age we lived in had a lot to answer for; everything was stored on your phone, and nobody knew people's numbers anymore. They were programmed in for ease of use, which was all very well, but when you lost the handset or, in my case, when a scumbag nicked it, the precious details it held went with it. Dad didn't want us backing up personal stuff in case somebody tried to steal the information and use it against us. He'd also banned us from storing anything in the cloud. Their security was tight, but it wasn't infallible and cyberattacks still happened. I got where he was coming from, but I wished I hadn't listened to him now.

Mum had tried to trace the receiver using the Apple tracking device, but she'd had no luck locating it. What was the point of having all the security measures when thieves knew how to disable the facility before selling the phone to somebody else at a fraction of what it was worth? I would gladly pay to buy it back again. The inconvenience it had caused was immeasurable. Being without my mobile was a huge pain in the arse.

'Scarlett, are you still there?' Hugh asked.

The sound of his voice brought me back to reality. 'Yes, I'm still here, but I'm afraid I haven't got any photos of CJ.'

Hugh must have picked up the despondent tone in my voice because his response was incredibly upbeat and positive.

'Not to worry. It makes the job easier to have an image to refer to, but the surveillance can still be done without it. Do you have any other questions?' Hugh asked.

'No. I think you've covered everything.'

'I'll get the quote emailed across to you so you can decide whether you want to go ahead or not,' Hugh said.

'On second thoughts, don't worry about the quote. I'd like you to start straight away if that's possible,' I replied.

My life had been in limbo since I'd been attacked. The police investigation was still continuing, but so far they hadn't been able to track CJ down. If I was going to put this behind me and have any sort of closure, I needed answers. At this moment in time, I didn't care how much it cost. I wanted Hugh to stake out CJ's Canary Wharf apartment and find out what he was up to.

'That's not a problem. If you text me the man's description and his last known address, I'll go over there shortly,' Hugh replied before we ended the call.

A couple of hours later, my phone pinged, and a tremor of excitement flowed through my body. My fingertips felt like they had pins and needles as I opened the WhatsApp message. Hugh had sent me some photos of a young man and asked if it was CJ. Although his physical description matched, he wasn't my ex, so my joy was short-lived. I flung my phone down on the bed in frustration. This could end up being a very costly exercise, I thought.

16

Mia

'Here goes,' Mum said, pausing outside Scarlett's room. She looked over her shoulder and smiled at me before she knocked on the door.

'Come in,' Scarlett called.

Mum pushed the door open and stepped inside. 'Hello, darling. Have you got a minute?'

'Yeah. What's up?' Scarlett asked.

Mum beckoned me towards her with her hand. Scarlett was sitting on the edge of her bed with her mobile clasped in her hand. She put it down next to her, then swept her long red hair over her shoulder and straightened her posture.

'Blimey, it must be serious if you've brought the cavalry.' Scarlett scowled.

'There's no problem either way.' Mum glanced sideways at me before she continued speaking. 'But we were wondering if you feel ready to start working for the family firm. We were thinking part-time until you're fully recovered.'

Scarlett raised an eyebrow. 'Really? What's brought this on?'

'We thought it would do you good to have something to focus on,' Mum replied, looking over at me for some moral support.

'Keeping Dad's business running has been the making of me. I really think it might help you get over everything that's happened to you,' I added.

Scarlett's response had blindsided me. I wouldn't have

invested the time and energy into talking Mum around if I'd realised Scarlett was going to be so underwhelmed. I'd been expecting her to leap off the bed and whoop with joy, but she just stared at us with a stony expression on her face. Mum and I were dumbstruck.

I'd stuck my neck out when I'd convinced Mum to bring Scarlett on board, but she didn't seem very grateful. I'd go so far as to say she'd thrown the offer back in Mum's face. I couldn't fathom the way her brain worked. Why make such a fuss about something if you didn't care either way about it? But I suppose that pretty much summed up Scarlett's personality. She made a song and dance act about everything and loved creating drama whether the situation called for it or not. It was true she had a lot on her plate, but it seemed like now that we were offering her what she'd said she'd wanted for ages, she'd changed her mind.

'Scarlett,' Mum prompted, looking at my sister as though she was the only person in the room.

But Scarlett didn't respond. She sat staring into space, so I perched on the edge of the bed next to her, which got her attention.

'I thought you wanted to work for the family firm,' I said.

'I did, but this has come out of the blue. I don't get it. Why the sudden change of heart?' Scarlett narrowed her blue eyes.

'Like I said, Mia and I thought it would be good for you…' Mum let her sentence trail off.

'I need to think about it,' Scarlett said.

She picked her phone up from the bed and started scrolling through it. She seemed distracted. It was as though her mind was somewhere else.

'Fair enough,' Mum said.

She turned on her heel and walked out of the room. As she passed me, she discreetly shook her head. Scarlett didn't even bother to look up when I got up from the bed. I glanced over at my sister as I closed the door, but she didn't seem to notice. Her eyes were still glued to her phone.

Mum paced down the stairs, across the hallway, through the kitchen and out into the garden. Her arms were swinging like pendulums down either side of her body as she made her way to the office, and I had trouble keeping up with her. Mum was standing in the corner of the room with her back to me when I arrived. I could tell by the way her shoulders were moving that she was trying to calm herself down. I took a seat behind my desk and observed her in silence. Mum was always so cool, calm and collected; nothing ever seemed to faze her. It was interesting watching her deal with the strains of motherhood. My sisters and I all tested her patience in different ways, but she did her best never to let us see how much we were stressing her out.

Mum had an ingrained need to take care of people. She was an expert at reading them and pre-empting situations. She spent a considerable amount of time trying to derail drama and manage the strong feelings of her offspring. But she had her work cut out for her in our household. With three very different daughters, there was never a dull moment.

Mum turned around with a smile pasted on her beautiful face, then went over to her chair, pulled it out from the desk and sat down on it.

'That went well, didn't it?' Mum laughed, running her fingers through her blonde pixie cut.

My cheeks flushed. I suddenly felt fiercely apologetic. 'I'm sorry I suggested bringing Scarlett on board now. I honestly thought she'd snap your arm off for the opportunity.'

'So did I. It just shows you, doesn't it? I've lost count of how many times she begged me to let her take her rightful place in the family firm. I listened to her whinging and whining about how I wasn't being fair over and over again. And now that I've finally relented and was giving her the chance to prove herself, she throws it back in my face.' Mum shook her head. 'Scarlett's played the martyr so many times she does it automatically now. When she was little, she always thought she was the odd one out and being hard done by. She used to accuse you and Kelsey of leaving her out of things.'

'You don't need to remind me. It used to do my head in. You know, most of the time, that wasn't the case.' I didn't know why I felt the need to justify something that had happened nearly twenty years ago.

'I know that, but Scarlett loved to create a scene and be the centre of attention. She developed an "I want it, and I want it now" mentality from an early age. The mention of your dad's name used to have grown men quaking in their boots, but he was a complete pushover where his girls were concerned. He didn't believe in disciplining you; our parenting styles differed. I think children need boundaries. Otherwise, how do they know what's right from wrong? Scarlett's behaving like a brat, and I feel like telling her a few home truths, but she's been through hell recently, so I'm going to have to bite my tongue and cut her some slack.'

Mum leant back in her chair and folded her arms across her chest. She looked fed up, and who could blame her? She was right; Scarlett was forever bleating on about how she wanted nothing more than to run the firm with Kelsey and me. She'd really thrown her toys out of the pram when Mum put her foot down and insisted she finish her education first. Maybe she was just being stubborn for the sake of it now that she'd been offered the job.

'I don't know why I'm so surprised by her reaction. It's typical Scarlett behaviour; it's a classic case of I want it because I'm not allowed it. Then when you back down and offer it to her, she doesn't want it after all! God give me strength!' Mum closed her eyes and blew out a slow breath.

'I feel bad for causing this situation,' I said.

Mum opened her eyes and fixed her blue gaze on me. She had a look of genuine concern on her face. 'You've got nothing to feel guilty about. None of this is your fault.' Mum's voice was soft and comforting. 'Do you hear me?'

'Yes.'

'I know what you're like; you'll start blaming yourself for something you had no control over. You were trying to do something nice for Scarlett and had her best interests at heart. You didn't know she was going to react the way she did.'

Mum always seemed to say the right thing.

'I sometimes wish your sisters could be more like you. You're responsible and reliable and give one hundred per cent to everything you do.'

Mum's compliment made me smile. 'Aww, thank you,' I replied.

We all had different strengths and weaknesses, so there was a place for all of us in the firm. Kelsey had excellent people skills and was a great motivator. She was a natural leader who thrived at influencing and persuading others. Scarlett used to have boundless energy and enthusiasm. Once she was back on her feet, I was sure it would return by the bucketload. If we could convince her to join us, the office would be a happier place with her in it. She had a great sense of humour, and her sunny outlook could lighten the darkest of situations. And what could I say about Mum? She was just a great person to be around, calm, patient and level-headed. She valued hard work and solved problems. She was a fantastic role model, loyal and supportive. The list went on, but most importantly, she was the glue that held the family together.

'Maybe Scarlett will come back around to the idea when she's had time to let it sink in.'

'Well, I can tell you something for nothing; I won't be asking her to work for the firm again,' Mum replied.

17

Kelsey

Part of me was relieved I knew the person I'd spent the night with, but the other part was terrified. What kind of man resorted to injecting a woman with drugs? A guy like that was a danger to society. He had to be a complete headcase who belonged in prison. Then another worrying thought crept into my mind. Whatever Todd had given me could be highly addictive, and that wouldn't be good news for me.

Todd and I hadn't parted ways on good terms, so this wasn't going to be a cosy reunion. He'd more than likely have revenge on his mind, and I wouldn't put it past him to go to pretty extreme lengths to get back at me. I wasn't sure what he had in store, but he could rest assured I intended to fight fire with fire.

My eyes focused on the door when I heard the key turning in the lock. A moment later, Todd pushed it open and stood in the doorway, staring at me. The sight of him was making my blood boil under the surface, so keeping a lid on my temper was going to be almost impossible.

'Have you calmed down now?' Todd asked with a smug smile on his face.

I felt my nostrils flare; that was the worst thing he could have said to me. But I couldn't afford to lose my shit, no matter how tempting it was. Giving Todd a lash of my tongue wasn't going to get me what I wanted. If I was going to make it out of this room, I'd have to use charm. Luckily I had bucketloads of it, and men like Todd were ruled by their dicks, so if I had to let him think I'd been pining for him and was desperate to rekindle what we'd had, then so be it.

'I'm sorry I freaked out.' The words stuck in my throat, but needs must. 'You can't really blame me for being angry, can you? Imagine if I'd drugged you and then wouldn't tell you what I'd given you,' I said, hoping he'd see things from my point of view.

I couldn't remember anything about last night, so I had no idea what had led up to the moment I'd been jabbed with a needle. Todd walked over to the bed and stood inches away from where I was sitting on the edge. His aftershave hung in the air between us. Now that I was a little more coherent, a memory sparked in my brain. That was the same aroma I'd smelled in my car, the one I hadn't been able to place at the time, even though it had seemed so familiar.

'Have you been stalking me?' I'd been doing my best to be pleasant, but my good intentions were suddenly heading out the window.

Todd's face broke into a huge grin. 'What makes you say that?'

'I'm fairly certain I smelt your aftershave in my car yesterday. And then, when I went to Bluewater, I'm pretty sure someone was following me. It wouldn't have been you by any chance, would it?' I narrowed my eyes and glared at Todd.

'You have a very vivid imagination, Kelsey.' Todd laughed.

'Just as I was leaving the shopping centre, I had a weird call from a private number. You know, the sort where the creep on the other end doesn't say anything because they're trying to scare the shit out of you. God, I'm so stupid sometimes. I should have realised it was you.'

I balled my hands into fists of frustration. I wished I'd told Rio about my concerns now instead of brushing them off as though they were nothing and going out to the event, completely disregarding the danger I might be in. I wasn't easily spooked, but this situation could have been avoided if I'd trusted my gut.

'What happened to the little charmer who was here a minute ago? Where did she go to?'

When Todd laughed again, I saw red and tried to lash out at him. He grabbed me by the wrist and yanked me onto my feet.

'Play nicely, Kelsey,' Todd said, his lips inches from mine. 'I wondered how long it would take you to show your true colours.'

'I don't understand why you're doing this.'

Todd and I locked eyes. He was a good-looking guy, but he didn't have any other redeeming qualities. I couldn't deny we'd been physically compatible. The sex between us had been off-the-charts amazing, but we'd never shared a strong emotional connection. If we'd had, I might have questioned whether I'd made the right decision by ending things. But I hadn't dwelled on my decision because I'd never been Todd's official girlfriend; we'd just been having a casual fling. Admittedly it had gone on for a while until Todd humiliated me, so he'd had to go.

Ending things hadn't been a knee-jerk emotional response; it had been a rational one. Todd and I had had a good thing going until his wife crawled out from the woodwork. Who knew how things would have panned out if she'd stayed out of the picture? We could have ended up married with kids...

As if I would have allowed that to happen. I couldn't think of anything worse!

I wasn't going to be somebody's bit on the side, no matter how good they were in the sack. I didn't do second best; I had too much respect for myself. If I wasn't a man's first choice, he could sling his hook as far as I was concerned. I wouldn't be forming an orderly queue and waiting in line with a bunch of other hopefuls on the off chance that he had time to show me some attention. Life was too short, and there were plenty of fish in the sea.

'Would you like me to tell you how you ended up here?'

Todd's tone was condescending, and if I hadn't been so desperate to know how I'd ended up in bed with him, I'd have told him to stick his account where the sun didn't shine.

'Yes,' I replied, pulling my arm free and sitting back down on the bed to put some distance between us.

'You've proved to be a lot more perceptive than I gave you credit for. I was tailing you. I wouldn't go so far as to say I was stalking, though. I hadn't expected you to notice, but I knew something was up when you abandoned your shopping trip.' Todd grinned.

'So you were following me at Bluewater.' My heart started hammering in my chest. Why hadn't I bothered reading the signs?

'I wasn't sure you were going to bother going to the party, but I should have realised it would take more than a little wobble to put Kelsey off a night out,' Todd taunted.

I felt my anger start to rise. But I couldn't afford to flip my lid.

'Were you at the event?' I asked in the politest tone I could muster while biting my tongue to stop it from tearing a strip off him.

I didn't recall seeing him there, but then again, there were a lot of question marks hanging over last night.

'You were in a right state by the time you made it home. I was surprised you remembered your address, let alone managed to make it up the stairs unaided. You really shouldn't drink so much when you go out. Some nutter could easily take advantage of you when you get off your face like that.'

Todd burst out laughing, and I felt myself bristle. I was too busy trying to process what he'd just said to give him a response. He'd been surprised I'd managed to make it up the stairs unaided. That implied he wasn't with me. As he'd so kindly pointed out, I'd been completely out of it, so I didn't remember talking to him at the function or even seeing him there, for that matter. I'd just presumed that was where we'd bumped into each other. But he'd neither confirmed nor denied that, so I was none the wiser.

'So we didn't share the taxi then?

'No.'

Todd's one-word answer gave nothing away.

'Are you going to tell me what happened or not?' I planted my hands on my hips and glared at my former bodyguard.

'Patience never was your thing, was it, Kelsey?' When Todd smiled, I flashed him an evil look. 'I can see the suspense is killing you, so I'll put you out of your misery. I didn't go to the event; I broke in while you were having a bath.'

My mouth dropped open, and I felt a shiver run down my spine. What was the point of having all the high-tech security my dad had installed to ensure our safety if it didn't keep out threats? My mind was whirring. Mum would have a nervous breakdown if she knew her fortress wasn't secure.

'How did you manage to do that without any of my family seeing you?'

'Mia and your mum were still in the office, and Scarlett was in her room,' Todd replied.

'Where were you hiding?'

We had a big sprawling house, so there must have been loads of places he could have been lurking without being spotted.

'Under your bed.' Todd's smile stretched from ear to ear.

No wonder I'd felt like somebody was watching me while I was applying my makeup. It was bad enough that he'd managed to break into our house in the first place, but the fact that he'd got into my bedroom without anybody noticing shocked me to the core. It shouldn't have done though. Todd knew our security system inside out and was used to sneaking into the house without getting caught to have sex with me. I used to find his stealth a turn-on. Not anymore.

'I'd been lying on my side, curled into a ball, waiting for the perfect moment to strike when you dropped your phone and started scrambling around in the darkness looking for it. I thought you'd spotted me. But luckily for me, you were smashed out of your skull. Once you'd found it, you lay back down and were sparko within minutes,' Todd said.

A feeling of dread washed over me as I remembered what Todd was talking about. The low level of light and my drunken state had tricked my eyes into believing that the dark mound I'd spotted under my bed was a well-established floordrobe. Seeing a graveyard of tried-on and discarded outfits hadn't alarmed me; they were an ever-present feature in my room. I couldn't believe I'd mistaken Todd for a pile of clothing. I wished I'd realised it was him. I might not be in this position now if I'd taken a closer look.

'Why did you bother to drug me if I was that drunk?' My temper had spiked, so my words came out in an angry tone.

'I didn't want you to start screaming or thrashing around when I moved you.'

It was terrifying to think that Todd had planned all of this in advance.

'What the hell did you give me? A horse tranquilliser? I still feel like shit.' The level of my voice started to rise as anger grew inside of me again.

'I gave you a shot of ketamine.'

'Ketamine?' I questioned. 'I'm pretty certain that's an anaesthetic.' No wonder I felt drowsy.

'Well done, Kelsey, it is; so it's very good at incapacitating a person, but because of its potency, it's also very easy to overdose.' Todd smirked.

'Is that meant to be a threat?'

I ran my fingers over my aching limb. My arm was so heavy it felt like it was made of stone.

Todd didn't reply. His eyes lingered on me for a few seconds before he walked over to the door and then stepped out into the corridor. My heartbeat speeded up. Even before he closed it behind him and turned the key, I knew he was going to lock me inside again. Todd was in his element. There had always been a power struggle between us, and now he felt like he had complete control over me.

I didn't bother protesting. There was no point; my words would have fallen on deaf ears, and I didn't want to give him the satisfaction of begging for my freedom. I wasn't a roll over and accept it sort of girl, but the ketamine he'd given me last night had sapped my strength. I felt as weak as a newborn kitten.

I'd have to try and use the time I had away from him wisely. Todd thought he was smart, but he was no match for me. He had the upper hand right now, but he wasn't going to be able to keep me here indefinitely. Once my family realised I wasn't at home, they would start to wonder where I'd gone. It was only a matter of time before they came looking for me, and then Todd would get what he had coming.

18

Scarlett

I couldn't get over my mum sometimes. I'd been nagging her for ages to let me join the firm, but she wouldn't hear of it. She was dead set against me becoming involved. Now that I'd given up, she'd decided the time was right and offered me a position. Did she seriously expect me to drop everything? The look on Mum's face was priceless when I told her I'd have to think about it. It was as though she'd been slapped around the face with a wet fish, and I'd had to stop myself from laughing out loud. I don't know what she thought I was going to say but judging from her reaction, she'd expected me to burst into song while doing a series of backflips. It was about time my family realised I wasn't a performing seal.

I could tell Mum was livid by the way she stormed out of my room, inwardly seething. She was trying to hide it, but she was in such a hurry to put some space between us that her chiffon dress frothed up around her long legs as she moved. Mia trailed along in her wake, playing the dutiful daughter to perfection as she always did. I knew my ears would be burning once they left, but I wasn't going to dwell on our conversation. I had more important things on my mind right now than taking root in a glorified Portakabin with my mum and sisters, chasing up the family's latest debt.

Before I'd been rudely interrupted, I'd been scrolling through the pictures that Hugh had sent me. I hadn't appreciated how many members of the public fitted CJ's description until Hugh had started sending through countless photos of men who could potentially be him. It was frustrating enough for me; I couldn't imagine how bad it was for Hugh. Carrying out undercover surveillance work must be about as exciting as watching back-to-back episodes of *The Great British Bake Off*. Sitting in your vantage point for hours on end, hoping the person you were looking for would hurry up and materialise, must bore a person rigid. Rather him than me, I thought after I'd gone through the latest photos. It was like being on a rollercoaster ride. The excitement of receiving a new message was soon replaced by a feeling of hopelessness when the sightings turned out to be false.

I let out a sigh as I typed my reply.

I'm sorry to say none of the pics are of CJ.

The apartments in the new development where CJ lived cost a small fortune, so I was surprised how many young people were able to afford to live there. They must have earned huge salaries or been the offspring of mega-rich parents to be able to call that place home. I'd been expecting a much older demographic, so I'd thought Hugh's job would be easier than it was turning out to be. At this rate, I was going to be in for an eye-watering bill the size of the Third World debt.

19

Kelsey

Being locked in a room with only my thoughts for company wasn't my idea of fun. I didn't enjoy alone time; solitary confinement was playing havoc with my sanity. It was absolute torture, even though my surroundings were luxurious. I was a party girl at heart and craved the company of others. Todd knew me well enough to know I'd be climbing the walls by now, but I wouldn't give him the satisfaction of asking to come out. I'd look for a way out instead.

I walked over to the windows that stretched along one side of the room. After trying every handle and finding them locked, I peered through the glass. I'd thought I might be able to jump to freedom, but I hadn't realised it was such a long way down. I glanced from left to right, but all I could see were uninterrupted views of water, so I couldn't even signal to somebody in a neighbouring building. My options were limited; allowing Todd to break my spirit wasn't one of them, and neither was giving up.

There must be something I could do. I couldn't believe how stupid I'd been and was about to learn a tough lesson the hard way. If you wanted to sleep peacefully at night, be careful who you got involved with. Todd had once been a trusted member of the team, but he'd burned that bridge when he'd kidnapped me. There was no going back from this situation. I possessed an incredible will to fight. Todd had underestimated me if he thought I'd fall apart easily.

I was lying on the satin sheets staring up at the ceiling, wishing my head would stop pounding, when I heard the key in the lock. I pushed myself up from the mattress and stared at the door.

'Are you hungry?' Todd asked from the hallway.

I wasn't. I felt nauseous, and the thought of swallowing anything solid made me want to be sick, but I decided not to share that with Todd. I couldn't imagine he'd allow me to eat in this room. He was a military man and very particular, so I was sure he'd want me to sit at a table rather than get crumbs in his bed.

'I'm ravenous,' I replied, which brought a smile to Todd's lips. I wasn't sure why he found that so amusing. Did he think I was flirting with him?

'You always did have an insatiable appetite,' Todd replied, grinning from ear to ear.

We both knew he wasn't talking about food. I felt my temper spike, but I had to hold my anger in. I hadn't had any contact with Todd since the day I'd fired him and ended our affair, so I'd never considered the possibility that he would turn up out of the blue. I was well aware that some people fought to win back an old flame, while the thought of that made others run a mile. Sometimes the rejected party became obsessed with getting back with the person who'd called it quits. If that was what all of this was about, he was barking up the wrong tree. I wouldn't touch him with a bargepole. I wasn't prepared to sleep with him, not even for old times' sake. I had more respect for myself than that.

I swung my legs off the huge leather-framed bed and stood up, steadying myself on the mattress as Todd walked past me. He picked up a black holdall that was on the floor at the end of the bed and then threw it down next to me.

'There are some spare clothes in the bag. I suggest you get changed into something more appropriate.'

'Some privacy might be nice,' I replied.

'It's not as though I haven't seen it all before,' Todd said with a laugh.

I sat back down on the bed and crossed my arms over my chest. I had no intention of undressing while he was in the room. Thankfully, he took the hint. He pulled the door closed behind him but left it unlocked. I thought about making a run for it but decided against it. I could barely support my own weight, so there was no way I'd be able to leg it out of here. I stared at the back of the door as though frozen in time for several minutes, trying to work out what to do for the best before I pulled the bag towards me and unzipped it. The underwear, clothes and everything inside belonged to me, but I knew I hadn't packed any of them. The thought of Todd going through my things brought a fresh wave of nausea crashing down on me. There were multiple items of clothing, a lot more stuff than I'd need for an overnight stop. How long was Todd planning to keep me here?

My heart started hammering inside my chest, but I swallowed my fear and put the black trackies and bright blue boxy sweatshirt on before walking out of the bedroom. My legs were wobbling more than unset jelly as Todd stood in the hallway watching me. Once I got close enough, he cupped my elbow with the palm of his hand and steered me into an open-plan living area. I could see a city skyline from the window. We weren't in a hotel suite after all; this was an apartment.

'Where am I?' I asked as I stared out of the window, trying to get my bearings.

'All will be revealed in good time,' Todd said, pointing over at a bowl of cereal and a glass of juice laid out on the granite worktop.

'Are you going to tell me what's going on?' I pressed.

An awkward silence spread out between us, so I used the opportunity to scan the room. Todd's apartment was flash. In all the time we'd been together, he'd never brought me here. I wondered if this was where he and Michelle had lived, but somehow I doubted it. The minimal ultra-modern space had bachelor pad written all over it. By the looks of this place, my dad must have been paying him well over the odds for his services. I wouldn't have thought it was the kind of pad a bodyguard could afford.

'Why did you bring me here?' I asked, planting my hands on my hips.

'That's enough questions for now. Eat your breakfast,' Todd gestured towards the counter with a flick of his head.

'I'm not hungry. I'd like to say it was lovely to see you, but I'd be lying,' I said, looking him straight in the face before I started to walk down the hall towards the front door.

My pulse was pounding harder with every step that I took. As I went to reach for the handle, Todd put his hand on my shoulders and pulled me around to face him.

'Where do you think you're going?' he asked with a smile playing on his lips.

'I've got to get back. I'm due in at work, and Mum will wonder where I am if I don't show up.'

'You seem to have forgotten I used to work for the firm, so I know first-hand how flaky you are.' Todd smirked. 'Your commitment to the job was appalling, so nobody's going to take the blindest bit of notice that you didn't show up today. Anyway, don't concern yourself about that; I've got it covered.'

I had no idea what Todd was talking about, but I was livid that he was making out I was a bad employee. I wasn't the only one who used to slope off while I was on the clock. He'd always been more than happy to accompany me to hotel rooms for marathon sex sessions when my dad was paying his wages.

'What do you mean you've got it covered?' I could feel my nostrils flaring as I glared at Todd.

He stuck his hand in the back pocket of his black combats and pulled out a phone that looked suspiciously like mine.

'I texted your mum earlier and told her you had the hangover from hell and wouldn't be in today,' he said, holding the screen in front of my face so that I could see for myself.

Fury leapt into my throat. 'You did what? I want my phone back right now,' I demanded, turning the palm of my hand over.

Todd grabbed hold of my wrist and applied just enough pressure to remind me how strong he was.

'No, can do, I'm afraid. Get back in the bedroom.' Todd pointed towards the door.

I shook my head, so he bent down and jabbed me in the stomach with his left shoulder before hoisting me over it, fireman style. Todd paced down the corridor, walked over to the bed and dumped me down on the mattress. Being dropped from a height knocked the wind out of me.

While I was catching my breath, Todd produced a bag from the bedside cabinet. Then he put his weight on me. For one awful moment, I thought he was going to rape me. Even though we'd had sex in the past, it had been consensual. I writhed and bucked to try and break free, but he was too strong for me to overpower.

Todd pulled a tourniquet and syringe out of the bag and tied off my arm while keeping me pinned to the bed with his body weight. I started screaming for help, so he clamped his hand over my mouth. I carried on, but all that came out was a muffled noise. He reached for a roll of gaffer tape, unravelled a strip and then tore it off with his teeth before sticking it over my lips.

With the skill of someone who'd performed this act a thousand times or more, he deftly slid the needle into the crook of my arm. He drew back on the syringe, and I saw some of my blood fill the tube, which made me feel faint.

'Just checking I've hit the vein,' Todd said, peering at the dark red substance. 'We don't want this pooling under your skin, or you'll end up with an abscess.'

When he pushed the contents into my arm, I had to look away. I couldn't bear to watch. Not knowing what was in the syringe was mental torture. I clenched my eyes as tightly as I could, hoping that if I didn't see it happen, I could somehow fool myself into thinking I'd imagined the whole thing. The thoughts tumbled around in my head for a couple of seconds before I felt a warm sensation travelling up my arm and then radiating into my shoulder and chest. It spread throughout my body, but there was absolutely nothing I could do to stop it. I'd never experienced anything like it; I felt terrified as the drug rampaged through my system, and the next minute I was at peace. I could feel its effects almost immediately. There was a rush of euphoria and a feeling of intense pleasure and then I started to become drowsy.

'Now I suggest you behave yourself until I decide if you can come out again,' I heard Todd say as the key turned in the lock.

20

Mia

'My God, she's unbelievable,' Mum said.

I was sitting behind my desk, and I looked over when I heard the sound of Mum's voice. She was shaking her head while staring at the screen of her phone.

'No prizes for guessing who you're talking about,' I replied.

'This is all a big joke to your sister,' Mum continued. 'I should have realised it wouldn't take her long to go back to her old lifestyle. I don't know what made her think she was cut out for this line of work in the first place; everyone could see party planning and hobnobbing with celebrities suited Kelsey down to the ground.'

Kelsey hadn't been to work for three days, and Mum was struggling to deal with the stress her absence was causing.

'What does she think she's playing at ?' Fury coated Mum's words.

'I have no idea.' I shrugged.

I never understood how my sister's mind worked and doubted I ever would.

It was another glorious summer's day, so we'd opened up the glass-fronted office to let the sunshine in. When Rio put his head around the door and said, 'Good morning, ladies,' it startled me as I hadn't heard him approaching.

I pressed my fingertips over my heart. 'You frightened the life out of me.' I laughed.

'Strangely enough, you're not the first person who's said that to me.' Rio grinned.

'I bet,' I replied.

It was hard to imagine it now seeing Rio with the smile on his handsome face, but the six-foot-plus, well-built man cut a very imposing figure when the need arose, which was frequently in our line of work. Trying to recover a debt from an unwilling party was no mean feat.

'Still no sign of Kelsey?' Rio quizzed, scanning his eyes over her empty chair.

'No.'

Mum's tone was abrupt, which surprised me. It was out of character for her to be snappy and short-tempered. She was normally so poised and patient. But if her response bothered Rio, he didn't let it show.

'That's not good news, Amanda.' Rio raised an eyebrow and fixed his dark brown gaze on Mum.

'I know that. She hasn't shown her face for days.' Mum blew out a sigh of frustration.

'Have you heard from her?' A look of concern spread over Rio's face.

Mum turned the screen of her phone around, but there was no way he'd be able to read the message unless he had supersonic vision. The distance between them was too great.

'What did she say? Rio looked troubled.

My sisters and I were like the daughters he'd never had. He was fiercely protective of us, and his desire to keep us safe stretched to Mum too.

'Kelsey told me not to worry; everything's fine. She's just met up with an old friend she hasn't seen for a while, and they're doing a bit of catching up, whatever that's supposed to mean.'

Mum rolled her eyes. She wasn't impressed by Kelsey's latest excuse. Who could blame her? It had been my younger sister's idea for us to take over Dad's firm. She'd been the driving force behind the whole thing and had nagged Mum repeatedly until she'd given in. But so far, she hadn't been very reliable when it came to turning up at the office, let alone running the show. It didn't take a brain surgeon to work out that Mum had lost faith in her abilities.

'Given Kelsey's track record, my guess would be she'd got a new man on the go. She probably hooked up with a guy at that party the other night and is giving him her undivided attention. Work and everything else has gone out the window.' Mum couldn't hide the frustration in her voice.

Mum was probably right. Kelsey's aim was to concentrate on being young, free and single, which wasn't that surprising given that she was twenty-three. She didn't want to be shackled by the chains of responsibility. Having no commitments and as much fun as possible were way more her style.

'Do you want me to see if I can find out what she's up to?' Rio asked.

'No, don't bother. Leave her to it. You know what Kelsey's like – she'll be bored of whoever it is by the end of the week, and then she might see fit to grace us with her presence.'

'I don't like not knowing where she is. It's a dangerous world out there. I don't want to worry you, but what if something's happened to her?' Rio had morphed into Papa Bear mode in front of our eyes.

'We're talking about Kelsey. I'm sure I don't need to remind you – she does what she pleases when she pleases. It's impossible to keep tabs on her, always has been,' Mum replied, dismissing his concerns.

'It's about time you put your foot down, Amanda. You shouldn't let her just take off like this when the mood suits her,' Rio said, telling Mum a few home truths.

'How can I stop her? She's her father's daughter. And besides that, she's a grown woman. If she didn't listen to me when she was a child, she's hardly going to start now, is she?'

The tone of Mum's voice changed. She was getting angrier

by the minute. Even though Rio was trying to help, he was only making matters worse in the long run.

'It's probably not my place to say, and you can tell me to mind my own business, but Davie was too soft on the girls. He wanted his princesses to have everything their hearts desired, but two out of three of them have ended up spoilt as a result.'

My cheeks flushed as the words left Rio's mouth. I glanced over at Mum. She looked horrified that he'd spoken so freely. But he'd known my dad since they were kids and was part of the family, so she couldn't blame him for being frank with her. My guess was he was trying to shock Mum into dealing with the situation.

'That's as may be. But it's too late to change them now. Davie had a formidable reputation as a hard guy when it came to business, but he was a complete pushover where his daughters were concerned. Kelsey and Scarlett used to run rings around him,' Mum replied with tears glistening in her blue eyes.

Things were getting worse by the minute. I would have given anything not to be in the office right now. It was embarrassing being present while they were having this conversation.

'I'm so sorry, Amanda. I didn't mean to upset you.'

Mum was showing her vulnerability, so now it was Rio's turn to look awkward. A moment ago, he was accusing my dad of being a softie, but truth be known, he wasn't so different himself. He was like putty in Mum's hand.

'I'm fine,' Mum lied. 'But right now, I'm so furious with Kelsey, I don't even want to think about her. I've got a good mind to box up her stuff and leave it in the front drive for when she finally decides to show her face again. If she thinks she can treat my house like a hotel, she's got another thinkg coming. Do me a favour, let's concentrate on the business and not my wayward daughter.'

'No problem,' Rio replied as he retreated out of the office.

21

Kelsey

My eyes felt heavy when I woke. I had no idea how long I'd been asleep. All I knew was that my temples were pounding, so I pressed my fingertips on them to try and stop them from throbbing. But it did nothing to help. I inched my head off the pillows, propped myself up on my elbow and squinted around the room. It took my foggy brain a while to register that my surroundings weren't familiar. Then I remembered I was in Todd's apartment.

The last thing I recalled was that he'd injected me with something again, but I had no idea what was in the syringe. He'd told me he'd given me ketamine when he'd first brought me to his apartment. But from what I could remember, he'd jabbed that shot into the muscle of my upper arm, and as it was a powerful sedative, I'd been out of it shortly afterwards. Whatever he was drugging me with now was different as he'd slid a needle into a vein in the crook of my arm before he'd pushed the contents in. The drug delivered a euphoric rush of pleasure, which lasted a few minutes, and then an intense relaxation followed.

I had no idea how long I'd been at Todd's apartment. I'd have to try and devise a way to keep track of the time. I had a sinking feeling that I might be held captive for a long while. I didn't want to consider the fact that the days might stretch into months or even years. But whether I liked it or not, it was a possibility. I knew that sometimes kidnapped victims were held in confinement for over a decade before they were freed. And there was that horrific case of the Austrian girl imprisoned in a dungeon in her parents' home for twenty-four years, wasn't there? The thought of that sent a chill down my spine.

I was stuck in an impossible situation, and even though I wanted to, I wasn't sure I'd be able to find a way out. I kept hoping my family would realise something was wrong and that I was being held against my will, but they weren't even bothering to look for me, thanks to Todd's lame messages. My blood was beginning to boil and I felt like tearing my hair out. Why couldn't Mum see through the kinds of things he was sending? I'd never ended a text with xx before, so why would I start now? And contacting her daily should have rung alarm bells. I'd always valued my privacy and didn't take kindly to people poking their noses into my affairs. I wouldn't normally give her a running commentary on my movements. It was much more my style to turn up when the mood took me without offering any explanation as to where I'd been or what I'd been doing. What was wrong with Mum? Why hadn't she realised Todd's messages were fake and that I was in trouble?

I turned my face towards the bedroom door when I heard a key slide into the lock. A moment later, Todd stood in the doorway with a big grin plastered across his face.

'Dinner's ready,' he said as he walked over to the bed.

I wasn't hungry, but Todd only let me out of the room at mealtimes, so I wasn't about to tell him that. I lowered my legs over the side of the bed and attempted to stand, but I'd lost all strength in my muscles and had trouble supporting my own weight. Todd put his hand under my elbow and helped me onto my feet. Then guided me out of the bedroom, along the hallway and across to the dining table.

'I got you katsu curry and rice from Wagamama,' Todd said.

I usually loved that dish, but when I opened the lid on the dark grey takeaway bowl, my stomach did a cartwheel, so I didn't bother picking up my fork.

'What's up? Isn't the food up to Lady Kelsey's standards?' Todd laughed.

'If you must know, I've been suffering from nausea and cramps. Whatever you've been injecting me with isn't agreeing with my stomach. Are you going to tell me what it is?'

'Now there's a question,' Todd replied before fixing me with his dark brown eyes. He tilted his head to one side as he considered what I'd just said. 'I gave it a lot of thought before I decided which drug to inject you with; crack cocaine was possibly the more addictive of the two, but heroin was going to play havoc with your looks. So in the end, it was simple really: losing your appearance would hit you the hardest.'

My mouth fell open as Todd's words registered. He definitely wanted payback.

'You've been giving me heroin?'

'Yes. Are you happy now the mystery's been solved?' Todd grinned.

I'd been hoping I'd misheard him, but he'd just confirmed my worst nightmare. I wasn't a nervy person; I usually took everything in my stride and was a water off a duck's back kind of girl, but I could feel panic start to rise up within me. The room suddenly felt darker, like somebody had closed the curtains or turned out the lights. I wasn't sure how many times Todd had injected me now, but I knew I was on a slippery slope.

'I can't believe you'd do that to me.' I felt my eyes start to well up, but I managed to hold back my tears.

'Why not? There's no love lost between us. It's not as though you meant anything to me.'

Todd's words were like a slap around the face. I'd briefly considered trying to convince him that I still had a soft spot for him. I'd thought I might be able to manipulate him into letting me go, but that wasn't going to work. He hated me as much as I hated him if that was possible.

'Aww, that's not very nice. Are you deliberately trying to hurt my feelings?' I'd been attempting to be on my best behaviour, but my inner bitch was riled up and desperate to come out to play.

'Just giving you a few home truths,' Todd replied with a smug look on his face.

'I'm sure I don't have to tell you the feeling's mutual. But the lengths you've gone to in the name of revenge are extreme if you ask me. Are you sure you don't have feelings for me? Your actions seem to suggest that you do. You look very much like a man scorned who wants to ruin the life of their former lover from where I'm sitting. Did I break your heart by any chance?'

I saw Todd bristle.

'As if. You're so far off the mark. But you're right about one thing: I do want to ruin your life. Like I said, I thought long and hard about what to get you addicted to before I made my choice. Enjoy your looks while they last.' Todd laughed.

'Do you really think I'm that shallow?'

'Who are you trying to kid? I know you are,' Todd replied.

He was right. I'd spent my whole life trading off my physical appearance.

'If you're not going to eat the food I bought, you can go back to your room. I'm finding your company jarring, to say the least.' Todd pushed his chair back from the table, walked over to where I was sitting and pulled me onto my feet. There was no point in resisting.

'Get your hands off me,' I said through gritted teeth.

Todd did as I requested, but he kept prodding me in the back with two of his fingers as I inched my way to the bedroom, which was infuriating me, but I wasn't going to give him the satisfaction of getting a rise out of me.

I lay on the bed, staring up at the ceiling, wondering how this was going to pan out. Becoming a drug-addled mess who only cared about where their next fix was coming from would be my idea of hell. Todd knew me better than I cared to admit, and he'd chosen my punishment well. He was going to make sure the payback was as cruel as possible. But I wasn't going to give up. There had to be a way out; I just hadn't found it yet., and there didn't seem to be a damn thing I could do about it.

22

Scarlett

I was still asleep when I was woken by gentle knocking on my bedroom door.

'Come in,' I said, lifting my head from the pillows. My voice sounded husky, so I cleared my throat.

Mum pushed open the door. 'Sorry, I didn't mean to wake you, but it's nearly eleven o'clock. Happy birthday, darling,' she said with a huge beam on her face.

'Thanks,' I replied, scooping my long red hair over one shoulder.

I was glad to see the tense atmosphere that had been hovering over the two of us seemed to have lifted. I'd been giving her a wide berth since she'd asked me if I wanted to work for the firm. She'd made it obvious that she wasn't happy I hadn't jumped at the opportunity, but her timing was lousy. I was pouring my energy into tracking down CJ, and until that happened, I didn't have the inclination to focus on anything else. But I couldn't exactly tell her that.

'Happy birthday.' Mia grinned as she came into view carrying a huge pile of presents wrapped in pale pink pearlescent paper and decorated with ribbons and bows.

I was more than a bit disappointed to see there was no sign of Kelsey. The last time I saw her, she was dressed to the nines and about to go to some boozy celebrity event. She hadn't been home for days, but I thought she'd make the effort as it was my twenty-first. We used to be so close; she was my go-to person and partner in crime.

'It's beautiful outside, just like the day you were born,' Mum reminisced. 'What would you like to do today?'

My brain was still thick with sleep, so making plans was the furthest thing from my mind.

'I'm not sure yet, but I'd be happy to start by opening those presents.' I smiled.

Even though I didn't feel like celebrating, I appreciated the effort my mum and sister had gone to and didn't want them to feel bad for me, so the best thing I could do was put on a brave face.

'Have you heard from Kelsey?' Mum asked.

I shook my head and then started ripping the expensive paper into shreds. I didn't want to get drawn into a conversation about my sister in case I got upset. It was my choice to have a low-key day, but I'd hoped the four of us would spend it together. Kelsey obviously had other ideas. I wasn't even sure she'd remembered it was my birthday.

'I know you didn't want me to make a fuss, but I have to do something to mark the special occasion.' Mum smiled. 'Maybe we could walk down to one of the pubs along the river and have lunch?'

Mum's suggestion was a safe bet. She knew I loved my food, so it would normally have been met with great interest. The truth was I didn't feel like doing anything or being in other people's company, but I didn't have the heart to tell her that.

'That's a nice idea,' I replied, inwardly groaning.

Mum's face lit up; she was delighted that I'd agreed to leave the house. I'd become a virtual recluse since I'd been discharged from hospital. Much as I really didn't want to venture out, spending a couple of hours being fed and watered wasn't going to kill me, and I might even end up enjoying the experience.

'I'll text Kelsey and see if I can tempt her to join us.'

Mum pulled out her phone. The pads of her thumbs moved

across the screen before I had a chance to reply. I was midway through opening my presents when her phone beeped. She didn't need to tell me what Kelsey had written. The thunderous look on her face said it all.

'I'm sorry, darling, it looks like she won't be able to make it.'

'That's OK.'

I pasted on a smile and went back to the job in hand, tearing at the paper with renewed enthusiasm. I didn't want Mum to know that I was more than a bit miffed that my sister had snubbed the invitation. Lunch would have been a lot more fun with Kelsey there livening things up, but if she couldn't be bothered to join us, it was her loss. I wasn't going to dwell on the matter.

I made light work of opening my presents, which no doubt took Mum an eternity to wrap. I'd been spoilt rotten as usual, and although I was grateful for the beautiful things I'd been given, material possessions only brought you happiness on a superficial level. They wouldn't stop me from feeling empty.

'Thanks for all of the prezzies.' I smiled, not wanting to come across as an ungrateful bitch.

'Our pleasure,' Mum replied, answering for Mia as well. 'We'll leave you to get spruced up, and then we'll head out once you're ready,' she said before leading the way out of the door.

I waited until they were out of earshot before I let out a sigh. People always made such a fuss of turning twenty-one, but it was just another birthday as far as I was concerned, and if I'd been given the choice, I would have gladly carried on as though it was any other day. But that wasn't going to happen if Mum had anything to do with it.

23

Kelsey

I had no idea what time it was when I woke drenched in sweat, but I could see it was still dark outside. My teeth were chattering, and every muscle in my body ached. At first, I thought I'd gone down with flu, but then another thought came to mind. Was I suffering from withdrawal? The idea of that sent my blood pressure spiking. I tried to remember if Todd had injected me before he'd locked me back in the room, closing my eyes in a bid to concentrate while I searched my memory. But any recollection I might have had was clouded under a thick blanket.

I couldn't ever remember feeling as ill as this before. I lay on my side with my knees pulled up to my chest, rocking back and forth, hoping that my symptoms would pass, but the waves of nausea kept coming at regular intervals. Every time I tried to go back to sleep, an overwhelming desire to vomit ripped through my body. 'Kelsey, Kelsey, it's me,' I heard Scarlett say as a vision of her gripping me by the hands danced in my head.

The image was so vivid I was sure she'd come into the room to rescue me. I forced my eyes to focus, but she wasn't there. It was just my imagination playing tricks on me. My lids were heavy, so I let them close as I attempted to block out the sight of my sister. Suddenly there was some activity outside the bedroom door. I prised open my eyes when I heard a key in the lock.

'Do you want some breakfast?' Todd asked from the hallway.

I wanted to tell him to go to hell, but I needed his help, but

I needed to stay on his good side while I worked out a way to escape, so I had to bite my tongue.

'I don't know what to do with myself. I feel awful.' I wrapped my arms around my stomach to try and ease the cramping.

'What's up?'

Todd crossed his tattooed arms over his chest. He didn't look the slightest bit concerned that I was feeling like death warmed up.

'I'm aching all over. I feel like I've got the flu.'

The moment I stopped talking, my nose began to run as though it wanted to confirm my symptoms. It took every ounce of effort I had to reach across to a box of tissues on the bedside cabinet and pull one out.

'Sounds to me like you're in the grips of withdrawal. Junkies always complain of having flu-like symptoms,' Todd replied.

Junkie? Who did Todd think he was? If I'd been feeling like my usual self, I would have ripped him a new arsehole for calling me that, but I felt so horrendous that I didn't bother to respond. Tearing a strip off him wasn't my top priority right now. It would have to wait.

'Really? Would that happen so soon?' I questioned as I didn't have a clue about these things.

Unlike a lot of the people who went to the same parties as me, I'd never been into drugs. Alcohol was definitely my thing. Give me a stiff drink anytime over something class A.

Todd nodded. 'I read up on heroin addiction before I gave it to you, and apparently, users begin experiencing withdrawal symptoms anywhere between six and twelve hours after their last dose. And I also found out that nearly a quarter of first-time users become completely hooked.'

That wasn't what I'd wanted to hear. I would have rather had a bad case of flu any day of the week. The fact that Todd had done his homework added to the misery and sent a shiver down my spine.

'Do you want me to get you a top-up?' Todd grinned.

What kind of a question was that? His desire for revenge was huge. I must have broken his heart because he was taking such pleasure in making me suffer.

'It'll make you feel better,' Todd continued.

Then he walked out of the room, leaving me alone and the door unlocked. If I hadn't felt so awful, it would have been the perfect opportunity for me to make a run for it. But there was no way I'd be able to drag my sorry arse out of bed. Escaping from this nightmare wasn't on the cards today. I lay back against the pillows and waited for Todd to return.

Each to their own, but I'd never been into drugs. My dad had hated them with a passion, and he'd drummed the message into us when we were kids to stay away from them at all costs. I was glad he couldn't see me now.

When I saw the needle coming, I wanted to scream and beg for mercy, but I needed another dose to ease my suffering. Who knew dependencies and addictions could form so quickly? The stab of the metal pricking my skin made me flinch, but I didn't try and resist. A moment later, I felt a rush, then a warm sensation started floating around my bloodstream, numbing the state of my mind and body, which took my pain away.

'You really should try to eat something,' Todd said once the heroin had started to take effect. 'You're losing those killer curves and starting to look a bit scrawny.' He grinned.

Under normal circumstances, I would have loved to wipe the smirk off his face. Todd's words were designed to hurt me, but I was floating along on a wave of euphoria right now, so I let his bitchy comments go over my head.

I'd been clamped in the jaws of hell a few moments ago, but now I didn't have a care in the world. Much as I didn't want to be in Todd's company any longer than I had to be, he was right – I needed to eat. I couldn't remember the last time I'd touched anything solid.

Todd hovered two steps behind me in case I needed assistance, but I gritted my teeth and got on with putting one foot in front of the other. I was determined not to lean on him every time I left the room. The smell of bacon filled my nostrils as I walked down the corridor towards the kitchen, and my stomach rumbled in response. The thought of tucking into a salty fry-up momentarily lifted my spirits. That was just what I fancied.

I was bitterly disappointed when the table came into view, and I saw a box of Cheerios and an empty bowl sitting there instead of the mound of food I'd imagined. The sight of the little hoops made me think of Scarlett; they were her favourite. I had no idea why my thoughts kept turning to her, so I forced them in a different direction. I wondered what my family were doing now. The idea of them carrying on with everyday trivialities while a vindictive maniac injected me with heroin was all it took to break my daydream. Where the hell were they? Why hadn't Mum sent Rio and the boys around to bash Todd's door down and give him a hiding he wouldn't forget in a hurry? Surely they'd expected me back by now. As if I'd go this long without changing my clothes. What could possibly be going on in their lives that trumped looking for me?

As my fury bubbled under the surface, I couldn't help noticing that Todd hadn't cleared his plate away. He'd left it discarded with a ketchup smear, a couple of crumbs and the tiniest bit of bacon fat behind just to drive the point home that he'd made himself a nice cooked breakfast while all I was offered was cereal. How childish could a person be? He knew I loved a bacon butty. I never realised how petty Todd was, but he was trying to torment me from every conceivable angle. I'd have to swallow down my anger; there was no way I'd give him the satisfaction of getting a rise out of me.

'Do you want coffee?' Todd asked, breaking my chain of thought.

I nodded in response, then picked up the box and let the cereal rain down. I became mesmerised by the motion, and by the time I stopped pouring, the bowl was full.

'Somebody's hungry.' Todd raised his eyebrows when he spotted the near-overflowing bowl.

When I ignored his comment, he reached for his dirty plate just in case I hadn't spotted it and placed it in the sink.

'Don't let me stop you – eat up,' Todd said.

I picked up the carton of milk and poured it onto the dry cereal. My hand wasn't very steady, so it took all my powers of concentration not to spill the Cheerios over the side of the rim.

'Have you got any sugar?' I asked.

'I'm not sure,' Todd said before he started rifling through all of the kitchen cupboards.

I hadn't realised such a simple request would cause him such a problem. He didn't seem to know where anything was, which made me think he must eat out a lot. Todd eventually found a glass jar in the cupboard above the kettle. It was stocked with the tea and coffee, which I would have thought would was the most obvious place to look.

'Here you go,' Todd said, handing me the jar.

I unscrewed the lid and sprinkled the sugar over the hoops, aware that Todd's eyes were watching my every move. I scooped up a large mound, but before I put it in my mouth, I looked up.

'Don't you think this is a sick and twisted thing to do? How long do you intend to hold me here against my will?'

Todd's dark brown eyes bored into mine as I tipped the Cheerios balancing on the spoon into my mouth and began to chew.

'I haven't decided yet.'

'Why are you doing this? Are you after revenge because you lost your job and your wife?' I asked between spoonfuls of cereal.

'I have so many reasons for wanting to get back at you. How does it feel not to have the upper hand for once? Poor little rich girl,' Todd sneered.

There had always been a power struggle between the two of us, and while he'd been working for my dad, I'd always had the advantage; how the tide had turned.

'Are you going to kill me?' I wasn't sure I wanted to know the answer to the question, but I'd decided to cut to the chase. I'd had enough of pussyfooting around.

'Now that would be telling.' Todd smiled, but his words had a chilling edge to them.

24

Mia

'I can't believe Kelsey didn't show her face yesterday. I'd love to know what was so important that she couldn't make an effort for Scarlett's birthday,' Mum said.

'I'm shocked too. The two of them used to be joined at the hip,' I replied.

'Didn't they just. I don't know what's got into her. Staying away was such a spiteful thing to do. But then again, Kelsey always loves to be the centre of attention, and she hates attending anything where the focus isn't one hundred per cent on her.' Mum hissed the words; she was absolutely seething.

Mum was adamant that Kelsey was just being selfish, but I couldn't help wondering if there was more to it than that. Although things had been a little strained between them recently, Kelsey still shared a close bond with Scarlett. I couldn't imagine her not showing up for her little sister's twenty-first birthday.

The conversation Mum had with Rio the other day had been playing on my mind; maybe she should have let him do some digging to find out what Kelsey was up to. I thought about suggesting it, but I didn't want to risk plunging Mum into a bad mood. Suffice to say; Mum wasn't her number-one fan at the moment. But if Kelsey hadn't shown up by tomorrow, I was going to raise the matter. Admittedly, Kelsey could be selfish and self-centred, but I didn't believe she'd have intentionally wanted to upset Scarlett or cause a whole lot of drama for no reason. I'd seen the look on Scarlett's face when Mum told her Kelsey had turned down the invitation. My younger sister was a born actress and had done her best to gloss over it, but her disappointment was plain for us to see.

The sound of my husband's voice brought me back to reality.

'That would be great, but don't go to too much trouble. I'll see you later on,' Jack said before he hung up the phone.

'Who were you talking to?' I asked when he walked into the office.

'My mum,' Jack replied while rifling through a filing cabinet on the far side of the room.

'I'll come with you.' I smiled.

Dale and Nancy doted on Jack, so every time we went to their house, they rolled out the red carpet and put on a huge spread. Nothing was too much trouble for their son.

'Maybe next time,' Jack replied.

I felt my face drop. I got on well with Jack's parents, so I was a bit miffed that I wasn't invited.

'Don't look at me like that, Mia,' Jack said.

'Like what?' I shrugged.

Jack shook his head and let out a sigh. 'I can tell you're disappointed, but I'm not trying to exclude you. It's just that I'm working around the corner from their place today, so I said I'd pop in to see them while I was in the area, that's all. It's not a big deal, so please don't start reading anything into it. Anyway, I'd better go, or I'll be late.'

Jack stooped and planted a kiss on my cheek before he disappeared back out of the door. I'd been tempted to turn my face away, but I managed to stop myself from being so childish in the nick of time. He had every right to visit his mum and dad without me.

'Where's my favourite son-in-law off to in such a hurry? Mum asked.

'He's working on something near his mum and dad's.'

'Good morning, ladies,' Rio said when he appeared a few moments later.

'Good morning,' Mum and I replied.

'Still no sign of Kelsey?' Rio's eyebrows settled into a frown.

Mum's expression changed at the mention of my sister's name, and she gave Rio a one-word answer. 'Nope.'

If he read between the lines, Rio would realise that meant she didn't want to talk about it, but the subtlety of her response had gone over his head, and he carried on regardless. 'I've got a bad feeling about this, Amanda.' Rio folded his arms across the front of his grey suit jacket.

'So you said.' Mum's reply was curt.

'I really think you should let me do a bit of digging…'

Mum put her hand up to stop Rio mid-flow. 'What's the latest on Oscar Myles? Everything seems to have gone quiet.'

Mum drummed her long slender fingers on the front of her desk. Judging by the look on Rio's face, he was puzzled that my mum had dismissed his concerns.

'Did you and Darius manage to find anything out when you went to Northampton?'

I wasn't sure why Mum had asked that. Rio would have informed her immediately if there'd been any news. I reasoned she wanted to change the subject, and he didn't seem to be getting the message.

'No, I'm afraid there's nothing to report on that slimy little weasel. Darius is still on his case, though. I do have some other business I want to run past you. A guy called Al Dempsey has asked to borrow two hundred and fifty grand.'

'That's a lot of money. What do we know about him?' Mum asked. Her blue eyes were like saucers when she fixed them on Rio's.

'I haven't had any contact with him for years, but he knew Davie back in the day.'

'Really? I can't say I ever remember Davie mentioning him

before.' Mum tilted her head to one side as she searched her memory.

'They were just casual acquaintances. They never did business together,' Rio replied.

'Did Al say what he wanted that amount of money for?'

Rio nodded. 'He's trying to expand his business, and he doesn't have enough collateral to secure a bank loan.'

'What line of work is he in?' Mum quizzed.

'The rag trade.'

'Ooh, that sounds interesting.' Mum's ears pricked up.

Being a former model, she loved anything to do with the fashion world.

Rio's full lips stretched into a broad smile. 'Don't get too excited. Al doesn't sell anything high-end. He supplies stallholders in the markets.'

'Two hundred and fifty thousand will buy him a lot of cheap clothes. Do you think it's genuine?'

Rio pulled a face. 'Who knows?'

'Why has he come to us if he never did business with Davie before?' Mum's earlier interest seemed to be waning.

'I got the impression we weren't his first choice, more of a last resort if you get the picture,' Rio replied.

'What do you think? Mum looked at me for several seconds, and then her eyes fixed on Rio's.

I shrugged. 'It's a lot of money, so we'd need to make sure we're going to get a good return.'

My inner accountant suddenly put in an appearance, and I started number-crunching in my head.

'Do you think this Al Dempsey character is a safe bet?' Mum asked.

Rio turned his huge hands over so that his palms faced the ceiling. 'As safe a bet as any.'

25

Scarlett

Being the one who got left out of everything made me feel distanced from my family, and I'd become quite alienated from them. They made a habit of being economical with the facts where I was concerned, preferring to cover things up, so I didn't always have a lot of confidence in what they told me. But I was beginning to think employing Hugh was a lost cause and that my family had been telling the truth when they'd said that CJ had done a runner after the attack and wouldn't be stupid enough to come back because the police would arrest him. Then something happened to change my mind.

I'd been sitting at the kitchen table mindlessly stirring my Cheerios around in the bowl when my phone pinged. I picked it up with my left hand while still gripping the spoon with my right. I typed in the PIN code to unlock the screen with the pad of my thumb as I scooped cereal into my mouth. Hugh had sent a WhatsApp message. I'd got so used to the disappointment at this stage I didn't get butterflies anymore when he contacted me.

I opened the message and started scrolling through the latest batch, then suddenly stopped chewing. The man in the photos looked alarmingly familiar. I dropped the spoon as though it had scalded me, and I swallowed down my cereal. My heart was hammering in my chest, and I was pretty sure my blood pressure had spiked.

Holding the phone in my trembling left hand, I examined them in more detail. Using my thumb and forefinger, I expanded the pictures so that I could get a closer look. The first three images were too far away for me to be certain, but when I zoomed in on the fourth, I was left in no doubt. Todd, our former bodyguard, was staring back at me. I was so startled to see him that I almost dropped my handset. As I hadn't had any photos to give Hugh, he'd had to make do with my description, and he'd mistaken Todd for CJ. I supposed it was easy to see why; on paper, they were both around six feet with dark brown hair and eyes, so they fell into the same bracket. Although I'd never have said the two of them looked a bit alike – they had completely different features and bone structures.

I hadn't clapped eyes on the man since the day Kelsey had fired him. What was he doing coming out of CJ's apartment block? Had he been visiting my ex? I had no idea the two of them knew each other. When I'd met CJ at Bluewater, Todd had maintained he didn't know him from Adam. But our former bodyguard was a practised liar, so now I wasn't sure what to believe. Bile rose up my throat when the next question came into my mind. Was Todd somehow linked to the attack that had left me in hospital, fighting for my life? He couldn't have been riding one of the motorbikes because he'd been at a function with Kelsey, but that didn't mean he hadn't been involved in the planning. That thought sent a shiver down my spine.

I let my phone slide from my fingers and pushed my chair back with such force I knocked it back onto the tiles. It landed with a clatter, but I didn't have time to pick it up. I barely made it to the sink before my breakfast made a reappearance. Mum heard the racket and came rushing into the kitchen. When I heard her coming, the first thought that popped into my head was the photos on my phone. I didn't want her to see them, but there was nothing I could do about it. With any luck, the screen would have gone black by now.

I'd been worried about nothing. My welfare was Mum's only concern. As soon as she came into the room, she rushed to my side. I was still gripping the work surface, retching into the sink, when she came up behind me and started rubbing my back to soothe me.

'Are you OK, Scarlett? she asked, but I didn't reply. Actions spoke louder than words, didn't they?

Mum walked over to the cupboard and lifted out a tumbler, then she pressed it up against the door of the fridge and filled it with ice-cold water.

'Here we go, darling,' she said, handing it to me.

I was trembling so badly that I almost spilt the contents and had to use both hands to try and hold the glass up to my lips. When I took a sip of the water, I couldn't face drinking it; my stomach was too raw. So instead, I used the cool liquid to rinse out my mouth.

'Whatever brought that on? Would you like me to call the doctor?' Mum asked.

'No thanks, I'm OK now.'

Mum placed her slender hand on my forehead. 'Are you sure? You look deathly pale.'

'Honestly, I'm not ill. Those Cheerios have got a lot to answer for; one of the little hoops went down the wrong way, that's all,' I lied and then pasted a full smile on my face.

'You had me worried there for a minute.' Mum smiled back at me. 'If you're sure you're OK. I'll get back to work.'

'That's fine. I'm going to have a shower anyway.'

Mum was clucking around me like a mother hen, so I was glad to have some space. I watched from the window as she walked down the garden path and disappeared inside the home office she shared with Mia, Kelsey and Jack. Once I was sure she was out of sight, I went back to my bedroom.

Thoughts of Todd were swirling around in my head, and I was desperate to have another look at the photos. Showering was the last thing on my mind. Now that I was alone in the privacy of my room, I scrolled back through the photos trying to make sense of it all. I scrutinised every detail just to be certain it wasn't a case of mistaken identity, but there was no doubt the man was Todd.

For the life of me, I couldn't work out the connection between Todd, CJ and the swanky new development. I kept turning possibilities over in my head and drawing a blank. The one thing I hadn't considered up until now was that it could be a complete coincidence that Todd was coming out of the building where CJ had an apartment. People who lived there all had one thing in common: they had pots of money, so it wouldn't be unreasonable to think that one of them might require the services of a bodyguard. But somehow, I doubted the explanation would be as simple as that. And to think I'd been about to tell Hugh to call off the search.

I usually just sent Hugh a WhatsApp message to say the latest batch of photos weren't of CJ but the ones he'd sent through today warranted me phoning him.

'Hello, Hugh Oliver speaking,' he said when he answered the phone.

'Good morning, Hugh. It's Scarlett Saunders.'

'Hi, Scarlett. How are you?'

'I'm good, thank you. I've just been looking through the photos you sent me.'

'I take it they were of interest to you then.'

I could tell Hugh was smiling by the tone of his voice.

'They were indeed.' I was smiling too.

'So the search is over, is it? Have I managed to solve the mystery and track down the elusive CJ?' Hugh quizzed.

'Unfortunately not, but the man in the photos is still of interest to me.'

'So you know him then?' Hugh sounded intrigued that while he'd been looking for one man, he'd uncovered another.

'Yes, his name's Todd Evans. He used to work for my family as a bodyguard.'

'I see. Do you still want me to continue keeping the building under surveillance?'

'Yes, please. I'd still like you to try and find CJ, but I'd also like you to keep an eye on Todd and see what he's up to. I'd love to know whether there's a connection between the two of them. Is it possible for you to keep tabs on both of them?'

'Of course; that's not a problem. Leave it with me. I'll be in touch when I have more sightings,' Hugh said before ending the call.

26

Kelsey

Being on my own was torturous. Where the fuck were my mum and sisters? Why had they abandoned me? I was the beating heart of the family. The house would be lifeless without me. They must have noticed I was missing by now. How long did I need to stay away before they became suspicious? The business would barely be functioning without my input. That should have given them incentive enough to send out a search party.

It was hard to know for sure how long I'd been locked up because I had no way of keeping track of the time. But one thing I was certain of was the powerful cravings for heroin were becoming more frequent, and the severity of my symptoms as the drug wore off were more extreme than they had been before.

The sun was just starting to come up when I woke from my sleep. I threw back the cover and hurled myself out of bed. I just managed to make it to the en suite bathroom before the contents of my stomach hit the pan. I gripped the toilet seat as the vomit kept coming. I'd retched myself dry, but my stomach was still spasming, twisting and turning, trying to rid itself of any tiny morsel that might be left behind.

When the sickness finally stopped, I felt like I'd been drained of life. Once I was stable enough to stand, I flushed the toilet before walking over to the sink on a set of legs that were so flimsy I felt like they'd been hollowed out. I washed my hands and then scrubbed my teeth, attempting to get the revolting taste out of my mouth, but it lingered as though it had been tattooed onto my tongue and the insides of my cheeks.

I peered at myself in the mirror while holding on to the sink. My stomach was so tender I couldn't fully straighten. I did a double take when I saw the state of the person staring back at me. My skin was grey, my cheeks hollow, and the circles around my eyes were so dark they didn't look real. I had a sudden urge to burst into tears and had to fight to hold them back. I couldn't bear to look at the person I'd become, so I decided to go back to bed. I was just climbing under the covers when my body started convulsing. The feeling was all too familiar now, but I wasn't going to suffer in silence this time. I wasn't prepared to wait until Todd got around to paying me a visit. So I started banging on the bedside cabinet with my fists, screaming and yelling at the top of my voice.

I heard Todd's footsteps pace along the hall; then, he began rattling on the other side of the door as he fumbled to get the key in the lock. I was sitting on the edge of the mattress when Todd burst into the room. He pushed me back on the bed and clamped his strong fingers over my mouth. He was obviously keen to silence me as quickly as possible.

'Shut the fuck up before you wake the whole building.'

Todd mounted me and pinned me to the mattress. My throat was raw, but the agony I was currently enduring made it pale into insignificance.

'I'm going to take my hand away, so don't start screaming again.' Todd's dark brown eyes bored into mine.

I gulped down air when he released his fingers.

'Can you give me something to take the pain away? I feel like shit.'

'No can do. For once, Kelsey's not going to get what she wants.'

'Please give me a top-up.'

I was disgusted at myself for being so weak, but I couldn't help it. At first, I'd bitterly resisted getting my jab, but now I found myself begging for another fix to ease the intense craving for the drug. I was stuck in a never-ending cycle where I needed to use heroin to stop the pain from the withdrawal.

'Now pipe down. I'm going back to sleep.' Todd stepped back from the bed, and I grabbed hold of his arm to stop him from walking away.

'You can't leave me like this.'

'Says who? I want to really make you suffer for what you did to me.'

'I'm sorry. I promise I'll make it up to you if you give me some more...'

A fresh wave of cramping smothered me, and I wrapped my arms around myself as I fought against it. I looked up at Todd with pleading eyes, and he stood watching me with a smile playing on his lips. I didn't know what I'd ever seen in the man. I'd been a bitch to him, but anyone would think Todd was the innocent party in all of this. He was no more a victim than I was.

Todd turned on his heel as I writhed around on the bed in agony. He came back a moment later with a syringe in his hand.

'Enjoy it while it lasts,' he said as he slid the needle into my arm.

The feel-good buzz the heroin created was short-lived in comparison to the drowsiness and mental impairment that followed. I didn't remember dropping off, but when I came to again, the sun was already high in the sky. I nestled my head into the pillows as I came to; I'd been lying there for a couple of minutes before I realised I wasn't alone in the room. Todd had been watching me while I was sleeping. My heart leapt into my mouth when I spotted him.

'You scared the shit out of me,' I said, clamping the quilt to my chest.

The sight of him sitting in a chair in the corner of the room jogged a memory that had been buried at the back of my mind.

'Can I ask you something? Apart from the day you followed me to Bluewater, had you been keeping tabs on me?'

Todd's lips parted, and the corners of his mouth tilted up. He seemed to find my questions entertaining.

A couple of weeks before I'd woken up in Todd's apartment, I'd started receiving some weird phone calls. The type when somebody was heavy breathing down the receiver but not saying a word. A withheld number would call me, and when I answered, they would wait for several seconds before hanging up. It was happening too regularly for it not to mean something, but I'd foolishly kept it to myself and not told Rio what was going on. I should have known better than to ignore the warning signs. I'd had trouble in the past with unwanted attention, and ignoring the problem didn't make it go away. Some people just couldn't take a hint. But the situation I'd ended up in was much more serious than I could ever have imagined.

'I might have been,' Todd replied. 'But I got bored tailing you, so I decided to put your dad's expensive security system to the test. I was surprised how easy it was to slip past it. I set myself a challenge to shave off a couple of seconds every time I broke in. My personal best was the night you went to the party.'

I felt myself shudder. I wasn't sure I wanted to know how many times Todd had been an intruder.

'You probably aren't aware, but you thrash around a lot while you sleep.'

Todd was deliberately trying to rattle me, and it was working. What he was telling me was really unsettling. It gave me the creeps to know he'd been watching me. Once would have been bad enough, but he'd openly admitted he'd broken in multiple times. The thought of that threatened to send me into a tailspin.

'And the mess you leave behind when you're getting ready is outrageous. You should spare a thought for the poor housekeeper who has to tidy up after you. Is it really too much to expect a grown woman to hang her wet towel up in the bathroom when she's finished with it or put her dirty clothes in the washing basket? Not in my book, it isn't. You wouldn't last five minutes in the military,' Todd said.

So he hadn't just been spying on me while I'd been sleeping. This was getting worse by the minute. I wished I'd trusted my gut now. I wasn't normally of a nervous disposition, but there were times when I'd felt like I was being watched while I'd been in my room. Nothing had looked out of place, but I couldn't seem to shake off the uneasiness. It didn't sit well with me. I was unaccustomed to feeling that way.

It was clear that Todd had got a kick out of violating my privacy in the worst possible way. I'd been blissfully unaware that I'd been alone with somebody who'd wanted to harm me while I'd been at my most vulnerable. The thought of that was terrifying. Anything could have happened. My heart was galloping in my chest as endless possibilities started running through my head.

'I could have slit your throat in the middle of the night and left you to bleed out if I'd wanted to,' Todd said as though he'd just read my mind.

'So why didn't you?'

Now that I was in the grips of addiction, death felt like an easy option.

'Believe me, I thought about it, but I didn't want to let you off the hook that easily. Tarnishing my reputation and publicly humiliating me comes at a price. I wanted to ruin your life the way you've ruined mine,' Todd said in a venomous tone.

No truer words had been spoken; Todd had indeed ruined my life. He couldn't have picked a worse punishment for me if he'd tried.

27

Mia

In Kelsey's absence, Mum and I went with Rio and Darius to hand over the cash. The men sat side by side in the front. Darius was behind the wheel of the Range Rover. Mum and I sat in the back, flanking the black holdall containing the cash. The M4 was busy, considering it was just before lunchtime, but thankfully, the traffic was moving steadily. Darius drove into the service station and parked up at the prearranged spot next to a white transit van that had seen better days. As he manoeuvred into the space, I couldn't help noticing the crumbling wheel arches and patches of rust that had got under the paintwork and eaten the metal away.

'Do you think we should be lending a man who drives a van like that this amount of money? Mum questioned.

Rio turned to look over his shoulder, and we locked eyes.

'As long as he pays back what he owes, I don't think we should concern ourselves with the vehicle he drives. Al told me he's using some of the money to get himself a new set of wheels.'

Even though Rio had brushed Mum's concerns away, she'd made a valid point. I also had a bad feeling about this, and we all knew you should listen to your gut. I was just about to voice my concerns when Rio interrupted me.

'Seriously, Amanda, you should see the state of some of the dodgy characters Davie lent money to over the years. If he'd been put off by outward appearances, he'd never have made a living in this game. The whole reason guys like Al borrow from people like you is that they don't have any other options, but that doesn't mean they're an unsafe bet. Geezers like Dempsey deal in cash most of the time, so they have problems proving their net worth. The banks or more legitimate lines of credit won't touch them, which gives us free rein to charge exorbitant amounts of interest. All's fair in love and war at the end of the day.'

'I hear what you're saying, but I still feel uneasy about it,' Mum replied.

That made two of us.

Rio offered Mum a weak smile. 'I've checked out his story, and he does supply market traders from a warehouse in Bovingdon. Darius and I have had eyes on him for a while now. If he tries any funny business, we'll seize his stock and warehouse assets.'

'Fair enough. Let's go through with the deal then.' Although Mum had agreed, her words were coated in hesitation.

'Al wants to import a new line from India. He's found a new supplier that produces top-quality counterfeits, but he needs the readies to get it off the ground,' Rio added as further reassurance.

Rio turned his attention away from Mum and let his dark brown eyes rest on his nephew.

'Right then, son, let's get down to business. Are you ready?' Rio asked as he stepped out of the car.

Darius nodded; he was a man of few words. I could count on one hand the amount of times I'd heard him speak. He was the strong silent type, but I was sure if you gave him a few years to gain more experience, he'd be a force to be reckoned with. He was in the same boat as Kelsey and me, so I wasn't in a position to judge. Learning on the job was harder than it looked. Half the time, I ended up having to do things on the fly.

Rio opened the back passenger door. 'All set, Mia?'

I glanced sideways at Mum, and she beamed back at me. If she felt nervous for me, it didn't show. I hoped her confidence was infectious.

'Mia?' The sound of Rio's voice brought me back to reality. 'Are you OK?'

'Yes.' I smiled, wrapping my fingers around the handle of the holdall.

Once I was out of the car, Rio took the bag from me. I pushed my shoulders back and tried to channel the inner badass lurking deep inside me. I had to start as I meant to go on and lead from the front. I walked over to the driver's door, staying two paces ahead of Rio and Darius.

Al was barely able to see over the steering wheel. I had to stifle a laugh as he climbed down from the van and stood in the car park, craning his neck so that he could look up at Rio, Darius and me. The light bounced off a chunky gold signet ring on his little finger as he reached his hand out in greeting. Al's thinning hair was parted on the left and swept over to one side, skimming his shiny line-etched forehead. He was wearing faded blue jeans and a pink Fred Perry polo shirt buttoned right up to the neck.

'Nice to meet you, Mr Dempsey. I'm Mia Saunders,' I said, extending my right hand towards him.

I was technically Mia Eastwood these days, but I preferred to keep my maiden name where business was concerned as it carried more clout than my married one. Even though my dad was long gone, the fear his name instilled in people existed even to this day.

'The pleasure's all mine,' Al replied, and his beady eyes scanned over me.

'The money's in the bag,' Rio said, flashing Al a glare without exchanging pleasantries.

'Thanks, chief.' Al grinned.

'Don't thank me, thank the boss.' Rio's tone was abrupt, and he curled his lip as he spoke.

His dislike for Al was apparent, and I was glad he was on my side. My dad's best friend was a powerhouse of a man and a force to be reckoned with. I felt totally safe in Al's company even though he was a sleazebag, as I was flanked on either side by two generations of the de Souza family. Uncle and nephew were carbon copies of each other, and Al looked more than a little uncomfortable as they stood eyeballing him.

'Sorry, my mistake – thanks, sweets.' Al held his hands up in front of him.

I offered Al a weak smile.

'Right then, I best be off. The dosh is burning a hole in my pocket already.' Al tapped the side of the holdall as he beamed from ear to ear.

An uneasy feeling began nesting in the pit of my stomach, but before I had a chance to act on my concerns, Al turned on his heel, leapt into the driver's seat, started the reluctant engine and began reversing. My ears felt like they'd started bleeding as the van let out a high-pitched squeal in protest.

'Sounds like his fan belt's on the way out,' Rio said as we walked back to the car.

Mum had unclipped her seatbelt and was now sitting in the middle; she was leaning forward, holding on to the passenger headrest as she stretched her neck towards the windscreen, trying to eavesdrop on the conversation. She moved back over to the left-hand side as we got closer to the car.

'How did it go?' Mum asked when I sat down next to her.

'Fine,' I replied without mentioning my unease about the situation.

There was no point worrying Mum any more than she already was over what, at this stage, was a gut feeling.

28

Scarlett

My phone pinged, and when I opened the WhatsApp message, I saw that Hugh had sent me some pictures of Todd and another man in a bright blue sports car with a caption underneath.

Is this our man?

My heart started galloping as I expanded the frames. I could clearly see Todd in the passenger seat, but the driver's face was obscured by the headrest, so I couldn't get a good look at him. I couldn't be sure if it was CJ or not.

I'm not sure. It's hard to tell. It could be. Can you get more pics?

After I typed my reply, I put my phone down on the counter. Was it a stroke of luck that Hugh had spotted Todd in CJ's apartment block or just a weird coincidence? It was impossible to second-guess the situation. My thoughts turned to Kelsey; she'd always been my go-to person when I needed to confide in somebody, and I suddenly felt lost without her. Things had become strained between us, but I wanted more than anything for our relationship to go back to the way it used to be.

I wished I could warn my sister that Todd was back on the

scene. They hadn't parted on good terms, and a man like Todd with an ego the size of outer space was bound to be feeling bitter about the way things had ended. I couldn't help thinking Kelsey should watch her back now that he'd been spotted in the local vicinity.

Jack was the perfect match for Mia. She'd been lucky enough to find her soul mate. The same couldn't be said for Kelsey and me. Neither of us seemed to be lucky where men were concerned. Todd had been a womaniser, and as for CJ, it was hard to find words to describe what a lowlife he was. He'd been incredibly cruel to me. You'd be hard pushed to find a nastier human being.

Details of our brief fling drifted back into my mind. The memories were so vivid that I found myself choking back tears. They'd started to roll silently down my cheek, but I wasn't going to let myself crumble; I needed to pull myself together and try to put thoughts of Todd and CJ out of my head for the time being. As the minutes dragged by, I found it impossible to concentrate on anything else. A million thoughts were floating around in my brain. I sincerely hoped that I wouldn't have to wait too long for news from Hugh. Otherwise, the suspense would kill me.

29

Kelsey

I was becoming well and truly hooked on heroin, so I had to keep facing the choice to fight the urge and try and stay clean or give in to temptation. Logic dictated that if something was bad for you, you'd stop doing it, right? Wrong. I'd never experienced a craving like it. It was persistent. I was on a very slippery slope, and logic had gone out of the window. There was only one way this was heading. I was developing a habit that might end up being impossible to break. My dependence was building by the day, and there was nothing I could do about it. I had no control over it; my willpower was at an all-time low.

I was getting good at spotting the tell-tale signs that my last dose of heroin was wearing off. When my nose began to run and I started experiencing flu-like symptoms, it set off a desperate chain reaction within me. I knew I needed to get some opioids into my body as soon as possible, or I was going to be struck down with sickness so terrible that I'd do almost anything to prevent it. The cold sweats, nausea and body aches were hell. I found myself craving heroin not just because I wanted the high but because it brought with it instant relief.

After a night of no sleep, rolling on the bathroom floor to ease the cramping in my stomach before vomiting into the toilet, I couldn't take any more. I dragged myself onto my feet, gritting my teeth from the physical exertion, and slowly made my way out of the en suite. My coordination was all over the place. My limbs felt heavy, and I struggled to stay balanced.

'Todd. Todd. Help me. I feel terrible.' Desperation coated my words as I banged on the bedroom door.

I gripped the chrome handle while pressing my ear against the wood, listening for sounds of activity. A ball of anxiety began to grow in the pit of my stomach when he didn't immediately respond. My mind and body were starting to unravel at an alarming rate.

'Keep the noise down,' Todd said when he flung the door open.

The speed at which he opened it nearly knocked me off my feet. My reactions were so laboured that I only just managed to stand clear.

'I feel awful. I need a top-up,' I said, wrapping my arms around myself.

'I don't think I heard you say please. I know that word doesn't usually feature in your vocabulary, but now might be a good time to learn some manners.' Todd tilted his head to the side as his dark brown eyes scanned me.

'Please, Todd, I'm begging you,' I replied. My speech was slurred.

Hearing me grovelling brought a smile to Todd's face. 'There you go. That wasn't so difficult, was it?'

I fixed him with my eyes as I stood shaking from head to toe.

'Sit on the bed,' Todd said, taking a needle out of the pocket of his black combats.

I shuffled across the room on legs that felt like they were made from concrete, and then I flopped down on the mattress. I didn't take my eyes off Todd as he removed the cover.

'How the mighty have fallen,' Todd said as he slid the contents of the syringe into my vein.

As the heroin started to course around my body, travelling through my bloodstream, my breathing became heavy. When the drug reached my brain, it produced a rush that only lasted a couple of minutes, but in terms of pleasure, it was orgasmic, and

I enjoyed the moment lost in my own world. The buzz didn't feel quite as intense these days, but at least the hit still took the pain away. On the upside, the high lasted for a while. But without access to a clock, I had no real idea how long, although if I had to guess, I'd say a few hours. I felt content and wasn't bothered by my confinement until the effects wore off again. On the downside, when the rattling started, the suffering that came with it was indescribable.

'You look a complete mess.'

The sound of Todd's voice brought me back to reality. His insult didn't concern me in the slightest. I'd lost all interest in my appearance.

'You're absolutely humming. When was the last time you had a shower?'

Todd's nose twitched, and then his smile stretched from ear to ear. Ridiculing me had become his favourite pastime; he couldn't get enough of it. At this moment in time, I couldn't give a flying fuck if I stank. Washing wasn't as high a priority as it used to be.

'I wonder what Davie would say if he could see you now,' Todd continued.

It was obvious he was hoping to provoke a reaction from me, and he seemed surprised when I let his comment slide. Not so long ago, he would have received a well-deserved lash of my tongue.

'I don't think I've ever met a man who was more anti-drugs than your dad. I'd say he'd be disgusted if he knew that one of his precious princesses had become a junkie.' Todd smirked.

His words stung like a slap around the face. I'd adored my dad, so he knew his comment would hurt me. Dad and I had been very close, and his death had hit me hard. It wasn't as though he'd died in his sleep. Todd's wife had killed him in cold blood. Michelle had intended to snuff out my life to get back at her cheating husband, but I'd moved just as she'd pulled the trigger, and she'd accidentally hit Dad. Knowing the bullet that hit him was meant for me would haunt me for the rest of my life. The memory of that day came to me so vividly that I found myself struggling to hold back my tears.

'Davie hated druggies; thought they were the scum of the earth. How does it feel to know he had no time for the likes of you?' Todd rambled on.

Since when had he become such an expert on Davie Saunders? He'd only been employed by the firm for a short while, yet he seemed to think he knew the inner workings of my dad's mind.

'The old man wouldn't be impressed, Kels.' Todd shook his head to emphasise his point. You used to be such a stunner, and now you look a right mess.'

'Thanks for the compliment,' I said through gritted teeth.

Todd's efforts to rile me were relentless, and the fact that I wasn't taking the bait was really starting to piss him off, which gave me a small sense of satisfaction. He was being a ginormous bellend, but that didn't really surprise me. Behaving like a dick head came as naturally to him as breathing. I wasn't sure how he was expecting me to react. If he was hoping I was going to break down in tears and sob my heart out because he didn't find me attractive, he was about to be disappointed. I felt like I was floating on air now that the heroin had got into my system, so his attempts to verbally abuse me were falling on deaf ears.

'Not such a pretty girl, these days, are you?'

That was true. My skin was so pale it had a bluish tint to it. I looked tired and haggard, and the dark circles around my eyes rivalled any panda's. I appeared to have aged ten years since he'd brought me here, but none of that concerned me.

I'd had enough of listening to Todd for one day, so I lay back on the bed and closed my eyes. I wanted to enjoy the rush while it lasted. As I drifted off, I heard him repeatedly calling my name and then his voice faded into the distance.

30

Mia

'Hello, stranger,' Jack said when I walked into the bedroom. 'How come you're so late?'

'Mum and I had to drop some money off, and the traffic was murder on the way back.'

'You know I don't like you putting yourself at risk for no reason. I would have gladly done that for you.' Jack was such a sweetheart. Nothing was ever too much trouble.

I kicked my shoes off and walked over to my husband. He was standing in the doorway of the en suite bathroom with a towel wrapped around his waist. His honey-blond hair looked two shades darker as it was still damp. He had droplets of water all over his muscular torso, having just stepped out of the shower, so I got up on my tiptoes and planted a kiss on his lips.

'You smell nice,' I said.

An aromatic cloud of sandalwood surrounded Jack, and it wafted up my nostrils when I got close to him. I found myself being drawn back for another sniff.

'Thanks. Although I can't really take the credit. It's Tom Ford that's responsible.' Jack smiled.

'How were your mum and dad?'

I'd got over my earlier disappointment at not being invited to Dale and Nancy's house and was keen to know how my in-laws were keeping as I hadn't seen them for a while.

'The same as usual. Mum cooked up the entire contents of the fridge while Dad told me all about his latest round of golf,' Jack replied. 'I didn't know you were dropping money off?'

'We went to meet a guy called Al Dempsey. He's expanding his clothing business, and he needed to borrow a fair bit.'

Jack looked puzzled. 'I'm surprised Rio didn't mention that to me.'

'I'm sure he would have done, but you've been out of the office for most of the day,' I replied.

'Even so, I would have thought Rio would have run it past me before lending a large amount of money. As the firm's accountant, I'm responsible for balancing the books. How much are we talking?'

'Two hundred and fifty thousand.'

Jack looked like he'd been slapped around the face by a wet kipper. Then he shook his head before fixing me with his blue eyes.

I felt my anxiety begin to rise in response as an uneasy feeling swept over me. It was obvious Jack thought we'd made a bad call lending so much money. But it was too late to voice his concerns now; we'd already handed over the cash.

'Jesus, Mia, that's a huge amount of money. I'm not trying to worry you, but I hope this doesn't go tits up.'

Famous last words. I was sure it wasn't intentional – Jack was always so sensitive about my issues – but negativity was coming off him in waves, and it was infectious. I found myself doubting what we'd done more and more with every second that passed.

'What do you know about this Al Dempsey? I've worked for the firm for years, and I can safely say I've never heard that guy's name mentioned before,' Jack queried.

I swallowed down the lump in my throat. Mum had said the same thing.

'He's a new client, but apparently, Dad knew him back in the day.'

The palms of my hands were sweating, but I didn't want

Jack to know I was starting to have serious doubts, so I tried my best to bury them.

'I can't say I've ever come across him before, and I thought I knew all of your dad's contacts.'

'Rio knows him,' I jumped in, hoping that would put an end to the conversation. 'He said Dad and Al were casual acquaintances years ago, but they'd never done business together before.'

'Let's hope for all our sakes that Mr Dempsey isn't a con merchant. The company can't afford to make a loss like that.'

'Who says we're going to make a loss? You'll be beaming from ear to ear when the payments start rolling in every month.'

I was doing my best to sound confident, but all of it was for show. My insides were churning like clothes in a washing machine.

'That's what I like to hear. I'll look forward to seeing the bank balance swell.' Jack offered me a weak smile before he walked over to the chest of drawers and took out some clothes.

After we'd had dinner, I helped Mum clear the table before she started rustling up some banana and blueberry muffins for tomorrow morning's breakfast. While Mum sifted flour into a bowl, Scarlett made her excuses and then she took herself off to her room.

'Let's go and watch TV,' Jack said, catching hold of my hand.

Alone time for us was rare these days, so I happily trailed after him. Jack and I sat side by side on the sofa as he flicked through the channels.

'Do you mind if I watch this?' Jack turned to face me. He was always so considerate.

His blue eyes were wide with excitement, so I could hardly say no, but my insides were groaning. Half an hour later, Jack was still glued to the programme about high-performance cars, and it was boring me rigid.

'I'm shattered. I think I'll get an early night,' I said.

The roar of the cars' engines was giving me a headache.

'I'll turn it off if you're not enjoying it,' Jack offered, ever the gentleman.

But I couldn't be that mean. I could see he was in his element watching the Porsches, Ferraris and Lamborghinis being test-driven at speed.

'It's not that, it's just it's been a long day, and my bed is calling me.' I smiled.

'Fair enough. I won't be too long. I'll be up when this finishes,' Jack said, planting a kiss on the side of my head.

I got up from the sofa and walked into the kitchen. 'I'm off to bed. Goodnight, Mum,' I called, poking my head around the door.

Mum looked up from her mixing bowl at the sound of my voice. 'Goodnight, darling. See you in the morning.'

I let out a yawn as I climbed into bed a few minutes later. Then I pulled the summer-weight duvet up over my shoulder before nuzzling my chin into the cool cotton fabric. There was something so comforting about the smell and feel of fresh sheets. I always seemed to drift off easier when the bed had been changed. I'd fully expected to fall into a deep sleep within minutes, but tonight seemed to be an exception to the rule.

I lay in the dark tossing and turning, desperately trying to get the conversation I'd had with Jack out of my mind. Every time I tried to blank out the details, I'd hear his voice questioning the decision we'd made. We hadn't taken it lightly or reacted on a whim. Mum, Rio and I had discussed it at length before we'd decided lending Al the money was a risk worth taking. He'd tried not to be too hard on me, but he hadn't hidden the fact that he thought we'd made a mistake. It was at times like this I wished I hadn't mixed business with pleasure.

Jack had the firm's best interests at heart, so I got where he was coming from and understood his concerns, but we stood to make a lot of money from this particular deal. And sometimes, you had to stick your neck out and gamble a little to make money. In this business, every debt was risky in its own right. We weren't in the line of work to play it safe.

As I tossed and turned in the bed, visions of the rusty van with crumbling wheel arches kept coming into my head. I tried to block them out, but they were playing over and over on a loop. I hoped we weren't about to be taken for a ride.

I'd had my doubts before Jack had voiced his opinion, which had ended up making me feel ten times worse. His fears had come from a place of concern, but uncertainty was now running riot in my head. I had to try and force myself to think about this logically. There was no point in panicking about being double-crossed at this stage or worrying about what-ifs. Al hadn't even done anything underhanded, so we should be giving him the man a chance to prove he could be trusted before we destroyed his credibility.

My dad always used to say loyalty counted for everything, and it was something that couldn't be bought. Rio's had been tested on countless occasions. It had been unwavering; he'd never let my family down. Dad's childhood friend had our best interests at heart. He would never knowingly bring trouble to our door, so I was going to keep that thought firmly in my mind.

And anyway, Rio had checked out Al Dempsey's story. He did supply market traders with clothes from a warehouse in Bovingdon. It had already been decided that if Al didn't pay back what he owed, we'd seize his stock. Unlike some of our customers, the man had assets, which could only be a good thing, and that should have offered us some peace of mind.

31

Kelsey

Once upon a time, I thought I'd known what made Todd tick even though he'd never told me much about himself. From the way he'd acted, I knew we shared a similar outlook on life. We were both commitment-phobes who loved our freedom and hated it when people invaded our personal space too closely. And he was every bit as selfish and self-centred as I was. In fact, I'd go so far as to say he'd knocked me off the top spot.

In hindsight, I realised I'd been completely clueless. His face and body were all too familiar. We'd shared an intimate relationship for eighteen months, so I knew the physical side of him inside out, but I had no idea what was going on in his head. He'd been leading a double life and had covered his tracks so well I hadn't realised what was going on behind the scenes. Keeping a secret of that size required skill. He was a master of deception and didn't have a legitimate reason for creating an alternate existence. It wasn't as though he was an undercover cop or a member of MI5. He was purely and simply a cheat, and a sociopathic one at that. As far as Todd was concerned, variety was the spice of life. He had an insatiable appetite for sex and amazing stamina, but he bored easily.

I was walking a fine line between pleasure and pain. Todd had become both my executioner and saviour, and he was bathing in the glory of his new elevated position. He decided if and when he'd relieve me of my suffering. My arms were like pin cushions;

puncture marks dotted the skin on the insides of my elbows, and a couple of small abscesses had appeared around the injection sites.

Where the hell were my family? I couldn't believe they weren't concerned for my welfare. I hadn't been home in ages, but instead of sending out a search party, none of them seemed the slightest bit bothered by my disappearance.

But I needed them to be worried about me. Otherwise, I was never going to get out of this nightmare. A lot of the time, I couldn't think straight, so I couldn't work out an escape plan. Todd could keep me in this apartment against my will for as long as he wanted, and there was nothing I could do about it. I had no idea what he had in store for me. I had to try not to dwell on that.

'If I wasn't funding your habit, you'd have to resort to selling yourself for your next fix. But that wouldn't be a problem for a whore like you, would it?' Todd looked down his nose at me.

'I've got my own money, and you'd do well to remember that. You seem to have forgotten who used to pay your wages.'

As soon as the words left my mouth, I regretted saying them. My outburst was a knee-jerk reaction; I'd always had a feisty side, and I didn't want him to think he had the upper hand. Who was I trying to kid? I was completely at his mercy, and we both knew it. I'd been snatched from my home and was being held against my will by the man who had formerly been paid to protect me, and he was taking great pleasure in making me suffer.

Todd was out for revenge; that didn't surprise me. I'd killed his wife and fired him from his job, but there was no love lost between Michelle and himself. From what she'd told me, he'd been a serial cheat the whole time they were married. It wasn't as though he'd have been heartbroken by her death, but Todd was a proud man and didn't take humiliation well. He liked to be the giver, not the receiver. Even so, I was shocked that he was prepared to go to such great lengths to right the wrong. I must have really got under his skin.

'No, I haven't. I clearly remember that Davie paid my wages. The money didn't come out of your bank account, did it?' Todd said through gritted teeth. 'You're pathetic, Kelsey. You're a grown woman, and you still used to let your dad pick up the tab for everything and, now that he's gone, your mum funds your lifestyle. I can safely say she'd cut you off in a heartbeat if she knew you were a junkie.' Todd smiled.

Wasn't that the truth? Mum would have been horrified to see me desperate for a fix. The fact that I was now an addict through no fault of my own was a difficult pill to swallow. Todd's words stung, but I'd have to take them on the chin. I could see I'd pissed him off. I'd done enough damage for one day and couldn't afford to take another step wrong. Todd was holding all of the cards. He stood between me and my next hit, so if I had any sense, I'd wind my neck in and be on my best behaviour.

When Todd turned on his heel and went to walk out of the room, I felt panic start to crawl up from my stomach. He hadn't given me my next dose, and without it, withdrawal symptoms would soon set in.

'How long are you going to keep me locked in this room?' I asked.

I'd almost given up hope of ever seeing my family again and wished I'd told Rio about my concerns when they'd first surfaced.

'Don't tell me you're feeling homesick.' Todd smiled.

I would have liked nothing more than to be back in my house with everyone and everything that was important to me, but I wasn't about to admit that to him.

'If I'm away for much longer, my family are going to get suspicious that something's not right, and Rio will start trying to track me down,' I said, clutching at straws.

'Nice try, Kelsey, but I'm not falling for that. Your folks aren't the slightest bit bothered. I've been texting mummy dearest regularly, so she thinks she's being kept in the loop. And judging by the replies you've been getting, she just thinks you're being flaky and self-centred, putting yourself first the way you usually do.'

I felt myself inwardly groan. How was I ever going to get out of this nightmare if I couldn't raise the alarm? My family were completely oblivious to how much danger I was in. They had no idea that Todd had kidnapped me and was holding me captive until he decided what to do with me. In the meantime, he was getting immense pleasure out of making me suffer and wanted to use every opportunity to exert his power over me. He wasn't going to stop until he broke me.

'Time management never was your thing, and you've always been a selfish bitch, so you can't really blame your family for not being concerned about your welfare.'

A lump formed in my throat and, for one awful minute, I thought I was going to burst into tears, but thankfully, I managed to pull myself together. I didn't want to give Todd the satisfaction of seeing me cry, so I came back fighting. His insults had got me riled up.

'Is that the best you can come up with?' I retorted.

Up until now, I'd tried to be on my best behaviour, but I couldn't keep the pretence up any longer. If my comment angered him, I'd just have to deal with the fallout.

'Feeling brave all of a sudden, are we?'

Todd stood grinning at me. I would have loved to have wiped the smirk off his face, but my limbs were like lead, and I didn't have the energy to slap him around the chops.

'I didn't think it would take long for your true colours to come shining through,' Todd said as he backed himself out of the door.

'Where are you going?' I asked with desperation coating my words.

'Out. Don't wait up!' Todd replied.

His words bounced around inside my head like a ball in a

game of tennis. Todd was wearing such a smug look as he closed the door behind him.

Hollowness burrowed inside me when I heard the front door of the apartment close. Even though deep down I had a horrible feeling all was lost, I had a stoic refusal to let him win. I knew the worst thing I could do was give up. It wasn't in my nature to throw the towel in. I was glad to see my stubborn streak was doing its best to shine through. Dad had brought me up to be a fighter, not a quitter. And real fighters fought dirty. They didn't abide by any rules, and they did whatever they had to do to get the upper hand. I'd never been a pushover, and I didn't intend to start now.

But it was impossible to work out what he might do next or how he was going to react in the coming days. The man was a trained killer, which in the past had sent ripples of excitement flowing through my body; now I was all too aware I might be sleeping in my deathbed. Todd might decide to finish me off, and if he did, there would be very little I could do about it. I'd been doing my best to be compliant and not antagonise him so he'd release me unharmed. He'd know that once Rio got wind of what he'd done, his days would be numbered. There was a very real possibility, he'd never let me leave here alive. The thought of that sent a wave of panic rippling through me. Maybe if I tried to connect with Todd and make him think I still had feelings for him, I'd be able to persuade him to let me go. It was probably a long shot, but I didn't have a lot of options, so it had to be worth considering. A split second later I decided against that idea. There was only so far I was prepared to stoop and that was way too low.

Todd was a predator who took pleasure from exploiting others. When he'd gone out and left me, he knew I was going to suffer. The clock was ticking. It wouldn't be long until the rattling started, but I wasn't about to sit here and wait. Now that Todd had given me this opportunity, I was going to grab it with both hands. There must be a way I could draw attention to myself.

My eyes scanned around the sparsely furnished room and settled on a lamp on the bedside cabinet. I'd been hoping to find something more substantial, but Todd's place was minimal to the extreme, so it would have to do. I closed my fist around the metal stem and wrenched the lamp from the socket, ducking out of the way to avoid the plug as it swung past my face. Then I paced over to the windows and started welting the glass with the base. But instead of shattering, the lamp just kept bouncing off the surface. I threw it down on the floor in frustration, then wiped my runny nose on the back of my hand. Time was running out.

I took a few deep breaths while considering what to do next, but I couldn't seem to get my brain to work properly. It felt fuzzy as though it was made from cotton wool. I was having trouble concentrating. All I could think about was my next fix.

In one final act of desperation, I tore across the room and hurled myself at the door. It didn't budge, so I began bashing the wood with my fists while screaming for help at the top of my lungs. I carried on until I lost my voice. I looked down at my trembling hands; they were throbbing and bruised. Nobody came. Silent tears ran down my cheeks as I walked over to the bed with aching limbs. I climbed into it, pulled the covers over my head and cried myself to sleep.

32

Mia

'Hello, beautiful,' Jack said when he walked into the bedroom.

I'd been sitting on a mat in the middle of the floor, cross-legged with my eyes closed and my hands on my knees, practising my deep breathing and doing my best to destress after an eventful stint in the office. But I opened my eyes when I heard the sound of my husband's voice, and my face broke into a beam at the sight of him. He'd been working away again today, so I hadn't seen him since first thing this morning.

'How was your day?' Jack asked.

He fixed me with his blue eyes as he loosened his tie. He always wore a suit to work even though most of the time he was based in the home office. He liked to look the part, and he wouldn't hear any complaints from me. Nobody could deny Jack was a good-looking guy, and he scrubbed up well.

'It was pretty hectic, but not too bad,' I replied before I untangled my legs and got to my feet.

That couldn't be further from the truth. Despite our best efforts, Oscar Myles was still giving us the run-around. We were stuck in a game of cat and mouse, and there didn't seem to be any end in sight. Trying to track him down was incredibly stressful, but I didn't want to get involved in a conversation about work. The only time Jack and I ever argued was where business was concerned. We didn't see eye to eye on the running of the firm at all, so I tried to stay off the subject.

'You look so at home in your gym wear. Don't you miss being a yoga instructor?' Jack pulled me towards him and then wrapped his arms around my waist before planting a kiss on my lips.

'Not really.'

Don't get me wrong, I enjoyed nothing more than meditating after a stressful day, but I loved being involved in the family business, and there was no way I'd want to give that up, especially now that Kelsey had gone AWOL. Mum needed my help more than ever, and after everything she'd done for me, I wasn't about to let her down. Kelsey and I had made a promise to her. I wouldn't go back on my word even though my sister had. Times had been tough since we'd stepped up to the mark and begun running the firm, but for me, nothing could dim the quiet satisfaction of knowing that, in my heart, I hadn't given up. What was the saying? In the end, you only regretted the things you didn't do.

'I'm not sure I believe you,' Jack said.

The sound of his voice brought me back to reality.

Jack held me at arm's length, and I looked up into his blue eyes.

'Can I ask you something?' I asked, preparing to go off on a tangent.

I felt mentally drained, and I didn't want to talk about work.

'Of course.' Jack smiled.

'Mum doesn't seem at all bothered about the fact that Kelsey's done a disappearing act. Do you think we should be worried?'

Jack shook his head. 'I have to say, I'm inclined to agree with your mum. I wouldn't lose any sleep over it if I were you.'

I let out a sigh. 'I know she has a tendency to be a bit flaky…'

'That's an understatement if ever I heard one,' Jack cut in before I finished my sentence. 'Kelsey's the most unreliable person I know. You can't depend on her for anything.'

'I know, but I don't remember a time when she's taken off for this long without coming home for a change of clothes.'

'Seriously, Mia, don't start fretting about her. You know what Kelsey's like. She doesn't give a shit about anybody but herself.' Jack put his finger under my chin and tilted my face towards his. 'She'll be home before you know it, but in the meantime, do me a favour – don't stress about it, or you'll make yourself ill. Kelsey's a big girl now. She can look after herself and fight her own battles. She doesn't need her big sister worrying about her welfare.' Jack leant towards me and kissed the end of my nose.

I supposed he was right. I'd give myself an ulcer if I carried on like this. But I couldn't help the way I felt. I had a bad habit of overthinking situations, so I was glad I'd run my concerns past Jack. He had a level head when it came to things like this, and that's why I'd turned to him for reassurance. He had an analytical mind and was a good person to have around in a crisis, unlike me.

I put so much effort into worrying about anything and everything that sometimes my own needs had to take a back seat. All too often, anxiety took over my life. I had to fight a daily battle to keep it at bay.

Jack had gone some way to putting my mind at ease by reinforcing what my mum had said. But I knew for certain I'd sleep much sounder once Kelsey did finally get around to showing her face.

33

Scarlett

Time had dragged by agonisingly slowly while I'd waited for news from Hugh. Instead of being a haven, my bedroom had become like a prison cell. I lay in my bed for hours on end, scrutinising the last message Hugh had sent. But it was impossible to get a good look at the man behind the wheel. I had a gut feeling it could well be CJ. I'd never seen the car before, but it was super flashy and reeked of money, so it would have suited him down to the ground. It would have been exactly the sort of motor he'd have liked to drive around in.

I was pinning my hopes on the fact that Hugh had come up trumps this time. I imagined the moment I got to confront CJ with a hint of malicious glee. But before I could do that, I needed better shots to be able to confirm my suspicions. Waiting for them to come through was doing my head in. I hadn't been blessed with patience, so the suspense was literally killing me.

My phone was on the bedside cabinet when it suddenly pinged, so I grabbed the handset. The adrenaline rush had kick-started my nerves, and the palms of my hands began to sweat, so my fingerprint wasn't recognised. I typed in the PIN, but I was all fingers and thumbs, and I got the sequence of numbers wrong twice. I almost hurled the phone across the room and screamed in frustration. When I eventually managed to unlock the screen, I saw a WhatsApp notification, so I clicked on the app.

Hugh had sent through another batch of photos, which sent

butterflies fluttering around in my stomach; my heart began hammering in my chest as I scrolled through them. This time, I was pleased to see that he'd managed to get clearer photos of the driver of the blue sports car. Hugh had sent a series of frames of the man getting out of the car and of him standing on the pavement talking to Todd. My heart sank when I realised that it wasn't CJ. The guy in the pictures was a total stranger. Now that I'd had a chance to have a proper look at him, I could see he had a slight frame and was considerably shorter than our former bodyguard; I'd say around five feet nine. His hair was light, mousy brown, but it was impossible to make out his eye colour from a distance. The mystery man had a goatee, which was so sparse it was more like bumfluff than a proper beard. All in all, he looked nothing like CJ, which was both a relief and a disappointment.

I'd been convinced that Hugh had managed to track CJ down this time, so I'd been gearing myself up for the showdown between the two of us. Part of me wanted all of this to be over and done with, but the other part knew I needed more time to get myself into the right headspace before I confronted him. It was something I was looking forward to and dreading in equal measure. Mentally preparing myself to confront the person who'd treated me appallingly was an incredibly stressful thing to do, especially as I had nobody to confide in or take advice from.

I'd had years of practice dealing with rejection while I'd been a drama student. Auditioning for a role I didn't get was the pits and something I never got used to, but there was always intense competition, so it was inevitable. Every time it happened, I'd wanted to throw my toys out of the pram. It was hard to take knockbacks on the chin, be gracious about them and chalk them up to experience. But by the time my course was ending, I liked to think I'd got it off to a fine art and handled rebuffs like a pro. One of my tutors used to tell us not to go burning bridges. It was far more sensible to keep the door open as we might cross paths with that prospective employer again in the future.

But being spurned on a professional level wasn't the same as being dumped by a person you were romantically invested in. That stung like a bitch. It was debilitating and a huge blow to my self-esteem, which was something I'd been hard-wired to protect at all costs. Negative emotions fed off vulnerability, so I'd had to adopt a different strategy and coping mechanism to get me through the ordeal.

Rejection happened to all of us at some point; it was part of life. It was impossible not to feel bitter, resentful and angry after the way I'd been treated, but I owed it to myself to come out of this stronger and wiser. I wasn't going to wallow in self-pity. I was going to focus on putting all of this behind me and on making a fresh start. It wasn't going to be easy, but Scarlett Saunders was a fighter. Always had been, always would be. CJ wasn't going to know what hit him when I got hold of him. He was in for a rude awakening.

34

Kelsey

I woke with a start. It was pitch-black in the room, and I had no idea what time it was. Where the hell was Todd? Although it was impossible to know for sure, it felt like he'd been gone for hours. Much as I couldn't stand the sight of the man, I hoped he hadn't gone and done a runner. I didn't want to think about what would happen to me if he'd upped and left. A sense of unease descended on me, making my empty stomach cramp in response.

A wave of nausea came from nowhere, so I rolled onto my side and pulled my knees up to my chest. As I lay in the darkness, a terrifying thought popped into my head. If Todd didn't come back, how was I going to score? I could feel desperation begin to set in. The only constant I had was my addiction. My previous life, the glamorous one where I used to rub shoulders with celebrities, was blurring into the distance. I wiped away a tear with the pads of my fingertips as it rolled down my cheek.

A sudden intense pain sent me rushing into the bathroom as fast as my lead-filled legs would allow. I held on to the sink, waiting for the moment to pass or for the vomiting to begin. This was the new norm between drug doses. While the contents of my stomach churned, I glanced in the mirror. I barely recognised myself. Sores and scabs covered my deathly pale cheeks. They were going to leave scars if I didn't stop picking at my face, but my skin was so itchy I couldn't help myself. Todd was right; I looked an absolute mess.

My heartbeat went into overdrive when I heard the front door close, and a moment later, the floodgates opened. The tears were a result of mixed emotions. I was relieved that Todd was back, but I was furious that he'd left me to suffer like this. As his footsteps started to retreat along the hall, I banged on the tiles with the palm of my hand. It was a half-hearted attempt; that was all my bruised flesh would allow. I opened my mouth to call out his name, but only a hoarse squeak came out.

I was just making my way back to bed when I heard Todd approaching. He turned the key in the lock and stood in the doorway watching me for several seconds before he began to speak.

'I'm surprised you're awake. I was expecting to find you out for the count.'

Todd locked eyes with me. He was waiting for a response from me, but I knew I'd give the game away if I spoke.

'You'd normally be screaming blue murder for a top-up by now.'

Todd narrowed his eyes, but his glare was met by a wall of silence.

'Maybe you don't want the gear I've got for you,' he said as he dangled a syringe in front of my face.

'I do,' I croaked, dragging myself towards him.

'What the fuck's up with you? You better not have been screaming your head off while I was out.' A flash of anger spread across Todd's face.

I swallowed the lump that was stuck in my throat, but his stare was so intense, I had to look away. I couldn't afford to upset him in case he refused to give me another dose. Todd closed the gap between us and grabbed hold of my upper arms. He clenched his jaw as his dark eyes scanned over me.

'Answer me, you bitch. Were you trying to get yourself noticed while I was out?' Todd spat the words into my face.

'I'm sorry,' I replied in a voice barely above a whisper. There was no point trying to deny it.

'Well, you're wasting your time. The apartment's soundproofed, so nobody's going to hear you cry for help. Now I need to find a suitable punishment for you.'

Todd paused and tilted his head to one side. My heart sank as I watched him. I had a horrible feeling I knew what was coming.

'Say goodbye to the gear, Kelsey.' Todd burst out laughing. 'You should see the look on your face; you're absolutely petrified that I'm going to go down that route, aren't you?'

He was loving every minute of this. Taunting me was giving him such a buzz, but I couldn't find the words to retaliate. They kept jumbling together and swirling around in my brain.

'Don't worry, Kels. It's an idle threat. I want to ruin your life, so that means keeping you hooked. Get on the bed.'

I fixed my eyes on Todd as he searched for a place to put the needle. Once he'd found the right spot, he secured the tourniquet. I had to focus to stop my arm from jittering as he emptied the contents of the syringe. I slumped back against the pillows and allowed my eyelids to close as the fight seeped out of me. My life had become a living hell; death seemed like an easy way out.

'Payback is the sweetest thing,' I heard Todd say as I drifted off.

35

Scarlett

The photos of Todd kept coming at regular intervals, and my curiosity was getting the better of me. People were creatures of habit and followed the same routine unless something happened to throw them off course. He seemed to come and go at the same time every day, so I was seriously considering getting Rio to drive me over to the new development so that I could shed some light on what he was doing there. There was only one way to find out if he was involved with CJ, and that was to confront him.

But I'd have to try and pluck up the courage to leave the house before I could do that. I knew that wasn't going to happen any time soon. I was too scared to go anywhere alone. I wasn't sure I'd ever be able to venture out on my own without being crippled by fear. The police had assured me that an attack like the one I'd sustained wasn't a regular occurrence. But that didn't stop me from being scared. The repercussions of that night had far-reaching consequences beyond the injuries I'd received. Physically, I'd turned a corner. Don't get me wrong, I was by no means back to normal, but there'd been a dramatic improvement just recently, so I'd come off the really strong tablets. Hopefully, in the not too distant future, I'd be able to ditch the rest. Even though I was fitter than I'd been in a long time, I was still psychologically scarred by the experience.

If I didn't push myself out of my comfort zone, I was going to be trapped in a state of perpetual limbo. It was time to think about what was important to me and what I was hoping to achieve by employing Hugh. I'd always been an active person, so it was driving me insane being stuck in the house, but I was finding it extremely difficult to get out of the frame of mind preventing me from taking steps on the road to recovery. It wasn't rocket science; the only way I was going to make any headway was to set myself a goal. An achievable one, but a goal all the same. If there was no goal, there wouldn't be any advancement because progress always moved towards an end result.

I'd been doing a lot of thinking and realised I'd run out of excuses. I was feeling stronger by the day and wasn't in constant pain any more. Sometimes you had to face your fears head-on if you wanted to overcome them. It would be a challenge, but I never used to be the sort of person who shied away from things. And I definitely wasn't comfortable playing the role of the victim, so it was time to shrug off the label before it completely stole my identity.

My desire to confront Todd was finally outweighing my reluctance to leave the house. Now that I'd talked myself into seeing what he had to say for himself, I needed to work out how to put the plan into action. First things first, I'd have to call Hugh's surveillance off. Because otherwise, he'd end up WhatsApping me saying he'd spotted a random girl accosting Todd in the foyer. The idea of that brought a smile to my face as I typed out the message.

We'd come to the end of the road. I had to complete the next stage of the journey on my own.

Thanks for everything, Hugh. You've done a brilliant job. If I ever need another private investigator, you'll be the first person I contact!

The next issue would be harder to overcome. Mum wasn't going to let me go out unaccompanied. She'd gone into overprotective mode since I'd been attacked. And even if I managed to sneak out, I'd never find my way to Canary Wharf. I had no sense of direction. I couldn't find my way out of a paper bag. There was no way to avoid it, I'd have to tell her I was going out, but I knew she'd insist that Rio shadowed me. The more I thought about it, the more I knew I couldn't risk that happening. If Rio clapped eyes on Todd, he'd string him up before I had a chance to speak to him. That wasn't going to work, so I'd have to think again. There had to be another way.

I'd been racking my brains for what seemed like hours when an idea suddenly sprang into my head. Darius had only started working for the firm after Todd was fired, so he wouldn't know him from Adam. Even if he came face to face with our former bodyguard, it wouldn't ring any alarm bells. But the timing needed to be perfect if my plan was going to work.

I was in the kitchen finishing off a sandwich when Rio walked past the open window. I didn't know who he was talking to, but he had his mobile clamped to his ear as he paced along the path.

'I'll be with you in half an hour, give or take,' Rio said.

That was music to my ears, so I shoved the last piece of crust into my mouth and quickly put my plate in the dishwasher before I went off in search of Mum.

'Hello, darling,' Mum said when I walked into the office space a moment later.

'Hi,' I replied before smiling over at Mia.

'What are you up to? Mum fixed me with her blue eyes.

'I'm thinking of going out. One of my uni friends has invited me over.'

I didn't mention any names or places. I wanted to keep things as vague as possible.

Mum's face lit up. She couldn't hide her delight.

'That's fantastic. You've spent so much time in your room; you were in danger of turning into a recluse.'

'Tell me about it. Is Rio about?' I asked, doing my best to

keep my tone light, but my nerves were building, and I hoped my voice wasn't going to quaver and give the game away.

Mum looked over at Mia. 'Do you know where Rio is?'

'He's out on a job with Wesley,' Mia replied.

That was excellent news. Rio must be on a difficult job. Wesley looked after the dog unit, and his services were only called upon when extra intimidation was required. Dad always maintained people weren't so lippy when they were faced with a couple of ferocious-looking Rotties. With any luck, he wouldn't be back any time soon.

'Is he likely to be long?' My arms were hanging down by my sides, and I had my fingers discreetly crossed.

Mia pulled a face. 'He might be a while.'

I let out a sigh that could have won me an Academy Award.

'What's the matter?' Mum fixed me with a look of concern.

I glanced at my watch; then, I pasted a mournful look on my face. I was a frustrated actress, so playing the part came as naturally to me as breathing.

'I was hoping he'd give me a lift, but I wanted to go now...'

I knew she'd feel much happier about me venturing out if one of the team were in tow. And I'd earned extra points because I'd come up with the idea all on my own, and she hadn't had to force me into agreeing to be chaperoned.

'Darius could take you,' Mum said.

That was what I was hoping she was going to say. I knew Mum was never going to let me go out on my own at the moment, so being accompanied by Darius was the best option.

'Fantastic.' I beamed. 'I'll just get my bag.'

Darius had brought the car around by the time I stepped out of the front door. I climbed into the back seat and gave him the address. As we drove along, a satisfied smile spread over my face. It had been a genius idea, even if I said so myself, and it felt good that everything was going to plan. So far. I knew Mum wouldn't ask for any details as long as I wasn't going out alone, which was just as well because she'd never have fallen for it if she'd asked me where my friend lived. There was no way the swanky apartment block was going to be the home of an impoverished student. But to be on the safe side, I'd better come up with a convincing backstory in case Rio asked Darius where he'd taken me. But nothing complicated. One with not enough detail to forget.

After running through several possibilities, my imaginary friend Anastasia came to life. She was the daughter of a wealthy Russian diplomat and was studying in London to improve her English. The background I'd created for my fictional character was perfect. It was simple enough for me to remember, and it sounded totally believable if you asked me.

'I'm not sure how easy it's going to be to get a parking around here,' Darius said as we cruised past the River Thames.

I'd spent the entire journey carving out my new friend's life, so it startled me that we were almost at CJ's apartment. The palms of my hands started sweating, and I was struggling not to hyperventilate.

'I'm not going to be too long; it might be easier if you just wait in the car, then you'll be able to pull up outside,' I suggested, taking advantage of the fact that Rio's nephew was new on the scene so he wouldn't be overly familiar with how things were done.

'Fair enough,' Darius replied.

His response brought a smile to my face. I would never have been able to get Rio to agree to that; he would have definitely followed me into the building and shadowed me from a discreet distance. A few moments later, Darius pulled the Lexus up outside CJ's apartment block.

'I'll wait for you over there,' Darius said, pointing towards the visitor parking bays.

'Thank you. I won't be too long,' I replied, pasting on a smile.

'There's no rush. Take your time.' Darius flashed me a perfect smile.

I opened the back passenger door and then stepped out onto

the pavement. My pulse speeded up as I walked across to the glass-fronted multi-storey property. This was the first time I'd left the safety of the family home on my own since I'd been stabbed, and although I'd expected to feel anxious, it was more nerve-racking than I thought. I kept reminding myself that I was in a public place with loads of people around me, so nothing was going to happen to me, but that had also been the case when my attacker had struck not too far from here. The memory sent a shiver down my spine before I managed to shrug it off. What happened to me wasn't a regular occurrence, so I had to keep that thought firmly planted in my mind, but it was going to take time for me to overcome my fear.

I took a deep breath through my nose and held it for ten seconds in an attempt to calm my galloping heartbeat. *You can do this*, I repeated over and over to myself as I walked through the revolving door. I crossed the tiled lobby and took a seat in the far corner on one of the leather seats. My desire to confront Todd was only just outweighing my underlying panic now that the time was growing closer.

I glanced at my watch; I'd been in the reception area for almost ten minutes, and I was starting to get cold feet when I saw Todd appear on the other side of the revolving door. My pulse went into overdrive when I clapped eyes on him. Before I knew it, he was striding across the tiled floor, a man on a mission, looking like he didn't have a moment to lose. I had to spring into action, or I was going to miss my opportunity. I wiped my clammy hands on the skirt of my cotton dress before I followed him over to the lifts. Todd had already pressed the up arrow before I made it across the foyer. I had no idea which floor he was going to and briefly considered getting in the lift with him, so I could see where he got out, but I decided against it in case things turned ugly. I wasn't sure how my surprise visit was going to be received.

'Todd,' I called out when I was inches away from him.

Kelsey's ex turned around at the sound of his name.

'I thought it was you,' I continued.

Todd looked me up and down with a scowl on his face. He tried his best to hide it, but I could see the look of shock spread across his features. And as I'd expected, he didn't look best pleased to see me.

'Scarlett,' Todd replied in a less than friendly tone. 'What are you doing here?'

The arrogance was rolling off Todd in waves. For the life of me, I couldn't work out what Kelsey ever saw in the man. He was good-looking, but he was a complete tool. I didn't want him to know that was what I thought of him. He had information that I wanted to extract from him, so I'd have to humour him until he coughed up what he knew. Todd wasn't the only one who could be manipulative.

'I could say the same to you,' I countered. My tone was frosty.

Todd and I had always had a difficult relationship, and it was clear nothing had changed; there was no love lost between us. Once he'd come on the scene, Kelsey and I started spending less and less time together. We'd been each other's shadows and done everything together until they'd hooked up. I'd felt a bit miffed that he'd taken my place, and instead of being her go-to person, the one she spent all her free time with, Kelsey only allowed me to tag along with her and Todd when she wanted me to be her alibi. Playing the third wheel sucked, so we'd begun to drift apart. I never in a million years thought she'd drop me like that.

'I asked you first,' Todd said.

The sound of his voice snapped me out of my daydream, and when I looked up at him, he was staring at me with a smug grin fixed on his face. He'd caught me off guard. I was expecting to be the one asking the questions. I should have realised it wouldn't be as simple as that. I needed to respond quickly as the silence between us was dragging on. Possible explanations were whirring through my mind, but none of them seemed viable or believable. I felt flustered and couldn't think straight. I could hardly tell Todd that I'd had the building under surveillance; my reason needed to be more organic than that, not planned or premeditated. I wanted him to think this was just a chance meeting.

'I've come to see CJ. He lives in this building,' I eventually said.

Todd's lips spread into a wide smile. 'I'm afraid you're going to be disappointed if you were hoping to meet up with him.'

What the hell was that supposed to mean?

'I don't think our business has got anything to do with you. CJ can decide whether or not he wants to see me. He doesn't need you to answer for him,' I snapped back.

I'd tried to keep a lid on my temper, but Todd's cocky attitude was making me see red. And when he rolled his eyes, it wound me up even more, if that was possible.

'I don't give a fuck about your business. I'm just trying to tell you CJ doesn't live here anymore. So if you're hoping to bump into him, you're out of luck.'

Todd stood grinning from ear to ear as an awkward silence stretched out between us again. I was a bit peeved that he seemed to know more about my ex's movements than I did, but I didn't want to give him the satisfaction of thinking he'd got one over on me, so I tried not to let it show.

'As you're still attempting to track CJ down, you mustn't have been let in on the sordid family secret.'

My mouth dropped open, and I felt my breath catch in my throat. What family secret? I had no idea what Todd was talking about. Panic clung to me like a second skin. I sensed whatever Todd was about to divulge wasn't going to be good news. All manner of possibilities started running riot in my head, but my delay in responding cost me dearly.

'See you around, Scarlett,' Todd said, and the lift doors closed behind him.

I felt my knees buckle, and my head started to swim, so I leant against the wall before I keeled over. All I could think about was what Todd was keeping from me. He hadn't gone into detail; he hadn't needed to. I could sense it was going to be something bad.

I reached over to the up arrow and pressed it several times in succession. I'd been hoping to stop the lift before it started ascending, but I was too late. Todd was long gone. And he'd taken the answers to all my questions with him.

I was still rooted to the spot, trying to decide what to do for the best, when the doors of the lift started to open. A surge of adrenaline raced around my body; maybe I might be about to get lucky, and Todd would step out. But the gods weren't smiling on me today; nobody was inside. I had no idea where Todd had disappeared to, so there was no point in scouring every floor of the apartment block looking for him. He could be anywhere by now. Finding him would be an impossible task.

I felt like screaming at the top of my voice, but what good would that do me? There was only one thing for it; I'd have to come back and confront him another day, which wasn't as simple as it sounded because I'd have to make sure Rio was occupied so that he wouldn't be able to accompany me.

'You were quick. Is everything OK, Scarlett?' Darius asked when I climbed into the back of the Lexus a few minutes later.

I glanced up at the sound of his voice. He was watching me in the rear-view mirror. We held eye contact for a moment before he turned to look at me over his shoulder.

'I'm fine,' I said, pasting on a smile.

'You don't look fine; you're as white as a sheet,' Darius replied.

'I'm just a bit tired, that's all. Socialising's hard work. I didn't realise I was so out of practice.'

36

Kelsey

The sound of the front door closing woke me from a fitful sleep. I wasn't sure if Todd had just come in or gone out, but I needed to know. After several attempts, I pulled back the covers, pushed myself up from the mattress and swung my legs over the side of the bed. I sat on the edge, yawning as I came to before shuffling over to the door on reluctant feet. Pressing my ear against the wood, I listened. You could have heard a pin drop, so I was pretty sure Todd wasn't here.

'Todd. Todd,' I said.

My voice was still croaky, so I didn't want to strain it any further by shouting. When he didn't reply, I tapped on the wood with my fingertips. The sides of my hands were still sore and bruised. There was no response, which gave me the green light. I went over to the bathroom door and slammed it as hard as I could over and over. Todd had told me the apartment was soundproofed, but he got angry every time I shouted for help, so I reckoned he'd just say that to deter me from trying to raise the alarm.

Slamming the door didn't seem to be working, so I crossed the room, opened up the cupboard and took out my crystal-encrusted Manolo Blahniks. My eyes drank in every detail of them as I held them in my hands. It seemed wrong on so many levels to potentially destroy a pair of expensive shoes, but if they bought me my freedom, it would be worth every penny.

Objects were replaceable, I reminded myself as I took several steps back, then hurled one after the other at the wardrobe door. They landed with a loud clatter which was music to my ears. Hopefully, somebody would hear the commotion. I picked them up, still basking in the glory of the racket I was making and was just preparing to fling them again when I heard the key slide into the front door.

Panic crawled up from the pit of my stomach. Todd would go mental if he realised what I'd been doing. I rushed over to the wardrobe so that I could throw the shoes inside, but I wasn't quick enough.

'Going somewhere?' Todd asked as he opened the bedroom door.

I was like a deer caught in the headlights. I couldn't think of anything to say, so I just stared at him with a blank expression on my face.

'Trying them on for old times' sake, were you? Anyway, you'll never guess who I just bumped into,' Todd said.

He was leaning against the frame with his arms wrapped over his chest and a huge grin plastered across his face.

'It was somebody you know very well. Any ideas?'

Todd seemed desperate for me to join in, but I really couldn't be bothered. I wasn't the slightest bit interested in playing guessing games.

'I give up,' I replied, hoping to put an end to the conversation.

'I just saw Scarlett.'

My eyes sprung open. Now he had my full attention. I felt the weight of Todd's stare. He was gauging my reaction as his words filtered into my thoughts.

'Scarlett?'

The pounding of my pulse made my eardrums feel like they were about to explode. What the hell was she doing here? My spirits suddenly lifted. Maybe she was coming to break me out of jail. But a moment later, my hopes came crashing down again when my cotton-wool brain realised that wasn't the case. I was still locked in Todd's apartment, and Scarlett was nowhere to be seen.

Knowing that I was almost within touching distance of my sister left me with a feeling of hopelessness that threatened to wipe the legs out from under me. My knees buckled, and I had to put the palm of my hand on the cupboard for support.

'I was surprised to see her in the lobby too,' Todd said.

'Did you speak to her?'

I wasn't entirely sure why I'd asked him that question. It wasn't as though Todd was going to confess to keeping me a prisoner in his apartment. But if they'd exchanged even a few words, I wondered if he might have said something that would have made Scarlett suspicious.

'Yeah, we had a bit of a chat as it goes.' Todd smiled.

Jealousy pulled at my heartstrings. I would have given anything for a chance to see my family right now. I missed them so much, which was a turn-up for the books. I wasn't the soppy, sentimental type by any means. A lump formed in my throat as my thoughts turned to home, and I found myself on the verge of tears. I had to sniff them back before Todd noticed.

'What did you and Scarlett talk about?' I asked, keeping my fingers crossed that my name came up in the conversation.

'This and that. She was banging on about CJ, and I was sorely tempted to let her in on the family secret.'

Todd's words bounced off the inside of my brain. 'Didn't she mention me?'

'I can't say that she did. This must be hard for you to accept, but everything doesn't revolve around you; you're not the centre of attention.' Todd laughed as he walked out of the door.

The old Kelsey would have loved to wipe the smirk off his face, but it was all I could do not to hurl myself at his feet and beg him to set me free. I couldn't stay in this room for much longer. As I listened to the key turn in the lock, I leant back against the pillows and stared up at the lights on the ceiling.

37

Scarlett

Why did time always go so slowly when you were desperate for it to pass? The last twenty-four hours had dragged by. I'd barely slept a wink last night because I'd kept mulling over what Todd had said. I was desperate to know what secrets my family were keeping from me. I'd considered confronting them just to put myself out of my misery, but how could I grill them about something when I didn't know any of the details?

The journey to Canary Wharf was taking an age. Everything seemed to be against me. We'd got caught at every red light since we'd left the house, and there seemed to be roadworks waiting for us around every corner. It felt as though even the traffic was playing a hand in prolonging my agony. The only thing that had been in my favour so far today was Rio was tied up on a job, which meant Darius was driving me again instead.

The Lexus inched its way closer, but the traffic was gridlocked, and I was worried I was going to miss my window of opportunity. Hugh always seemed to take photos of Todd at 2 p.m., give or take a minute. By the time we made it to the apartment block, I had roughly five minutes to spare. Darius glided the Lexus to a halt at the kerb, and I leapt out of the car, which made my stomach twinge. I didn't have a moment to lose, but I had to respect my injury and not do anything to aggravate it.

'I'll park in one of the visitors' bays,' I heard Darius say as I slammed the door behind me.

I'd barely sat down in the foyer when Todd walked through the revolving door. He rolled his eyes and shook his head when he saw me approaching.

'I need to speak to you,' I said when I closed the gap between us.

'Not now, Scarlett. I'm busy.'

Todd went to sidestep me as he attempted to brush me off, but I wasn't having any of it, so I kept pace with him as he walked over to the lift.

'Please, Todd, this is important. What did you mean when you said my family were keeping secrets from me?'

Todd turned toward me, and his face broke into a huge grin.

'So that's what all this is about? And there was I thinking you were just craving my company.'

Todd's chest swelled as he straightened his posture. He loved being in a position of power, and I could tell he wasn't going to give away the information easily by the silence that had stretched out between us. Todd was going to eke this out to really make me suffer. But I was prepared to work hard and put in the graft, even beg if need be. I wasn't going to leave here until I found out what he knew.

'Please tell me what my family are hiding from me,' I said to break the long pause.

'I've already told you I'm busy,' Todd replied before he pressed the up arrow.

The doors to the lift opened almost immediately, and he stepped inside. I would have loved to have said something to wipe the smug look off his face, but the clock was ticking, so I had to think on my feet. I wasn't about to be fobbed off that easily so I walked in after him.

'What are you doing?' Todd asked. His finger was poised, ready to press the floor number, but he drew his hand back, and his face settled into a frown.

'I'm coming with you. I'm not going to leave your side until you tell me what you know.'

My need for answers had blocked out my fear. And so the battle of wills commenced.

'Get out of the lift, Scarlett.' Todd pointed towards the lobby. His dark eyes were blazing.

I shook my head. Quite a few people were milling around, so I'd already decided if I needed to cause a scene, that was exactly what I was going to do.

'Please, Todd, I'm begging you.' I fixed him with a look of desperation.

Every fibre in my body despised Todd. Even more than I had before, if that was possible. I hated having to sink so low as to grovel at his feet. But needs must, so I wasn't going to beat myself up over it. Todd could see I was serious. As he weighed up what to do, my prayers were answered when a man got into the lift.

'Which floor do you want?' the man asked as he pressed seven, which illuminated the number.

Todd looked sideways at me. I knew he didn't want me to know where he was going, but his hand had been forced.

'Sorry, mate, you go ahead,' Todd replied.

When Todd left the lift, I was hot on his heels.

'Persistent, aren't you?' Todd stood in the foyer with his hands on his hips, glaring at me.

I wanted to grab him by the throat and say just get on with it, but I had to bite my tongue. I knew I'd have to be on my best behaviour, or Todd wouldn't put me out of my misery.

'I'm sorry, I'm not trying to be a pest, but I really want to know what my family are keeping from me. And if there's anything I can do for you in return, I'd be only too happy...'

I let my sentence trail off when Todd began to laugh. I felt like giving him a piece of my mind, but I couldn't afford to continue in case I tore a strip off him.

'That's an interesting concept, but there's nothing I want from you.' Todd grinned.

Despair gripped me like an iron fist. I'd tried pleading and bargaining, but none of it seemed to be working. There wasn't anything else I could do. If Todd wasn't prepared to tell me what he knew, there was absolutely nothing I could do about it. Todd looked so smug, and I was beginning to wish I hadn't decided to confront him. He was running rings around me, and we both knew it.

Tears stabbed the backs of my eyes, but I was determined to hold them in. Turning on the waterworks wasn't going to do any good, but it would make Todd gloat even more than he was already doing. It was time to admit defeat and walk away with my tail between my legs while I still had a shred of dignity left.

The door to the lift opened again, and this time, a loved-up couple got out, so I used that as an opportunity to make a move.

'I'll let you get on,' I said, pointing to the open doors. 'I know you're in a hurry.'

I was heading across the tiled lobby on my way to the car when Todd suddenly spoke.

'Hey, Scarlett, wait up.'

I turned around to face him.

'I've decided to do the gentlemanly thing and share the family secret with you.'

You could have knocked me down with a feather.

'Why the sudden change of heart?'

As I walked towards him, Todd fixed me with his dark brown eyes. His gaze was so intense my heart started hammering in my chest.

'I was trying to be nice.'

Todd flashed me a sarcastic smile, and I wished I'd kept my mouth shut.

'It's no skin off my nose, Scarlett. If you'd rather not know what your mum and sisters are keeping from you, that's fine by me...'

When Todd reached forward and pressed the up arrow, I wanted to kick myself. It was time to eat a large slice of humble pie.

'Please don't go. I do want to know.' I hoped I hadn't just gone and blown things.

Todd took a step closer to me. 'They found out a while ago that your beloved CJ was Craig Coleman, but they decided it was best not to share that with you,' he said, keeping his voice low.

'CJ was one of the Colemans?' I couldn't believe what I'd just heard. Surely that couldn't be right.

'Yes. He was the nephew of your dad's arch-rival, Barney.'

I felt my lips part, and I gulped for air as the realisation that I'd been sleeping with the enemy hit me.

'Oh, and there's one more thing.' Todd leant in even closer. 'Rio executed him as a payback for what he did to you, so you might as well stop looking for him. You're not going to find him.'

My head started to spin as Todd's words hit me like bullets from a gun. Before I could question him further, he stepped inside the lift, the doors closed and then he was gone. I glanced at the display to see what floor he was on, but my heart sank when I realised it only showed an up arrow.

38

Kelsey

My eyes opened a crack, and as they began to focus, I realised I wasn't alone in the room. Todd was standing at the bottom of the bed, watching me sleep. It gave me the creeps when he did that.

'What time is it?' I asked, rubbing my eyes with the back of my hand.

'Almost three. I don't know how you can still be tired. You've been asleep for hours.' Todd shook his head as he looked down his nose at me.

But I'd lost all concept of time; the days and nights rolled into one another.

'I bumped into Scarlett again earlier.' A smile played on Todd's lips; he looked extremely pleased with himself.

Todd's words jogged my hazy memory. I vaguely remembered having a conversation with him about Scarlett, but I couldn't really recall any of the details.

'Scarlett came to your apartment?' I questioned. I felt my spirits lift.

'No, she was in the foyer.'

'What was she doing in the foyer?' I felt my eyebrows knit together.

'She was looking for CJ again.'

'Who?' I fixed Todd with a puzzled expression; my mind had gone blank.

'Don't tell me you've forgotten CJ already. Does the name Craig Coleman ring any bells?'

I shrugged my shoulders and then started racking my brain, hoping I'd find more details floating about the fuzzy space. But I couldn't come up with anything.

'I know he was fairly unremarkable on the surface, but you must remember him. He was the guy behind Scarlett's attack, and Rio executed him as payback...'

The words slipped from Todd's lips as though they were nothing, but the damage they were doing inside my head was catastrophic. It was like a bomb had gone off. Millions of tiny fragments were spinning around in my grey matter. I was desperately trying to piece them back together so that I could get a clear picture of what he was talking about. Then suddenly, I felt my expression change as the penny dropped.

'There you go; now you remember him. I knew you would.' Todd's lips stretched into a smile.

'But Craig's dead, so why is Scarlett looking for him?'

Todd let out a belly laugh. 'I can't believe you just asked me that. Your memory's shot to pieces.'

He didn't need to tell me that my brain wasn't working properly; it felt like it was short-circuiting.

'So I guess I've got two choices. I can either tell you the truth, or maybe I should rewrite history. Now, what's it going to be?' Todd tapped his lip with his index finger, and then he allowed a long pause to stretch out between us.

I sat on the edge of the bed in silence, trying to play him at his own game. The more he thought I wanted to know the part I couldn't remember, the keener he'd be to withhold it. We stayed locked in a standoff for what seemed like an eternity waiting to see which one of us would crack first. It was clear Todd was itching to spill the beans, so I didn't think it would be too long before he told me the answer to my question. He paused for effect to stretch out the build-up, but I could see holding it in was killing him. He was desperate to get it off his chest. Todd needed to tell me for his sake as much as mine.

'Let me put you out of your misery. Scarlett was looking for CJ because she doesn't know he's dead. You, Mia and your mum decided not to tell her that Rio had blown his brains out. She seemed very shocked when I put her straight. I'm not even sure she believed me.' Todd grinned.

My head began to spin, and before I knew what was happening, the contents of my stomach emptied all over the bedroom floor. The sickness came on so quickly that I didn't have time to get to the bathroom.

'Well, if you think I'm cleaning that up, you've got another thing coming. Don't wait up. I'm going out.'

From the tone of Todd's voice, I knew he was disgusted, so I didn't bother looking up. I closed my eyes when I heard him lock the bedroom door behind him. Moments later, the front door slammed. I should have been trying to escape, but I felt so rough I didn't have the energy to stand up, let alone fight for my freedom. If I was honest with myself, I was starting to lose hope once more, but I'd have to keep that a closely guarded secret. Todd would try and use it against me if I showed any weakness.

The silence was deafening. The sense of isolation crippling. I opened my eyes, and they were drawn to the vomit glistening on the bedroom floor. The sight and smell of it brought on a fresh wave of nausea. I forced myself onto my feet and headed for the bathroom. Armed with a bin bag, toilet roll and some Flash wipes, I started cleaning it up. Once I'd finished, I padded back into the en suite to wash my hands. I was exhausted from the effort, so I crawled back into the bed and turned onto my side to face the windows.

Desperate to distract myself from the living hell I was stuck in, I pushed my thoughts in a different direction. A vision of Scarlett popped into my head. Now that she knew the truth about Craig, she must be beside herself. But more to the point, she'd be furious with me. I hated the thought of us being on bad terms. She was more than my sister; she was my best friend. I wished I could reach out to her and tell her how much I missed her. But I was wading through a pit of darkness, lost in the depths of a black hole with no way out.

A fist of despair wrapped itself around me, and began squeezing the life out of me. Everything didn't revolve around me; Todd's words taunted me, haunted me. I hated being this vulnerable. I knew nobody was coming to rescue me, and that made me feel empty.

My chest ached as tears streamed down my cheeks. I wanted them to stop, but they just kept coming. I cried, and cried, and cried as though I was mourning something that had died within me. I felt defeated and deflated. I didn't know what else to do, so I burrowed down under the quilt to block out my surroundings. And block out the world.

39

Scarlett

Todd's words had hit me like a tidal wave and were now swimming around in my head. When would my family learn that nothing good came from shutting people out? After my dad was murdered, they'd intentionally kept me out of the loop by denying me access to the business, and that hurt more than I could say. I'd felt shunned by their behaviour, and that had driven me into CJ's arms in the first place. Now they were trying to keep me in the dark again. What was wrong with them? I felt like it was them against me. Why hadn't they just told me the truth? It might have helped me make sense of the situation if I'd known all along that CJ was Craig Coleman.

I supposed CJ's motive for hurting me was clearer now, but one thing I still didn't understand was why he'd bothered to start a relationship with me. He could have arranged for somebody to plunge a knife into my stomach without hooking up with me. It made the attack so much harder to deal with because the betrayal had become personal. Maybe that was what drove him, knowing the outcome would be twice as bad. What had I ever done to him? I didn't deserve to be treated like that. The feud was between our fathers. It had nothing to do with me.

My entire world felt like it had come crashing down around me. Not only had CJ betrayed me, but so had my family, the people that were closest to me. I'd been left reeling after Todd had dropped the bombshell and couldn't face going back to the car after the shock I'd had. Darius would know something was wrong for sure if he clapped his eyes on me. I gave myself a moment's breathing space and then decided to drop him a message to buy myself some time, but my hands were trembling so badly I'd have to calm myself down first.

I hope you don't mind. I'm having such a great time. I'm going to stay a bit longer.

I'd barely sent Darius the text when his reply came through.

No worries. Stay as long as you like. I'm happy to wait.

When Todd had cleared off, having pulled the rug from under me, I'd been so overwhelmed I needed some time to fully digest his words and collect my thoughts, so I'd taken myself off to a quiet corner of the lobby to lick my wounds.

I was still coming to terms with what he'd told me when my eyes fixed on the lift doors as they opened. My heart skipped a beat as I watched Todd step out. I couldn't believe what I was seeing. I hadn't been expecting to bump into him again so soon.

'Todd,' I called out, getting to my feet.

I walked across the tiles so that I could close the gap between us. Todd turned around to look at me. From the expression on his face and the eye-roll he threw in my direction, I could tell he wasn't banking on me still being in the lobby.

'So you're still here.' Todd didn't try to hide the irritation in his voice.

'Please, can we talk? I promise I won't take up much of your time.'

Todd glanced at his watch. 'You've got five minutes.'

'Should we go somewhere more private?' I asked.

I wanted to ask questions about CJ, and as the details

surrounding his disappearance were sensitive, I didn't want anyone milling about in the lobby overhearing our conversation.

Todd gestured to the leather sofa I'd been sitting on a minute ago, which was an ideal spot as it was tucked out of the way.

I walked back across the tiles and sat on the same seat as before. Todd dropped down next to me, then tilted his right shoulder towards me.

'I'm confused,' I began.

'About what?' Todd's tone was abrupt.

'CJ. It does seem feasible that Rio hurt him in retaliation for what he did to me.'

Todd let out a loud sigh in case I was in any doubt about how he felt. He wanted to make it perfectly clear that he was bored by the conversation we were having.

'Rio didn't just hurt CJ. He went one step further and killed him.'

I felt a lump form in my throat. I still couldn't get my head around all of this.

'OK, whatever, I believe you,' I said, brushing away an image I didn't want to picture. 'The part I'm struggling with is that CJ was Craig Coleman. You must have got that wrong.'

I straightened my spine and then rested my hands on my knees. I was all ears.

'I haven't got it wrong. It's true,' Todd insisted.

Then he glanced at his watch, and I felt my heart rate speed up. I was scared he was going to pull the plug on our chat before he'd answered my questions.

'But you and Kelsey both met CJ. Why didn't you tell me his family were Dad's enemies before I got involved with him?'

Kelsey had tried to warn me off him, but she'd never given me a good reason, so I'd taken no notice of her. Things could have turned out very differently if I hadn't been so pig-headed and listened for once.

'We didn't find out until after you were attacked, and by then, it was too late.' When Todd spoke, he looked directly at me.

I narrowed my eyes as I considered what he'd just said.

'I can see you're not buying it, but I can prove I'm telling the truth.'

Visions of an unmarked grave suddenly popped into my head, which sent a shiver down my spine.

'Not that I need to,' Todd muttered under his breath.

I had selective hearing, so I pretended not to notice. I couldn't work Todd out, one minute, he was reluctant to talk, and the next, he seemed to be bending over backwards to convince me that what he was telling me was true. What had happened to cause his change of heart? I couldn't help feeling suspicious. Why would Todd suddenly offer to help me? I asked myself. There must be something in it for him.

'I can take you to meet his mum, Lorraine,' Todd suggested.

I didn't want to question him about his integrity in case he withdrew his offer. But I wasn't sure I could trust him. Todd might be trying to lure me into a trap to get back at Kelsey.

'Make up your mind, Scarlett. I haven't got all day.' Todd flipped his wrist over and checked the time on his watch again.'

I only had a split second to make my decision.

'You said CJ was dead.'

'He is.' Todd blew out a breath as he slowly shook his head. His frustration was apparent.

'So how can I verify that Lorraine's his mum? He can't exactly confirm it, can he?' I was interested to see how Todd was going to answer that.

'No, but her house is like a shrine to him. She's got framed photos on the wall and scattered over every surface. You'll be able to see for yourself that CJ was Craig Coleman.'

'I suppose that would be one way to prove it,' I replied.

'I can't think of another way unless you want me to take you to the family plot and dig up his body so that you can identify his remains.' Todd laughed.

I wasn't sure why Todd found that idea so amusing.

'You don't have to look so worried; I was only joking. I'm on my way to see her now. Do you want to come along for the ride?' Todd asked.

That was the million-dollar question, and thoughts started bombarding my brain. I wanted to get to the bottom of this, but was it safe to go to Lorraine's house? What if Todd was setting me up? They could have something awful in store for me.

I took a deep breath to calm my frazzled nerves and willed myself not to overthink this situation. I'd taken Todd by surprise when I'd showed up at the apartment block, and we were having this conversation off the cuff, so he hadn't had the opportunity to pre-plan anything with Lorraine. If I let my imagination run away with itself, I'd never uncover the truth. But I'd have to dig deep to block out my fears.

'I haven't got all day, Scarlett. Do you want to come or not?'

Now it was my time to check the time on my watch.

'Unless, of course, there's something more important you'd rather be doing.' Todd's sarcasm wasn't lost on me. 'I've had enough of this shit; your five minutes are up.'

Todd turned on his heel and started to walk away.

'Todd, please wait.' The sound of my shoes echoed around the lobby as I tried to catch up with him. He was striding across the tiles like a man on a mission.

'Stop fucking me about, Scarlett. You either want to come with me, or you don't. It's not that difficult a decision. Anyone would think I'd asked you to strip naked and dance around the foyer with your knickers on your head,' Todd said in my ear so that he wouldn't be overheard.

'I do want to meet Lorraine, but Darius is waiting outside in the car for me, so if he sees me come out of the building with you, I don't know what I'm going to tell him.'

Lorraine was the only link left to CJ, so I pushed my previous concerns out of the window. I sincerely hoped I was doing the right thing. It would be my own fault if my body was discovered two weeks from now in a shallow grave.

'Who the fuck is Darius?' Todd turned the palms of his hands out.

'He's Rio's nephew.'

A flash of anger spread across Todd's face, so I decided not to add, *he's your replacement*, as I wasn't sure how well that would go down, but I had a strange feeling that it might worsen his mood, and I didn't want to risk it.

'I should have realised you wouldn't have been allowed to leave the house on your own,' Todd sneered. 'Does anyone else know you're here?'

'No,' I replied without missing a beat.

When I saw Todd mulling over my answer, I instantly regretted being so honest. If he was lining something bad up for me, I'd pretty much given him the green light to carry out his plan without the worry of being caught. But I'd been hoping to run into him today so, like last time, I hadn't come to the meeting unprepared. If things turned ugly, I had a little something hidden in my handbag. I knew Mum kept a mouse gun in her bedside cabinet. I'd decided to borrow it, and bring it with me, just in case. Fingers crossed, I wouldn't have to use it, as I had no idea how to fire it, but it bolstered my sense of security knowing I had it with me if the need arose.

'That's good, and let's keep it that way. You'd better not bring trouble to my door, Scarlett.'

I held my hands up in front of me. 'I won't, I promise.'

I needed to keep Todd on side, or I was never going to get closure.

'I'll go and get the car, and I'll meet you at the back of the building, so Darius won't see you leave,' Todd suggested.

'OK, but how do I get around the back?'

I'd only ever used the front entrance before. I didn't even know there was another way out.

'If you go into the stairwell, you'll see a door marked exit. I'll pick you up outside.'

My hands started sweating as I watched Todd disappear

through the revolving door. I'd decided to wait for a couple of minutes to give him a head start, and then I walked over to the stairwell, taking deep breaths as I moved in the hope of calming my frazzled nerves. I blew out a breath before I pushed open the door that led to the street behind the apartment block. Todd was just pulling up as I stepped outside, so I climbed into the front passenger seat of his black BMW.

'Why are you going to see Lorraine?' I asked once the car was moving.

I glanced over at Todd, but he kept his eyes fixed on the road. After a sizeable pause, Todd turned his face towards mine. 'If I tell you, I'll have to kill you.' Todd raised his eyebrows up and down before he burst out laughing.

Why would he joke about something like that? I didn't think it was funny at all, and my heart started hammering in my chest in response.

'For fuck's sake, lighten up. I was only pulling your leg. You used to find everything funny. When did you lose your sense of humour?'

That was true. I used to be a perpetual giggler, but if Todd couldn't work out for himself what had affected my outlook on life, he was more stupid than I thought.

'To answer your question, Lorraine's my boss,' Todd said, reverting back to the original conversation.

I had to admit that Todd's openness took me by surprise.

'You seem shocked to hear that.' Todd briefly turned his head in my direction before his eyes returned to the road.

I shrugged my shoulders. 'It's none of my business who you work for.'

'Good answer.' Todd grinned. 'I actually think there's a chance we could end up establishing a good partnership. I'll keep your secrets, and in return, you need to keep mine.'

I never thought Todd and I would end up on the same side, but sometimes allies appeared in the strangest forms.

'That suits me fine,' I replied, but at the back of my mind, I wondered what he wanted from me. I hoped he wasn't going to ask me to feed him information about Kelsey.

When Todd pulled into the driveway of the large detached house, my eyes were drawn to the bright blue sports car parked in the far right corner of the block-paved frontage. I was no expert on makes and models, but the car was such a distinctive colour I was almost certain it was the same as the one in the photos that Hugh had sent me. The intense rays of August sunshine reflected on the surface, making the paintwork shimmer. It was mesmerising watching the metallic finish change colour.

'How are you feeling?' Todd asked as he parked his BMW outside the front of the house.

The sound of his voice broke my train of thought, and I tore my eyes away from the gleaming sports car.

'I'm OK,' I replied, wondering why he'd asked.

'I thought you'd be bricking it; meeting your other half's family is always a bit nerve-racking. Well, it was for me anyway. Michelle's mother was an old hag and gave me a right grilling the first time I met her. The experience scarred me for life. I can still remember it to this day.' Todd laughed. 'Craig did you a favour by not bringing you home to meet the parents.'

I couldn't bring myself to join in. Instead, I sat stony-faced, looking up at the perfectly symmetrical neo-Georgian house. Its red-brick walls, white columns and portico were impressive, but I'd rather have our place in Bow any day of the week. It had far more character and charm than Lorraine's new build. I was trying to block out what Todd had said. Whether it was intentional or not, his comment was cruel, and I felt tears stab the backs of my eyes. I was determined to put on a brave face and not let the heartbreak I was feeling shine through.

Todd hadn't needed to take such a cheap shot. If things had turned out differently, meeting CJ's family would have been a huge deal to me. Introducing somebody to the people closest to you was a big step and cranked things up a level.

I already felt like a complete idiot for allowing myself to be duped so easily without Todd rubbing my nose in it. But in my defence, I hadn't had a lot of experience with the opposite sex, so I was naïve when it came to matters of the heart. I'd been flattered by the attention CJ had given me and thrown caution to the wind. He'd swept me off my feet, and I'd allowed myself to get carried away and completely lose touch with reality. It had been wonderful while it had lasted, but now I had to deal with the fallout. I'd have to put all thoughts of my doomed relationship out of my head; or otherwise, I was going to lose my nerve.

'Are you coming?' Todd leant down and looked in the car at me.

I'd been so wrapped up in my own thoughts I hadn't noticed him open the driver's door and get out.

'Yes,' I replied, fumbling with the handle.

I walked up to the glossy black door, and Todd pressed the bell. We stood side by side, waiting for Lorraine to answer it. I could feel myself becoming more and more apprehensive as the seconds ticked by.

'Hello, Todd.'

As the woman, who I presumed was Lorraine, flung open the door, the smell of her musky perfume hit me at the back of the throat, and I coughed in response. She was older than I'd expected, in her fifties or sixties, I'd say. But I wasn't a good judge of age. I was basing my guess on the condition of her skin. Her face was tanned and had a leathery, lined appearance, and the plunge-fronted, leopard-print top she was wearing gave me a bird's eye view of her crepey cleavage. I'd put money on the fact that she was a sun worshipper and spent every spare moment chasing rays.

'What are you doing here?'

The woman seemed surprised to see Todd, which puzzled me as he'd given me the impression she was expecting him. He hadn't gone into details in the lobby, but by the way, he'd been talking, I'd presumed they'd had a meeting arranged when he'd said he was on his way over to see her.

'I've brought you a present,' Todd replied.

My heart started hammering in my chest. What did he mean by that?

'I'd like to introduce you to Scarlett Saunders.' Todd gestured to where I was standing.

Lorraine's blue eyes widened. 'You'd better come in,' she said.

Lorraine took a step to the right to allow us to pass, but I suddenly had a bad feeling about the visit and was reluctant to go inside. I'd far rather stay out in the open in full view of the neighbours. Todd could obviously sense my hesitation, so he prodded me in the small of the back with his fingers to get me to move. Lorraine closed the front door, and my pulse went into overdrive.

40

Kelsey

I barely recognised myself these days. I wasn't the same person that I'd been before. I found it difficult to concentrate on anything other than my aching limbs. Any thoughts I had were clouded and confused. And my will to fight was ebbing away with each passing day. Getting high had become my one and only purpose in life. Heroin had me in its grip, and it wasn't letting go. The harsh reality was that I needed the drug like I needed air to breathe. It controlled everything. My life revolved around it. Being an addict was a full-time job.

The bathroom was calling. I sincerely hoped I made it in time. It was one thing cleaning up a pile of vomit, but now my bowels were rumbling, so sorting out that mess would be a whole different story. I got off the bed with a sense of urgency and staggered over to the en suite. I'd barely sat down when the world dropped out of my backside. I'd never experienced anything like it. The only way to describe it was to imagine the worst case of food poisoning and then multiply it by one thousand. My insides were in bits. Having done some serious damage in the toilet, I needed to lie down so that I could recover. I felt completely drained. I tried to focus on something else, but my stomach was churning like a washing machine.

I lay on my side, squeezed my eyes close, hugged my knees up to my chest and willed the feeling to pass. Then something on the other side of the room caught my attention. It was the unmistakable sound of footsteps, but I hadn't heard the door open. I looked over my shoulder, expecting to see Todd. Nobody was there. So where had the sound of shoes connecting with the floorboards come from? Maybe I'd imagined it. I listened again. Nothing. A moment later, a distant voice floated through the wall. It was a woman's voice. Was it Scarlett? I scrambled out of bed and rushed over to the door.

'Help. Help. Scarlett, it's me,' I called over and over again while hammering on the wood with my fist.

41

Scarlett

A knot had formed in the pit of my stomach, and it was growing by the minute, but I willed myself to keep calm even though I had good reason to feel anxious.

Lorraine flashed me a smile. 'Follow me,' she said. Her dangly earrings came alive and moved when she spoke.

'Ladies first,' Todd said, pressing his hand into my back.

He used his fingertips to steer me along the shiny marble floor. As I trailed along behind Lorraine, I couldn't help thinking the timber-panelled hall seemed to go on for miles. She led the way into the lounge, which overlooked the front garden and well-stocked flower beds. The heady scent of lilies hit me when I walked into the huge space. From the way the house was decorated, it was clear the Colemans had a few quid in the bank, but money didn't equal taste. Everything was gaudy.

Lorraine stood with her back against a baby grand piano as my eyes drank in my surroundings. Heart-shaped family photos stared out from the mantelpiece, but they were too far away for me to get a good look at them. It seemed surreal that I was standing in CJ's house. I'd always hoped this day would come, but I'd been expecting him to be the one to introduce me to his mum. I pushed that thought from my head so that I could focus on the here and now.

'I haven't been completely honest with you,' Todd said, and I felt my heart skip a beat. 'I didn't bring you here just to meet

Lorraine; I was hoping to get in the boss's good books. She'll pay good money to see your family come to harm. Isn't that right, Lorraine?'

'That makes me sound terrible, but it's true. I lost my wonderful son and my husband of almost thirty years because of the ongoing feud between our rival firms,' Lorraine explained as though she was trying to justify what Todd had just said.

I'd been hoping that Todd had been lying and that he'd made up the story about CJ to hurt me and cause a rift within our family. But Lorraine had just confirmed my worst nightmare.

'How much is she worth?' Todd asked.

'Now there's a question, but you know very well there's no limit to the amount I'd pay to see the people who wronged my family brought to justice. I don't care how much it costs.' Lorraine's voice was cold.

My head felt like it was about to explode. Todd had tricked me into believing that he'd brought me here for my benefit when he'd intended to throw me to the wolves all along. I was kicking myself. I should have known better than to trust him. My eyes scanned the room as I looked for a means of escape. I'd come here to get closure; I wasn't ready to pay the ultimate price.

'Have a seat,' Lorraine said a moment later.

She looked at me with hate-filled eyes before she gestured to a shocking pink velvet sofa that looked as though it had the ability to swallow me whole.

'Thanks,' I replied before lowering myself onto the pillowy surface, making sure I perched right on the edge to avoid any unnecessary embarrassment if I couldn't get up again or, worst-case scenario if I needed to make a run for it.

I'd been naïve coming here. Lorraine wasn't a meek and mild housewife who spent her days cooking and cleaning, she was the head of the firm. The big cheese. The one who gave the orders. She was a serious threat to my family. My heart sank as my stupidity hit me.

Todd and Lorraine began talking as though I wasn't even in the room.

'You've already met Mia and Kelsey. This is the other sister, the one Craig was porking.'

I felt myself shudder at the way Todd had described our relationship. Was I the only one who'd been fooled by it all? My lip began to tremble, so I bit down on it until the tears that were threatening to run down my cheeks subsided.

'How delightful. You have a real way with words.' Lorraine cackled.

When Todd joined in, I felt like getting to my feet and storming out of the room. But who was I trying to kid? I wasn't in a position to go anywhere, and besides that, I wanted to hear what they had to say, so I'd have to grin and bear it for the time being, which would be pure torture. Being the laughing stock wasn't fun by any means.

'My Craig was a big hit with the ladies. He always had his pick of the crop and was never short of admirers, which was hardly surprising, he was a good-looking lad.' Lorraine had a faraway dreamy look on her face, which was miles away from the expression she'd worn when my family was mentioned.

'I thought you'd like to finally put a name to a face.' Todd grinned.

Lorraine's eyes scanned over every detail of my facial features before she turned her attention to the rest of me. 'It's good to see her in the flesh, but I'll tell you one thing, never in a million years was I expecting her to be a ginger nut!' Lorraine laughed.

The cheek of the woman. I'd had enough of being the butt of their jokes for one day. Why did people think it was acceptable to make derogatory comments about my hair? I'd been teased mercilessly at school by the other kids, but these two were grown adults and should have known better.

'It never fails to amaze me why my colouring seems to amuse people so much.'

Lorraine's comment had hit a nerve, so I swallowed down my fear and forced myself up from the sofa.

'Sit down, Scarlett, you're not going anywhere,' Todd said.

He put his hand on my shoulder and pushed me back onto the pink sofa. I bit down on my tongue while glaring at Lorraine. I'd have loved to have told her a few home truths too. Lorraine was no oil painting herself; she might be all dolled up to the nines, but she was about as attractive as a hippo in a tutu. She was neither slim enough nor young enough to wear a top like the one she had on. It did nothing for her pot belly, and if she'd had blonde hair, she could have passed as Pat Butcher's twin.

'I'm sorry, Scarlett. I've been a terrible host. I'm glad I got the chance to meet you. I can assure you that I didn't mean to offend you. I was just stating a fact,' Lorraine said, but her apology was lame.

Why was she suddenly being nice to me? The Saunders family were scum in her eyes, weren't we?

I sat perfectly still like a waxwork dummy while Lorraine drank in every inch of me again. I felt like I was on display at Madame Tussaud's. As she scanned me looking for flaws, I let my mind drift back to what she'd said about CJ being a ladies' man. By the way she'd spoken about him, I suspected nobody would have been good enough for him, whether they'd had red hair or not.

'I really am sorry. Please accept my apology. For what it's worth, I think your hair's beautiful.'

I didn't know what to make of Lorraine. One minute she wanted my guts for garters, and the next, she was filling my head with flattery.

'It might surprise you to know I like being a redhead,' I said through gritted teeth.

'And so you should. It makes you stand out in the sea of blondes and brunettes.' Lorraine smiled.

I held eye contact with her, but I kept a stony expression on my face. I was silently seething. Lorraine had riled me, and her compliment had come too little too late as far as I was concerned. I couldn't switch it on and off like some people could. When something triggered my temper, it took me a while to calm down.

'What do you want me to do with her?' Todd asked, changing the subject.

My pulse began leaping around in my wrist as Lorraine considered his question. A lump formed in my throat while I waited for her to reply. I was going out of my mind, paralysed with fear. I'm fucked, totally and utterly fucked, I screamed inside my head. Every muscle in my body tightened. Tension hung heavy in the air between us. I couldn't believe I'd been stupid enough to walk straight into a trap. I must be the most gullible person on the planet.

'I'm not sure. Let me think about it,' Lorraine eventually said.

I had to focus on staying positive and not let fear take over. Being alert was critical; things could develop very quickly, and I might have to make decisions fast.

'Are you serious? Rio blew Craig's brains out right over there.'

I felt myself shudder when Todd gestured to the immaculate wall opposite. Lorraine had obviously had the place redecorated since then as there was no trace of anything untoward happening in the room.

'You don't need to remind me.' Lorraine threw Todd a look. Her face was like thunder. 'The vision of that bastard Rio sticking a gun into my son's mouth and pulling the trigger is etched into my brain.' Lorraine turned her attention away from Todd and fixed her eyes on me. Hatred was coming off her in waves. 'The bullet blew a huge hole in the side of Craig's face. There was blood and gore splattered all over the wall, and one of his eyes was left hanging down on his cheek. It was like a scene from a horror movie. Seeing my gorgeous boy reduced to that will haunt me for the rest of my days.'

I drew a sharp intake of breath, then clasped my hands to my chest as Lorraine sniffed back tears. She was beside herself. Her emotions were all over the place, swinging like a pendulum. She was tormented by what had happened.

I'd been desperate to know what my family had been keeping from me, but now I was beginning to wish I hadn't started digging. Nothing could have prepared me for what I'd just heard. I hadn't expected Lorraine to tell me all the gruesome details, but she wanted me to know how much bad blood there was between the Colemans and the Saunders family. The feud ran deep. CJ had suffered a truly horrific death, and despite what he'd done to me, my heart went out to Lorraine. It must have been unbearable for her to witness the murder of her son.

Todd held his hands up in front of him. 'I'm sorry, Lorraine, I didn't mean to rake up bad memories. I was just trying to give you a little nudge in the right direction. I thought you'd be happy that I brought you one of the enemy. An eye for an eye and all that...'

'I'm pleased that you brought Scarlett here,' Lorraine replied.

I swallowed down the lump in my throat. What had I got myself into?

'So, what's the problem?' Todd stared at Lorraine with unblinking eyes.

'Killing Scarlett won't bring my beloved son back from the dead,' Lorraine said.

'I know it won't, but it'll make you feel like you got justice for him. Anyone can see how much Craig meant to you.' Todd's eyes scanned around the room, which was like a shrine to CJ.

'I adored the bones of that boy. He was my world, and I will get justice for him, but I'm torn between punishing my arch-rivals and the connection I feel to Scarlett. It doesn't seem right hurting the woman who'd been carrying his baby, my first grandchild. She's practically family.' Lorraine glanced over in my direction.

I didn't want to get my hopes up, but it sounded as though Lorraine was considering letting me walk away because I'd been pregnant with CJ's child. In Lorraine's book, that gave me a get-out-of-jail-free card as long as Todd didn't manage to convince her otherwise.

'You can't just let her go.' Right on cue, Todd piped up. 'What are you going to do when she goes telling tales to Rio? He warned you to leave this house and never come back. You were meant to go into hiding for your own protection. If you don't stick to your side of the deal, he'll come after you. He told you that.'

Todd had laid it on thick, and I could tell by the look on Lorraine's face that she didn't know what to do. Panic started to crawl up from the pit of my stomach.

'I won't say a word, I promise. As far as I'm concerned, this meeting never happened.' Now it was my time to try and sway the balance in my direction.

'Don't fall for that bullshit. Her loyalty doesn't lie with us.' Todd looked down his nose at me.

'Do you seriously think I owe my family anything after what they've done to me? They've been lying to me the whole time, so I'm hardly likely to reward them by throwing either of you under the bus.' I turned my attention to Todd. 'If you hadn't told me the truth about CJ in the first place, I'd still be completely in the dark.'

Much as I couldn't stand the sight of the man, I was doing my best to flatter Todd. He had a huge ego, so I was hoping to win him over by buttering him up. He might not believe me, but I wasn't lying. What I'd said was true. I wasn't about to tell Rio or my family that Todd had defected to the other side, so he had nothing to worry about. I was so disgusted by the way they'd treated me; the last thing they deserved was me sharing that nugget of information with them. Giving them a tip-off was the last thing on my agenda.

Neither of them responded, so I decided to fill the silence by making one last-ditch attempt to appeal to their better nature. I was on their turf, miles away from home with no backup in sight. I had the little mouse gun for protection but I had no idea how to use it, so I couldn't exactly try and do a runner. I had to think on my feet, and there was nothing else I could do given the situation but throw myself into the role of damsel in distress.

'When I started looking for CJ, I'd been hoping to put this traumatic chapter of my life to bed once and for all. But now, the secrets are coming out of the woodwork like cockroaches, and I don't feel like I fit in anywhere. Not with the Saunders family nor with the Colemans. I'm a complete outsider.' My voice cracked with emotion as I finished my sentence.

Todd seemed unmoved by my heartfelt speech, but Lorraine gave me a sympathetic smile. As she appeared to be sitting on the fence, I turned my attention to her.

'I promise you, if you let me go, I won't say a word to anyone. My lips are sealed.'

I ran my finger and thumb from one side of my mouth to the other, miming that I'd closed the zip.

'I wish we'd have met under happier circumstances,' I continued.

'So do I, love. I think we have a lot in common; I was a young mum too,' Lorraine said.

I could sense that I was just starting to win her over, so I battled to keep the surprised look off my face. My estimation of Lorraine's age must have been well off the mark if that was the case. CJ had been in his twenties, so she must only be in her forties. I'd had her down for being ten or twenty years older than that. It just showed you how much damage the sun did to your skin, and with my pale complexion, I made a mental note never to venture out wearing anything less than factor fifty.

'I had my first child when I was fifteen.' The sound of Lorraine's voice brought me back to reality.

I tilted my head to the side. Lorraine had just said she'd given birth to her first child when she was fifteen, but she hadn't said it was CJ. He must have had an older brother or sister. This was getting more complicated by the minute. I'd always thought he was an only child as he'd never spoken about having siblings, but then again, I hadn't known much about him at all, had I?

'It didn't go down too well with my parents, I can tell you, but that feels like a lifetime ago now.' Lorraine's eyes misted up. She paused for what seemed like several minutes before she began to speak. 'I want you to take Scarlett home now, Todd.'

Relief flooded my body, and I felt like doing a happy dance, but I managed to resist the urge.

'You can't be serious.' Todd threw the palms of his hands up, and then he leapt to his feet.

'I'm deadly serious.' Lorraine fixed him with a thunderous look. 'If I find out she's come to any harm while in your care, you'll be a dead man walking.'

Todd let out a loud sigh as he shook his head from side to side.

'Do I make myself clear?' Lorraine planted her hands on her hips and locked eyes with Todd.

'Yes,' Todd said in the tone of a sulky schoolboy.

'Thank you for letting me go,' I said as Lorraine showed us out.

I reached for the passenger door handle but then drew my hand back. I was more than a bit reluctant to get in the car with Todd again.

'Don't be scared,' Lorraine said, picking up on my hesitation. She stepped towards me and rubbed the side of my arm. Her touch repulsed me, and I almost flinched. But I didn't want to throw her kindness back in her face, so I forced out a lopsided smile. I'd done the hard work talking her around. I couldn't afford to upset her at this stage in case she changed her mind.

'Remember what I said, Todd. Scarlett better not come to any harm,' Lorraine insisted, wagging her finger in Todd's face.

Now that Lorraine had reiterated her ultimatum and it was hanging over Todd's head, I felt slightly more relaxed. I got in the front and fastened my seatbelt, deciding to discreetly run my fingertips all around the inside of the car to plant evidence, just in case Todd didn't keep his promise.

As Todd drove towards London, you could cut the atmosphere

in the car with a knife. The sooner we were back in Canary Wharf, the better. I stared out of the front windscreen with my arms folded across my chest, grinding my teeth. I was absolutely furious with him and found it difficult to bite my tongue. There was so much I wanted to say, but I wasn't brave enough to tear a strip off him while we were alone. I had more sense than that. If he kicked off, I'd be no match for him.

There was a lot of power in letting a person know you were angry with them without losing your temper. The tricky part was keeping the *Jesus, you're even more of an arsehole than I thought you were* look off my face. We'd have words at some stage about this, but now wasn't the time, so I'd have to wait for the right moment.

42

Kelsey

'Who were you talking to?' Todd asked when he opened the bedroom door.

He stood staring at me, waiting for me to reply, but my mind was fuzzy; I couldn't seem to find any words.

'What's up, Kels? Cat got your tongue? And yet a moment ago, you were rabbiting away to some unidentified person.' Todd grinned.

I'd have to take his word for that. I had no recollection. All I could think about was my body shaking uncontrollably.

'I thought you'd got an imaginary friend in here with you. I've been listening at the door for a while, but I couldn't make out what you were saying. There was just a lot of incoherent rambling going on.'

Todd locked eyes with me as I stood in front of the bed, sweating buckets with my hair stuck to my head.

'P-p-please Todd...'

I was about to ask him for something, but I lost my train of thought halfway through the sentence. I was sure it was something really important. But the harder I tried to remember, the further it slipped away.

'What the fuck! Since when did you have a stutter?' Todd let out a belly laugh.

I wanted to reply, but I was finding it difficult to concentrate. Every single muscle in my body ached.

'Given that you're rattling like a seasoned junkie and have the same brain capacity as a goldfish, I'd say you need a top-up. Is that what you were going to ask me for?' Todd didn't bother waiting for me to answer. 'Sit down, Kelsey.' He gestured to the bed with a nod of his head, then took the cover off a syringe and fed the needle into the crook of my arm. 'Now, if you had any manners, you'd say, thank you, Todd.'

I went to repeat his words, but they came out jumbled and incoherent.

'In an ideal world, addicts should get medical help as soon as they notice changes in their speech. It would be such a shame if you lost the ability to talk and communicate with people, wouldn't it? Pity you're not in a position to call a doctor.'

Todd smiled, and I burst into tears.

'Aww, you poor thing,' Todd mocked as I cried hysterically. 'It must feel awful being all alone, knowing you're unravelling at the seams and nobody's coming to help you. This is the beginning of the end, Kelsey...'

I slumped back against the pillows when I heard Todd lock the door, clinging to hope as though it was a life raft, but then it drifted away from me as my heavy limbs pulled me towards sleep. I tried to fight it, but drowsiness won the battle.

43

Mia

Rio had circulated pictures of Oscar and the missing car to all his contacts as we'd wasted enough precious manpower trying to track him down ourselves. His importance had started to pale into insignificance with every day that passed as Al Dempsey had top-trumped him. All eyes were now firmly fixed on the rag-trade man. We wanted to make sure he didn't do a runner with the large sum of money we'd lent him.

'Good morning, ladies,' Rio said from outside the office.

'Good morning,' Mum and I replied.

Rio looked full of the joys of spring.

'What are you looking so happy about?' Mum asked.

'I've got some good news.' Rio grinned. Then he glanced sideways as Darius joined him in the doorway.

'We'd like to speak to you if you've got a minute,' he said.

'Of course,' Mum replied. 'Please come in.'

Rio and Darius were wearing matching grins as they stood side by side in the opening.

'My boy's done well.' Rio slapped Darius on his broad back, and his full lips parted, exposing his naturally straight white teeth. 'Tell them what happened.'

'Take a seat,' Mum said, gesturing towards the black leather sofa.

She put her pen down, rested her elbows on the corner of

the desk and interlinked her long fingers. Rio had her undivided attention.

'You know Darius has been trying to track down the Aston Martin.' Rio glanced between Mum and me, and we both nodded. 'Well, you're not going to believe this, but he's only gone and found it.'

'That's great news!' Mum's smile lit up her face. 'How did you find it? Did DC Fallow come up trumps?'

'No, we haven't heard a dickie bird from him, so I asked some of my contacts to keep their eyes peeled,' Darius began.

'The motor was such a distinctive colour. Flugplatz Blue was a limited edition, so it was only a matter of time until somebody spotted it,' Rio cut in. 'Sorry, I interrupted, but I couldn't help myself. I'm absolutely buzzing. I promise I'll keep my trap shut from now on; carry on with the story, son.'

Darius smiled at his uncle before turning his attention back to Mum.

'I got a call last night. One of my guys was out doing a bit of business when he saw the car cruising through Canary Wharf,' Darius continued.

Mum slammed her hands down on the desk, and the sudden sound made me jump. My hand flew up and covered my heart. It was beating like a drum.

'Oh my God, you scared the life out of me.' I laughed.

'I'm so sorry, Mia, I didn't mean to startle you.' Mum offered me a weak smile before she turned away and fixed her eyes on Darius. 'That's fantastic; you've done a brilliant job. I can't praise you enough.'

Darius appeared to shrink down in the chair as though Mum's compliments were weighing him down, but she wasn't trying to embarrass him or make him cringe; she just wanted him to know how much she thought of him. Mum had great leadership skills. She made her staff feel appreciated, which was a great business strategy as it made the workforce want to go the extra mile for their employer.

Feeling valued made a person's day, didn't it? It was a basic human need. Mum was an expert when it came to finding something nice to say and making people feel good about themselves. I should know; she was forever surrounding me with positive vibes even though I sometimes bitterly resisted the aura radiating from her. When my self-esteem was low, I was highly motivated to hold on to my negativity. All too often, my mood set the tone for the household.

Darius sat next to Rio, looking awkward. By his reaction, it was clear he didn't know how to respond to the praise but seeing the warmth in Mum's smile, and the genuine affection in her eyes finally won him over. I knew that Mum hadn't intentionally invited the uncomfortable silence filling the air around us into the room.

'Well, like I said. I think you've done a fantastic job,' Mum repeated.

'Thanks, Amanda, that's nice of you to say.' Darius's mouth stretched into a smile before he cast his eyes to the floor.

Almost as soon as the words left his mouth, Jack appeared in the doorway. His blue eyes scanned around the room before they settled on Mum.

'I seem to have missed something. What's going on?' Jack fixed her with a quizzical expression as he walked over to his desk.

'Darius has found the Aston Martin.' Mum grinned.

The news should have delighted Jack as it meant we were one step closer to recouping the money owed to the firm, but a scowl was resting on his handsome face, which told a different story.

'Really? So you've taken possession of the car?' Jack asked.

I should have realised my husband wouldn't be premature with his excitement. He wasn't going to whoop with joy like the rest of us until the Aston Martin was parked in the drive.

All the pairs of eyes in the office looked in Darius's direction.

'No. We haven't recovered it yet,' Darius replied.

'But we're working on it, and when I get my hands on Oscar

Myles, the scrawny little scrote will wish he'd never been born,' Rio added.

Jack ran his fingers through his honey-blond hair. He seemed a bit agitated by what Rio had said. He was probably worried it might not materialise.

'Anyway, we'd best get out of your way and let you get on,' Rio said, stealing a glance at Jack before he turned to look at Darius.

'Make sure you keep us in the loop,' Mum said when they were in the doorway.

'We will,' Rio replied as he retreated along the path that led back to the private lane by the side of the house.

'Poor Darius, I thought he was going to die of embarrassment,' I said when they were out of earshot.

'It wasn't my intention to make him squirm in his seat.' Mum pulled a face. 'But you know what I'm like; if I think somebody's done something well, I like to sing their praises. Everyone has qualities that deserve complimenting. I always think a little bit of flattery goes a long way.'

'Don't worry about it; he'll get used to it.' I smiled.

Mum had such a lovely way about her. She was always the first in line to pat somebody on the back and give credit where it was due, which helped to give a person like myself a more optimistic outlook on things. But I suppose if you weren't used to her cheerleading style, it might be a bit overwhelming.

'I hope so; I can't change the way I am. I like to make a concerted effort to notice all the good things about a person. I think it's important. When I used to model for a living, some agents and photographers were unnecessarily cruel when we were on a shoot. I could never understand what they got out of reducing people to tears. Being exposed to that bitchy environment made me want to be a better person.'

'It must have been tough.'

I wouldn't have lasted five minutes being scrutinised under

the microscope. We lived in a world filled with cynicism and negativity, so Mum was setting a good example.

'It was hard sometimes, but that goes with the territory. When you're being judged on your appearance alone, you have to develop a tough skin, or you'd end up becoming a paranoid mess.' Mum laughed.

Much like myself, I thought. I wished I'd inherited more of my mum's personality, not just her looks. She wasn't a needy person in the slightest and oozed confidence from every pore.

'I need to pop out for a bit,' Mum said, getting to her feet. 'Will you be OK holding the fort?'

'I'll be fine.' I smiled.

'Aren't you going to fill me in on what's happened? What did Darius say about the Aston Martin?' Jack asked after Mum left the office.

He looked a bit put out that he hadn't been involved in the conversation.

'Sorry, I thought you'd heard what he said,' I replied.

'I caught some of it, but I missed the beginning of the conversation,' Jack said.

'One of Darius's contacts spotted the car in Canary Wharf,' I said.

Jack raised his eyebrows. 'Is he sure it's the right one?'

I shrugged my shoulders. 'I think so. He's as sure as he can be. Rio said Flugplatz blue was a limited-edition colour, so I can't imagine there are too many of them on the roads around here.'

Jack fixed me with a neutral expression. 'Well, I don't think you should get too excited at this stage until he knows for certain.'

Being the voice of reason came naturally to Jack. The words had barely left his mouth when the office phone began ringing. As soon as I realised it was Rio, I put him on speakerphone so that Jack could hear the conversation as well.

'I thought you'd like to know, my contact's just sent me some images of the car, and the plates don't match the one we're looking for.'

Rio sounded deflated, so I glanced over at Jack. He threw me an *I told you so* look, and I felt my heart sink.

'But all is not lost. Oscar wouldn't be the first crook to switch the plates on a motor. It's the oldest trick in the book,' Rio added.

'What are you going to do?' I asked.

'We'll try and seize the car, and once we've got possession of it, we'll be able to check the chassis number, which will confirm whether or not it's the right Aston Martin. I can't imagine it's not. The paintwork's the right colour, and there aren't many of them in circulation. I'll let you know when I've got more news,' Rio said before he ended the call.

'I told you there was no point getting too excited,' Jack said, looking at me over the top of his monitor.

That was easy for him to say. Jack had such a calm, measured approach to everything, but I was more easily influenced than him.

'I know, but I got caught up in the moment,' I replied.

Mum had been over the moon when she'd heard the news, and her reaction had impacted mine. She was a glass-half-full kind of person, and her happiness had a habit of rubbing off on those around her. Her optimism was infectious, which wasn't a bad thing by any means, especially to somebody like me whose glass was nearly always just above empty. It was no secret that I struggled with depression, so it was good to surround myself with positive forces. There was no doubt about it, cheerful people helped to buoy my mood.

'Rio might sound confident, but if you ask me, he still got a long way to go before he has the keys in his hand, and that's if he's even pursuing the right car,' Jack said, bursting my bubble.

44

Scarlett

Why did everyone I came into contact with lately end up double-crossing me? I should have known better than to trust Todd Evans. Don't get me wrong, I was glad I'd had the opportunity to meet Lorraine, although I could have done without hearing the gory details of how CJ lost his life. Her account was going to stay with me for a long time. But I didn't appreciate being handed to the enemy on a plate.

Todd pulled up at the back of the building, but before I'd got out of the car, he'd made me swear not to tell anyone I'd been in contact with him and to promise not to come to the building again. He'd said he'd kept his side of the bargain, and if I didn't keep mine, I'd be history. Anger had been boiling up inside of me on the journey back, but once he gave me the chilling ultimatum, it seemed to vanish into thin air. I would keep my word to Todd, not out of loyalty, but for my own safety.

Once I was out of the car, I didn't look back. I made my way towards the car park where Darius was waiting, I was becoming more and more distressed by the minute. It was really weird, but now that I was heading to safety, it was hitting home how much danger I'd been in and the thought of what could have happened began to terrify me. My naivety could have cost me dear. I'd had a lucky escape from my encounter with the opposition. I'd learnt a valuable lesson from the experience; I'd be more careful in future. But I'd been so desperate to validate what Todd had told me that my common sense had gone out of the window.

A wave of panic flowed through my body, and I staggered out of the foyer on pipe-cleaner legs. They seemed to have a mind of their own and buckled every time I put weight on them. As I walked along the pavement, tears started streaming down my face. By the time I reached the Lexus, I was on the verge of having a full-blown panic attack; there was no way I could hide the state I was in, so I didn't even bother to try.

'Are you all right, Scarlett? Aren't you feeling well? You look awful,' Darius said.

He leapt out of the driver's door when he saw me approaching and reached towards me. Darius cupped my left elbow in the palm of his large hand and steered me towards the Lexus as I battled to stay upright.

'What's the matter? Scarlett? Scarlett? What's up?' Darius asked when I didn't reply.

His eyes scanned my face for the answer to his questions. I could see he was concerned, but I felt too overwhelmed to speak. When I threw myself against him and buried my face in his broad chest, I felt his posture stiffen, and instead of putting his arms around me to comfort me, he let them hang down by his sides. The last thing I wanted to do was make him feel awkward, so I pulled away and looked up into his face.

'Can you take me home, please?' I managed to blurt out between sobs.

I didn't want to go back to the house, but I had nowhere else to go. I'd never felt more alone. My world felt like it was crumbling all over again. Was there ever going to be an end to the misery? I didn't utter a single word on the journey back to Bow; I just stared straight ahead, pretending not to notice the way Darius kept glancing over in my direction as he drove along.

We were getting closer now, so I tried to psych myself up for the showdown with Mum and Mia that was about to happen. I also needed to invent a plausible story to explain how I found out what they'd been keeping hidden in the closet. I couldn't mention that Todd had told me the truth about CJ without breaking my promise to him. Not that I owed the traitor anything, but I was too scared of what might happen to me if I didn't keep my word. Admittedly, he'd done as Lorraine had asked and hadn't laid a finger on me when he'd driven me back to Canary Wharf, but I didn't want to push my luck by turning on him. Todd wasn't the sort of person you wanted as an enemy, especially now that he was working for Dad's biggest rivals. If Lorraine had a change of heart, my days would be numbered.

As the Lexus sped towards the house, I racked my brains, trying to come up with a convincing lie, but I couldn't think of anything. Time was running out; we were getting closer, and the pressure was mounting. I let out a defeated sigh, and a split second later, an idea suddenly popped into my head. I could say Kelsey phoned me and told me what they'd been keeping from me. It was perfect. She'd disappeared off the face of the earth and wasn't here to contradict the account I'd concocted.

I already had my keys in my hand when Darius pulled up in front of the house.

'Thanks,' I said as I got out of the car.

I didn't hang around long enough to hear Darius's reply. I walked up the steps, shoved my key in the lock and burst through the front door. I started rampaging through the house like the Tasmanian Devil, creating as much noise as possible to make my presence felt.

'Mum,' I called, sticking my head around the kitchen door, but she wasn't there, so I went to the bottom of the stairs and shouted at the top of my voice. 'Mum. Mia.'

The house was in silence; they must still be at work, I thought. I glanced at my watch; it was almost six thirty. They would normally have clocked off by now. I walked back into the kitchen, and flung open the side door, which led into the back garden.

'Whatever's the matter?' Mum asked when I appeared in the office doorway a moment later, visibly out of breath.

'Why didn't you tell me that CJ was Craig Coleman?' I panted.

I could feel my nostrils flaring as I stood in the opening, waiting for her to reply. Mum had the good grace to look embarrassed by my question. Mum glanced over at Mia, and then she fixed her eyes back on me. I couldn't help noticing the colour had drained from her face.

'Let's go into the house so we can talk in private,' Mum said, no doubt hoping to buy herself some time.

As soon as she finished speaking, I saw her look sideways at Mia.

'Mum's right; let's talk about this inside. We don't want the whole world listening in to our affairs, do we?' Mia added to back Mum up.

I threw her a look and saw her sink back into her shell.

'Fine, but I'm not going to let either of you wriggle out of this.' I pointed my finger at Mum and then at Mia.

Mum got up from the desk and walked over to where I was standing. She put her hand on the small of my back to usher me out of the office. I was so livid I felt like slapping it off, but instead, I shrugged her away and stayed rooted to the spot. I was so angry; I was physically shaking and stood in the doorway with my fists clenched, grinding my teeth, trying my best to contain my temper.

As Mum walked past me, Mia jumped up from her desk. She bowed her head and hid behind her curtain of long blonde hair while she did her best to close the gap spreading out between them. I glared at her as she drew closer, but she refused to meet my eye and scampered after Mum. They didn't bother hiding the fact that they were whispering to each other as they made their way back to the house, trying to decide on the best course of action.

I stood in the office doorway for a minute or two, attempting to calm myself down, but my insides were boiling with rage. Taking deep breaths was a fruitless exercise. All I was doing was wasting precious time. I stomped up the garden after them, and by the time I made it into the kitchen, they'd taken a seat next to each other at the large circular glass table that overlooked the garden and outdoor pool. Mum and Mia had their eyes locked on one another, but they turned to face me when I dragged a chair out and plonked myself down opposite them. I could see they were ready to put on a united front, but I wasn't about to let them worm their way out of this situation.

'Who told you about Craig?' Mum asked.

Her voice indicated she was annoyed that the secret they'd been hiding from me was now out of the bag. She hadn't answered my question earlier, so I declined to answer hers and began drumming my fingers on the glass surface.

'Was it Kelsey?' Mum pressed.

'What does it matter? The only thing that matters is that you lied to me. Why didn't you tell me about CJ? Didn't you think I had a right to know?'

I'd tried to stay strong, but my voice cracked with emotion when I finished the sentence.

Mum reached her hand across the table towards me when tears started streaming down my cheeks, but I pulled back so that she couldn't make contact with me.

'We were trying to protect you,' Mum replied, glancing sideways at Mia.

I'd heard her use that line a thousand times before. It was one of the go-to phrases she liked to wheel out at a time like this when tea and sympathy were required. Rage began filling every inch of my body. It took every ounce of my strength to stop myself from getting up from the table and swiping the huge vase of white flowers sitting in the centre onto the floor before tearing around the kitchen, destroying everything in my path. I knew that would be childish, but I wanted to hurt Mum like she'd hurt me. Material possessions meant everything to my mum, so smashing up her beautiful home would really get to her. I felt out of control and knew I was about to blow my top. My pressure relief valve had reached its upper limit, and there was only one way things were going to go.

Mum must have read the warning signs. She knew I was prone

to trashing things when I threw a hissy fit, so she sprang into action and tried to defuse the situation before my temper got the better of me. But there was no point in being a fiery redhead if you didn't have the personality to match, was there?

'I can see you're upset, and you have every right to be, but we're all adults, so let's discuss this in a rational manner.'

At least Mum had the good sense not to tell me to calm down. It had taken her years to realise that those two words always ended up having the opposite effect.

'Why didn't you just tell me the truth?'

Knowing CJ was Craig Coleman went a long way to explain why he'd treated me the way he had, and in time, it might just help me come to terms with his betrayal. I'd thought we were falling in love, but all he was interested in was getting revenge for his Uncle Barney's death. My family needed to pay the price one way or another, and I'd blindly walked into the trap with my head stuck in the clouds. I was like a lamb to the slaughter. But if I lived to be one hundred, I'd never understand how CJ could have been so heartless. The man was pure evil, rotten to the core.

'I'm so sorry, Scarlett, we made a terrible mistake.'

'Yes, you did. You messed up big time,' I fumed.

Mum glanced at Mia, but she was staring out the window with her eyes fixed on something in the distance. She hadn't said a word since she'd walked into the kitchen, and even though she was trying to hide it, I could see her body shaking ever so slightly as stress rippled through her insides. Mia hated confrontation, so I knew this would be killing her, but I didn't feel sorry for her. My sister's welfare was low on my list of concerns right now.

'You owe me an explanation, but don't you dare give me the watered-down version and leave out details you think might upset me. Don't try to spare my feelings; I want the full, unedited version.'

Mum's eyes were glistening with tears, and I felt my breath catch in my throat, so I paused for a moment before I began speaking. 'When did you find out that CJ was Craig Coleman?'

Now that I knew the truth about CJ, my hatred for him grew bigger with each passing minute. My pulse was pounding beneath my skin while I waited for Mum to reply.

'I swear we only found out after you were attacked. Kelsey recognised him when she went to Victor's house with Mia, Todd and Rio,' Mum said.

We were off to a good start, I thought. Todd had said the same thing, which made me think it must be true.

'Craig was hiding in the kitchen like a coward,' Mia suddenly piped up. 'When Kelsey confronted him, he admitted that he'd been involved in your attack.'

'That was big of him.' Bitterness coated my words.

'Believe me; he didn't face up to what he'd done without some real persuasion. I can still see the smug look on his face when he announced that his name was Craig Jordan, and sometimes he was called CJ for short.'

Pain ripped through my insides with such ferocity I had to gulp down the lump that had formed in my throat before it escaped as a sob. I almost considered asking Mia to stop. I wasn't sure how much more of this I could take.

'Do you want me to give you a minute?' Mia asked.

She'd read the signs. She was on the verge of tears herself. Her bottom lip was trembling as she filled in the blanks for me.

'No. I need to know what happened,' I replied, even though hearing the truth was tearing me apart.

Mia sniffed back her tears and took a deep breath, replacing her weepy state with a steely expression. 'Craig was delighted that he'd duped us, but his smugness was short-lived. Rio saw red when he confessed, and if it's any consolation, he made sure Craig suffered for what he'd done.'

Mia didn't need to say any more. Lorraine's account of what Rio did to CJ was still fresh in my mind. At first, I'd been horrified to think that Rio had executed him on my account, but now I'd like to pat him on the back. He'd wanted to get justice for me. Dad would have done the same thing if he'd still been alive.

'This must be so distressing for you, darling,' Mum said, breaking my train of thought. She didn't try and reach out to me this time. I knew my earlier rejection would have stung. 'Perhaps we should leave it here for today and give you time to absorb everything. We can talk more at a later stage.'

I inhaled a deep breath through my nostrils and straightened my posture. Mum was right: there was such a lot to take in, and what they were telling me hurt like hell, but I wanted to get this over and done with. I needed to have the full facts so that I could try and get my head around things. It felt like Mum was doing her best to fob me off and keep the details buried deep underground. And now that I'd started digging, instead of answers, I only seemed to be uncovering more questions.

'Regardless of what CJ did to me, knowing the father of my unborn child had a hand in its death is the worst feeling in the world. I can't think of anything more tragic.' My voice changed pitch as I tried to force the words out.

'You've been through such a lot. I'm surprised you're still standing. I'm not sure I would be if I was in your position.' Tears welled up in Mum's eyes.

She turned her face away and swept her blonde pixie cut over her forehead, then rested her elbows on the glass table top, clasping her hands in front of her.

'I can honestly say I've had enough devastation to last me a lifetime. I know you were trying to protect me, but keeping me in the dark didn't spare me the gut-wrenching pain. How could telling me the truth be worse than what I'd already been through? The man I'd hoped to spend the rest of my life with left me to bleed out on the pavement…' I let my sentence trail off.

Mum broke down and started sobbing, and a second later, Mia joined in, but I was fresh out of tears, having already cried a river. So I sat opposite them, stony-faced and numb. As I listened to them wallowing in self-pity, anger started to build up inside me. I was the victim here, not them.

I pushed my chair back from the table with such force it

toppled backwards and crashed onto the tiles just as I slammed the palms of my hands down on the glass surface. It made such a noise Mia jumped out of her skin, and her tears stopped mid-flow.

'I can't believe you tried to keep this from me. I'm disgusted at both of you,' I yelled, jabbing my finger into their faces. My temper had finally got the better of me.

Mum looked up at me with tear-filled eyes while Mia bowed her head to avoid my glare. She'd retreated behind her long blonde hair that fell like curtains in front of her face, trying to block out the reality of the situation. By ignoring what was in front of her, she hoped it would go away. They both looked gutted, but they deserved to have a guilty conscience for what they'd done to me.

'I hate you, and I never want to see either of you again.'

I suddenly felt claustrophobic, like there was no air in the room. I put the palm of my hand on the base of my throat and tipped my head back, attempting to force air into my lungs, but it was as though somebody had put a plastic bag over my head and pulled it tight around my skin. I could tell I was on the verge of having a panic attack. I'd seen Mia have them in the past, and I didn't want my mum and sister fussing over me, so without saying another word, I began pacing across the kitchen floor as fast as my stomach would allow.

'Scarlett, wait,' Mum called after me.

I wasn't going to hang around. I kept going and didn't pause to catch my breath until I was out in the hallway and away from prying eyes. Realising that CJ was related to my dad's biggest rival explained a lot of things. I'd been a pawn in the game, and he'd used me to get back at my family without giving a second thought to my feelings. I was starting to get my head around that, but I'd never be able to understand why the people closest to me closed ranks around me and blatantly lied to me. That was unforgivable and made no sense at all.

45

Mia

The moment I clapped eyes on Scarlett, I knew something was wrong before she even opened her mouth. Her face was pale and troubled, and her blue eyes were glistening with unshed tears.

'What the hell have we done?' Mum's eyes questioned mine. 'I know we thought we were sparing her the pain by keeping the truth from her, but we've made matters ten times worse.'

'It was a judgement call,' I replied.

'And we totally messed it up.'

I could see Mum was stressed, and I wanted to take the pressure off her shoulders. She'd always been there for me in my time of need, so it would be nice to do something for her for a change.

'It isn't humanly possible to make the right call every single time. Don't beat yourself up about it. It wasn't just your decision. Whether Scarlett believes it or not, we had her best interests at heart.'

'We all agreed it was the right thing to do. Who would have told her? It wasn't either of us, and there's no way Rio would break his promise. It must have been Kelsey. I don't understand why she'd do that. What a spiteful thing to do.' Mum shook her head.

Guilt slammed into me and knocked me sideways when I saw Scarlett so distressed. She had every right to have the mother of all tantrums and rant and rave. Emotions were running high in the room. To be fair, her reaction had been quite tame under the circumstances. I felt like the worst person in the world for withholding the truth from her. Nobody liked being lied to, but we'd been trying to spare her feelings. All we'd done was prolong her agony.

'Bitching about me again, are you?' Scarlett said when she came back into the kitchen.

Mum and I looked around at the sound of her voice. She was standing in the doorway with a holdall in her hand. Her face was like thunder.

'I can't stand the sight of either of you, so I'm going to stay with a friend. I'm not prepared to live under the same roof as you anymore. You're toxic,' Scarlett yelled before she turned on her heel and stomped out of the kitchen.

'We can't let her leave like this,' Mum said, leaping up from the table and rushing after her. 'Scarlett, please don't go...'

I was two paces behind, but Scarlett was on a mission, and she had no intention of being stopped. By the time we got to the hall, she'd flung open the front door. She glanced over at us with a satisfied smile pasted on her face.

'You're both dead to me,' Scarlett said.

'Don't say that.' Mum sniffed back tears. 'We love you, Scarlett.'

She looked down her nose at us, then she tossed her long red hair over her shoulder and stormed out of the house, slamming the door behind her for good measure.

Mum's hands flew up to cover her chest, and then her tears began flowing freely. I spent at least an hour trying to comfort her, but she was inconsolable. I felt completely helpless and underqualified to deal with the situation. Mum always offered emotional support to the family, so I was ever so slightly relieved when she said she was going to lie down.

*

'We think Kelsey told Scarlett that CJ was Craig Coleman,' I said when Jack walked into the bedroom later that day.

'She did what?' Jack questioned.

He stood staring at me with a startled expression on his face. He looked so horrified, if I hadn't known better, I'd have thought a rat had run up the leg of his trousers and started gnawing his balls.

'I know. I couldn't believe it either, and we're not one hundred per cent sure it was her, but by a process of elimination, she's the only person it could be.'

'Jesus. What the hell made her do that?' Jack fixed me with his blue gaze.

'Who knows? We'd all agreed it would be better if Scarlett didn't find out.'

'When did Scarlett speak to Kelsey?' Jack asked.

'She didn't say, and I didn't like to ask. You should have seen her; she was in a right state. She was screaming and yelling. She needed to get things off her chest, so it didn't seem right to question her.'

'Try and find out, will you?' Jack said.

'What difference does it make? Surely the most important thing is that Scarlett knows we all lied to her. I don't know about you, but I feel terrible that we kept her in the dark. She said she hated Mum and me, and she never wanted to see us again.'

When my eyes misted over, Jack took a step towards me and threw his arms around my shoulders. He held me close for a short while before he loosened his grip.

'I wasn't trying to upset you, I just thought Scarlett might know where Kelsey is if she spoke to her recently, that's all. Please don't fret about this. Everything will be all right. Scarlett will come around when she's had time to calm down. Do you want me to go and talk to her? Jack let go of me and started to walk towards the door. 'Is she in her room?'

I shook my head. 'No, she packed a bag and said she was going to stay with a friend. She said she couldn't stand the sight of any of us, and there was no way she was prepared to live under the same roof with us anymore.' My lip began to wobble.

'Don't cry, Mia. Things will sort themselves out; they always do. I bet your mum wasn't happy that Scarlett left. What did she say?'

'What could she say? Even though we all treat her like she's the baby of the family, Scarlett's a grown woman.'

'I know, but your mum's like a lioness when it comes to her girls, so I'm surprised she let her go that easily.' Jack pulled a face.

'She tried to stop her, but you know what Scarlett's like. She's headstrong, so she wasn't having any of it.'

'I'm not trying to worry you, but I have a bad feeling that this isn't going to end well.' Jack said the words I'd just been thinking. 'I don't want you stressing out about this. If you can find out where she's gone, I'll try and talk her into coming home. We've always got on well, so she might just listen to me.'

Jack was so kind and caring. What would I do without him?

46

Scarlett

Packing a bag and walking away from my family might seem like an extreme thing to do, but I didn't care. I'd felt like I was living in a goldfish bowl and had to get away from the house. I was burning bridges left, right and centre, but I couldn't bear to be around Mum and Mia right now, so I'd decided to check into a hotel in the shadow of CJ's apartment block so that I could keep a closer eye on Todd. After our last encounter, he'd proved he couldn't be trusted, so I wanted to know what he was up to at all times.

Todd seemed to come and go at roughly the same time every day, but I still hadn't worked out why he was there in the first place. Given his connection to Lorraine, it must have something to do with the Colemans. I was more convinced than ever that he had access to CJ's apartment. I'd sell my soul to step over the threshold of the bachelor pad one last time. Even though he was dead, I had a burning desire to trash everything he owned. I felt energised by the thought of tossing CJ's designer clothes out of the window or taking a pair of scissors to them and cutting them to shreds. That way, I could erase his existence and rebuild my life. It was a great idea in principle, but no matter what happened in the future, I would always have a scar across my stomach to remind me of him.

*

I was sitting on the balcony of my hotel room sipping a glass of pink lemonade enjoying the early evening sunshine, when a bright blue sports car came into view, which immediately grabbed my attention. I was pretty certain it was the same car that was parked on the driveway of Lorraine's house and the one in the photos that Hugh had sent me.

I put my glass on the table and stood up to see what was happening. The car pulled up outside CJ's apartment block on the opposite side of the road. I was fully expecting to see Todd walk through the revolving doors, but instead, a black Lexus screeched to a halt behind the sports car. A moment later, Rio and Darius jumped out and paced up to it. They seemed to appear from thin air, which must have surprised the occupant. In one smooth movement, Darius got into the passenger seat as Rio wrenched open the driver's door.

My heart started hammering in my chest, and I hurried across to the glass railing. Now I had a bird's-eye view of the unfolding drama. Rio dragged the driver out of the car and slammed him against the bonnet. He pulled the man's arm right up his back, which made him wail so loudly I heard it over the hum of the traffic six flights up. Rio produced some plastic restraints from his pocket and slid the two interlocking straps over the man's hands, securing them behind his back. Then he frogmarched the guy back to the Lexus. Rio towered over his prisoner, who was short and slightly built, which was probably why he didn't bother resisting. Rio pushed him onto the back seat before he got behind the wheel of the car and pulled out into the traffic.

My eyes drifted back over to the sports car. Darius was crouched down at the back of it, peering at the number plate. He stayed like that for several seconds, and then he straightened up and walked over to the open driver's door. Ducking down, he slid behind the wheel. A moment later, I heard the low rumble of the engine as it came to life. I watched as Darius pulled away from the kerb, driving off in the same direction as Rio. What the hell was all that about? I thought as I sat down and took another sip of my wine.

I was still rerunning the scene in my mind when I saw Todd come through the revolving doors. He walked over to the kerb where the sports car had been parked moments earlier and looked up and down the road before checking the time on his watch. I watched him with interest to see what he was going to do. He'd come within a hair's breadth of bumping into Rio; what I wouldn't have given to see that encounter. Todd might think he was a big shot, but he was no match for Rio. Mr de Souza would make mincemeat out of him. And I, for one, would pay good money to see that. My lips stretched into a lazy smile as I visualised the scene. While I fantasised about Todd yelling out in pain, I saw him check the time on his watch again before he turned on his heel and stormed back inside the apartment block.

I'd come out onto the balcony to enjoy the last rays of sun. I hadn't expected to have a front-row seat watching the family firm at work. If I'd had any loyalty to my blood relatives, I'd pick up the phone and tell them I was almost one hundred per cent certain the sports car had been parked in Lorraine Coleman's driveway a couple of days ago and that Todd was somehow connected to the driver, but after the way they'd treated me, that was never going to happen. I owed them nothing.

47

Mia

Mum and I could hear the commotion before Rio came into view.

'What's going on?' Mum got up from her desk and walked over to the glass doors.

They'd been folded back so that one side of the office was completely open, which gave us an uninterrupted view of the garden and allowed the warm September sunshine in. Mum stood in the middle of the opening and peered down the path in the direction of the private lane.

'It's Rio,' she said, looking over her shoulder to where I was sitting.

I got out of my seat and went to join her. We were standing shoulder to shoulder as Rio drew closer. He was towing along a young brown-haired man whose arms appeared to be pinned behind his back. Mum and I stepped back to allow them to come inside the office.

'We finally caught up with the scumbag. This is Oscar Myles,' Rio said. He put his large hand between the man's shoulder blades and pushed him over the threshold.

'Did you find the Aston Martin?' Mum asked.

'Yes, which is just as well. The car's a lot more valuable to us than this scrawny, barely out of his teens guy standing in front of you shaking like unset jelly,' Rio replied.

'That's good news,' Mum said, and a look of relief washed over her face.

'I'm glad to see you're shitting bricks,' Rio said, getting up in Oscar's face. 'That's the first sensible thing you've done since you started giving us the run-around. For the life of me, I can't understand why you thought you'd be able to outsmart us.'

As my eyes scanned over Oscar, questions started bombarding my brain. How did he even afford to buy a car like that in the first place? He must have had to put some kind of a deposit down, and he would have needed a decent credit rating to get approved for a loan. Neither of those things were easy for a young person of his age to come by. It made me question Larry's sanity. Surely he must have realised that Oscar wouldn't be able to afford the repayments or the upkeep of a luxury car. Didn't he check out his clients' finances or do a risk assessment before he allowed them to sign on the dotted line?

'I told you we'd catch the little git,' Rio said.

'I didn't doubt it for a second.' Mum smiled.

I wished Jack had been here to see this. He'd tried to play it down so that he didn't worry me, but I knew he was concerned that this day would never come. Having the car back would be a huge weight off his mind. I couldn't wait to tell him the good news.

'Where's Darius?' Mum asked, and a moment later, his large frame appeared in the doorway.

He obviously moved like a ninja as none of us had heard him approaching, which was quite an achievement for a man of his size. Darius didn't have a sylph-like figure, so he wasn't exactly light on his feet.

'What have you done with the motor?' Rio asked.

'It's in the lane. I parked it behind the Lexus,' Darius replied.

'Good. Now let's get down to business.' Rio cracked his knuckles. 'You might want to close the door, Darius. I think our friend Mr Myles might start getting a bit vocal in a minute or two.'

Oscar's face paled as it suddenly dawned on him that he'd bitten off more than he could chew, but I didn't feel sorry for him. He'd wasted enough of our time.

'You must have got shit for brains if you thought you were going to get away with this.'

Rio got up in Oscar's face, and the young man's Adam's apple started dancing in his throat.

'I'm telling you now, son, you don't know who you're messing with.'

When Rio clenched his fists as he bared his teeth, I thought Oscar was going to start crying. His eyes widened, and even from where I was standing, I could see they were glistening with tears.

'Trying to track you down has been one massive ball-ache. You've put us through untold stress, so the way I'm looking at it, we're entitled to some much-needed payback. And I fully intend to get my pound of flesh.'

Oscar's face froze with fear then his bottom lip began to quiver, so he clamped his teeth into it to stop it from moving. I was sure all sorts of horrors were running through his mind as he anticipated what Rio had in store for him.

'What have you got to say for yourself?' Rio puffed his chest out to display his strength and power like a male bird during a mating ritual.

He was playing mind games and enjoying every minute of making Oscar squirm. It was clear Rio intended to stretch out Oscar's agony until he was at breaking point.

'I'm sorry I took off with the car.' Oscar looked up at Rio with a sincere expression pasted onto his face.

'I bet you are. You knew we'd come after you. Why did you take off?' Rio was just getting started on the grilling.

Oscar's eyes darted around the room as he did his best to piece together a suitable answer.

'Don't tell me, you panicked when Larry sold the debt on to us. You wouldn't be the first geezer to shoot through after they'd been paid a visit in the middle of the night,' Rio said.

'It wasn't that,' Oscar replied, taking us all by surprise.

'Come again?' A confused expression had settled on Rio's face.

'Don't get me wrong, you scared the shit out of me when I woke up and found you'd broken into my flat, so I would've been seriously tempted to do a disappearing act. But that wasn't what happened. I shot through because I was paid to take off,' Oscar said.

'Hold on, son. I think you need to rewind a bit,' Rio said. 'Either my ears were deceiving me, or you said you were paid to take off.'

'That's right.' Oscar nodded with more enthusiasm than necessary.

Mum's eyes widened. 'Who paid you?' she asked.

'I'd rather not say.' I could see Oscar's pulse throbbing in his neck.

Rio grabbed the front of his T-shirt and twisted the material around in his fist.

'That's not the answer Mrs Saunders was looking for. I'd start talking if I were you.'

When Rio straightened his posture, he towered over Oscar. Time seemed to stand still while we waited for Oscar to find his voice. When nothing happened, Rio glanced over in Darius's direction.

'Keep an eye on this little fucker; I'm going to get my tool kit,' Rio said, breaking the silence.

'Wait,' Oscar wailed.

Rio flashed him a smug smile. He knew his comment would provoke a reaction.

'Who paid you?' Mum asked for a second time.

Oscar was visibly shaking. 'I'm going to be a dead man if I tell you.'

'And you're going to be a dead man if you don't.' Rio got up in Oscar's face, and the young man's knees buckled.

Oscar closed his eyes for a couple of seconds, then he let out a slow breath. 'I know I haven't got a lot to offer, but can we make a deal? I'll tell you what you want to know if you promise to let me go.'

Oscar didn't have a lot of options, so he wasn't really in a position to bargain. The name of his paymaster was the only thing that was of any interest to us.

'Do we have a deal?' Oscar repeated with an undertone of desperation in his voice.

Rio glanced over in Mum's direction, and she gave him the nod.

'Yes,' Rio replied.

'Todd Evans paid me to make myself scarce.'

I felt my mouth drop open. I couldn't believe what I'd just heard.

'Todd Evans?' Mum questioned.

'Yes,' Oscar confirmed.

My eyes scanned between Mum, Rio and Darius. Each one of us looked as confused as the next. You could have heard a pin drop until the sound of Oscar's sobbing filled the air between us.

'I think you've got some explaining to do,' Rio said.

Oscar's tears stopped in their tracks as he stared up at the huge man looming over him.

'How do you know Todd?' I asked.

'I don't know him well at all, really,' Oscar replied.

'So why were you working for him?' I narrowed my eyes and fixed them on Oscar while I waited for him to speak.

'I needed the money.'

Oscar looked at me with pleading eyes, no doubt hoping I was going to be a soft touch, but he was barking up the wrong tree. I had a steely side where business was concerned.

'Rio, can you take his cuffs off, please?' I asked. 'Something tells me we're in for a long story, so we might as well get comfortable.'

'Are you sure? Rio questioned.

I nodded. 'I don't think Oscar would be stupid enough to try and do a runner.'

Rio picked up a pair of scissors from Mum's desk and cut the restraints off. Once he was free, Oscar stretched out his shoulders before bringing his hands around to the front of his body. Relief was written all over his face as he rubbed the skin on both of his wrists.

'Thank you,' he said, offering me a weak smile.

'Take a seat,' I replied. 'You'd better start at the beginning and tell us how you got involved with Todd in the first place.'

'The first time I met him, I was in my local drowning my sorrows at the bar. I was chatting to the landlord about how expensive it was to live in London. I'm from Northampton originally,' Oscar began.

We knew that already because Rio and Darius had driven up there when the car first went missing to see if he'd parked it at one of his relative's. We were off to a good start, I thought; he seemed to be telling the truth.

'What brought you to London?' I asked.

'Work, and I got the chance to move out of home and rent my own place, which was something I'd wanted to do for a while,' Oscar said.

That seemed like a valid reason for a young man.

'But I hadn't realised how difficult it would be to manage. My wages only stretched so far. That's where Todd comes into the picture. He overheard the conversation I was having about my money worries, and he made me an offer I couldn't refuse.'

'Which was?' My pulse had speeded up a notch.

'Todd offered me a grand to buy a car for him,' Oscar replied.

'And you didn't think it was odd that he didn't just go and buy it himself?' I questioned.

Oscar's cheeks flushed. 'I didn't think too much about it. A grand is a lot of dosh to somebody like me, and it seemed like an easy way to make money at the time, but if I'd known what I was getting myself into, I would have turned him down.'

'So what happened after you accepted his offer.'

I glanced over at Mum. Her eyes were glued to Oscar.

'Todd picked me up from my flat the next day and drove me to a car lot at the back of Shoreditch High Street. He gave me the deposit in cash and asked me to put it down on the Aston Martin. Then he told me to sign a credit agreement to pay the balance off in monthly instalments.'

I felt my eyes widen. 'Weren't you worried that your name and personal details were on the loan document?'

Oscar was more naïve than I'd thought, and Todd had taken complete advantage of him. I couldn't believe he'd signed the credit agreement.

Oscar looked up through his eyelashes. 'What can I say? I'm not the sharpest tool in the box, am I?'

'You said it, son,' Rio chipped in.

Oscar's cheeks flushed again in response to his comment.

'I'm embarrassed to admit it, but I didn't give it that much thought. All I was focused on was the grand he was going to give me when I handed him over the car.'

'Surely you expected there to be consequences when you didn't pay the instalments?' Mum chimed in.

Oscar clamped his mouth shut and then cast his eyes to the floor. I could see he was slowly dying inside. He knew he'd been stupid without us rubbing his nose in it.

'So you gave Todd the car straight away?' I wanted to get the conversation back on track.

'No. I was expecting to, but he told me to hang on to it for the time being. He said he'd be in touch in the next couple of days, and in the meantime, he gave me permission to drive around in it. I was gassed. I'm twenty-two. Not many guys my age get to sit behind the wheel of a motor like that.'

'You really got taken for a ride, didn't you, son,' Rio said.

Oscar let out a loud sigh. 'I trusted Todd. I thought he was a decent bloke.'

'And then something happened to change your mind.' I smiled.

Oscar's eyes met mine. 'I realised what an idiot I'd been when I woke up and found those guys in my bedroom.' Oscar gestured to Rio and Darius.

'Why didn't you tell them about Todd at that stage?' I asked.

'I don't know. I panicked. Waking up and finding I'd got unexpected company scrambled my brain, so I wasn't thinking straight,' Oscar replied. 'It only sank in after the guys left that your firm expected me to repay the loan. I phoned Todd the next morning and told him what had happened. He assured me that it was all a big misunderstanding and that he'd get it sorted, but he asked me to make myself scarce and take the motor with me while he smoothed things over.'

I glanced over at Mum, Rio and Darius. They were wearing blank expressions as they listened to Oscar's account.

'Where did you go?' I was curious to know as we'd searched high and low for him.

'I went to Essex...' Oscar let his sentence trail off.

So near and yet so far, I thought. He'd practically been on the doorstep the whole time we'd been looking for him.

'What were you doing at Canary Wharf?' I asked.

'I was running an errand.'

Considering he'd started off being very open, Oscar's answer was very non-committal.

'The car had been seen in the area more than once,' Rio suddenly piped up.

'What sort of an errand were you running?' I quizzed. We seemed to be going around in circles.

'I was dropping off a parcel, but don't ask me what was inside. I haven't got a clue.' Oscar fidgeted in his seat.

'Who was the parcel for?' I had a horrible feeling I knew the answer to the question before Oscar replied.

'Todd.'

Rio's expression changed, and he took a step closer to Oscar. I could almost smell fear radiating off him.

'Does Todd live in the building you were parked outside of?' Rio was wearing a frown.

'Yes, but I don't know which apartment is his.' Oscar looked drained.

'I'd like to speak to you ladies alone. Darius, can you take Oscar to the official HQ at the industrial estate?' Rio asked.

'Of course,' Darius replied.

'Hey. I've told you everything I know. I thought we had an agreement? I gave you the info, and in return, you were meant to give me my freedom.'

Oscar was making a stand, but Rio took no notice of his outburst. He reached into the inside pocket of his suit jacket and produced a set of restraints. Then he clamped them around Oscar's wrists before he had a chance to voice his objection any further.

The expression on Oscar's face when Darius led him out of the office was that of a man about to face the firing squad. I wasn't sure what he thought we had in store for him, but no harm was going to come to him for the time being. He might not realise it, but he was a valuable asset. Rio wanted him held at the firm's commercial property until he was of use again. Dad had installed a detention unit at the premises for occasions just like this. They were as secure as any prison. Rio stood in the opening and watched them walk towards the house and the private lane that lay beyond. Once they were out of earshot, he turned around to face us.

'I hope you didn't mind me asking Darius to take Oscar to the lock-up, but I didn't want to discuss things in front of him.'

'I think that was a very sensible idea,' Mum replied.

'Todd being back on the scene is bad news. It only spells trouble if you ask me,' Rio said.

'I agree. Why did he pay Oscar to buy the Aston Martin and then disappear with it?' Mum fixed Rio with a puzzled expression.

'Todd would have known that Larry would come to us for help when the debt turned bad. My guess would be that your ex-employee had revenge on his mind,' Rio replied.

A niggling thought crept into my brain, and even though I was trying to shake it off, it started burrowing deep inside, making its presence felt.

'Do you think Todd has anything to do with Kelsey's disappearance?' I blurted out, finding the need to voice my concerns.

'Disappearance? I'm not sure I'd call it that. Don't blow this out of proportion. Your sister's work-shy, and she's gone AWOL from the job, that's all.' Mum batted away my concern like she was swatting an irritating fly.

I felt a bit embarrassed that Mum thought I was overreacting and was about to banish my uneasiness to the depths of my brain when Rio began to speak.

'To be honest, Amanda, the same thing crossed my mind. I don't mean to speak out of turn, but you shouldn't dismiss Mia's concerns just like that. Kelsey has had plenty of unwanted attention from weirdos in the past, so if you ask me, I think her absence warrants a bit of investigation.'

Rio fixed Mum with an intense stare, but Mum didn't want to get drawn into the conversation, so she stayed quiet. He wasn't going to give up that easily, and after a short pause, he started trying to wear her down again.

'For what it's worth, I think Mia's right to be worried. I feel the same way. I know Kelsey can be selfish and unreliable at times, but maybe you could humour an old man and let me do a bit of snooping, just so I can put my mind at rest.' Rio flashed Mum his winning smile.

If anyone could convince Mum to do something, Rio could. He was the right man for the job, so I left him to it. I decided to watch and learn from the expert instead of trying to stick my oar in.

'You know Kelsey doesn't like people meddling in her affairs,' Mum replied.

'I promise I'll be very discreet, and if everything turns out to be kosher, I'll let the matter drop once and for all,' Rio said.

Mum threw her eyes up to heaven and shook her head. 'Oh, for God's sake. Go on, then. And I'm expecting an apology from both of you when it turns out you were worried about nothing.'

'Thanks, Amanda. You don't know how happy you've made me.' A look of relief spread over Rio's handsome face. 'I'll check back in with you as soon as I've got some news.'

48

Kelsey

My dependence seemed to be getting worse. I didn't think I was imagining it; I was pretty sure I was craving a fix more frequently than before. I pulled back the edge of the curtain to try and gauge the time. The sky was still pitch-black, and the road below was pretty deserted, which made me think it must be the early hours of the morning. Todd wasn't going to be happy that I was about to wake him from his sleep, but I'd been writhing in agony for a while now, and there was only one way to cure my discomfort.

My body was drenched in sweat. The Egyptian cotton sheets were clinging to me like a second skin, and it took every ounce of strength I had to untangle myself from them so that I could sit up. I threw my legs over the side of the bed and paused for a moment before I managed to haul myself onto my feet. But my limbs weren't cooperating and were refusing to move. They felt heavy and achy, so I knew crossing the room was going to be an uphill battle. Once I reached the door, I dropped down onto the floor and started banging on it with all my might, but I was as weak as a kitten.

'Todd, Todd,' I cried out.

I'd tried to call at the top of my lungs, but my voice sounded strangled and distant. By the time Todd appeared at the other side, the heels of my hands were red and throbbing. Todd unlocked the door and pushed it open with such force he nearly knocked me spinning. I rocked backwards and out of the way in the nick of time.

'What did I tell you about making a racket? Shut the fuck up. It's the middle of the night,' Todd said, crouching down next to me and getting up in my face.

'I'm in ag-ag-agony.' My words were garbled.

Todd looked down his nose at me before he scooped me up in his arms like I weighed nothing. He walked over to the bed and flung me down on it. When I hit the mattress with a thud, I curled into a ball as a fresh wave of pain ripped through my body.

'Stay there and be quiet. If there's another peep out of you, you won't be getting a top-up. Do I make myself clear?' Todd spoke through gritted teeth.

I nodded.

Silent tears rolled down my cheeks when Todd pushed the needle into my flesh a few moments later. As the heroin started travelling around my system, I closed my eyes and flopped back against the pillows.

'Look at the state of you. You're pathetic, Kelsey.'

I opened my eyes at the sound of Todd's voice and saw him leaning over me. The corner of his lip was lifted into a snarl. 'You're an absolute mess. I've got a good mind to give you an extra-large dose and put you out of your misery.'

Daily life had become a miserable existence, and I half wished he would carry out his threat. But I couldn't imagine that was part of the plan, not at this stage anyway. Todd wanted to make me suffer and was getting great pleasure out of taunting me. I could see he was hoping to get a rise out of me, but I was in no position to take the bait.

49

Scarlett

My life had been turned upside down yet again, so checking into the hotel was the best decision I'd made in a while. Having time on my own had given me the space I needed to think clearly without Mum sticking to me the way porridge welded itself to the surface when it was left to dry in a bowl.

We lived in such a noisy world full of distractions. Sometimes it did a person good to take themselves out of the equation. From the moment the key card opened the door, I felt like I'd entered luxury hotel heaven. My room was huge, but the soft glow of the lights made it feel cosy, and the bed was so comfortable it was hard to drag myself out of it. If it hadn't been for the lure of the L'Occitane toiletries and the roll-top bath in the en suite, I might not have bothered.

I was a sociable person by nature and usually craved the company of others, so I thought I might get bored holed up on my own, especially in the evening when the spa facilities were closed, but I couldn't have been more wrong. Leaning back against the pillows while gazing out of the window had become my new favourite pastime. I couldn't tear my eyes away from the London skyline; the view from the full-length windows was amazing. What more could a girl ask for? At this rate, I'd never want to go home.

My thoughts drifted back to my mum and sisters. I wished they'd been honest with me from the start. I'd tormented myself over the possible reasons CJ had lied to me. Why tell me that I was the best thing that had ever happened to him if he was going to arrange for somebody to stab me? That had haunted me from the moment Kelsey had revealed he was behind the attack that cost the life of our unborn child. I'd speculated about what had driven him to do such a wicked thing, but there was no point in dwelling on it – I was never going to hear his side of the story.

I was finding it so much easier to hate CJ now that I understood what a ruthless bastard he'd been. He'd robbed me from ever having proper closure by taking my desire for justice to the grave with him. But I was struggling to forgive my mum and sisters for keeping me in the dark. It made me question if there was anything else going on that I didn't know about.

Todd was coming and going from the building at regular intervals, but I still hadn't got to the bottom of why he was there. There was no way I could follow him to find out which apartment he was going into, and I didn't want anyone to go on my behalf.

I couldn't remember the last time I bothered to do my hair or put makeup on, but if I was going to pick the bartender's brain and get him on my side, I'd need to look my best. The dark shadows under my eyes and my whiter shade of pale complexion would have him running for the safety of the storeroom if I wasn't careful. I had no idea if the guy still worked there, and even if he did, he might not be on shift, but it had to be worth a try.

Luckily for me, the guy who'd served me when I was waiting for CJ in the residents' lounge was behind the bar, and from the way he responded when I walked into the exclusive members' club, it looked like he recognised me. I'd decided to put on the same outfit I was wearing the last time I'd seen him in the hope of jogging his memory. It seemed to have done the trick. As I approached the counter, he smiled warmly, so I flashed him a big grin. It was a long shot, but I'd decided to play the damsel in distress.

'Hello again,' I said to try and jog his memory. I was hoping he'd remember that we'd met before.

'Hello, stranger. Long time no see. What can I get you?' the barman asked.

'I'll have a cherry blossom lemonade, please.'

'Coming right up,' he replied.

I glanced over my shoulder to where the receptionist was standing guarding the entrance. I'd told her my boyfriend lived in one of the apartments in the complex, and I was meeting him for a drink, but I was a bit early and asked if it would be possible to wait for him in the bar. She'd waved me through, and when I saw she was preoccupied vetting some other people, I leant over the bar as the guy was preparing my drink.

'I'm in a bit of trouble and could do with some friendly advice,' I said in a very quiet voice so that the receptionist wouldn't overhear. I batted my eyelashes and fixed him with my best doe-eyed stare while I waited for him to speak.

'I'm sorry to hear that. I don't know how much use I'll be as an agony aunt, but I'd be happy to give it a shot,' he replied, placing a coaster down on the bar before he lowered the tall glass onto it.

The pale pink lemonade, which was scattered with fragrant rose petals, looked almost too nice to drink, I thought as I took a sip through the black straw.

'My boyfriend and I have split up.' I cast my eyes to the floor, then pretended to sniff back tears while wiping imaginary wet patches off my cheeks with my fingertips. I was laying it on thick, but it had to be done.

'Oh, I'm sorry to hear that,' he replied but judging from the smile threatening to spread across his face, he wasn't that disappointed to hear my news.

'My ex is being a dick, and he won't give me my things back. Do you know if there's any way I could gain access to his apartment?'

His lips twisted to one side as he considered what I'd asked.

'The management company has an in-house cleaning team. Did your ex sign up for that service?'

I had no idea. But CJ didn't strike me as the domestic type, so it was possible that he had.

'I'm not sure. What difference will that make?'

'They'd have a key to his apartment if he did,' the barman said.

'Ooh.' I felt my eyes grow wide with excitement. 'Is there any way I could find out?' I flashed him a warm smile, and he grinned back at me.

'If you don't mind waiting for a few minutes, I'll have a quick chat with one of the supervisors. I know him quite well,' he said.

'That would be great, thank you,' I replied.

'What number does your ex live at?'

It was the question I'd been dreading. 'I can't remember, but his name's Craig Coleman.'

It felt alien to call him that, as I knew him as CJ.

'No worries. I'm Greg, by the way. What's your name?'

'Scarlett,' I smiled at him full beam.

I sat at the bar with everything crossed while I waited for him to come back. I was mindlessly twirling the stirrer around the cherry blossom lemonade when Greg reappeared, and judging by the smile on his face, he had good news.

'Well, what's the verdict?' I fixed him with my blue eyes.

'I had a word with the supervisor, and Craig did sign up to have his flat cleaned. But she said there's a note on the system asking the cleaners not to come until further notice,' Greg said.

My heart hammered in my chest. 'Did she say why?' I quizzed.

'No, but I'd say the apartment's probably empty,' Greg replied.

Todd was here so regularly that I'd assumed he was living here, but Greg could be right. If the flat was unoccupied, Todd was using it for something he wanted to keep private. He'd insisted that I wasn't to tell anyone I'd seen him, and he'd made me promise not to come to the building again. What did he have to hide? I had a feeling I was one step closer to finding out.

'Does your friend, by any chance, have a key to Craig's apartment?'

'I would have thought so,' Greg replied, and I felt my spirits lift.

50

Mia

'Amanda, I'm sorry to disturb you. Have you got a minute?' Rio asked when he appeared in the open doorway.

He was wearing the expression of a man about to deliver bad news, and I felt my heart sink.

'Of course. Take a seat.' Mum gestured to the leather sofa. She straightened her posture and was ready to give him her undivided attention.

'I've looked back at the CCTV from the night Kelsey went to the party to see if there were any clues. I noticed that it was disabled at 23:47 and then reconnected an hour later,' Rio said.

Mum got up from her desk, walked around to the front of it and perched on the edge so that she was closer to where Rio was sitting.

'What do you think that means?' Mum's hands were resting in her lap, and she began wringing them.

'I'm not sure. But it might indicate a break-in,' Rio replied.

My pulse speeded up at the thought of an intruder roaming freely through our house while we were in bed, oblivious to their presence.

'Why would a thief bother reconnecting the security system when they left?' Mum quizzed.

'Your guess is as good as mine. Have you noticed if anything is missing, apart from Kelsey, that is?' Rio asked.

His question startled Mum, and she glanced over in my direction.

'I can't say that I have. What about you, Mia?' Mum asked.

'Nothing of mine has been taken. Do you really think we were broken into while we were all in the house?' I wasn't sure my nerves could handle Rio's answer, but I'd asked the question all the same.

Rio held his hands up in front of him. 'I can't say for certain. But it happens sometimes...'

I knew that was true, but I was an incredibly light sleeper, and the slightest noise disturbed me, so I'd be amazed if Rio's theory turned out to be correct.

'Maybe we had a power cut,' I suggested, looking for a more straightforward explanation.

Rio shook his head. 'That wouldn't have disabled the system.'

The three of us sat in silence, lost in our own thoughts for several moments, trying to make sense of it all.

'Don't you think it's a bit strange that Kelsey's switched her phone's "find me" facility off?' Rio asked Mum.

'Not really. Kelsey's done that because she doesn't want to be disturbed. The action means exactly what it says on the tin. It's important not to lose sight of that,' Mum replied.

'I'm not sure I agree with you. What if she's been kidnapped?' Rio's words took both of us by surprise.

'It's easy to let your imagination start running riot at a time like this, but I think you're reading too much into it,' Mum replied.

'I don't think I am. Kelsey hasn't been home for weeks.' Rio was standing his ground.

'I know, but she's been in regular contact over text,' Mum countered.

Her words hung in the air between them as they locked eyes with each other.

'I've taken the liberty of contacting DC Fallow. As Kelsey's disabled the "find me" facility, I've asked him to trace the location of her phone,' Rio said.

Mum raised her eyebrows, and her mouth dropped open. 'I wish you'd run that by me first before you took matters into your own hands.'

Rio cast his eyes to the floor.

'I don't see how that's going to help anyway, as she's switched it off.' Mum folded her arms across her chest. She looked annoyed that Rio had gone behind her back.

'The police have ways of getting around that problem. I told Fallow it's urgent and asked him to put a rush on it. We should have some news soon. I'll keep you posted,' Rio said, getting up from his seat.

He didn't wait for Mum to reply before he walked across the floor, ducked back out of the office and disappeared down the garden path. He hadn't added any words of reassurance like: *don't stress yourself out too much. I'm sure it's nothing to worry about. I just wanted to check to be on the safe side.* He just dropped the bombshell and left Mum and me to our thoughts. I couldn't speak for my mum, but my mind was whirring at a million miles an hour. Something told me there wasn't going to be a good outcome to this. It was true Kelsey had a selfish streak a mile wide, but if she was in trouble and we just sat back and did nothing, I'd never be able to forgive myself if anything happened to her.

51

Scarlett

My dad was a firm believer that everything had a price, and I was inclined to agree with him. After a bit of gentle persuasion, Greg's friend had agreed to have a copy of the key to CJ's apartment cut. I was hoping she'd accept a small fee, but she stood between me and what I wanted, so she'd milked the situation for all it was worth.

Greg had gallantly offered to come with me, but I'd said there was no need as I was pretty sure the place was empty. I knew for a fact CJ wasn't there, and if I timed it right and waited for Todd to go out, I was certain I'd be able to let myself in without anyone finding out.

I took up position on the balcony and trained my eyes on CJ's apartment block. My heart started hammering in my chest when I saw Todd come through the revolving door and walk off in the direction of the car park. I didn't have a minute to lose, so I texted Greg and asked him to meet me in the foyer. He was standing by the lifts when I appeared about five minutes later.

'I'm sorry. I didn't mean to keep you waiting,' I said as I walked towards him. 'Have you been here long?'

'No.' Greg smiled. 'I've only just got here. The bar was deserted, so I took the opportunity to pop out while there weren't any customers.'

Greg and I got into the lift, and I handed him the envelope

containing five hundred pounds in cash. It was quite a hefty fee for a copy of the key, but I wouldn't be able to get into the flat without it, so all things considered, it was a small price to pay. Cleaning staff were generally low-paid and worked hard for their money, so I couldn't really blame the supervisor for being a bit greedy. She was putting her job on the line, after all. If anybody found out what she'd done, she'd be sacked on the spot. Her secret was safe with me, and Greg didn't seem like the type of guy who'd be a snitch.

'I feel bad paying the supervisor for her trouble while you're getting nothing in return. Are you sure I can't give you something?' I asked as the lift started its ascent.

'Don't be silly. I'm just glad I was able to help,' Greg replied.

'Well, for what it's worth, I really appreciate what you've done for me. You're a lifesaver,' I said.

Gregg's lips stretched into a huge smile. A moment later, the lift came to a stop on the eighteenth floor, and the doors opened.

'Are you sure you don't want me to go with you?' Greg asked.

'Thanks for the offer, but I'll be fine.' I couldn't help thinking I sounded more confident than I felt.

'Good luck. Feel free to pop into the bar later and tell me how you got on,' Greg said as he stepped out of the lift.

My heart was hammering in my chest as I stood outside CJ's front door with the key in my hand. But I didn't have time to hesitate. I only had a small window of opportunity before Todd returned to the apartment. That was probably a blessing in disguise because the longer I stalled, the more time I had to think about what I was about to do, and the closer I was to chickening out. With that thought in mind, I slid the key into the lock, opened the front door and stepped over the threshold.

The butterflies that had been resting in the pit of my stomach suddenly took flight and began flapping around my insides. I wasn't sure how I was expecting to feel, but instead of being swept away by a wave of nostalgia, I was engulfed by an overwhelming sense of dread. I stood frozen to the spot, looking down the hallway towards the open-plan living area.

As I made my way towards CJ's bedroom, goosebumps appeared and covered my arms. I placed my fingertips on the handle, and the palms of my hands started to sweat. I wasn't sure whether I was pleased or disappointed when I pushed down on it and discovered the door was locked.

I glanced down at my watch. Time was travelling at the speed of light, so I'd have to get a shift on. I hot-footed it into the living area, and my eyes scanned around the space. As they did, a lump formed in my throat, and I had to battle to hold back my tears. The memories were coming thick and fast. I looked out onto the balcony and saw the bamboos rustling in the September breeze, and the wicker bucket seat made for two that CJ and I used to cuddle up in was swaying backwards and forwards. I was on the verge of breaking down, so I had to tear my eyes away and focus on something else.

The apartment was spotlessly tidy and just how I remembered it. If Todd was living here, he wasn't making his presence felt, so I walked over to the huge built-in fridge and pulled open the door. A half-used carton of milk and a couple of ready meals were the only tell-tale signs that somebody had been in here. I peered at the dates on the cardboard sleeves to check whether they'd been bought recently. For all I knew, they could have been left behind by CJ himself.

The two chicken Madras and pilau rice had seven days left before they expired. It struck me as odd that he'd bought two of the same dish. You'd think he'd get bored eating curry all the time, but then again, not everybody was a foodie like me. Some people had no interest in what they ate; it was just a necessary thing they had to do to fuel their bodies.

I stole one last glance at my watch before I decided to head for the door. I'd done enough snooping for one day, and I didn't want to risk being caught by Todd. Now that I'd plucked up the courage to venture inside, I knew I'd be able to do it again. I'd come back tomorrow and see what he'd been up to.

52

Mia

Rio put his hands up in front of him. 'Don't freak out about this, but I'm glad I got Fallow involved now. Something's come to light, and it's changed everything. He managed to track Kelsey's phone, and when he gave me the address, it rang alarm bells.'

Mum glanced over in my direction. She had a worried look on her face. 'I don't like the sound of that one little bit.'

'I've had a bad feeling about this from the start, but when I found out the location of Kelsey's mobile, it pretty much confirmed my worst nightmare. It's in the apartment block where we caught up with Oscar.'

Mum's eyes filled with tears, and her hand flew up to cover her mouth. As Rio's words registered, a wave of nausea smothered me and my stomach twisted into a knot.

'Is that the place where Todd lives?' Mum looked horrified as the realisation hit her.

Rio nodded.

'I'm sorry to interrupt you, but I think I should mention I took Scarlett over there a couple of times too.' Darius's Adam's apple bobbed up and down when Rio fixed a set of blazing eyes on him.

'Come again?

I could almost see Rio's brain working overtime.

'I think her friend lives in the same building,' Darius continued.

'The one from uni?' Mum quizzed.

Darius shrugged. 'Scarlett didn't say.'

'What did they look like?' Rio asked.

'I don't know. She asked me to wait for her in the car...'

Rio's head rocked back on his neck, and he let out a loud groan. 'And you did as you were told without asking any questions. Really? What about her safety? Anything could have happened...'

'I'm sorry.' Darius cast his eyes to the floor.

'It wasn't his fault. I was so delighted Scarlett wanted to go out, I asked Darius to drive her,' Mum piped up.

'Why didn't you tell me about this?' Rio clenched his jaw as he spoke.

'You were out on a job with Wesley.' Darius was literally squirming.

'And you didn't think to mention it afterwards? Not even when we caught Oscar outside the building?' Rio looked like he was about to blow his top.

'I was so caught up in the moment I forgot all about it.' Darius hung his head in shame.

'I'll deal with you later,' Rio said to his nephew through gritted teeth before turning his attention to Mum. 'I don't know where Scarlett fits into all of this, but that will have to wait for another time. We need to get a move on. I've asked Fallow to meet Darius and me outside the building.'

'Why?' Mum asked. 'We wouldn't normally bother involving the police.'

'I know, but his badge carries a lot of weight. If I bowl up to the reception and demand to know the number of Todd's apartment, they're going to tell me to sling my hook. Whereas, if it's a matter of police business, they'll have to co-operate,' Rio replied.

'Fair enough. I see what you mean,' Mum said.

'We'd better make tracks. I want to get there as soon as possible,' Rio said.

'Keep me posted.' Mum had tried her best to hide her concern, but a slight undertone of panic had crept into her voice.

Thoughts had begun whirring through my mind. But I was determined not to let the ideas run away with themselves. I took several deep breaths and then considered what this might mean with a logical head firmly planted on my shoulders.

Now that Rio had traced Kelsey's phone to Todd's apartment, everything started to slot into place. Initially, I'd thought we should be worried as they hadn't parted on good terms, but as she was making regular contact with Mum, it was unlikely that anything untoward was happening. It seemed far more likely that they'd become an item again. Kelsey and Todd had history. They'd been in the throes of a passionate affair until she'd discovered he was married. It could be a simple case of them rekindling the romance and her wanting to keep it a secret because she knew the news would be met with as much enthusiasm as a dose of food poisoning from the rest of us.

'Todd Evans has brought nothing but misery into our lives. You don't think she's got back with him, do you?' Mum was wearing the expression of a woman who had stepped into a freshly deposited cowpat while she had nothing on her feet.

Mum and I were clearly on the same page.

'It's weird you just said that. I was thinking that too.'

'It would explain a lot, wouldn't it? The secrecy, the lying, switching off her phone's location. Kelsey's a lot of things, but she's not stupid. She'd know damn well we wouldn't be happy about her bringing that man back into our lives,' Mum fumed. Her voice was bitter.

'The fact that she's been making regular contact with you makes me think she doesn't want us to worry. Kelsey would never admit it, but I think she was head over heels in love with Todd. I've never known her to be in a relationship as long as she was with him,' I said.

'I know what you mean. Kelsey usually bores so easily, and once she's got the guy she was after, she kicks him to the kerb again and moves on to the next one. She's the son your father never had. But she didn't do that with Todd. She kept going back for more. He must have had something none of the others did,' Mum replied.

I nodded. Todd definitely had a hold over my sister, and I was sure it broke her heart when things came to such an abrupt end. Kelsey had toned down her social life since she'd finished with Todd. She barely went out these days, and as far as I knew, she hadn't had another man in her life since him, so if you read between the lines, it left a lot of clues behind. The more I thought about it, the more I was convinced that when Rio turned up at the apartment, he'd find the two of them together, blissfully unaware of the drama they were causing.

'How could she get back with him after what he did to our family?' Mum's lip was quivering, and her blue eyes were brimming with tears.

I got out of my chair and walked over to where she was sitting. By the time I got there, she'd placed her elbows on the edge of the desk and had covered her face with her hands. I knew she was crying even though she wasn't making a sound because I could see her shoulders moving. I crouched down and placed a kiss on the top of her head, and then I gently began stroking her back to try and soothe her. It was rare for Mum to show her vulnerability and the sight of her made a lump form in my throat, but I swallowed it down. I had to be strong for her for a change. Mum needed me, and I wasn't about to let her down.

53

Scarlett

'Scarlett.' Rio looked startled when I stepped out of the lift.

My right hand flew up to my chest, and my heart began hammering against my ribcage when I clapped eyes on him.

'Oh my God, you frightened the life out of me.'

'What the hell are you doing here?' Rio asked.

'I could say the same to you,' I replied, hoping to buy myself some time.

My mind was racing. Talk about being caught off guard. Rio and Darius were the last people I'd expected to bump into when I was leaving the building.

'Were you visiting your friend again?' Darius piped up.

Rio's head snapped around, and he glared at his nephew. Darius's shoulders stooped in response. I watched his Adam's apple move in slow motion as he swallowed a lump in his throat before he bit down on his lip. Rio seemed peeved that Darius had spoken to me. Luckily, his annoyance halted the conversation before I had to answer any awkward questions. Rio threw him one last look before he turned his attention back to me.

'We're looking for Kelsey. I'm pretty sure she's in Todd's apartment. You wouldn't happen to know anything about that, would you?' Rio narrowed his eyes and fixed me with a stare.

I could see he was suspicious; his unblinking gaze tried to burrow into my brain and read my thoughts, which I found quite unnerving.

'Despite what you're implying, I haven't got any insider knowledge,' I replied.

'Yeah, right. Do you think I came down in the last shower?' Rio shook his head. 'You and Kelsey are as thick as thieves.'

'We used to be.' My voice trailed off.

'It's important you tell me what's occurring. Has Kelsey hooked up with that dickhead for old times' sake?' Rio pushed his shoulders back and appeared to grow two inches in height.

'I swear to you, I don't know,' I insisted.

'Listen to me, Scarlett, I'm not leaving here until I find out what's going on. I'm worried Kelsey's in trouble.'

The words *Kelsey* and *trouble* started rattling around in my brain, and a feeling of unease washed over me, so I decided to put my differences with my sister aside and tell Rio what I knew.

'I was in Todd's apartment a few minutes ago, but there was no sign of Kelsey,' I said.

From the look on Rio's face, it was clear this wasn't making any sense. His expression was pained, as though his balls were trapped in a vice.

'Kelsey's phone was traced to this building, so where is she?'

I threw the palms of my hands up.

'Why did you go to see Todd?' Rio's tone was demanding.

'It's a long story. I'll tell you about it later,' I replied.

Now that I knew Kelsey's phone had been tracked to the apartment block, her safety was at the forefront of my mind. I didn't trust Todd as far as I could throw him.

'Can you take me to Todd's apartment?' Rio asked.

'I can do one better than that. I can let you in. I've got a key.' I smiled.

I held it up in front of Rio to back up my claim, then turned away from him and pressed the up arrow on the lift.

'Let's take the stairs. We need to get there as quickly as possible,' Rio said.

'The apartment's on the top floor,' I replied.

Rio's dark brown eyes widened. 'Of course it is. The flash bastard was bound to have the penthouse. Lift it is then.' Rio paused for a moment before turning to face Darius. 'Phone DC Fallow and tell him not to bother coming. The useless fucker won't be any help to us now.'

'Who's DC Fallow?' I asked as the lift doors slid open.

'I'll tell you another time. Let's just get to Todd's apartment,' Rio replied.

Thoughts of my window of opportunity slipped my mind as the lift began climbing. All I could focus on was opening the front door. Once I'd unlocked it, I led Rio and Darius into the swanky bachelor pad.

'So where's the cowardly fucker then?' Rio fumed. He paced down the hall and stuck his head through the open doorways.

'He's not here,' I said.

'I thought you'd just been to see him?' Rio's eyebrows knitted together as a frown settled on his face.

'I said I'd been in his apartment...' I corrected.

Rio blew out a breath, then put his hand up to cut me off. He turned his face away before I had a chance to explain and walked back down the corridor towards the closed door. Rio stopped outside CJ's bedroom, put his hand on the handle and pushed it downwards.

'It's locked,' I confirmed as a feeling of dread rose up from the pit of my stomach.

Rio turned sideways and hurled himself at the door, but it didn't budge.

'Darius, give us a hand, son,' Rio said as he prepared to barge the door again.

At first, there was no movement, but the human battering rams didn't give up, and after several attempts, the door sprang open. My heart leapt into my mouth when I saw Kelsey lying on the bed, curled into a ball. She had her back to us, but there was no mistaking it was my sister. I'd recognise her dark brown glossy hair anywhere. It was alarming that she didn't look around at the sound of the noise. I stood in the doorway, trembling with my fingers pressed to my lips.

'Kelsey,' Rio called, rushing over to the bed.

He dropped onto his knees, put his hand on Kelsey's shoulder and gave her a vigorous shake, but she was unresponsive. When he turned her onto her back, her eyes flickered ever so slightly, which gave me a small glimmer of hope.

'Should I call an ambulance?' I said, suddenly finding my voice.

Rio was leaning over her, checking for signs of life. Panic started swirling around my insides like a tornado.

'Is she breathing?' I asked. I was dreading his reply.

Rio pressed his ear up to her lips. 'Yes,' he said.

'Thank God for that.' I'd never felt more relieved to hear that one word.

Kelsey looked absolutely dreadful. Her skin was so pale it had a bluish tinge to it, and I thought for one horrible moment, she was no longer with us.

Rio turned Kelsey's limp arm over and pressed two of his fingers onto her wrist. He had large bear-sized hands, but Kelsey's arm was so thin his fingers seemed bigger than normal.

'Her pulse is very weak,' Rio said.

He looked over his shoulder to where Darius and I were standing like a couple of extras waiting in the wings for the moment the director needed us on set. Rio didn't wait for either of us to reply. Instead, he turned his attention to Kelsey. I watched as his eyes scanned over her. A moment later, his head snapped back to Darius and me, and he let out a howl like an animal trapped in a snare. I felt myself jump as the loud noise ricocheted around the minimal space.

'That bastard must have been drugging her. She's got puncture marks all over the inside of her arms. I'm going to fucking tear Todd limb from limb when I get my hands on him.' Rio's lip curled when he spoke.

'I'd like to see you try,' Todd said.

We all turned towards the sound of his voice. He'd snuck into the apartment without any of us noticing and was standing just behind Darius and me. Rio pushed past the two of us and squared up to Todd. They stood facing each other in a death stare contest, sizing each other up.

A moment later, Rio swung his killer right hook. He was a former bare-knuckle fighter, so he never missed his target. He executed his destructive punch with skill. It had just the right amount of power and speed to catch Todd off guard. There was something to be said about the element of surprise. Blood and saliva flew out of Todd's mouth as Rio's huge fist connected with his jaw. The solid crack sent his head spinning. It rocked around on his neck in slow motion, and he stumbled back several steps. Todd was in trouble. He must have been seeing stars.

Real fights were nothing like boxing matches; any time I'd witnessed Rio in action, his punishing blows disabled his opponent within a few minutes. But Todd had no intention of playing by the rules. Once he'd corrected his stance, he reached around to the back waistband of his trousers and pulled out a gun. I gasped when I saw it in his hand. Time seemed to be moving at a snail's pace. The concept of a gentleman's code of honour had gone out the window. This wasn't going to be a fair fight; only one of the men was armed. I knew Rio would definitely have been carrying a weapon, but he hadn't had time to draw it. My heartbeat had gone into overdrive. There was no way of knowing how this was going to pan out. Rio had become a father figure to me. I couldn't bear the thought of losing him as well as my dad.

Todd went to aim the gun, but he'd underestimated Rio's long reach. Rio managed to knock the weapon offline with his right hand. I felt myself squirm as I watched him plunge his left thumb into Todd's eye and gouge it. It was a brutal technique, but it had to be done. Todd yelled in agony as he dropped the gun and then covered his face with his hands.

The speed at which Rio had moved took my breath away. He

was a huge man, but his reflexes were like lightning. Todd must have thought he'd have the upper hand coming from a military background, but Rio was streetwise and had been ready to react to the unexpected.

'You probably should know, if you start something with me, I'm going to finish it,' Rio growled before he pulled out a set of nylon restraints and cuffed Todd's arms behind his back. 'You hold on to him while I see to Kelsey,' Rio said to Darius.

I stood rooted to the spot as Rio bent down next to Kelsey again. He used the hand that had just smashed Todd around the chops to gently smooth my sister's hair back from her face.

'It's OK, sweetheart. I'm going to take you home now,' Rio whispered into Kelsey's ear.

His words were so tender that I found myself sniffing back tears.

54

Mia

'Hello,' I said, picking up the office phone after the first ring. 'It's Rio. I've got something important to say. Is your mum with you?'

'Yes, hold on, I'll put you on speakerphone.' I took the receiver away from my ear and pressed the icon, so Mum was included in the conversation. 'Go ahead, Rio.'

'We've found Kelsey.'

'Oh, thank God.' Relief coated my words.

'Please tell me she wasn't with Todd,' Mum said.

'We're in the car, on our way over to you. I need you to call the doctor and get him to come over straight away. We'll be with you shortly,' Rio replied without responding to what Mum had just said.

'Why? What's wrong? Has something happened to Kelsey?' Mum sat bolt upright as a look of concern washed over her face.

'I haven't got time to explain. Please just do what I've asked, Amanda.' Rio's tone was firm.

He hung up the call without going into any more detail. Mum and I locked eyes with each other for a few moments before she did what Rio had asked.

'Thanks for coming, Dr Burton,' Mum said when she opened the front door.

I was hovering outside the kitchen, trying desperately to swallow down my anxiety before I had to face the man who'd been our family GP for my entire life. I didn't want my mental state to distract him from the home visit. I'd developed a technique, and it seemed to work very well. If I forced myself to focus on tiny details, it stopped me from freaking out when stressing about something. I slowed my breathing and began concentrating on the markings in the travertine tiles.

'So where's the patient?' Dr Burton asked as his eyes swept around the hallway.

'On their way,' Mum replied.

The words had barely left her mouth when the sound of tyres crunching over gravel filled the air. Mum flung open the door and ran down the steps. Dr Burton followed her, and they stood side by side, waiting for the car. I edged nearer so that I could see what was going on, but I stayed in the shadows.

As soon as the car came to a stop, Rio jumped out of the back passenger door. He leant back through the opening, but I couldn't make out what he was doing from where I was standing. I craned my neck, and that was when I saw Scarlett get out of the opposite door. My mouth dropped open. She didn't glance in Mum's direction but kept her eyes fixed on Rio.

Darius left the driver's door open as he hurried to help. Rio backed out of the car, straightened his posture and turned to face the house. Dr Burton raced into action when he saw Kelsey. She was lying like a limp rag doll in Rio's arms. As soon as he reached her, he pressed his fingers onto her pulse.

'Take her inside, please,' the doctor said a moment later.

'Don't leave him out of your sight.' Rio gestured with a flick of his head to the front passenger seat.

'Oh my God, what's happened?' Mum asked as Rio walked past her.

She'd been rooted to the spot in a state of shock watching the scene unfolding.

Rio carried Kelsey up the steps, across the hallway and into the living room. I scampered along behind him, safe in the knowledge that my sister had Dr Burton's full attention. Rio laid her down on the sofa. She looked dreadful. I was genuinely shocked when I saw the state she was in; she'd lost a lot of weight, and her skin was alarmingly pale. Mum and Scarlett came to stand next to me while the doctor went to examine Kelsey. He took a stethoscope out of his bag and began listening to her breathing.

'Do you know what happened to her?' Dr Burton asked.

Rio shook his head. 'I'm afraid not, but she's got needle marks all over her arms.'

Mum let out a gasp, so I reached for her hand.

Dr Burton pulled up Kelsey's eyelids and shone a torch into them. 'Did you know Kelsey had a drug problem?' he asked, turning to face Mum.

'No,' Mum replied.

'Excuse me a moment,' Rio said before pacing out of the room. A moment later, I heard him whistle and then call out. 'Darius, bring that scumbag in here. He's got questions that need answering.'

We all looked over when Todd approached the doorway, flanked by Rio and Darius. As soon as he stepped into the room, Mum flew at him, her eyes blazing with rage.

'What have you done to my daughter?' Mum's voice cracked with emotion.

'I gave her a shot of heroin, and before I knew it, she developed quite a liking for it.' Todd smirked.

I couldn't believe Todd had freely admitted to something so awful. I would have thought he'd try to gloss over what he'd done, not confess as though he was proud of the fact. But it was clear to see that he was delighted with himself. Todd stood in front of us with his head held high, grinning from ear to ear. I'd never held him in high regard, but I would never have thought he'd stoop so low. The man was pure evil.

Dr Burton shook his head as he looked down his nose at Todd, mirroring all our thoughts.

'You're behaviour was reckless. You had no way of knowing the purity of the drug, so the chances of giving Kelsey an overdose were extremely high. Heroin makes a person relax, but sometimes it suppresses their respiratory system to such an extent that they forget to breathe. Did you know that?' Dr Burton fixed Todd with a glare.

Todd shrugged his shoulders in response.

What we'd just discovered was beyond my worst nightmare. I couldn't speak for the others, but I was pretty sure they would have agreed that this was by far a worse outcome than our original concern. I would have preferred to see Todd and Kelsey get back together any day of the week. And to think we were worried that that was the case. That would have been a much better alternative.

'I can't bear the sight of him. Get him out of my house right now.' Mum spat the words into Todd's face. Her usual composure had deserted her, which was perfectly understandable.

'I will, but I don't want to take any chances with this slippery bastard. We don't want him doing a runner before he pays for what he's done, do we?' Rio locked eyes with Mum. 'Don't worry, Amanda. I'll get it sorted.'

'Thank you.' Mum offered Rio a weak smile.

Rio smiled back, and then he turned to face Darius.

'Get Wesley to come over, so you've got back-up, and then deposit the slimy fucker at Davie's HQ. Rotting in a cell will soon wipe the smile off his face,' Rio said, squaring up to Todd. 'Keep him alive for now. He might turn out to be useful.'

55

Scarlett

'I'm sure I don't have to tell you that this is a very serious situation,' Dr Burton began. 'That young man was playing a dangerous game. No matter how it's taken, once heroin enters the body, it starts changing the way the central nervous system functions.'

'Do you think Kelsey has become hooked already?' Mum asked. I could see her holding her breath while she waited for the doctor to reply.

'I'd say the likelihood is very strong. Even first-time users find themselves wanting more. The risk of developing a dependence rises with repeated use. I'll need to assess her properly once she wakes to see how badly she's been affected,' Dr Burton said.

Mum, Mia, Rio and I were sitting around the table in the adjoining dining room, lost in our thoughts, when Kelsey began to stir. We all leapt out of our seats and rushed over to the sofa. We'd only just gathered around her when she opened her eyes. It took a moment for our faces to register in her brain, and when they did, a lazy tear rolled down her left cheek.

'Don't cry, darling; you're safe now,' Mum said, dropping down onto her knees in front of the sofa. She dried Kelsey's face with the pads of her fingertips before placing a tender kiss on the side of her head. 'Can one of you phone the doctor, please?' Mum asked without tearing her eyes away from my sister.

'Consider it done,' Rio replied before he stepped out of the living room.

Kelsey was still lying on the sofa, trying to take everything in, when Rio walked back in with Dr Burton a short while later. She was groggy and seemed to be having trouble focusing on anything.

'Hello, Kelsey. How are you feeling?' Dr Burton asked as he approached her.

'Wh-wh-where am I?'

Kelsey seemed completely out of it. Her eyes were glazed over.

'You're at home with your family.'

Kelsey didn't react when we gathered around her, but she looked through us as though we were strangers. Mum turned towards Dr Burton and fixed him with a look of concern.

'It's not surprising Kelsey feels disorientated. Memory loss is a common side effect of heroin use, as is a lack of mental clarity,' he said.

I could see Mum wasn't reassured by his words.

'Do you have any recollection of how all of this started?' Dr Burton looked straight into Kelsey's face, but she stared blankly back at him.

A moment later, she burst into tears. I felt my heart lurch to see her so distressed.

'Even though you were in regular contact with your mum, I was worried because you hadn't been home for weeks, so I looked back at the CCTV from the night of the party to see if there were any clues,' Rio said.

Kelsey stopped crying and fixed her eyes on him.

'I noticed that it was disabled around midnight and then reconnected an hour later, but at the time, I couldn't work out why. Now I'm certain Todd was behind it. I think that's when he kidnapped you.'

Rio's words hung in the air as we all digested them.

'It wasn't me tex-tex-texting…' Kelsey's voice trailed off.

'It was Todd?' Rio's eyes were glued to Kelsey's as he finished her sentence.

Kelsey nodded, and I felt a shiver run down my spine.

'Why can't she talk properly?' Mum asked.

'It's a symptom of drug abuse,' Dr Burton replied. 'Was Todd injecting you regularly?'

Kelsey nodded before she began to cry again. It was torture seeing her like this. She'd always been the strong one who never wasted her tears on anyone or anything. So to watch her completely falling apart was devastating for all of us. She was like a different person. My feisty sister had been drained of her personality. The fight had gone out of her, and now she was dead behind her eyes. Todd had broken her spirit.

Kelsey suddenly began to shake. She wrapped her stick-thin arms around her emaciated body and rolled onto her side, whimpering in pain. She looked extra vulnerable because the weight had dropped off her.

'What's the matter with her?' Mum's eyes were filled with fear.

'She's suffering from withdrawal. It's like a really bad case of the flu: muscle aches, headache, a runny nose; you get the picture. Have you experienced this before?' Dr Burton asked Kelsey.

My sister didn't reply. Instead, she started writhing in agony. Standing by and watching her suffering made me feel utterly useless. Tears pricked my eyes, but crying about it wasn't going to make things better.

'Can't you do something to help her?' Desperation coated Mum's words.

I turned to look in the doctor's direction, but his eyes were fixed on Kelsey. He scanned every inch of her, checked her pulse and listened to her breathing as he carried out his assessment.

'A supervised medical detox in a substance abuse treatment centre is recommended in a situation like this, but overcoming heroin addiction isn't easy,' Dr Burton replied.

'N-no way.' Kelsey looked horrified.

She might have been having trouble articulating herself, but there was no mistaking her facial expression. She wasn't going to go into a clinic willingly.

'It's OK, darling, don't upset yourself. I don't like the idea of Kelsey going into rehab, either. Couldn't she go cold turkey instead?' Mum suggested.

'I'm afraid it's not that simple. Heroin is a highly addictive short-acting opioid that takes effect rapidly but also leaves the bloodstream quickly. She's going to be in for a rough ride without professional help,' Dr Burton said.

Kelsey was becoming agitated listening to my mum and the doctor discussing her treatment as though it had nothing to do with her. I could see she wanted to protest, but she didn't have the energy. She was in no fit state to speak up and express her wishes.

'You'll have a real battle on your hands if you don't take my advice, Amanda. I'm going to leave Kelsey to get some rest, but I'll be back in a couple of hours to check on her,' Dr Burton said, glancing at the time on his watch. 'If you need me to come back sooner, just call me.'

56

Mia

'Y̶ou heard what the doctor said. You need to rest. Let's get you up to bed,' Mum said, stepping naturally into the role of a mother hen.

Kelsey pushed herself up from the pile of velvet cushions she was lying against and slowly swung her legs over the edge of the sofa. They folded like pipe cleaners when she went to stand up, and she flopped back down onto the seat.

'Can you help Kelsey to her room and then come and see me in the office?' Mum asked Rio.

'Sure thing,' Rio replied.

Scarlett cast a sideways glance at Mum, then trailed along behind them. It was obvious she didn't want to get drawn into an awkward conversation, so she decided to make herself scarce instead. Once they were at the top of the stairs, Mum gestured for me to follow her.

'I don't know what to make of it all. There's so much to take in,' Mum said as we walked along the path.

'Kelsey looks dreadful. She's lost so much weight. I was worried something wasn't right, but I'd never have guessed in a million years what was going on,' I replied.

My words must have struck a chord, and I saw Mum blink back tears as she took a seat behind her desk. I hadn't been trying to make her feel guilty. I wished I'd kept my mouth shut now. I didn't know whether to apologise or pretend I hadn't noticed. I was still trying to decide when I saw Rio heading our way.

'I'm her mother. I should have realised she was in trouble. I feel terrible,' Mum said with regret written all over her face.

'It's not your fault, Amanda,' Rio said as he stepped into the office. Then he slid the folded glass panels back into place to block out the garden so that we could talk in private.

'Isn't it? You and Mia were worried about Kelsey, whereas I was carrying on as though everything was fine.' Mum shook her head. 'I was so furious that she wasn't taking the business seriously and thought she was just being selfish when she didn't show up to work...'

Mum let her sentence trail off. I could tell she was looking for reassurance, but before I had a chance to offer her any, Rio jumped in.

'Amanda, don't beat yourself up about it. We all know what Kelsey's like. And you were getting regular texts, so you weren't to know,' Rio said.

When his face broke into a smile, I saw Mum relax a little.

'The fact that she was making contact with me was the main reason I hadn't taken her disappearance seriously. I had no idea Todd was sending those messages.' Mum's lip trembled. She was close to tears. 'If I'd had the slightest inkling that she was in trouble, I'd have pulled out all the stops to find her.'

'You don't need to tell me that,' Rio said.

It was easy to look at things in hindsight and wish you'd done them differently. I could see Mum felt dreadful, but there was no point in dwelling on something that she couldn't change. It was a well-known fact that Kelsey thought everything revolved around her and that she could come and go as she pleased. If that hadn't been the case, Mum would have been frantic when she vanished into thin air. Don't get me wrong, I wasn't suggesting my sister was to blame in any way for what happened to her.

'What are we going to do with Todd?' Mum asked. 'He needs to pay for what he's done.'

The sound of her voice brought me back to reality.

'Don't worry about him. He's not going anywhere. Rest assured, I'll make him suffer. I think we should focus on Kelsey for now. We need to make sure she gets the right treatment,' Rio said.

I typed the words *heroin addiction* into the search bar of my laptop and then clicked on the first result.

'Oh my God, listen to this,' I said as I read out the information on the website's page. 'Heroin is one of the most addictive substances in existence, and an addiction to it is hard to overcome without help.'

'That ties in with what the doctor said,' Mum replied.

'It says here that heroin addiction causes a network of changes in the brain that are not easy to reverse. Daily cravings can last for years and sometimes for the rest of the person's life. It can also cause serious heart problems.'

That was a very sobering thought, and I couldn't force myself to continue reading. I closed the lid of my laptop as I swallowed the lump in my throat. Poor Kelsey had a long and bumpy road ahead of her.

I jumped out of my skin when Scarlett pulled back the glass office door.

'I need some help. Kelsey's in a bad way,' Scarlett said.

The words had barely left her mouth when Rio slipped through the gap next to her. I was amazed his broad-shouldered frame hadn't got stuck; considering he was a huge man, he was incredibly nimble. If I hadn't known better, I'd have thought he'd dislocated his body parts to squeeze through the space. Scarlett stood in the doorway pleading to us with her eyes. Rio had disappeared inside the house by the time we got there. We filed up the stairs one after the other, listening to the sound of Kelsey vomiting. Rio was in the en suite, holding back her hair as she retched into the toilet bowl.

'I'll phone the doctor,' Mum said, rushing out of the room.

Scarlett and I stood side by side as we watched Kelsey's

emaciated body heaving with the effort. I've never felt more helpless in my life than I did at that moment.

'Dr Burton. Can you come over straight away, please? Kelsey's in the grips of withdrawal,' I heard Mum say.

Seconds later, she walked back into the bathroom, slumped down on the floor next to Kelsey and ran her hand up and down my sister's back to try and soothe her.

57

Scarlett

By the time Dr Burton arrived, Kelsey was back in her bed.
'How are you feeling?' the doctor asked.

'T-t-terrible. My head is pounding, and I'm aching all over,' Kelsey slurred.

'I'm going to start you on methadone. It's a synthetic opiate prescribed to people trying to come off street heroin. It will eliminate the withdrawal symptoms you're experiencing,' Dr Burton said.

'Is it safe to substitute one lot of drugs for another?' Mum looked concerned by the doctor's suggestion.

'It's much safer for Kelsey to take methadone under medical supervision than it was for her to take heroin,' Dr Burton countered.

Kelsey glared at the doctor, which was perfectly understandable as he was talking about her like she was some kind of junkie, ignoring the fact that Todd had forced her into this situation.

'What if she becomes addicted to that as well?' Mum asked.

'That's not the intention. The first dose I give her will be low. Then I'll gradually increase it until the maintenance dose is reached,' Dr Burton explained.

'What's a maintenance dose?' Mia asked.

'It's the amount of methadone you need to enable you to give up heroin while avoiding the unpleasant withdrawal symptoms,' Dr Burton explained.

'W-w-what are you waiting for?' Kelsey asked.

I drew a sharp intake of breath when she held her arm out towards the doctor.

'I'm going to give you methadone liquid. I'm sure you've seen enough needles to last you a lifetime,' Dr Burton said.

He unscrewed the lid of an amber glass bottle and poured some of the green liquid into a small plastic cup. Then he held it up to Kelsey's lips. She pulled a face as she swallowed it.

'Yuck.' Kelsey shuddered.

'What does it taste like?' I asked.

'It's vile. I'm not t-taking that again.' Kelsey shook her head.

Mum sat down on the edge of Kelsey's bed and took hold of her hand. 'I was looking at a rehab website earlier, and it said that if a user hadn't abused heroin in massive doses for any length of time, it would be possible for them to detox and be heroin-free in about a week.'

'That's true, but it doesn't mean the addiction is cured. When someone hooked on heroin stops using it, withdrawal symptoms set in, they peak on the second or third day and are often so unbearable that the person relapses and avoids attempting to quit in the future. I can assure you the substitution treatment is much less severe than going cold turkey,' Dr Burton said.

I didn't doubt what he'd said was true, and that was a terrifying realisation. But judging by my sister's earlier response, Mum was going to have her work cut out, trying to get her to agree to go into rehab. None of us said a word for what seemed like an eternity.

'How are you feeling now?' Dr Burton asked, breaking the silence.

'A bit b-better,' Kelsey replied.

'Good. I thought that would be the case. The effects of methadone start quickly and last several hours. I'll be back to give you another dose later on. In the meantime, can you all please leave her to get some rest,' Dr Burton said as he made his way out of the door.

He didn't hang around to discuss Kelsey's treatment. As far as he was concerned, it wasn't up for discussion. Going cold turkey wasn't an option – doctor's orders. Whether Kelsey chose to follow them was another matter entirely.

I took myself off to my room. I couldn't face being part of the talks that were about to go on in the kitchen following the doctor's exit. Just the thought of it made my blood boil. Mum would hold court like King Arthur, with Mia and Rio playing the part of her loyal knights of the round table, discussing things that ultimately really only affected Kelsey. She should have been involved in the conversation, but that wouldn't be the case. I didn't need to be in the room to know they'd huddle together, forging plans regarding her treatment without taking her wishes into account. But for once, I was glad it was her and not me.

I lay on my bed and let my mind drift. Kelsey had been through a terrible ordeal. She must have been in the apartment the first time I went there, and I'd had no idea. I wasn't the most switched-on person, but how had I missed that? As I mulled it over, a troubling thought popped into my head. The day after Kelsey vanished, Hugh sent me a picture of Todd and another man. They were in a bright blue sports car outside the apartment block. Was the man with Todd involved in Kelsey's disappearance? I couldn't say for sure, but I had a horrible feeling that Rio might have found her sooner if I'd spoken up.

I battled with my conscience and asked myself: was it too late to come clean? I decided it was, so I'd have to bury that piece of information. What goes around comes around. My family had kept me in the dark plenty of times. Now it was my turn to repay the favour.

58

Mia

'I should have realised Todd would want to get even with Kelsey. I wish I'd listened to you and let you search for her sooner,' Mum said, casting her eyes towards the floor.

'It's not your fault. You mustn't blame yourself,' I said, but my words fell on deaf ears.

Mum looked up at me with tear-filled eyes. 'I'm not making excuses for the way I behaved, but I was so angry with Kelsey because she'd swanned off that afternoon to go shopping without giving us a second thought. And then, when she didn't come home that night, I presumed she was up to her old tricks. I never realised she was in danger...' Mum's voice cracked, and she let her sentence trail off.

Rio put his large hand on her shoulder and squeezed it in a show of support as I rushed over to her. I crouched down by her chair and threw my arms around her.

'I feel so guilty.' Mum sounded heartbroken.

'Well, don't. She's home now, and that's the most important thing,' Rio said, and his brown eyes scanned over us.

He was doing his best to make Mum feel better, even though he'd voiced his concerns on several occasions. He'd done his level best to persuade her to let him look for Kelsey, only stopping short at dropping to his knees and begging to be allowed to check that all was as it should be, but his requests had fallen on deaf ears. As far as Rio was concerned, all of that was forgotten.

He was taking great pains to deflect any accusation away from Mum at a time when he could have been pointing the finger of blame. I admired him for that.

'So where do we go from here?' Mum's eyes settled on Rio, and then she turned her attention to me.

'I know you don't like the idea of Kelsey taking methadone, but if the doctor thinks that's the best way for her to beat her addiction, I think we should be listening to him,' I said.

'I'm inclined to agree with Mia. No disrespect, Amanda, but none of us are qualified to deal with the situation. Kelsey needs professional help,' Rio added.

'She's not going to like being sent to rehab.' Mum sounded concerned.

'Maybe not, but it's for the best,' Rio replied.

'I know Todd was angry with Kelsey, but what on earth possessed him to do such an evil thing?' Mum's eyes glazed over with tears.

'I think it's time we found out. If it's OK with you, I'll go and get him and then we can confront him,' Rio suggested.

Mum and I were sitting behind our desks a short while later when Rio and Darius walked in. Todd was between them. From the angle of his shoulders, I could tell his wrists were secured behind his back.

'No prizes for guessing why you wanted revenge on Kelsey,' Rio said. He lifted Todd's arms up behind his back and made him squeal like a girl. 'There were plenty of ways to get even with her. Why did you give her heroin?'

'I had the good fortune to get some for a song, so I thought I'd kill two birds with one stone,' Todd sneered.

'Come again?' Rio fixed him with a questioning look.

'Davie hated druggies, so by getting Kelsey hooked on gear, I gave him a kick in the nuts as well.'

A flash of anger spread over Rio's face, and he grabbed hold of the front of Todd's black T-shirt, balling the material in his fists as he pulled Todd towards him.

'If you know what's good for you, you'll shut your mouth and don't speak ill of the dead. I don't take kindly to people bad-mouthing my friends.' Rio rammed his face into Todd's until they were millimetres apart.

Todd tried to stand his ground as he glared back at Rio. But I could tell by the way his Adam's apple was bobbing around in his throat that he wasn't as confident as he was trying to make out.

'What did Davie ever do to you to deserve your disloyalty?' Rio asked through gritted teeth.

Todd maintained eye contact, but he didn't reply.

Rio either didn't know about the dressing-down Dad had given Todd when he found him with his tongue down Kelsey's throat the night before my wedding, or he was calling our former bodyguard's bluff.

'Just as I thought, nothing. The boss paid you a handsome wage and gave you an opportunity other men would give their right arm for, and this is how you thank him.' Rio balled the fabric even tighter than before as he eyeballed Todd. 'What kind of lowlife scum deliberately injects another person with heroin?'

Todd's lips were sealed. He appeared to have lost his tongue and said nothing to defend himself, not that his words would have washed with Rio. There was no viable reason to justify what he'd done to my sister.

'Davie had his doubts about you from day one.' Mum's upper lip curled, and she threw Todd a look of disdain. 'He had a feeling that you weren't trustworthy and was worried that you might turn on the family. My husband was right to be wary of you.'

'We know Oscar Myles was working for you. He told us you paid him to buy the Aston Martin. No doubt because you knew we'd take on the debt from Larry,' Rio said.

'Who's a clever boy then? Not just a pretty face, are you, mate.' Todd laughed.

'We've got the car back, so I don't understand what you were

hoping to get out of that little exercise?' I felt my face fall into
a frown.

'I just wanted to cause you some aggro for old times' sake,'
Todd sneered.

Even though I'd been playing it down, trying to track the car
down had been a massive pain in the arse, so Todd had achieved
what he'd set out to do. Not that I'd share that with him.

'Is that so? Something tells me there's more to it.' Mum
narrowed her blue eyes and bored them into Todd as if trying to
read his innermost thoughts. 'That still doesn't explain why you
injected Kelsey with heroin. I suggest you start talking.'

Mum glanced sideways at Rio, who responded by cranking
the pressure back on Todd's arms. His shoulders looked like they
were close to dislocating, but he was still refusing to speak up.

59

Kelsey

Thanks to Todd, withdrawal symptoms and cravings had become part of my daily life, which made it hard to stop taking the heroin I'd become dependent on. I was trying to be strong, but this wasn't just down to willpower. The pain and physical symptoms I was experiencing were proving impossible to ignore. Even with the dose of methadone the doctor gave me, which was supposed to be a long-acting substitute for heroin, I still craved the real thing.

'How are you feeling, Kelsey?' Dr Burton asked.

Where did I start? I had insomnia, itchy skin and constantly twitched on top of everything else, but my brain felt like it was disintegrating, so it was impossible for me to put my thoughts into words.

'Awful. I can't t-take much more,' I replied, desperately trying not to pick at the open sore by the corner of my mouth.

I completely understood how people risked everything for heroin. It consumed your life whether you wanted it to or not. The sense of euphoria and oblivion it used to give me had faded away, and now I didn't feel normal without it.

'I'm afraid this is only the beginning; your symptoms will only get worse in the coming days,' Dr Burton said.

'C-can you g-give me some m-more methadone?' My teeth were chattering, so it was hard to speak.

I was shocked to hear the undertone of desperation in my

voice. I'd sworn I wouldn't go near the stuff again, but I had to do something to take away the pain.

Dr Burton nodded. 'Methadone will help to stabilise your symptoms, but heroin is a central nervous system depressant, and it's changed the structure of the reward pathway in your brain, which is why it's going to be hard for you to quit on your own.'

Mum stood in the corner of the room with the fingers of her right hand pressed to her lips as though she couldn't trust herself not to speak out. I knew how she felt about it, but I had to do what was right for me. Her eyes were fixed on the doctor as he produced the bottle from his bag. I watched her out of the corner of my eye as he put it on my bedside table and carefully poured the green liquid up to the line on the plastic cup.

'You need to reconsider getting professional help if you want to overcome your habit. Becoming an inpatient on a dedicated programme is the best chance you'll have to beat the addiction.'

Dr Burton's words were like a slap around the face. It was crystal clear that he wasn't in the business of sugar-coating anything; he just told it as it was. But what he'd said was hard to swallow.

'I can recommend an excellent treatment centre with a brilliant track record for dealing with issues like yours. Patients are medically assisted and closely monitored to ensure the detox process is as comfortable as possible. The sooner you get on the programme, the easier all of this will be.' Dr Burton fixed his eyes on mine to apply some extra pressure.

I wanted to push against him, but I could feel myself start to buckle. Dr Burton must have sensed that I was starting to come around to the idea because he began chipping away again.

'Tolerance to heroin builds quickly, which you already know, and as users increase their doses, they become at greater risk of a fatal overdose,' Dr Burton said.

'Why are you telling her this? She's not even taking heroin anymore,' Mum piped up.

'Maybe not, but you're underestimating how hard it will be for Kelsey to kick the habit. Her withdrawal symptoms are going to get much worse in the coming days, so she's at real risk of relapsing.'

'We won't let that happen,' Mum said.

The doctor threw my mum a look before he continued to speak. 'It doesn't matter how good a support network a person has around them; addicts find a way to get back on heroin. Trust me; you're not qualified to deal with this. It would be like me putting a plaster on a severed limb after a shark attack.'

Dr Burton's words left a chill in the air. They were a wake-up call, and it suddenly hit home that I was walking a very fine line. Heroin had stripped me of everything. I wanted to get it out of my system before it was too late. I didn't want to end up dead. Deep down, I realised I needed to go to rehab. But that didn't change the fact that I didn't want to.

Rio pulled the car up outside a nondescript-looking building nestled down a side street in the heart of London. My mum and sisters were by my side as I made my way to the reception, where a young nurse greeted me with a smile. The place felt like a dental surgery. And to be perfectly honest, at this moment in time, I'd rather volunteer for a root canal than embark on the detox programme Dr Burton had prescribed for me. I wished I was anywhere other than here.

Tempted as I was to turn around and head back out of the door, I had to stay strong. This didn't just affect me. My family were suffering too. I could see the pain in their eyes as they tried their best to support me. Heroin would destroy me if I let it. The worst thing about battling addiction was that I hadn't taken drugs out of choice. They'd been forced on me in a depraved act of revenge. And now I was stuck in what felt like a never-ending cycle.

'Good morning. How can I help you?' the nurse asked.

Suddenly feeling paranoid, I looked around to see if anyone was listening. 'Our doctor has booked my daughter in for some treatment,' Mum replied.

I was glad she hadn't gone into details as I found the idea of being a junkie hugely embarrassing. Even though we were the only people in the reception area, I was acutely aware of how judgemental people could be where drug addiction was concerned.

'What's your name, please?'

'K-k-kelsey S-saunders.'

The nurse looked at her computer screen. 'Oh yes. You're on the twenty-eight-day treatment programme.'

'T-twenty-eight days!' I turned towards Mum with a look of horror on my face.

'I thought it was possible to detox in a week,' Mum said before she cast her eyes to the floor as a wave of embarrassment washed over her. I was on the verge of walking out. I hadn't prepared myself for a shock like that, and in my fragile state of mind, I wasn't sure I could cope with being lied to.

'Sometimes it is, but being heroin-free doesn't mean the patient's been cured. To overcome your daughter's problem, the team will need to get to the root of what made her take drugs in the first place,' the nurse said.

A vision of Todd jumped into my head. If my speech hadn't kept coming out so disjointed, I'd have been tempted to tell her exactly what had happened to me. But trying to communicate with people was hard work and it wasn't going to achieve anything, so I buttoned my lip and stayed silent.

'The programme is quite intensive. During the next month, you'll take part in group and family therapy sessions, and you'll also receive intensive counselling on a one-to-one basis.'

The nurse was doing her best to sell it to me, but I couldn't think of anything worse than discussing something so private with a bunch of people I'd never met before. How could I participate in the sessions if I couldn't string a coherent sentence together? It would be almost impossible. This wasn't what I'd signed up for; it felt like an invasion of my human rights. Nobody mentioned being forced to attend group therapy. I'd thought I was just staying here for a week to make the detox process as comfortable as possible.

I'd lost control of everything and felt like I was on the verge of completely falling apart, so I looked at Mum with pleading eyes. My brain wasn't working properly; I needed her to speak up for me and say I wasn't going to enrol on the programme after all, but she wouldn't meet my gaze. She might be choosing to ignore me, but the nurse noticed the panic-stricken expression I was wearing.

'It's perfectly natural to feel anxious. This is the first step in a long journey. But we're here to help you put this destructive behaviour behind you once and for all so that you can begin living the full and happy life you deserve.' The nurse offered me a sympathetic smile.

I scowled back at her. I was no ordinary addict, but I was being treated like one. My mind was in turmoil. I was desperate to protest, but I was finding it impossible to express myself. I couldn't seem to push the words out, which was a totally new experience for me as I'd never struggled to make myself understood before. I'd underestimated the power of speech until I'd lost the ability to communicate what I wanted to say. I'd become a prisoner trapped inside my body.

The frustration was overwhelming. I felt like dropping to my knees and screaming at the top of my lungs. But what was the point?

60

Mia

Leaving Kelsey at the clinic was weighing heavy on all of our minds. Scarlett was taking refuge in her room. Mum and I were in the office trying to distract ourselves with work when Rio appeared on the other side of the glass. Now that it was mid-September, there was a slight chill in the air, so we'd closed the doors for the first time in weeks. Mum gestured for him to come inside with a wave of her hand.

'What's wrong?' Mum asked. Her forehead furrowed as she stared at him.

It was clear by the look on Rio's face that something was troubling him.

'I'm so sorry, Amanda, I've ballsed up big time.' Rio's shoulders slumped.

'What's happened?' Mum tilted her head to the side and waited for him to continue.

'The line that geezer fed me was a load of old flannel.' Rio shook his head.

'I'm afraid you've lost me. Which geezer are you talking about?' Mum bit down on the corner of her lip.

'Al Dempsey.'

'Now there's a surprise,' Mum replied, and I felt a shiver run down my spine.

'This came from a reliable source, so I have it on good authority that Al didn't want the money he borrowed from the firm to expand his knocked-off clothing empire,' Rio said. His dark brown eyes darted back and forth between Mum and me.

Mum shook her head, then folded her arms across her chest. 'What did he want it for?'

The familiar feeling of dread started to rise up from the pit of my stomach.

'The fucker used it to buy heroin,' Rio replied.

'Oh, for God's sake! You can't be serious,' Mum snapped before she closed her eyes and took a few deep breaths, letting Rio's bombshell sink in.

His words rattled around in my head for a moment or two, and when they finally registered, all I could think of was what Jack's reaction would be. He was going to be furious that Al Dempsey had taken us for a ride and possibly stung us for a huge amount of money. I had to put that out of my mind; I could feel myself becoming overwhelmed by the situation. The only way to stop that from happening was to break the problem into small pieces and deal with them one by one. Oh, and breathe, never forget to breathe.

'Are you OK, Mia? You're very pale.'

I looked up at the sound of Mum's voice and realised she was standing over me.

'I'm fine; I'm just a bit shocked.'

'That makes two of us.' Mum turned around to face Rio. 'How could you let this happen?'

Rio hung his head in shame, and my heart went out to him.

'I hate the idea of the firm's name being linked to heroin. Davie always stayed well clear of anything drug-related. He never entertained dealers; thought they were the dregs of society,' Mum said.

She was really giving Rio a hard time, which was out of character for her. They normally had each other's backs, but she obviously felt very strongly about what had happened. I almost felt like I was intruding on a private conversation and considered leaving them to it, but curiosity kept me rooted to the spot.

'I know how Davie would have felt about this cock-up. That's why I feel so bad about it,' Rio said, meeting my mum's glare before he bowed his head again.

'I'm still trying to get my head around the fact that Kelsey's in rehab without this latest drama. It's one thing after another. When's it going to end?' Mum's eyes were glistening with tears. She'd had as much as she could take.

'I'm so sorry, Amanda. I feel like a complete moron for letting him get one over on me.' Rio wore the expression of a man who'd forgotten to do the lottery the night his numbers would have turned him into a multi-millionaire.

Mum didn't reply, making an already tense situation even worse. My heart was breaking for Rio. He'd been nothing but loyal to our family over the years, and I didn't think he needed to be taken on a guilt trip. It was clear he couldn't have felt worse than he already did. Rio had made a mistake, but if it hadn't been for him, the firm would have crumbled after Dad's life was cut short. Without him, we wouldn't have had the knowledge or experience to keep the business going. So, as far as I was concerned, we owed him big time.

Mum adored Rio, so I was surprised she was giving him such an earful. But she was so stressed out about Kelsey she was venting her anger and taking her frustration out on him instead.

Mum stood in silence, mulling things over, chewing on her bottom lip, so Rio flicked his dark eyes towards mine. I gave him a sympathetic smile. We stared at each other for several seconds, and then he turned away. Rio straightened his posture and clasped his hands one over the other in front of his stomach.

'I don't know what to say. I'm so disappointed in you.' Mum shook her head, and hostility rolled off her in waves.

'I'm so sorry I've let you down, Amanda.' Rio paused. A moment later, he took a deep breath and continued speaking. 'There's no easy way to say this, but it wouldn't be fair to keep you in the dark...'

While Rio swallowed the lump stuck in his throat, I glanced

over at Mum. Her eyes were fixed on him, unblinking as she braced herself for what he was about to say.

'For God's sake, just spit it out, Rio.' Mum's tone was abrupt as impatience got the better of her.

'The heroin that Al bought was stolen,' Rio said.

Rio's words appeared to bounce around the space between us, and my head felt like it was about to explode.

Mum gasped and then grabbed onto the side of the desk to steady herself. 'What do you mean the heroin was stolen?'

'It belonged to a gang who'd imported it all the way from Afghanistan, so as you can imagine, they're not best pleased,' Rio said.

'How on earth did Al Dempsey get his grubby little hands on it? I wouldn't have thought he'd be clever enough to outsmart a professional operation,' Mum replied.

'I know what you mean,' Rio agreed. 'To be honest with you, I think it fell into his lap. Word has it that the lorry driver double-crossed the original gang. He'd been paid to bring the consignment from Rotterdam to Hull and then deliver it to the Wilkinsons, who pretty much run the West Yorkshire scene, but armed men mysteriously intercepted it before it arrived. The gang are baying for blood quite rightly. They've put money on the heads of anyone involved.'

'So Al's put himself in the firing line,' Mum said.

'Well and truly,' Rio nodded.

'It serves him right.' I shook my head. I didn't have any sympathy for the man.

'That's true, but he's also implicated us because we lent him the money…'

'But the loan was to expand his clothing line, not to buy class-A drugs.' My breath caught in my throat, which made my voice wobble.

'The gang don't care about that. As far as they're concerned, we're every bit as guilty.'

It was as though Rio had sounded the death knell. Mum's

face crumpled, and she began to cry. She'd had enough bad news to last her a lifetime. Rio rushed to comfort her, but she placed her hands on his broad chest and pushed him away. He looked genuinely hurt by her rejection. Rio had been Mum's rock since Dad had gone. He was the first person she turned to when she needed help. I could see how much her action had hurt him, but I didn't know what to do, so I stood where I was, staring blankly at Rio as the implications of Al's stupidity bounced around in my head.

'How could you let this happen?' Mum blurted out through her tears.

I rushed over to her and threw my arms around her. Mum began sobbing into my shoulder.

'Maybe you could leave us alone for a bit. I think Mum needs some space to try and take all of this in,' I said, offering Rio a sympathetic smile.

Despite what had happened, this wasn't his fault. Mum would realise that when the shock wore off.

61

Kelsey

'It lacks a few home comforts, but it's nice enough,' Scarlett said when she walked into my private room. 'Stainless steel and flat surfaces are easy to clean, but they make the place a bit clinical, don't they? Anyway, that's enough about that. I sound like Kirstie Allsopp rabbiting on. Let's talk about something much more important. How are you feeling?'

'D-d-do you want me to t-t-tell you the truth?'

Scarlett nodded, and the sun bounced off her copper-coloured hair.

'I'm in a-agony,' I said as crippling pain ripped through my body.

'I remember what that was like,' Scarlett said, running her fingertips across her stomach. 'Up until recently, I had to remember to engage my core just so that I could stand up, sit down or move about without flinching.'

'I f-feel like I've l-lost everything...' The tone of my voice sounded flat as I let my sentence trail off.

'I know. It's as though your whole world's crumbling around you, and there's not a thing you can do about it,' Scarlett said.

A pang of guilt stabbed at my conscience. I'd been so caught up in myself I'd almost forgotten what my younger sister had been through.

'It might seem hard at the moment, but you'll get through this,' Scarlett said.

I wasn't sure I believed her. There was so much more I wanted to say, but my brain wouldn't cooperate. The words were fully formed in my head. The problem was I couldn't get them to come out of my mouth. 'Honestly, you will, but you have to stay strong.' Scarlett walked towards me, caught hold of my hand and squeezed it.

Scarlett was doing her best to lift me, but I was at rock bottom. there was more to beating an addiction than willpower alone. Heroin was such a potent drug that it interfered with how your brain experienced pleasure and pain, so people took it just to feel normal. That option had been taken away from me, and even though I was undergoing the best treatment that money could buy, I was still struggling to kick the habit.

'You can do this, Kelsey. We're all rooting for you.' Scarlett smiled.

She tightened her grip, willing me to fight with every fibre of my being. I was glad the clinic allowed me to have contact with my family. Knowing they were behind me was definitely boosting my desire to get better. But it was so hard; even the methadone couldn't keep the cravings at bay. It did help. It gave me feelings of warmth, relaxation and detachment while relieving my anxiety. But it wasn't enough; my body was begging for the only relief that would stop my heart from racing with every beat.

'I'm n-not sure I can d-do this,' I said, shaking my head.

'I know it feels impossible right now, but dig deep,' Scarlett said, locking eyes with me.

I felt the waves of pity coming off her, which made tears well up in my eyes. I tried to tap into Scarlett's power of positive thinking, but it was hard to quash the feelings of hopelessness surrounding me. It had been days since I'd last taken heroin, and there didn't seem to be any end in sight to the withdrawal symptoms. I was still sweating profusely. My skin was crawling, I was cramping all over, and I felt like I was going to vomit.

'This won't be a quick fix. You're not going to get better in a couple of days. It's a marathon, not a sprint. But one way or another, you'll beat this. I know you will. Kelsey Saunders isn't a quitter.' Scarlett's cheerleading skills were being put to work. 'I'll be right by your side, but you have to try and stay positive. Take baby steps, so you don't get overwhelmed by things.'

'That's all I'm capable of doing.'

I wiped my tears away with the back of my hand. It was good to know, after everything we'd been through, Scarlett was here for me.

62

Mia

'You've got enough to worry about at the moment. Why don't you let me sort this mess out?' Jack's blue eyes bored into mine as he stood opposite my desk.

'Thanks, but there's no need.'

When he'd walked into the office a moment earlier, my heart had sunk at the sight of him. I'd been expecting an 'I told you so' lecture, but he'd done nothing of the sort. Jack seemed genuinely concerned by our predicament rather than worrying about money for once.

I glanced sideways at Mum to gauge her reaction, but she was staring into space. It was clear her mind was elsewhere. As expected, Jack had come riding in on his white horse when he'd heard about Al Dempsey, offering to sort things out, but I didn't want him to think we couldn't deal with the situation ourselves. I'd been hoping I'd have a bit of time to come up with a solution before he'd found out, but bad news had a habit of travelling fast when you didn't want it to.

'Seriously, Mia, you should just focus on spending time with Kelsey and let me handle the business. You'll only stress yourself out if you try and take on too much. We both know difficult situations like this trigger your anxiety.'

Jack's eyebrows knitted together. I knew he had my best interests at heart, but I'd feel like a complete failure if I did as he'd asked. 'You've got yourselves into a very serious situation, and you're in way over your heads. I'm not trying to undermine your authority, but I'm really worried about this.'

By being so vocal about his concerns, Jack was unintentionally heightening my fears.

'We're dealing with it, Jack,' I replied.

Although his intentions were good, I didn't appreciate Jack implying that Mum and I lacked the skills, knowledge, or resources to sort out the problem, even though I knew there was a fair chance that we did indeed lack the skills, knowledge and resources to dig ourselves out of the hole.

'How are you dealing with it, Mia? I'd love to know.' Jack put his hands on his hips. He'd started off with a softly-softly approach, but his tone was becoming firmer by the minute.

Heat rose up the back of my neck as I felt the weight of his stare. I sank my teeth into my bottom lip. I didn't want to answer his question.

'You haven't thought that far ahead, have you?' Jack paused and ran his fingers through his thick honey-blond hair. 'Well, I'm afraid burying your head in the sand isn't going to work this time.'

Talk about knocking my confidence; Jack's words hadn't just nudged it, they'd caused it to nosedive. I got up from my desk and walked over to the glass doors. I needed some air. The room suddenly felt claustrophobic, so I slid the handle back to allow the fresh September breeze inside. I stood in the opening, filling my lungs when Jack appeared next to me. He turned me towards him and held me at arm's length so that he could look into my face.

'Come on, Mia don't take offence. I'm not having a go at you, I'm trying to help you,' Jack said.

That was easy for him to say, but he was making me doubt myself.

'I'm sorry. I shouldn't have spoken to you like that. But I hate watching you struggle when there's a simple solution. I'd be only too pleased to take this off your hands,' Jack offered.

'I know, but honestly, we're going to sort it. We just need a bit of time to decide the best way to handle things.' I smiled.

'Taking a back seat would be a good place to start. Why are you pushing me away? We're both on the same side. Let me take the pressure off you. Spend some time with Kelsey and start to build bridges with Scarlett instead.' Jack was doing his best to persuade me.

'If I walk away, I'll lose face and then everything I've worked for will have been for nothing.'

Surely Jack understood that.

'You don't know what you're taking on. This situation is too dangerous for you to be involved in.' Jack fixed me with a look.

'Give me some credit. I'm not going to wade in unprepared.'

Things were getting heated between us. I hated arguing. Like Mum, I chose my battles wisely. But even though I didn't like confrontation, I pushed myself out of my comfort zone where business was concerned.

'I appreciate your offer, but I need to deal with this myself. I know you weren't happy we went ahead and lent Al the money without running it past you first, so I feel responsible. Especially now the firm's lost two hundred and fifty thousand pounds,' I said, breaking eye contact with Jack.

'Listen to me.' Jack put his finger under my chin and tilted my face towards his. 'Recovering outstanding money isn't always possible. Sometimes you just have to walk away. You can't put a price on a person's safety.'

'I couldn't agree more, but I'm surprised to hear you say that. You normally have such a tight hold on the purse strings.'

Jack rolled his eyes. 'Thanks for the compliment. You're making me sound like Scrooge.'

'I didn't mean it like that, but it's your job to balance the books, and a quarter of a million is such a lot of...'

'Don't worry about the money,' Jack cut in, stopping me mid-flow. 'Your safety comes first. What kind of a husband would I be if I didn't step in and help at a time like this? I know it's old-fashioned, but believe me, you need to let the men handle this. I promised your dad I'd look after you, and I fully intend to keep my word.'

Mum looked up at the mention of Dad's name, so I glanced over at her.

'I know most of the time you're more than capable, but this is one occasion where you won't be taken seriously, Mia.' Jack's words hovered between us.'

'Do you know how infuriating it is to be undermined?' I said through gritted teeth.

'I'm not trying to undermine you. I'm trying to protect you from a bunch of violent thugs. We need to let Rio front this. They'll think twice about crossing paths with him. Everyone knows he can switch his aggression on at the drop of a hat. You'd have to go a long way to find somebody with a more powerful swing than he has, and his height and long reach give him an advantage over most people,' Jack said.

'He's right, Mia: we should stay in the background,' Mum piped up, and the sudden sound of her voice made me jump.

I was kicking myself for reacting, but what could I say? I startled easily. Being naturally anxious wasn't ideal in a situation like this. I knew Jack had noticed, and I didn't want to give him any more ammunition.

'We can still be involved with the planning, though,' Mum said to soften the blow.

'I take it Todd and Oscar are being held at your dad's HQ?' Jack trained his blue eyes on me and tilted his head to one side while he waited for me to reply.

I couldn't trust myself to speak. I was still seething, and on the verge of bursting into tears, so I nodded instead.

'We need to deal with the mess Al Dempsey's landed us in ASAP. I'm going to talk to Rio. I'll see you later.' Jack placed a kiss on my cheek.

I had to stop myself from wiping it away with the back of my hand. I didn't appreciate being cut out of the equation one little bit, but that wasn't going to stop Jack from taking charge now that Mum had voiced her opinion and given him the green light. The tension lingered in the air long after he'd walked out of the office. I sat back down at my desk, pretending to be engrossed in something on my screen to stop myself from looking daggers at Mum until I calmed down.

63

Mia

The sound of the phone ringing interrupted my thoughts.

'Hello,' Mum said, answering the call.

It was the first time either of us had spoken since Jack had left. We'd sat behind our desks for hours, doing our best to ignore one another.

'That's fine by me. OK, we'll see you soon.' Mum put the phone down and then glanced over at me. 'Rio and Darius are bringing Al over. He wants to talk to us. They'll be here in a minute. I'm going to make a coffee. Would you like one?'

'No thanks,' I replied, trying to keep the sulkiness out of my voice.

Mum went to the coffee machine and placed one of the large white cups on the platform before hitting the button for a cappuccino. I saw Rio come into view as the unit sprang to life.

'We've got company,' I said, bouncing my knee under the desk.

'I'm sorry for all the trouble I've caused,' Al began. He paused for a moment, but when none of us acknowledged his apology, he continued talking. 'I should have known better than to get involved in the drugs game, but the guy I bought the gear off was practically giving the stuff away.'

There was something about this man that made me see red. I couldn't decide if it was the chunky gold signet ring he wore on his little finger or the way his thinning hair skimmed his shiny forehead. Whatever it was, I couldn't bear the sight of him, and that made a fire start in my belly. I probably should be acting with a calm business head, but he'd pushed me too far, so I was going to let Al have it with both barrels loaded.

'You're pathetic, do you know that? And now, thanks to you, the Wilkinsons are gunning for us,' I said without allowing him to reply as my pent-up frustration poured out of me.

Al held his hands up in front of him. 'I'm sorry about that, sweets. I wasn't expecting them to track me down.'

'If you didn't want the Wilkinsons to come knocking on your door, you shouldn't have flooded the market with their gear. It's not rocket science.' Rio shook his head.

'What can I say? I fucked up. But the guy I bought it from told me to shift it quickly. And anyway, I still don't get why they're giving you a hard time, chief. Their beef's with me, not you.' Al stared at Rio with a blank expression on his face as beads of sweat started running down his temples.

'The Saunders firm lent you the money.' Rio held on to each word to drive the message home.

Al looked like somebody had rammed a red-hot poker between the cheeks of his arse when the penny finally dropped.

'Our firm's lost a quarter of a million because of you.' I pointed my finger in Al's face as he craned his neck to look up at me. 'What are we meant to do? Chalk it up to experience?'

'I swear to you, I'm good for the money. Now that I've sold the gear, I've got a huge pile of cash. I'll pay you back every penny, but you've got to keep the Wilkinsons away from me,' Al begged.

'You're expecting protection?' Al's cheek was astounding. He'd double-crossed us, and now he was expecting our help. 'Your welfare is the least of my concerns.'

'Let me give you some advice. Try engaging your brain before you open your gob in future. Now I think you've taken up enough of the ladies' time. You and Darius should take a walk,' Rio said, pushing his shoulders back.

'Whatever you say, chief,' Al replied before trailing down the garden path in the shadow of Rio's nephew.

'From the moment I clapped eyes on him, I never liked that man,' Mum said.

'I know what you mean. He's a dirty little rat,' Rio agreed.

As we watched Al and Darius fade into the distance, a thought suddenly popped into my head. 'Do you remember Todd said he'd got the heroin he gave Kelsey on the cheap?'

Mum and Rio nodded.

'You don't think he bought it from Al Dempsey, do you?'

'You might be right. Oscar delivered Todd a package, but he said he didn't know what was in it. That might be true, but he could have been covering for Todd. There's only one way to find out. Can I bring Todd here, or would you rather not see him?' Rio asked, fixing his eyes on Mum.

'I suppose I can grin and bear being in his company if it means we get some answers,' Mum replied.

I understood where she was coming from. I was barely able to tolerate the sight of him either.

'Where did you buy the heroin?' I asked when Rio brought Todd into the office.

'It seems to have slipped my mind.' Todd raised his eyebrows as cockiness rolled off him in waves.

'Did you buy it from a man called Al Dempsey?'

My heart was galloping in my chest. Todd looked straight through me and didn't reply.

'What's Oscar got to do with all of this?' The tone of my voice was raised. I was becoming more frustrated by the minute.

'Oscar?' Todd threw me a look of confusion.

'He told Rio he was delivering you a package when the Aston Martin was spotted. My guess would be it contained heroin. Am I right?' My eyes bored into Todd's.

'Now that would be telling.' Todd smirked in an act of defiance.

'Right, we can do this the easy way or the hard way; it's your choice. But if you've got any sense, you'll start talking,' Rio said, wrenching Todd's handcuffed arms up behind his back.

Todd's yell went straight through me, and my forearms broke out in goose pimples.

'All right, I'll tell you. I guess you're going to find out sooner or later, but I want the restraints taken off first,' Todd replied.

When I gave Rio the nod, he walked over to Mum's desk and took a pair of scissors out of her stationery organiser. A moment later, he freed Todd. The two men stood eyeballing each other as Todd rubbed the skin on his wrists.

'Did you buy the heroin from Al Dempsey?' I asked again, prompting Todd to speak.

'No. He bought it from me.' The corners of Todd's mouth stretched into a big grin.

My eyes swept between Rio and Mum, but they looked as confused as I was.

'What do you mean Al bought it from you?' Rio asked. 'Did you intercept the gear when the ship docked in Hull?'

Todd shook his head. 'The Colemans did.'

Todd's words bounced around the room. I could barely believe what I'd just heard. We'd thought we'd defeated this family, but our oldest enemies were coming back to haunt us.

'So, how did you get hold of it?' My head was spinning. I wasn't sure I wanted to know the answer to my question.

'I'll tell you, but I need to cut myself a deal. I'll give you the full version, warts and all, once I'm a free man. And I want the Aston Martin thrown in as a thank you,' Todd said, laying down the terms of his agreement.

If we let him go, he was likely to go underground and then we'd never find out the truth. I glanced over at Rio. I didn't know where to go from here.

'I'll get Darius to bring the car to Coalhouse Fort. We'll meet him there,' Rio said, sweeping his eyes between Mum and me.

I felt sick to my stomach that we were negotiating with the lowlife scum who had ruined Kelsey's life. I couldn't believe Rio had agreed to Todd's demands and I felt like making my objections heard. But I was sure he had a plan even though he hadn't shared it with us, so I'd have to trust his judgement.

Todd sat in the front passenger seat of the Range Rover with his wrists and ankles bound. I was directly behind him, aiming a .22 calibre revolver at the back of his head, when Rio pulled into the disused landfill site. I hadn't been to East Tilbury for some time, and as I watched the smoke from the industrial chimneys snake its way into the sky and the fine mist roll off the water, giving the place an eerie feel, a shiver ran down my spine. It was hard to believe this was one of my dad's favourite childhood haunts. It gave me the creeps. I pulled down the sleeves of my long-sleeved T-shirt and wished I'd brought a jacket. But we'd left in such a hurry I hadn't given it much thought.

Darius got out of the Aston Martin as our car drew closer, crunching over the muddy surface littered with bits of broken rubbish from decades past. Once Rio turned off the engine, I glanced over at Mum. She was a million miles away, staring into space, her mind on other things.

'We're here,' I said, touching her arm gently to get her attention.

Mum turned towards me a gave me a half-smile, but her blue eyes seemed glazed over.

'I'll take it from here, Mia,' Rio said, looking over his broad shoulder at me before he pulled his gun out of his jacket and pointed it at Todd.

We stepped out of the car, and I wrapped my arms around myself. There was a definite chill in the air. It was several degrees colder than it had been in our sun-trap of an office, but nobody else seemed to notice. They were probably too wired with adrenaline to feel the cold.

As Todd swung his legs out of the car, Rio tucked his gun into the waistband of his trousers. Then he crouched down in front of him to cut off the restraint.

'Let's get this over and done with, shall we? Start talking,' Rio said, pulling Todd to his feet.

'Not so fast. I think you're forgetting a few things.' Todd held his bound hands out in front of him. 'All of you need to put your weapons down over there.' Todd gestured with a flick of his head to an empty pallet a distance from where we were standing. 'And I'm going to need the car keys.'

Rio cut the cable ties off Todd's wrists before taking our guns over to the pallet.

'I left the keys in the ignition,' Darius said as he went to put down his weapon too.

'You don't mind if I check, do you?' Todd smiled.

'Anyone would think you didn't trust us,' Rio replied.

We stood in an awkward huddle as Todd walked over to the blue sports car, pulled open the driver's door and peered inside. Once he was happy the keys were there, he sauntered back to us, wearing a smug expression implying he was holding all the cards.

'I've been working for Lorraine Coleman for some time now,' Todd began.

It didn't particularly surprise me that Todd had joined the opposition.

'Really? I never thought she'd have the guts to carry on the firm without Victor and Craig,' Rio replied.

Hearing Victor's name made me picture him inside the shipping container to the right of where we were standing. Rio had blown a hole through the back of his head with a pump-action shotgun. The memory of the gaping wound was as clear today as when it had happened, and if I lived to be one hundred, I doubted I'd ever be able to erase it from my mind.

'Were you part of the team that robbed the shipment?' I asked.

'No. But Lorraine told me to offer it to Al at a price he

couldn't refuse. And I did, but I couldn't resist siphoning some off as a little treat for Kelsey,' Todd said. 'Until the opportunity with Lorraine came up, I'd been planning to sell Kelsey to the highest bidder. Davie upset a lot of people over the years, and now that he was no longer in the picture, his rivals were happy to extend the feud they had with him to his family members, so I'd have had plenty of takers if I'd gone down that route.'

I saw Mum bristle out of the corner of my eye. Then my heartbeat speeded up as Jack's warning swam around in my head. I had to calm myself down; I couldn't afford to let my fear distract me before we got to the bottom of things.

'Why did you deliberately target Al?'

'I thought you were cleverer than that, Mia. Do I need to spell it out?'

I stared at Todd with the lights are on, but nobody's home expression on my face, which seemed to delight him.

'Your firm provided Al with the readies, and in the Wilkinsons' eyes, that makes you just as guilty as he is. Lorraine knew they'd come after you too, and after what you did to her husband and son, you can't really blame the woman for wanting to settle the score.' Todd's face stretched into a wide grin.

'How did you know we'd lent Al money?' I narrowed my eyes and fixed them on Todd.

'Let's just say I had an inside source.' Todd's head was swelling by the minute.

Kelsey immediately sprang to mind, but it couldn't have been her. Only Mum, Rio, Darius and myself knew about the arrangement. I turned my attention to Darius. He was the newest member of the team, and I couldn't say I knew him well at all. He was a closed book. I supposed it was possible he'd talked. But as I drank in his appearance, he looked at me with his clear blue Husky eyes, and I knew he hadn't sold us out. He might be quiet, but that didn't mean he wasn't trustworthy. Darius had de Souza blood running through his veins. And loyalty was Rio's strong suit.

'I've told you what you wanted to know, so I'm going to make a move,' Todd said.

As he was about to turn away, Mum pulled a small handgun out of her cardigan pocket. I hadn't realised she was armed until now as she'd concealed it with ease.

'You're not going anywhere,' Mum said, pointing the weapon at him.

Todd started laughing. 'That mouse gun looks like it came out of a Christmas cracker. You're not seriously thinking of shooting me with that, are you?'

'Don't tempt me. I have it on good authority that being shot hurts like a bastard, regardless of the calibre. Would you like to find out?' Mum's eyes bored into Todd's.

While Mum kept Todd occupied, Rio slipped away and retrieved our weapons. Todd let out a loud breath when we all aimed in his direction.

'If you finish me off, you'll never find out who the mole is, will you?'

Todd was hoping to save his own skin, but what he'd said was true. While I was weighing up what to do, Rio lunged and grabbed hold of the front of Todd's top, balling the material around in his fist as he yanked him forward. Then he forced the barrel of his gun under Todd's chin.

'I suggest you start talking,' Rio growled.

'Really? You're going to make me, are you?' Even though he had a weapon pointed at him, cockiness was rolling off Todd in waves.

Rio lowered the gun, then whipped Todd around the side of the head with the barrel several times. I felt myself flinch as the metal connected with his skull, sending chunks of flesh flying through the air.

'You fucking bastard,' Todd yelled as blood started running down the side of his face.

Rio dug his weapon back under Todd's chin as they stood eyeballing each other.

'Who told you about the loan?' I asked when I saw Rio's jaw lock.

I could tell he was moments away from losing it and I didn't want him to get carried away and beat the crap out of Todd before he'd answered the question. Rio was desperate to tear Todd apart. There was so much bad blood between them. You could almost see the hatred radiating between them.

'If you're going to kill me anyway, I might as well ruin your lives before you take mine.'

Todd paused and the air became heavy with tension. Rio cocked the trigger; his patience was wearing thin.

'Wait,' I shouted. 'Come on, Todd, put us out of our misery.'

Todd grinned. 'Jack's the leak in your firm.'

It was hard to imagine how a few words could cause such catastrophic devastation.

'My Jack?' I asked the question, but I didn't want to know the answer.

'Yes.' Todd's smile widened.

'I don't believe you. Why would he want to sell us out? He's part of the family,' I said.

'Call it a conflict of interests,' Todd replied.

'Come again?' Rio looked as baffled as I was.

'Lorraine Coleman's his mum.'

When Todd delivered the shocking piece of information, my head began to spin. The last thing I remembered was my knees buckling before everything went black.

64

Scarlett

'What's going on?' I asked when I walked into the kitchen and saw Mum, Mia, Rio and Darius huddled around the table.

When they turned to face me, I fully expected them to make their excuses and disperse, but that wasn't what happened, and you could have knocked me down with a feather.

'You'd better sit down,' Mum said.

I pulled out a chair opposite Mia, and the first thing I noticed was the fact that she'd been crying. Her head was bowed, and she was doing her best to hide behind her hair, but her skin, which looked paler than usual, was covered in blotches, and her eyes were red-rimmed. A dead giveaway if you asked me.

'What's up, Mia? You look like death.' I slid my hand over the table towards her, but she backed away and lowered her chin further.

'She fainted earlier, so she still looks a bit peaky,' Mum replied.

'Fainted? Why?' I was genuinely concerned for my older sister.

'She's had a bit of a shock. Well, we all have, actually. Jack's been telling the Colemans confidential information about the firm.' Mum's words poured out of her mouth like water from a tap.

'Why the hell would he do that?' I fixed Mum with a puzzled expression.

'Todd said his mum's Lorraine Coleman.' Mum glanced at Rio, who looked like he was chewing on a wasp.

'No way.' I felt my mouth drop open like a ventriloquist dummy. 'That can't be right; we met Jack's mum at the wedding, and I'm pretty sure she was called Nancy.'

Mia let out a loud sob.

'Don't cry, darling. We've only got Todd's word on this, and we all know he can't be trusted, so it might turn out to be complete rubbish,' Mum said, holding the palms of her hands up in front of her.

My mind started working overtime. Lorraine told me she'd given birth to her first child when she was fifteen, which had made me think CJ must have an older brother or sister. I hadn't dwelled on the matter because I hadn't for one moment thought it might be Jack. If I was Mum, I wouldn't be too quick to dismiss what Todd had said.

'What are you going to do?' I asked.

'We're waiting for Jack to come home and shed some light on the matter.'

The words had barely left Mum's mouth when we heard a key in the door. Moments later, Jack was standing in the kitchen, gawping at us.

'What's wrong, Mia?' Jack crouched down by her side and took hold of her hands.

Mia's lips trembled, but no words came out of her mouth. Jack tore his eyes away from her, and he looked at each one of us in turn.

'Is somebody going to tell me what's wrong with my wife?' Jack seemed bewildered.

'Todd told us you've been feeding him confidential information,' Mum said, looking daggers at her son-in-law.

I could see Mia was willing him to say that wasn't true.

'Why the hell would I do that?' Jack stood up and placed his hands on his hips as he glared at Mum.

'Because Lorraine Coleman's your mum.' Mum got straight to the point, openly accusing him of lying.

Jack was so startled he almost stumbled backwards. 'She's what?'

'You heard. What have you got to say for yourself? We're all dying to hear, aren't we?' Rio's eyes swept the room.

'Since when did I have to answer to you? It's so obvious Todd's out to cause trouble, yet here you all are, happy to believe the crap he's fed you,' Jack fired back before he went to storm out of the house.

'Where the fuck do you think you're going?' Rio shouted before clamping his hand down on Jack's shoulder and spinning him around to face us.

'If you ask me, Jack knows he's been caught out. I'm almost certain he's putting on a front. The tone of his voice and his body language makes me think Todd's definitely the one telling the truth,' I said without letting on that I was the one with insider knowledge this time.

Lorraine hadn't mentioned Jack by name, but after hearing this, I was convinced he was the love child she'd been referring to.

'How can you believe Todd over Jack? The man's scum.' Mia looked horrified by what I'd just said.

'I know he is. But Jack's also looking fairly dodgy from where I'm standing,' I replied.

Mia's eyes grew wide, and her mouth dropped open. 'Why are you being so nasty?'

'That's enough, Scarlett.' Mum threw me a look, warning me to back off.

I wasn't trying to be a bitch, but I didn't want Jack to worm his way out of this.

'Please, Jack, tell me it's not true.' Mia clutched her hands over her chest before she burst into tears again.

Mia had always been fragile, but she seemed even more so than usual as she stood opposite her husband, the man she referred to as her rock, waiting for him to tell his side of the story. She looked drained and tired. Her skin was almost translucent. I knew by the way she kept wringing her hands that she was stressed out of her mind. If Jack was innocent, why didn't he just put her out of her misery? He should be outraged and spouting words in his defence, not silent. The fact that he was reluctant to speak made me think he was trying to buy himself some time so that he could come up with a viable explanation. Good luck with that, I thought.

'Why the long pause?' Rio asked.

'I need to know what's going on. Just tell me the truth.' Mia fixed her tear-filled eyes on Jack, but he wouldn't meet her gaze.

'I'm sorry, Mia, I know you don't want to hear this, but I have a sixth sense when it comes to sniffing out a liar, and I think your hubby's been less than honest with us,' Rio said.

65

Mia

It was all getting too much for me. The general consensus in the room was that Jack was guilty, but I didn't want to consider the possibility that Todd might be telling the truth. I wanted to believe Jack because if Lorraine Coleman was my mother-in-law, my whole relationship was built on a lie.

Without saying a word to anyone, I pushed my chair back from the table and started to walk towards the back door. I needed some space. I couldn't think straight and was in danger of losing the plot.

'Mia, where are you going?' Mum called after me.

'I need some fresh air.'

I'd planned to sit alone by the pool, stare into the blue depths, and enjoy the solitude as I attempted to switch off from the earlier conversation so that I didn't overanalyse it. But despite my best efforts to shake them from my head, Rio's words stayed with me. I'd barely reached the water's edge when I decided it was time to get things out in the open. If anyone deserved to question my husband, it was me. I spun around and rushed across the grass towards the office with my heart pounding in my chest. Everyone turned to face me when I pulled open the glass door. I'd been expecting my family to be interrogating Jack, but nobody was speaking.

'We need to talk,' I said, looking Jack straight in the eye. You could cut the atmosphere in the room with a knife.

Jack took a step towards me and went to take hold of my hand, but I moved it just out of his reach.

'I think that's a good idea. Maybe we could go somewhere more private.' Jack's eyes swept around the room.

I shook my head. 'No. I want them to hear what you have to say.'

I was sure this was all a big misunderstanding. It had to be. I trusted my husband and didn't believe for one minute what Todd had said. He was just trying to stir up trouble by bad-mouthing Jack.

'Please, Mia, I want to talk to you on your own first,' Jack said.

'No. I'm not going anywhere.'

I was sticking to my guns. I wanted Jack's accusers to witness first-hand the moment they realised they'd judged him unfairly.

When I heard Jack say, 'Listen, Mia,' I knew I'd made a terrible mistake. My pulse began to race, and I could feel myself start to hyperventilate; this couldn't be happening to me.

'I don't want you to freak out about this.' Jack held his hands up in front of him before he paused to compose himself.

I could feel myself starting to fall to pieces. I wanted to run out of the room, so I didn't have to hear what was coming, but I felt too weak to take a step.

'Lorraine is my mum...'

'Oh my God!' Jack's words hit me with such force they nearly floored me.

'I knew it!' Scarlett shouted out.

'You rotten bastard.' Rio lunged forward and wrapped his huge hand around Jack's windpipe.

'Get off him!' I screamed.

Seeing my husband gasping for air made me spring into action, and I started clawing at Rio's hand until he loosened his grip.

'So Todd was telling the truth.'

My pulse pounded at the side of my neck as the contents of my stomach performed a succession of cartwheels.

'Have you been passing the Colemans confidential information?'

I held my breath. I wasn't sure I wanted to know the answer.

'Of course he has,' Scarlett piped up and then started jabbing her finger in Jack's direction.

I turned at glared at my sister. 'Stay out of this and give him a chance to speak. Well, have you, or haven't you?'

'I'm Lorraine's son, but I swear I haven't been in league with her. Todd's lying about that.'

'Yeah, right,' Scarlett sneered.

'Can you just keep quiet for one minute?' I locked eyes with my sister.

'This is why I wanted us to talk in private,' Jack said and I turned my attention back to him.

'Why didn't you tell me any of this before?'

Jack shrugged.

'What kind of an answer is that? Is that why you tried to persuade me to take a back seat and spend time with Kelsey and Scarlett instead of dealing with the mess Al landed us in?'

'Don't be ridiculous. I was just trying to take the pressure off you because I was worried about your health. I know how anxious you get when you're stressed about something,' Jack replied.

'And finding out you've been hiding a whopping secret like this won't bother Mia in the slightest, will it?'

'Please shut up,' I said.

I didn't look in Scarlett's direction. She was behaving like a deranged heckler, hurling unwanted remarks at Jack every couple of minutes.

'Are you sure you weren't trying to steer me off course so that I didn't work out there was a connection between Todd, the heroin and Lorraine Coleman in case it led me to your door? I'm right, aren't I?'

'This is precisely why I didn't tell you about Lorraine. I knew you'd jump to all sorts of conclusions when nothing untoward was happening.' Jack rolled his eyes.

'So what kind of relationship do you have with Lorraine?' I was shell-shocked that Jack had been able to keep something of this magnitude from me.

Jack looked me in the eye, but he seemed lost for words.

'I need to know what's going on; I think you owe me that much.' My tone was cold.

Jack let out a sigh. 'Lorraine gave birth to me, but she didn't raise me. I hardly know the woman.'

My heart was delighted by what Jack had said, but my head told me to proceed with caution.

'If everything's as innocent as you're making out, why didn't you just come clean?'

'I wish I had, but by the time I found out Lorraine was my mum, I was already working for your dad, and I knew he was arch-enemies with the Colemans, so I decided it was better if I kept her identity buried,' Jack said.

Jack had offered me a feasible explanation, but it wasn't enough. 'I want to know every last detail.'

'And I'm going to tell you everything I know. I'd always thought Dale and Nancy were my parents. It turns out I was wrong. They're my grandparents.'

'Really? They don't seem old enough,' I replied.

'I guess that's what happens when you have your kids young. Nancy was twenty when Mum was born, and Mum was only fifteen when she had me.' Jack let out a sigh.

I could see this was hard for him, but if we were going to put this behind us, I had to understand the background. It struck me as odd that he seemed comfortable calling Lorraine Mum, but he'd suddenly started referring to his grandmother by her first name.

'Mum had been the apple of her dad's eye until she got pregnant by his best friend. By all accounts, there was hell to pay, and she ran off to Spain with Bryan, leaving me behind when I was only three months old.'

That pulled on my heartstrings. I couldn't help it; I was a big softie.

'The romance was doomed, and they split up a year after leaving the UK. Mum rang her parents and begged for their help. She was all alone in a foreign country and desperate to go home, but they told her to stay in Spain. There was nothing for her to come home to, and they never wanted to see her again. Imagine saying that to your daughter.' Jack shook his head. 'It's hardly surprising they've been estranged ever since.'

The picture he was painting was grim, and it played on my conscience that I'd been too quick to jump to conclusions. Always thinking the worst was the habit of a lifetime of mine and not an easy one to break.

'So what happened then? Did Lorraine stay in Spain?' I asked to prompt Jack as he seemed lost in his thoughts.

'Yes. She met Victor Coleman when she was working in a bar in Torremolinos. He was on a stag do with a group of friends, but he was so fixated by her that he couldn't stop thinking about the gorgeous brunette who'd captured his heart after he'd gone home. A couple of months later, he went out on an extended holiday so they could get to know each other better, and she ended up coming back to the UK with him. They got married six months later. Talk about jumping out of the frying pan into the fire. Mum was only seventeen.'

'Did she make contact with Dale and Nancy?' I asked.

'She tried to heal the rift with them, but they refused to have anything more to do with her.' There was a bitterness coating Jack's words.

'And you said you didn't find out that Lorraine was your mum until you'd already started working for Dad.'

'That's right.' Jack nodded.

'If you believe that, you'll believe anything,' Scarlett muttered under her breath, but I was pretty sure everyone in the room heard.

'It's such a sad situation.'

'I know. It must have been awful for Mum. She had to watch me grow up from the shadows. She was scared to rock the boat with Nancy and Dale. But when she found out that I was working for her husband's biggest rival, she contacted me and offered me a job. There was always so much bad blood between the Colemans and the Saunders family. She was worried I might get hurt and reasoned if I was on her side of the fence, she could keep me away from the action to make sure I stayed out of harm's way.'

Jack's confession shocked me to the core. He'd had access to all of my dad's business dealings and handled sensitive information that could have caused chaos if it had fallen into the wrong hands.

'I'm presuming my dad didn't know about your connection to Lorraine.'

'No. As I said earlier, I decided it was best to keep that to myself as I wasn't going to have any contact with her. She was a stranger to me, so my loyalties lay with your dad. And you, of course. You'd already caught my eye, and I didn't want to do anything to mess up my chances.'

Jack reached for my hand, and this time, I let him hold it.

'I'm so sorry, Mia. I didn't want you to find out like this.'

'Why do you think Todd told us about your mum? It doesn't make any sense. He had nothing to gain from it.' I felt my eyebrows settle into a frown.

'By making all of you question my loyalty, it's taken the attention away from him and the way he treated Kelsey. I have to say, I'm surprised, and a bit hurt that any of you gave him airtime, really.' Jack's eyes glanced in Mum's direction.

I bit down on my lip. I felt ashamed that I almost hadn't given Jack the benefit of the doubt. 'I'm sorry I doubted you, Jack. But this all came as such a shock to me I couldn't think straight.'

'I wouldn't be so quick to apologise if I were you. Jack's been blatantly lying to you for years…'

'Oh, for God's sake, Scarlett, why don't you mind your own business?' I burst in, cutting my sister off mid-flow. She was getting right on my nerves.

'I wasn't blatantly lying; I was trying to protect my wife by shielding her from the truth,' Jack said before clenching his jaw.

'Is that so?' Scarlett let out a belly laugh, and I felt myself bristle.

'Now that we've cleared this up, I've got a bit of business to attend to,' Jack said before planting a kiss on my lips.

As he turned to leave, I felt the atmosphere shift.

'You don't mind, do you?' Jack flashed his winning smile, but this time it didn't achieve the desired result.

'I do mind, actually,' Mum said.

She'd been quiet while we'd had our conversation, but I could tell by the tone of her voice that she had things she wanted to discuss.

'Can you take Jack up to the house? I want to talk to the girls,' Mum said to Rio.

'I'd like to give my input. Maybe I could get Darius to drop Jack over to Davie's HQ. What do you think?' The corners of Rio's lips lifted into a small smile, and I felt my heart drop.

'That's an excellent idea,' Mum replied.

66

Scarlett

I was so glad Mum spoke up when she did and stopped Jack from slipping out of the house and disappearing into the ether before we'd had a chance to discuss what he'd said. I was certain Mia would be the only person convinced by his tale of woe. She was a sucker for a sob story and believed anything Jack told her. I wasn't so sure. Now that I knew he was a Coleman, it changed everything. I didn't trust him as far as I could throw him. And I'd be lying if I said it hadn't just crossed my mind that my brother-in-law could have been involved in the attack on me. Not surprisingly, I was highly suspicious of everyone.

'I never thought I'd hear myself say this, but I actually think Todd's more honest than Jack.'

Mia threw me an evil look before she dissolved into floods of tears. I shook my head. It was clear her emotions were all over the place, but she was in danger of losing the plot if she wasn't careful. She was unravelling at the seams in front of us.

'Scarlett, please tone it down,' Mum mouthed before she comforted Mia.

I blew out a breath before I crossed my arms over my chest. I felt like I was walking on eggshells, and all I was trying to do was express my concerns. I didn't want Jack to pull the wool over everyone's eyes. Mia was a lost cause. She thought the sun shone out of his arse. He could tell her black was white, and she'd agree. But I was sure he was up to no good. The Colemans were the enemy, and Jack was one of them.

'I don't understand what your problem is. Jack's explained his connection to Lorraine,' Mia said, wiping her tears away on the back of her hand and fixing me with a glare.

I was about to respond when Mum cut in. 'I know he has, darling, but there's so much bad blood between the Colemans and us; we just need to be sure that he's really on our side.'

Mum was taking the softly-softly approach. The way she always did, handling Mia with kid gloves.

'So you're suspicious of him too?' Mia stood facing Mum; her bottom lip was trembling. An awkward silence stretched out between them before Mia began to speak again. 'Of course he's on our side. He's my husband. He's not going to have chosen his mum over me.'

Mia spat the words out like they were burning her mouth. I hoped for her sake what she'd said was true, but I was cynical when it came to matters of the heart. Once bitten, twice shy and all that.

'Jack's been nothing but loyal to this firm, and this is how you repay him. I'm disgusted at all of you.' Mia's tear-filled eyes swept over us before she started sobbing again.

I had to stop myself from rolling my eyes. I'd always thought I was the actress in the family, but she was giving me a run for my money.

'You can't blame us for questioning his motives. This situation could have serious implications for all of us, so we need to make sure Jack's one hundred per cent kosher. We can't just take his word for it,' Rio said.

'Why not?' Mia threw her hands up.

She was the only person in the room who didn't have doubts about Jack, and she wasn't about to be swayed by our opinions. She'd stick up for him until the bitter end. I felt like bursting into a quick chorus of 'Stand By Your Man' but I didn't think it would go down too well, so I swallowed down my desire.

'Look, in the guy's defence, Davie always trusted Jack and not much got past him, but I wouldn't be doing my job if I didn't do a bit more digging, would I?' Rio smiled at Mia as he tried to soften the blow.

'Well, I don't buy his story for one minute. I reckon Jack's spinning us a line and is happily selling us out to Lorraine.' I couldn't hold my tongue any longer. All this pussyfooting around was doing my head in.

'I can't believe you just said that.' Mia looked horrified.

'I'm sorry, Mia. I used to like Jack. But that was before I realised he'd been lying to us for years. You can't expect us to ignore that. We'd be mad to sit back and carry on as though nothing's happened, knowing we have a spy in the camp.' I wasn't trying to be nasty, but I had to get my point across.

Rio glanced sideways at Mum and shifted on his feet before he spoke. 'I have to say, I agree with Scarlett,' he said, but I couldn't help feeling he looked uncomfortable.

Mum bit down on her lip and looked into the middle distance for a moment before she replied. 'I know. If I'm totally honest about it, so do I.'

That was a result. At least the three of us were on the same page, even if Mia was in complete denial. I was tempted to high-five Mum and Rio, but I managed to stop myself in my tracks.

'What's wrong with you lot? Why are you being so nasty? I can't believe you've all turned on Jack. Well, I'm on his side even if none of you are.' Mia looked at us in turn before she ran out of the office, clutching her hands over her heart like a jilted heroine on the set of a period saga.

'Do you think I should go after her?' Mum asked with worry pasted onto her features.

'No. Let her have some time on her own,' I replied.

Mum had a habit of smothering people, and when I'd been on the receiving end of her undivided attention, it made me feel stifled and claustrophobic.

'Mia's so sensitive. I don't want her to think we're ganging up on her,' Mum said.

'But we can't just turn a blind eye to what's happened. This battle's worth fighting. We've got to find out what Jack's been up to.' I fixed my mum with a look. I could see she was on the verge of backing off now for fear of upsetting Mia.

'I'm fucking fuming that Lorraine didn't take notice of my warning. I should have put a bullet in her when I had the chance,' Rio said through gritted teeth, diverting the conversation away from Mia. 'I only let her go on the condition that she went into hiding. But the dozy cow's thrown my generosity back in my face and chosen to ignore me. I made it crystal clear that if she didn't stick to her side of the deal. I'd come after her. I'm a man of my word, so I can't let her get away with this, Amanda.'

'I'm right behind you. I think we should go over there now and confront her about Jack. I'd love to hear what she has to say for herself,' I butted in before Mum had a chance to reply.

'That's not a bad idea. We need to get to the bottom of this and if we turn up unannounced, we might be able to catch her off guard,' Mum suggested.

Rio nodded. 'You've just got my vote. The element of surprise is a favourite strategy of mine.'

'No offence, but Lorraine's unlikely to welcome either of you with open arms. And Darius looks too much like Rio to knock on the door without raising suspicion,' I said. 'I might be able to convince her to let me in without any drama, though.'

'That's true. She doesn't know you, and you hardly look like an axe-wielding maniac.' Mum smiled.

'Sometimes appearances can be so deceptive.' I smiled back.

Mum had no idea that I'd met Lorraine before, but now wasn't the right time to get into a complicated explanation.

I gripped the handles of my petrol blue Radley bag as I stood outside the glossy black door. After several deep breaths, I finally plucked up the courage to press the bell. My pulse started pounding as I heard footsteps approaching. Lorraine pulled back the porch curtain and peered outside. She seemed surprised to see me on the doorstep, but thankfully, she opened the door.

'Hi, Lorraine. I hope you don't mind me turning up out of the blue, but I really need to talk to you. Do you mind if I come in?' I said, flashing her my brightest smile.

'Scarlett, what a lovely surprise. Of course I don't mind. Come in.' Lorraine was only too happy to oblige and stepped to one side to allow me to pass.

The smell of her musky perfume filled the space around her, and it caught me at the back of the throat when she placed a kiss on my cheek. I had to stop myself from recoiling. She was so busy looking at me she didn't notice Rio and Darius coming up the drive, moving with the stealth of two sleek panthers on the hunt. Their frames were so huge I couldn't even see Mum behind them, but I knew she was there. Rio was inside before Lorraine had a chance to react. Her face paled at the sight of him, and she backed herself into the wall.

Rio took hold of Lorraine's arm and led her along the timber-panelled hall and into the lounge. Darius followed closely behind while Mum and I brought up the rear.

'Why don't we all sit down? We've got some questions that I'm hoping you can help us with,' I began. I needed to put her at ease to gain her trust, but pure hatred rose up inside me as I faced the woman I once hoped would become my mother-in-law.

'I'll tell you anything you want to know as long as you promise not to hurt me.' Lorraine looked terrified as she fixed me with pleading eyes before glancing sideways at Rio.

'As long as you cooperate, everything will be fine. Is Jack Eastwood your son?'

'Yes,' Lorraine replied without hesitation as she lowered herself onto the pink velvet sofa.

'Why did Jack introduce Nancy and Dale to our family as his mum and dad?' I asked, looking daggers at her.

'He thinks of them as his parents. They raised him for me. There was hell to pay when it came out that my dad's best friend Bryan had got me pregnant. We ran off to Spain and left Jack behind when he was only three months old. I know I shouldn't have done it. I made a stupid mistake, but I was fifteen years old.' Lorraine's eyes misted over.

She was obviously scarred by her past and still found it hard to talk about, but if she was looking for sympathy from me, she'd be waiting until eternity. I didn't feel sorry for her. She'd made her bed so she'd have to lie in it.

'How did you end up with Victor?' Mum said, changing the course of the conversation.

'I met him when I was working in a bar in Torremolinos. We had a bit of a whirlwind romance, and got married six months later. Now that I had a ring on my finger, I hoped Mum and Dad would let me have Jack back, but they weren't having any of it. I finally made contact with him when he was fifteen. I figured he was old enough to understand family politics by then.'

'Fifteen,' Mum repeated as if she was trying to get Jack's age to register in her brain. My thoughts turned to Mia. There was such misery in her eyes when this first surfaced that I'd felt near to tears just looking at her. She wasn't going to take this well. Jack would have known Lorraine was married to Victor when he started working for Dad. What a vile piece of shit he was.

'He didn't believe me when I told him I was his mum. My parents' names appear on Jack's birth certificate, so he wasn't having any of it until I showed him the original before he was legally adopted, which named me as his mother and his father unknown.'

I glanced over at Mum. She was wringing her hands in her lap, but her eyes were glued to Lorraine.

'Jack took it hard, and he refused to have anything to do with me, but a few years down the line, I offered to financially support him while he studied for his degree, and we seemed to turn a corner. I started visiting Jack regularly when he went to uni, and we became really close.' The corners of Lorraine's lips turned upwards.

Jack was the most money-motivated person I knew, so of course, he'd allow himself to be bought. I was disliking him more and more with every second that passed. And the fact that Lorraine was gushing about him made my anger spike. My chest felt tight as my muscles tensed. I was a hothead, so showing no reaction was a huge challenge. But I needed to keep a lid on things, for the time being, at least.

'Something doesn't add up here,' Mum said. 'If you and Jack have this unbreakable bond, why did he take a job with Davie and marry my daughter?' Mum's question was loaded, and Lorraine didn't speak for several seconds.

'Jack felt indebted to me and wanted to repay me. He knew our families had been arch-enemies from the day dot. There's always been bad blood between us, so when an opportunity arose for him to work for Davie, he jumped at the chance,' Lorraine said.

So Jack had been working for the other side the whole time. What a slimy bastard, and what a stupid thing for Lorraine to say. Had she forgotten the ball wasn't in her court?

Mum shook her head. 'What a great son he turned out to be.'

'I think so.' Lorraine beamed with pride. The irony was lost on her.

A snake with legs, more like. Todd had been right all along. It seemed bizarre that he looked like the good guy, which just went to prove that Jack was rotten to the core. Mia would be devastated when she found out that he'd been only too happy to pass on his insider knowledge. Where did she fit into all of this? I'd always thought they were a match made in heaven. It was becoming clearer by the minute that Jack's loyalties lay with Lorraine.

My mind drifted back to the crap we'd listened to him spouting earlier about Lorraine being a stranger, which turned out to be complete horse shit. You'd be hard pushed to find anyone more dishonest than Jack, apart from CJ, of course. The two of them were well and truly cut from the same cloth. The pain and suffering they'd caused was immeasurable. Just thinking about all the terrible things they'd done made my emotions well up inside me. Anger was a powerful force, and I was reaching boiling point. I was desperate to take my fury out on Lorraine and had to battle to hold back my tears and contain my explosive temper. As the minutes ticked by, I could feel myself losing the fight.

I'd spent many a sleepless night wondering why CJ had bothered to get involved with me if he'd just wanted to add fuel to the long-running feud. But I hadn't known then that he was following his big brother's example and sleeping with the enemy, which made the betrayal sting twice as bad. This was going to crush Mia.

Since Dad had been murdered, Jack had slipped into the role of man of the house, and we'd all been happy to let him because we'd had no idea that he was selling us out. My distress turned to anger and I suddenly saw red. When something triggered my temper, I couldn't switch it on and off like some people could. I was my father's daughter, and I was ready to take action and do what had to be done; nobody I loved would ever be harmed by the Colemans again. I shoved my hand into my bag and pulled out a long-bladed kitchen knife. Lorraine's eyes filled with fear at the sight of it.

'Both Jack and CJ were pure evil. That must have come from you as they had two different fathers,' I said. Fuelled by pure rage, I rushed towards Lorraine and plunged the blade into her stomach. Lorraine stared up at me as she clamped her hands over the wound. I watched the blood seep into the fibres of her top before I pulled the knife back out. I wanted her to experience what I'd been through, feel the terror and the pain, but then I couldn't seem to stop myself. I stabbed her in the chest twice and once more in the neck for good measure. Blood started pulsating out of the gash when I removed the knife. I gripped the handle and watched Lorraine's life drain away. I didn't feel the slightest bit guilty; her family had put mine through hell. It was a case of kill or be killed. Lorraine could have finished me off when Todd brought me over here, but she didn't. As I watched her take her last breath, I wondered what was going through her mind. I bet she was wishing she'd put a bullet in me when she'd had the chance. Unlucky.

'You'd better go and clean her up, Amanda and give her something to calm her down,' I heard Rio say.

My limbs started trembling as adrenaline raced around my body. I was wired to the max after the frenzied attack. But I couldn't tear my eyes off Lorraine or drag myself away from her lifeless torso, which had slumped back on the blood-spattered sofa.

67

Mia

When I'd gone back into the house, the place was deserted, which was a blessing as it meant I wouldn't have to get involved in any more awkward conversations. The others had made it crystal clear how they felt about Jack, but I was still trying to process it all. The last thing I wanted to do was fall out with them over this, but I felt like I was playing piggy in the middle. I knew he'd had good reason to hide the truth from me, but that still didn't make it right. I was doing my best to be understanding, but the fact that he'd been lying to me was casting a dark shadow over everything.

I was sitting at the kitchen table nursing a mug of milky tea when I heard a car approaching, so I made myself scarce, racing across the tiles and bounding up the stairs two at a time. The last thing I wanted was company. I was still catching my breath when I heard someone knocking on my door.

I let out a sigh and then said, 'Come in.'

'Have you got a minute?' Mum asked, poking her head around the door.

'Sure,' I replied, but I didn't really mean it.

'Scarlett and I need to talk to you,' Mum said.

I felt my heart sink. I wasn't in the right frame of mind to deal with more confrontation.

Mum walked into my room and sat down on the edge of the bed. Something didn't seem right, so I immediately sat up straighter. Scarlett went the opposite way and stood in front of the window. I couldn't put my finger on it, but they'd brought a peculiar atmosphere into the room. Then I reasoned it was probably just the after-effects of our heated conversation.

Mum, Scarlett, Rio and Darius had gone to see Lorraine after I'd stormed out of the office. I wasn't sure how I felt about being left out of the meeting, but I listened intently as Mum relayed the details of their conversation. What Lorraine had told them didn't make sense, and Mum's words felt like they were floating around in the air above me.

'I'm sorry I had to be the one to break this to you,' Mum said, clutching my hand and squeezing it tightly.

My face crumpled, and it took me a moment to compose myself.

'That's not what Jack told me. You were there; you heard what he said. Their stories don't add up. One of them's lying. And I'm pretty sure it's Lorraine.'

I hoped I sounded more confident than I felt. I was suddenly scared that the husband I adored had been lying to me the whole time we'd been together. We lived in a vile world where people we trusted hurt us. Craig had betrayed Scarlett in the worst way imaginable, and then Todd took his revenge on Kelsey by turning her into an addict. I never for one minute thought that Jack would betray me too.

I closed my eyes in a bid to concentrate while I searched my memory, wondering if I'd find some recollection lurking there that Jack wasn't as sincere and loving as I remembered. Either he was an incredibly good actor, or Lorraine and Todd were conducting a witch hunt.

'Lorraine wasn't lying,' I heard Scarlett say.

I opened my eyes when I felt myself start to hyperventilate. Then I covered my chest with my hand until my breathing returned to normal.

'Are you OK, Mia?' Mum tilted her head to one side as she fixed her eyes on me, watching my reaction.

What sort of a question was that? Of course I wasn't OK. My whole world was falling apart at the seams.

'I know you don't want to hear this, but Jack's been lying to you from the start.

Scarlett's words stung. The last thing I needed was for her to rub salt into my wounds. My head was spinning. I couldn't think straight.

'You're right; I don't want to hear it. I've had enough of you bad-mouthing my husband for one day. My relationship's got nothing to do with you, so mind your own business.' There was a definite tremor in my voice, but that was the least of my concerns.

'We're not trying to upset you, darling. We just want you to know the truth.' Mum's tone was sympathetic, but her pity just made me feel worse.

'And do you seriously think you can trust a word that comes out of Lorraine Coleman's mouth?'

I could see Mum mulling over what I'd just said although it seem to go straight over Scarlett's head. I didn't know who to believe. Everyone seemed to have a reason to lie. It was all so confusing. I didn't know where to go from here. I loved my husband with all my heart and felt like I was losing my mind.

'I'm not ready to give up on Jack even if you are.'

Silent tears started to run down my cheeks. Mum went to wipe them away with her fingertips, but I pushed her hand away.

'For God's sake, Mia. What do we have to say to convince you the man's pure evil? He wormed his way in our family and has been playing games ever since.' Scarlett flung her hands up in frustration.

'Jack's very manipulative and because he's highly intelligent that makes him incredibly dangerous,' Mum added for good measure.

'I've had enough of this. Get out of my room.' I pointed to the door as I threw Mum and Scarlett a look.

'Please, Mia, we just trying to make you see sense.'

Mum held the palms of her hands out towards me, to try and defuse the situation, but I couldn't stand the sight of either of them right now.

'Get out,' I shouted.

Mum got up from the bed and glanced over at Scarlett, giving her a silent cue to follow her.

My bedroom walls felt like they were closing in on me, so once I was alone, I rolled onto my side and hugged my knees into my chest. My brain couldn't process what was happening. I couldn't make any sense of it. The idea that my life with Jack was built on a lie terrified me. He was my rock, my constant. The future looked too bleak without him in it. I didn't want to think about that, so I allowed myself to zone out.

68

Scarlett

Even after everything we'd told her, Mia was still convinced that Jack was telling the truth. How she could take his word over ours I'd never know. But then again, Jack had her brainwashed. She'd lost a lot of her identity since they'd been together, and she'd let herself become dependent on him. If I was in her shoes, I probably wouldn't want to believe Lorraine either. It would be far less traumatic to accept his version of events.

'I felt so bad telling Mia about Jack. The last thing I wanted to do was fall out about it.' Mum looked gutted.

'I know, but it would have been worse if we'd kept it from her. She doesn't believe what Lorraine said anyway. She sees Jack through rose-tinted glasses and at the moment, there doesn't seem to be anything we can do to change that,' I replied.

Mum walked over to the wine fridge and took a bottle of Chablis off the rack. 'Would you like a drink?'

'No thanks.'

She brought the chilled white and a long-stemmed glass over to the table and poured some out. Then she lifted the wine to her lips and savoured the moment it flowed down her throat.

'We have to do something to get through to her. He's manipulated all of us for long enough. He even had your dad fooled and not much got past Davie.' Mum looked troubled.

'Jack has a powerful hold over Mia, so she's going to take some convincing. She's in love with him and we all know she takes her marriage commitment seriously; she'll be loyal until the end. But this isn't just about Mia. It affects all of us, so whether she likes it or not, things are going to have to change,' I said.

'How are we going to persuade her that Jack can't be trusted when she's not even talking to us now?' Mum sighed.

We sat in silence, lost in our own thoughts for some time before I came up with a suggestion.

'Why don't we get Rio to bring Jack over here so we can break the news to him about Lorraine. Mia might be tempted to come out of her room if she realises he's here and even if she doesn't, with any luck she'll eavesdrop on the conversation. If they were as close as Lorraine maintained, Jack's going to go mental when he find out his mum's dead, which might give Mia the wake-up call she needs.'

'That's a brilliant idea,' Mum said, downing the rest of her wine. 'Don't judge me. I need a bit of Dutch courage.' She smiled.

A short while later, Jack walked into the kitchen, flanked on either side by Rio and Darius. His eyes blazed as he stood opposite us with his hands cuffed in front of him.

'I don't appreciate being treated like a criminal,' he said. 'I explained my connection to the Colemans, so why am I being held?'

'The thing is, we paid your mum a visit and she told us her side of the story. Surprise, surprise, it doesn't match yours.' Mum's voice was laced with sarcasm.

'You did what?' Jack shouted.

'Don't you dare speak to a lady like that,' Rio replied before his fist connected with Jack's left kidney.

When I saw him wince with pain it brought a smile to my face.

'The truth's out in the open now, so there's no way back,' I said.

'Shut the fuck up, Scarlett.' Jack's head jerked in my direction.

'You never learn, do you?' Rio's words were followed by two swift blows.

Jack clenched his teeth when Rio's fists connected with his body.

'As if Lorraine would tell you anything. You're hardly best buddies, are you?' Jack sneered.

'Funnily enough, she took one look at me and seemed very compliant.' Rio smiled.

'You better not have hurt her,' Jack replied.

'Now that would be telling.' Rio tapped the side of his nose with his index finger.

'What have you done to her?' Jack's face contorted in rage.

'Rio didn't do anything to Lorraine. It was me who killed her,' I admitted, looking him straight in the eye.

Before Rio could stop him, Jack lunged at me and pulled me onto my feet. We were only inches apart, so I could feel his breath on my face.

'You fucking bitch.' Jack's voice cracked with emotion.

'Get off her,' Rio bellowed.

Then, attacking from behind, he wrapped his arm around Jack's neck, forcing it into the crook as he applied a sleeper hold. Jack let go of me instantly. He started coughing as spluttering as Rio pulsed the pressure on and off.

'What the hell's going on?' Mia yelled.

Rio released Jack, who dropped to his knees and began gasping for air.

'Scarlett's killed Lorraine.' Jack's eyes glistened with tears as he looked up at her. Then a moment later he got back on his feet.

'Oh my God,' Mia cried out.

I almost rolled my eyes when her hands went up to cover her mouth. She was displaying all the dramatics of a heroine in a silent movie. Plunging the knife into Lorraine had felt strangely therapeutic, as though justice had been done. She'd brought him into this world and raised him, so ultimately she was responsible for the way he'd turned out. The bastard she'd given birth to had tried to ruin my life. But I wasn't going to let CJ win. I was stronger than that. I'd had enough of being stuck in the past, replaying the nightmare in my head. 'Oh, Jack, you look absolutely devastated. But I don't understand. I thought you barely knew Lorraine...' Mia said, taking us all by surprise.

I'd been expecting her to fall into his arms and weep and wail for the loss of the mother-in-law she hadn't known existed until just recently.

'That's what you told me, wasn't it?' Mia's question was left hanging in the air unanswered. 'I wonder if you could clear something up for me. Lorraine told Mum and Scarlett that you were fifteen when she made contact with you. You said you were much older. Which one's the truth?'

A flash of anger crossed Jack's face. 'Yes, I was fifteen. And before you ask. Yes, I knew my mum was a Coleman when I started working for your dad. And yes, marrying you was just part of the plan,' Jack spat the words out as though they were coated in venom.

Mia's face paled and her body started jerking over and over as Jack's spiteful comments registered in her brain like bullets hitting her from a gun.

What a horrible piece of work he was, I thought as Rio grabbed him by the throat.

'Rio, stop interfering,' Mia said when Jack started making a gurgling sound, so Rio released his iron grip. 'I need to talk to Jack, and I don't want any of you getting involved. This is between him and me. Do I make myself clear?'

Mia's eyes swept over us in turn as we agreed to her request. Emotions were running high, so it wasn't going to be easy to stay out of it, but we had to for her sake. Nobody was going to be able to convince Mia that Jack was an evil bastard. She had to find that out for herself.

'You told me Lorraine was a stranger, so your loyalties lay with my dad.' Mia's lip trembled as she spoke.

She'd chosen to ignore his remark about their marriage, but it must have been killing her. I knew how much Mia adored him, and I'd always thought the feeling was mutual.

'Well, I lied.'

When Jack dealt another cruel blow, I wasn't sure how much more Mia could take.

'You think you know so much about Davie's criminal activities, but you're a bunch of amateurs. We've been running rings around you, getting Todd to pull the stunt with the Aston Martin to distract you so that you didn't check Al Dempsey out as well as you should have. You ended up lending the loser a small fortune and played right into our hands. Having one up on the Saunders family feels so good.' Jack laughed. 'Then you spent all that effort looking for the car, and it was on my mum's driveway the whole time.'

Jack looked so smug, and I was kicking myself that I hadn't spoken up earlier. Talk about hiding in plain sight.

'I've spent more than a decade infiltrating your family,' Jack said, his blue eyes shining. 'None of you have any idea how badly I've screwed you over and I've enjoyed every minute of it.'

'How could you do this to me?' Mia's voice came out in a whisper.

'Oh, Mia, you look absolutely devastated,' Jack said throwing my sister's words back at her.

'Of course I'm devastated. I thought you loved me, but you were just playing games...' Mia shook her head.

She looked crushed by Jack's admission. And who could blame her? His betrayal was bad enough for the rest of us to deal with, but for Mia, it was ten times worse. Now that Jack knew the game was up, the knives had come out and he wasn't holding back.

'I was pretty convincing, though, wasn't I? You lot all fell for the doting husband routine.' Jack laughed.

'I was over the moon to have landed such a catch when I married a kind, strong, supportive man, and all the time you were putting on a front and concealing your true feelings.'

Tears started rolling down Mia's cheeks. She wiped them away with the back of her hand, but she didn't break eye contact with Jack. It was as though they were the only two people in the room.

'I'd like to say better luck next time, but you have such a lot of emotional baggage, there won't be many men rushing to fill my place. Face it, Mia, you're a burden to everyone.' Jack was really twisting the knife and the atmosphere in the room felt loaded.

Mia didn't need any help undermining her confidence; she did a great job of that herself.

'I feel like you've just ripped my heart out and smashed it to pieces.'

Mia's shoulders rounded and her hair fell forward. Beating her down was giving Jack so much pleasure. It was hard to stand by and watch. I glanced sideways at the others and saw a nerve twitching in Rio's jaw. I could tell he was poised and ready to pounce. Mia only had to say the word and he'd spring into action. Mum had one arm crossed over her chest while the fingers on her other hand covered her lips as though she couldn't trust herself not to speak.

'I devoted myself to trying to make you happy. What did I do to deserve this?' Mia's self-esteem was taking a battering.

'Now where should I start? Call it payback for the countless times I had to prop you up when you were depressed, put your mind at rest when you overanalysed every single situation you encountered and that's without adding in all the things your family did to mine over the years.'

Jack had reduced Mia to a quivering wreck, but that wasn't stopping him, he just kept gunning for her. A loud sob escaped from her lips before she rushed out of the room.

'I don't care what you do with him, but get him out of my house,' Mum said to Rio once Mia was out of sight.

'Gladly,' Rio replied with a glint in his eye.

69

Mia

I'd had to get out of the room. I couldn't bear the pain of Jack twisting the knife any longer. His words were so cruel; they'd ripped me to pieces. I'd thought our marriage was rock solid, but it had just disintegrated before my eyes. I stood in the living room shaking, my heartbeat galloping, my mouth dry. Jack's admission was so shocking it left me speechless. His words jumbled together as they bounced around my head. It was as though my subconscious thoughts were distorting the facts to shield me from the awful truth.

I'd never seen this side of Jack before, but he'd been hiding behind a mask all the time we'd been together. It was no wonder I didn't recognise the man who'd been standing in front of me moments earlier. I never thought Jack was capable of such deception, but he'd humiliated me in the worst way possible. And now I was on the verge of losing it. I wanted to rush up the stairs, smash his belongings to pieces, rip his clothes to shreds and throw the whole lot out the window. What good would it do? Acting like some deranged lunatic wouldn't change anything, but littering the driveway with his possessions might just make me feel better. Who was I trying to kid? I'd never have the guts to do that.

My mind drifted back to the way Craig had treated Scarlett. I suddenly appreciated how she must have felt. At the time, I hadn't understood what she was going through. I remember thinking being betrayed by your partner, the person you loved and trusted, must be completely devastating and thanking my lucky stars that I had Jack. He'd helped me through the worst moments of my life. I couldn't imagine not having him to lean on. Now I felt like a complete idiot. Never in my wildest dreams did I think he'd be so calculated and insincere, but it was clear my judgement was seriously lacking. I'd believed every word he'd fed me and couldn't trust my instincts. I was utterly useless, a waste of space.

I'd been blindsided, and now my head was scrambled. How do you make sense of the incomprehensible? I felt overwhelmed by the whole situation and didn't know what to do for the best. Nobody had ever hurt me like this before. What Jack had done was on another level. I wished I could turn back the clock to a time when I was blissfully unaware of the huge betrayal Jack was hiding from me, but I knew that wasn't possible.

The sound of Mum and Scarlett's voices, on the other side of the door, threw me into a blind panic. I couldn't bear the thought of facing people. I wanted to be left on my own, but I was trapped inside the living room with nowhere to go.

'I'm so sorry that Jack turned out to be such a total scumbag,' Scarlett said when she opened the door. As she walked towards me, she looked at me with pity.

My heart started hammering in my chest. I didn't want her to hug me because if she did, I knew I'd break down and be inconsolable. I'd already been stripped of my dignity and didn't want to make a fool of myself again. I'd been humiliated at the highest level and now a cloak of shame and embarrassment was hanging around my shoulders. I wasn't worthy of anyone's respect.

'What on earth possessed Jack to treat you like this? You look completely shell-shocked, darling. Why don't you come and sit down, and we'll talk things through?' Mum said, but I backed myself into the wall furthest away from her.

'No thanks. I'd rather go up to my room.'

'Do you want me to come with you?' Mum asked.

'No, I'd prefer to be left on my own. I need some time to think.'

I offered her a weak smile as I tried to put a brave face on things knowing I was about to face some dark hours, the darkest ones of my life. Nobody could begin to understand what I was going through.

'Scarlett and I might go and see Kelsey then if you're sure you don't want company,' Mum said.

'That's fine by me. Give her my love and tell her I'll pop in soon.'

I was doing my best to act as if everything was OK when it was anything but, because I didn't want to draw attention to myself. Kelsey was creating the perfect diversion, so now I could take myself away from the spotlight and hide. I needed to be alone with my thoughts. And much as my heart went out to her, I'd be eternally grateful that Mum's focus was on her and not me for once.

My heart was broken beyond repair. The pain was so real, I felt like I was physically sick and ached all over. Every step was an effort; sheer exhaustion set in as I began to climb the stairs. Once I reached the safety of my room, I threw myself face down on the bed and sobbed my heart out.

Jack had been my ideal man. He'd been sweet, drop-dead gorgeous, funny, smart, et cetera, et cetera... Until he'd betrayed me, I was guilty of almost hearing birds singing when I spoke about him. I'd thought we'd had something special, that our connection ran deep. How could I have been so wrong? My whole world had come crashing down around me, and I wasn't sure what to do.

I was at my most vulnerable, unhinged, losing the plot and desperate for help, but because I'd turned on my family when they tried to warn me about Jack, I'd driven a wedge between us. Mum and Scarlett had tried to reach out to me, but I could sense the tension between us, so I didn't feel like I could confide in them or ask for advice. Jack had been the decision maker in our relationship. I didn't trust myself to step into his shoes. Now that he was gone, I had nobody to turn to; I was lost, totally alone and the thought of that terrified me.

Jack, who I'd always considered my rock, had been lying to me from the first day I'd met him, which just went to prove that we all kept secrets from each other, didn't we? Inside I was dying. The seams of my world had burst open. I loved Jack with all my heart and thought our relationship would last forever. Knowing it was built on a lie made me feel hollow. I was broken. Unrepairable. Without Jack, my life would become an endless round of sleeping and eating. I'd just be going through the motions. And for what? To maintain a miserable existence? What was the point? Everything always went wrong for me.

The future seemed dangerous and unpredictable. I was already a slave to my anxiety without having all this to deal with. I wouldn't be able to cope. I wasn't proud of being needy, but I was acutely aware that I shouldn't lumber people with my issues. Thanks, Jack. The psychological damage of betrayal was profound. I didn't buy into the idea that time was a great healer. I doubted the memory would ever fade. I'd been to hell and back too many times and didn't have the strength to wait and see if better days were around the corner. I had no fight left in me; feeling worthless wore you down.

I dragged myself up from the bed and walked into the en suite, making a beeline for the medicine cabinet hanging over the sink. I opened the door and scanned the shelves laden with half-empty bottles of prescription drugs I used to treat my anxiety and depression. Moments later, I lifted them down and carried them back to my room.

I unscrewed the lids from the bottles and pushed tablets out of blister packs until all of them were empty. Then I stared at the mound in front of me, mesmerised by the different shapes and colours splayed over the quilt, willing me to swallow them.

I didn't want to be a burden. I would be doing everyone a favour if I took my own life, wouldn't I?

There was no coming back from a betrayal this size. How could I ever move on? I wasn't strong enough to bear the pain. I felt like less than nothing. Life had lost its meaning. Images of happier times flashed into my brain. There'd been so many over the years that it was hard to remember them all. They kept coming one after the other, reminding me of everything I had to live for. But then the bad visions pushed them aside and started running on a loop in my head, my dad lying dead on the chapel floor as I'd stood feet away from him, clutching my wedding bouquet with tears rolling down my cheeks. Jack had stood beside me, comforting me. He'd brought me back from the brink so many times in the past I wondered why he'd bothered. Probably just so he could twist the knife again. I could speculate forever, but I put it out of my mind. I'd never know if that was the right answer or not.

I reached over, took the large bottle of Volvic from my bedside table and opened the lid. The house was eerily quiet, but I felt strangely calm as I sat on the edge of my bed and swallowed the tablets one by one. Then I lay down and allowed my head to sink into the pillows while I waited for the drugs to take effect, wondering if I should have left a note...

70

Scarlett

It was late by the time Mum and I got back from the clinic, so we went straight to bed. It had been the day from hell, and shortly after my head hit the pillow, I was sound asleep. I'd gone out like a light.

'Oh my God, Mia, what have you done?'

Mum's voice was loud and shrill; it woke me from my sleep, so I decided to go and investigate. When I walked into Mia's room, Mum was sitting on the edge of the bed amid a sea of empty bottles and foil wrappers. My eyes fixed on the empty packaging. It was as though my subconscious was delaying the moment so that I had time to adjust to the horror I was about to see. I tore my gaze away and let it settle on my older sister. Mum was cradling Mia in her arms, rocking backwards and forwards. Panic flooded me.

'I don't know what to do. Should I run down the road and try and get help or stay with her?' Mum was beside herself.

'We need to try and revive her,' I replied, fighting down a rising sense of panic. My stomach was churning so badly, I could barely breathe.

'How? Call an ambulance,' Mum sobbed. 'And phone Dr Burton.'

I did as I was told, going one step further and phoning Rio too. I wasn't sure how to deal with the situation, but he would know what to do. I couldn't shake the horrible feeling that it was too little, too late. Mia's skin had lost all its colour, and she was unresponsive. A wave of guilt washed over me. I'd been sound asleep just moments ago, completely unaware.

We hadn't disturbed Mia when we'd got home last night; she'd made it clear she wanted to be alone. We'd thought she was licking her wounds as she tried to come to terms with everything. If we'd had any idea she was going to try and take her life, we'd never have left her on her own. But she'd seemed OK when Mum and I had gone out.

When I walked back into the room, I noticed the doors on the wall-mounted glass cabinet in Mia's bathroom lay open, the shelves bare. The sight of it was so shocking that silent tears started rolling down my cheeks. I'd been trying to get her to see sense, but maybe I'd been too hard on her. Mia was such a gentle soul and took everything personally.

Dr Burton was the first to arrive. I left the front door open and led the way to Mia's bedroom. He rushed over to where she was lying in Mum's arms and began checking her for signs of life. Time dragged by agonisingly slowly and fear started creeping through my veins as I watched him trying to locate her pulse and listening for her heartbeat. I looked on helplessly while being suffocating by dread. I was numb with terror.

'I'm so sorry, Amanda, but Mia has passed away,' Dr Burton said.

The scream that left Mum's lips sent shock waves through the house. The sound would haunt me forever. I rushed to her side just as Rio walked into the room.

'She can't be dead? Isn't there something you can do? Can't you pump her stomach?' Desperation coated Mum's words.

Dr Burton shook his head. 'I'm afraid it's too late for that,' he replied with a pained expression on his face.

His words shot through my brain like a bullet, and left behind the same amount of destruction. Spots appeared in front of my eyes and I thought I was going to faint.

'It can't be.' Mum rushed over to the bed and dropped down on her knees. 'Mia. Mia. Wake up, darling.'

Mum kept rubbing Mia's hand as she tried to rouse her, which was heartbreaking to witness, and I felt my breath catch in my throat.

Rio walked up behind Mum, cupped her elbow in his hand and helped her to her feet.

'She's gone, Amanda,' he said, choking back tears.

Mum shook her head. 'She can't be. She's just in a deep sleep.'

'Mia's not asleep, Amanda. She's with Davie now,' Rio said, locking eyes with Mum.

When I saw the tears streaming down his face, it set me off again.

'No, no, no. She can't be. This can't be happening.'

I couldn't blame Mum for being in denial; I could barely believe it myself. It didn't feel real; there was too much to take in.

'Mia's at peace now. Davie will look after her,' Rio said, trying to get through to her.

'I should have been the one looking after her.' Mum's lip trembled.

'Don't beat yourself up thinking you could have done something to prevent this.' Rio's eyes bored into Mum's.

We all fell silent, lost in our own thoughts. I glanced over at Mia. My sister was beautiful even in death. She looked so peaceful and serene, which gave me some comfort, but Mum was inconsolable. Crushed by the weight of her sorrow, she started howling in agony.

I saw Dr Burton approach the ambulance crew when they appeared in the doorway. He spoke softly to them, so I couldn't make out what he was saying over the sound of Mum sobbing.

'Make it stop. Make the pain go away.' Mum looked up at Rio through a sheet of tears.

He didn't say a word, but he wrapped his strong arms around her and let her cry her eyes out while holding her close to his chest.

After the paramedics wheeled Mia away on a covered gurney, Mum picked up the Tiffany pendant from the bedside table and clutched it in her hand.

'Dad and I bought that for her the last Christmas we were all together. I can't believe they're both gone.' Her hands were shaking uncontrollably.

'Let me put it on for you,' I said, taking the silver chain out of her hand.

I opened the clasp and fastened it at the base of her neck. When the heart settled against her chest, she covered it with her fingertips, pressing it into her skin as though trying to hold Mia close. Then she threw her arms around my shoulders, and we cried in each other's arms. When Mum pulled away, she looked utterly grief-stricken.

'I can't even begin to imagine what was going through her head in those final moments. She was all alone. What sort of a mother am I? I wasn't there for her when she needed me the most,' Mum said, and her eyes filled with tears.

'Don't you dare blame yourself. This wasn't your fault,' I replied.

Guilt was eating away at me too, but I kept that to myself. I didn't want Mum to feel worse than she already did. We'd both known Mia was struggling. We should have realised something like this might happen. Mia always seemed to be battling demons of some sort or another. But she'd collapsed in on herself since she'd found out about Jack. The sheer magnitude of her grief was so overwhelming she couldn't cope. From her perspective, she'd received the most devastating news in the universe. And her life was so entwined with Jack's, it was no wonder she couldn't face carrying on without him.

'Mia's relationship with Jack meant everything to her. Losing your husband hurts like hell. I know that better than anyone, and yet I still managed to let her down.' Mum broke down and began sobbing, so I wrapped my arms around her to try and comfort her.

'Mia was a grown woman. Nobody could have stopped her from doing what she did,' Rio said. I wished Mia hadn't alienated herself from us. She might still be alive if she'd talked things through with us instead of shutting herself away. It had distressed us to see her in such a state. We had her best interests at heart and could have helped her gain a better sense of perspective of the situation. It was dire, but things would have improved in time. Nobody was disputing how much she loved Jack, but losing him wasn't the end of the world. If she'd reached out to us, she might not have put her suicidal thoughts into action. She could have learned to live without him.

Mum and Dad had had the perfect relationship, but sadly none of us had been lucky in love. If you scrolled through social media, there was no shortage of advice on what happiness, success, and fulfilment should look like. And every man and his dog had an opinion on how to achieve lasting love. But I'd had my fingers burned, so I'd been put off men for life. Kelsey's track record was no better, so Mia would have been in good company. We could have grown old together and lived out our days with a house full of cats. I could think of worse ways to end up.

'Why didn't she change her mind at the last minute and decide not to go through with it? I let her slip through my fingers. You can't imagine how awful it feels to know that I failed her.' Mum's voice was barely a whisper.

'Stop torturing yourself. We didn't know suicidal thoughts were lurking at the back of her mind,' I said to make Mum feel better.

But we'd both heard the despair in Mia's voice the last time we spoke. We'd both seen the devastation carved into her features, the pain in her eyes. We both knew deep down she'd lost hope. And we still went out and left her alone. I felt like I'd betrayed her too. My stomach muscles started to spasm, and I thought I was going to vomit.

'I didn't realise Mia had taken an overdose at first. I just thought she was sleeping. I only noticed all the empty bottles when I couldn't wake her.' Mum broke down in tears again. She had no control over them.

I sat and held her until the moment passed, not speaking just letting her get her anguish out. Words were so inadequate at a time like this. There was nothing I could say to console Mum; her grief was all-consuming, inescapable.

Mia's suicide hadn't been meticulously planned. It had been a rash, impulsive spur-of-the-moment decision.

'Maybe she was having trouble sleeping. Do you think she took the tablets by accident?'

Rio and I could both hear the desperation in Mum's voice. Silence spread out between us. Neither of us wanted to answer her question. Even though it was difficult for my mum to accept, I was in no doubt that Mia had intentionally swallowed the entire contents of her medicine cabinet. It was no accident. Her actions were controlled by grief. She felt there was nothing left to live for; she wanted the pain to end. I couldn't imagine what was running through her head when she pressed each individual pill out of its blister pack, leaving discarded wrappings littering her bed.

'I can't bear to think that she took her own life on purpose.' Mum broke down and began to sob again. She was beyond heartbroken.

I've had enough of watching you beating yourself up about this. It wasn't your fault; it was Jack's.' Rio's eyes blazed as the words left his mouth.

Anger surged through every nerve ending in my body at the thought of what Jack put Mia through. The anguish and suffering he caused her in her final hours was unforgivable.

'You're right, and he needs to pay for this.' Mum's despair turned to blind fury. 'He robbed me of my daughter and the chance to say goodbye and tell her how much I loved her.'

I wish I'd intervened now when Jack was belittling her instead of standing by and letting him crush her self-esteem...' Rio let his sentence trail off.

He was devastated too. Mia was like a daughter to him.

'But Mia was adamant she didn't want any of us interfering. She wouldn't have thanked you for sticking your nose in.' It was Mum's turn to reassure Rio.

'The fucker made her feel like she was a burden to everyone. She was anything but. She was an angel. Far too good for a scumbag like him.' Rio stood tall and swallowed the lump in his throat.

'Isn't that the truth?' Mum's voice was flat.

'Jack's got a lot to answer for, but before we deal with him, we need to go and tell Kelsey,' I said.

'I'm not sure that's a good idea. Kelsey's getting better, but she's still very fragile. If we tell her the truth, I'm worried she might fall back into a pit of despair and lose the desire to beat her addiction.' Mum had the weight of the world on her shoulders.

'You can't keep this from her. She has a right to know what's going on,' I replied.

Mum closed her eyes for a moment as my words registered, and then she opened them again. 'How are we going to break this to her?'

'I'll go and tell her if you like,' Rio offered.

'I can't ask you to do that. Maybe we could all go.' Mum locked eyes with me. 'Do you feel up to coming with us?'

I nodded; I had to be there to support Mum. There was no telling how Kelsey would react. She already had enough on her plate without hearing news like this. But it also wasn't fair to keep her in the dark.

71

Scarlett

Kelsey was sitting on top of the covers, dressed in a tracksuit, with her back against the headrest when we walked into her room. She looked up from the magazine she was leafing through, and her eyes scanned over us.

'What's wrong?' Kelsey asked.

Even before we'd said a word, she'd guessed something wasn't right. Hardly surprising really, as we were red-eyed and wearing the expressions of undertakers.

'We've got some bad news,' Mum said, walking over and sitting down on the edge of the bed. 'Mia's dead.'

'She's what?' Kelsey's eyes started darting between us as she tried to process what Mum had just said.

'She died this morning,' Mum continued.

She was managing to stay very composed, which was more than I could say for myself. I stood watching them with tears pouring down my face.

Kelsey let the magazine fall from her hand. 'Oh my God. W-what happened? Was she in an accident?'

I was glad to see her speech had improved a lot, but she was still having a bit of trouble articulating herself.

Mum shook her head. 'She killed herself.'

Kelsey jolted as she tried to absorb the shock. 'How? Why?'

'She took an overdose.' Mum's voice wobbled as her composure slipped.

'But why?' Kelsey's eyes filled with tears.

I wondered how Mum was going to answer that.

'She broke up with Jack,' Mum said, leaving out all of the details.

'Why d-did they split up?' Kelsey clearly couldn't believe what Mum had just told her.

When Mum stayed silent, I knew I had to step in. I wiped my tears away and moved closer to the bed.

'It turns out Lorraine Coleman was Jack's mum. He denied it at first, but when Mia confronted him, he gave it to her with both barrels loaded. To cut a long story short, Jack told her he'd never loved her, and marrying her was just part of the plan. He's been selling us out for years, screwed us all over big time,' I said, trying to condense everything that had happened.

'And he also told her she was a burden to everyone. You can just imagine how that must have made her feel.' Mum swallowed hard, trying her best not to break down, but she couldn't hold in her grief and began sobbing.

'Oh no. Poor Mia.'

Kelsey's tears started to flow, so I threw one arm around her and the other around Mum. A few moments later, Kelsey pulled away.

Kelsey dried her eyes on the sleeve of her sweatshirt. 'What a h-horrible bastard he turned out to be. I wish I could get out of here and put a b-bullet in him.'

'Don't you worry. We'll sort that out for you,' Rio replied with a glint in his eye.

'You're doing brilliantly. You'll be home before you know it.' I reached for Kelsey's hand and squeezed it.

It was good to see the flame of passion reignite inside her. I was so proud of my sister. Instead of making her crumble, it looked as though this tragedy had given her the will to fight back. I was certain she was going to beat her addiction.

72

Scarlett

Flowers and sympathy cards started to arrive in the days that followed. Every surface in the house was covered in vases. But the envelopes remained unopened. Mum and I couldn't bear to read the condolences people were offering. It was hard enough trying to carry out basic daily functions. I hadn't washed or brushed my hair since Mia died. It seemed wrong to carry on with mundane things when she was lying on a slab in the mortuary.

Friends and neighbours were doing their best to rally around us, but nothing they did or said lessened the misery we were feeling. Grief was hard work, and it was taking its toll on our minds and bodies. Our hearts were broken. *Sorry for your loss* was stuck on a loop in my brain. The words did nothing to comfort us, but what else were people supposed to say at a time like this?

'I don't think I'll ever come to terms with what happened. I still can't make sense of any of it. It's such a waste of a life.' Mum fixed me with tear-filled eyes.

'I don't think any of us will get used to the enormity of the loss, the emptiness Mia's left in her wake,' I replied, reaching for Mum's hand.

I supposed our hearts would heal, but the scar would remain. It was early days; we had to give it time. The journey would be slow and painful. We still had a long way to go; a lot of travelling to do.

'When I close my eyes, I keep having a recurring image of Mia opening all the lids from the bottles and pushing the tablets out of the blister packs before swallowing them. It's on a loop in my brain, and I can't block it out. I know I wasn't there, but it's like I'm in the room with her,' Mum said.

We were all sleep-deprived and haggard with fatigue. I knew exactly what she meant. I kept picturing Mia frightened and alone. The shock and horror of her death consumed my thoughts. I'd spent hours going over it, ranting, crying, pacing back and forth, wishing there was something I could have done to prevent it.

'The night after we lost Mia was the longest night of my life. I feel so responsible. I was her mother. I should have been able to keep her safe. But I let her down,' Mum said, echoing my thoughts.

I'd slept chaotically too. My senses were under assault, my nerves frayed, so sleep was hard to come by. I'd kept having flashbacks of my sister. The memories were so vivid, they felt real. I could feel her presence and her absence at the same time; it was really weird. Daylight couldn't come soon enough for me.

'Losing Davie caused me untold heartache, but the grief I feel for Mia is on a different level. It's as though part of me died with her. When she went, she took my soul with her.'

Mum looked broken, and I felt my eyes well up as a lump formed in my throat. Mia's death had hit us all hard. I wanted to say something to ease her suffering, but I was having a hard time putting my feelings into words. There were so many conflicting emotions going through my head: anger, blame, despair, regret. The list went on.

'The older generations are meant to go first. That's the order of things, the way it's supposed to be. Parents shouldn't outlive their children.' Mum looked to Rio for reassurance.

'I know, Amanda, but sadly, that's not always the way things turn out,' Rio replied.

73

Scarlett

'The Colemans weren't going to stop until they'd taken out each and every one of us,' Rio said.

Mum looked shocked that he'd thrown that out there, but we shouldn't spend every minute of every day talking about Mia. It wasn't healthy. Life had to go on.

'Davie would be horrified if he was still here. You know how protective he was of all of you. It would have torn him apart to see how Jack, in particular, has turned out.' Rio shook his head.

He was right: Dad would have been disgusted. He wouldn't have sat back and done nothing while he mourned. He'd have put his grief on hold and dealt with the situation. It was time we settled the score.

'Davie treated Jack like the son he never had,' Rio continued.

Mum inhaled a deep breath, then let it out slowly. 'The business has cost us dearly on a personal level. I think it's time we stepped away from this line of work.'

Mum's words had given me food for thought.

'Really? Just as I was planning to show you what I'm made of,' I said.

Mum raised her eyebrows. 'I'm surprised to hear that. I said all along you weren't cut out for an office job. It was always your dream to tread the boards.'

'Not anymore. I want to get stuck into the business.'

Losing Mia to suicide and Kelsey's struggle with addiction

had paved the way to smoothing the rift I'd had with my family. It shouldn't have been the case, but sometimes it took a tragedy to bring people closer together.

'It's too dangerous, Scarlett. We're all going to end up dead if we don't walk away. We'll find other ways to make a living. We were all following different paths before we started working for the firm.'

Mum's mind was made up, so there was no point in arguing about it. The decision was no longer mine to make. It had been taken out of my hands.

'That's a bold move,' I said.

Mum nodded. 'I know, but it has to be done. We'll have to cut ties with everybody the firm had dealings with if we want to stay safe. The Wilkinsons are still breathing down our necks, and it's making me very edgy. I'm not the sort of person who'd be content living my life looking over my shoulder. I couldn't allow that type of power to be exercised over me.'

'I know what you mean,' I agreed.

'Once Kelsey finishes the programme, we'll sell the house and move away from here. This place is worth a fortune. We could use the money to have a fresh start, somewhere nobody knows us,' Mum said.

'It's been nice knowing you.' Rio laughed, but there was genuine sadness in his eyes.

'You can't get rid of us that easily. I was hoping you'd come too. What do you think?' Mum smiled.

'I'd love that.' Rio began nodding his head enthusiastically. 'But we've got a couple of issues to sort out first. We need to recover the debt from Al; then, we'll deliver him to the Wilkinsons. They've assured me they'll wipe the slate clean once we've dropped him off.'

'Can we trust them to keep their word?' Mum bit down on her lip.

'I'd say so?' Rio replied.

'How easy will it be to get the money back?' Mum asked.

'It won't be a problem. Al told us since he'd flogged all the heroin, he's sitting on a huge pile of dosh.' Rio checked the time on his watch. 'Can I interest you ladies in some target practice?'

'Why not.' Mum smiled.

Rio had completely lost me. 'What do you mean?'

'Would you like to learn how to fire a gun?' Rio smiled and tilted his head to one side.

Todd, Jack and Oscar were lined up like ducks in a row in the shipping container at East Tilbury. They were restrained at the wrists and ankles and had gaffer tape covering their mouths. Rio walked towards Oscar, and as he drew nearer, a trail of urine ran down Oscar's right leg, turning his pale grey trackies two shades darker. His eyes were wide and kept darting around the dimly lit space.

'Scarlett, come here,' Rio said, turning to look at me.

I walked over to him with my shoulders back, hoping my pounding heartbeat wasn't noticeable through my clothes.

Rio lifted the weapon and held it against Oscar's temple. 'Watch and learn,' he said before he pulled the trigger of the pump-action shotgun.

I jumped when it blew a massive hole in his head. Covering my mouth with my hands, I watched his splattered brains slide down the wall opposite.

'It's got a bit of a kick-back, but I think you'll be able to handle it.' Rio smiled. Then he handed me the gun, the barrel of which was still smoking.

Rio stood behind me, helping me aim the gun at Todd. I felt his eyes settle on me in a bid to put me off, but I was determined not to let him. My first shot whistled past his ear and bounced off the metal walls. My second attempt grazed his left arm, taking a lump of flesh with it. He whimpered like a wounded animal behind the tape, heightening the pressure. Rio took the gun out of my hands and reloaded it. Third time lucky, I told myself as

I squeezed the trigger. The bullet blew a hole in the base of his throat, and Todd dropped to his knees before rolling onto his side. I watched the blood seep out of him before I turned to look at Rio.

'Well done.' Rio beamed with pride.

'My turn,' Mum said, not taking her gaze away from Jack's. She stared at him for the longest time with hatred in her eyes before she walked up to him, placed the gun against his chest and pulled the trigger, firing it a second time for good measure.

'Nice work, ladies,' Rio said, taking the gun out of Mum's trembling hands. 'Wesley will be along soon to clean this mess up.'

We sat in silence on the drive back to Bow, so I allowed my mind to drift. It was a funny old world we lived in, I thought, contemplating everything that had happened. Was murder ever justifiable? Some would say not, but my moral compass told me I'd had every right to take the lives of the people who'd wronged me. When you faced your arch-enemies, it was a case of kill or be killed. I wasn't going to lose a moment's sleep over what I'd done. Society was a better place without lowlife scum wandering the streets. My family had been to hell and back because of the Colemans. The trauma they'd put us through had tested our mettle, but we weren't going to let them beat us.

Setbacks were part of life; everyone experienced them to a greater or lesser degree. Some were small enough just to slow you down a bit. Others were so big they stopped you entirely in your tracks. The experience might leave you scarred, but each scar made you stronger. You couldn't let difficulties throw you off course completely or limit your options. You had to learn from them, move on from them and look to the future.

Grief was exhausting. It left you feeling disorientated and broken, but it was the price you paid for love. When you lost somebody close to you, the shock, the sadness, and the unanswered questions made you look at things differently. Death was a part of the circle of life, and even though you felt like curling into a ball and giving up, you had to push through the pain and carry on. Mum and Kelsey had become more important to me than ever. The relationship I had with them was precious. I knew I was lucky to have them.

Burning our bridges was a brave thing for us to do. But facing new challenges would make us stronger, wiser, and more resilient. No matter what life threw our way, if we adopted the right mindset, we could overcome anything. I was certain of that.

Acknowledgements

Writing this novel was a huge challenge, a battle from start to finish. Almost as soon as the words began to flow, I became ill with shingles. I'd barely recovered from the virus when Covid got me for the second time. A month or so later, I face-planted onto the pavement and knocked myself out. My cuts, bruises and black eye made me look like I'd had a run-in with one of the characters from my books. Then just when I thought nothing else could possibly go wrong, I unexpectedly lost both of my parents in the space of two weeks. I can safely say it was the worst six months of my life, but writing got me through the darkest days.

Martina Arzu, my brilliant editor, was amazingly patient and supportive throughout all the turmoil, so I'd like to thank her from the bottom of my heart. It was a pleasure working with you, as always.

Thanks to the team at Head of Zeus and everyone involved in the production of this book, especially Helena Newton, Yvonne Doney and Cherie Chapman.

And finally, thank you to the readers. Without you, none of this would be possible. I hope you enjoy the book!

About the Author

STEPHANIE HARTE was born and raised in North West London. She was educated at St Michael's Catholic Grammar school in Finchley. After leaving school she trained in Hairdressing and Beauty Therapy at London College of Fashion. She worked for many years as a Pharmaceutical Buyer for the NHS. Her career path led her to work for an international export company whose markets included The Cayman Islands and Bermuda. For ten years, Stephanie taught regular beauty therapy workshops at a London-based specialist residential clinic that treated children with severe eating disorders. Stephanie took up writing as a hobby and self-published two novels and two novellas before signing a contract in March 2019 with Head of Zeus.